Praise

'A deeply touching, de[...]slow wr[...]'
Dinan Jefferies

'A big, beautiful, epic tale . . . I can't remember the last time I
was so transported by a book'
Louise Douglas

'A magnificent, sweeping tale that I haven't stopped thinking
about since I turned the last beautiful page'
Amanda Geard

'Beautifully written, powerful and poignant. Time and place are
brilliantly evoked, with a moving love story at its core'
Tracy Rees

'Utterly emotive and beautiful'
Lorna Cook

'Ashcroft writes with the perfect blend of elegance and emotional
punch'
Hazel Gaynor

'Emotional, evocative and enthralling'
Kate Furnivall

Jenny Ashcroft is the author of several historical novels, including *Beneath a Burning Sky* and *Island in the East*. She previously spent much of her life living, working and exploring in Australia and Asia, and now splits her time between Australia and the UK.

Also by Jenny Ashcroft

Beneath a Burning Sky
Island in the East
Meet Me in Bombay
Under the Golden Sun
The Echoes of Love

SECRETS

of the

WATCH
HOUSE

JENNY ASHCROFT

ONE PLACE. MANY STORIES

HQ
An imprint of HarperCollins*Publishers* Ltd
1 London Bridge Street
London SE1 9GF

www.harpercollins.co.uk

HarperCollins*Publishers*
Macken House, 39/40 Mayor Street Upper,
Dublin 1, D01 C9W8, Ireland
This edition 2024

1
First published in Great Britain by
HQ, an imprint of HarperCollinsPublishers Ltd 2024

ISBN: PB: 978-0-00-846909-2
TPB: 978-0-00-846906-1

This book contains FSC™ certified paper and other controlled
sources to ensure responsible forest management.

For more information visit: www.harpercollins.co.uk/green

This book is set in Sabon by HarperCollins*Publishers* India

Printed and Bound in the UK using 100% Renewable
Electricity at CPI Group (UK) Ltd

For you, Chloe

Hello old thing,

I've been meaning to write for such a terribly long time. I do hope you'll forgive the delay. I gather you're to have a new resident on the island. A young lady who, by my estimate, will arrive at Aoife's on the same boat that brings this letter. I'm picturing her now, clambering ashore, doe eyes taking in her wild new home. Quite striking, so I believe. Although, no patch on Elizabeth.

Who could be?

Still, a pretty lone woman, come to stay. My goodness, that must bring back some memories.

Although have you really managed to forget it all?

Forget what you did?

And got away with.

Could you truly have put a thing like that from your mind?

I know I've never been able to. And how strange, how utterly perplexing it is, that even as I sit here, imprisoned by sorrow, you remain at liberty, with life on Aoife's still continuing.

And now another woman invited to her shores.

What would she think, I wonder, if she was to learn the truth of how that ended for Elizabeth?

Oh, has that made you anxious, old thing? A little hot in the skin?

1

You've believed your secret safe, haven't you?

But I know it all, you see.

I know just what you did, and where you were, that October night in 1932.

And I'll be keeping a closer eye on you from now on. I have a little bird among you. A little bird who, when pressed, tweets.

A little bird who tweets to me.

You haven't got away with it, old thing.

I simply can't allow you to have got away with it.

Chapter One

Violet

April 1934

It was on an inauspiciously grey day that Violet Ellis made her move from London to Aoife's Bay, her world packed loosely into her father's battered suitcase, and no one left in that city she'd so fleetingly belonged to, to miss her. The landlady of her Lancaster Gate boarding house had already given her room to another – a primary school teacher who'd sighed at the damp marks adorning the floral walls, the missing hooks on the curtains, but paid a month's rent in advance anyway, because what more could one expect for a crown and six? – and her employer, Mr Barlow, of the legal firm Barlow Shipley, had hired a new secretary. Thenceforth, a Miss Lydia Atkins would be arranging his diary, taking his dictations, and reminding him to return his wife's telephone calls. Good luck to her, really.

Violet had travelled on the Tuesday night sleeper from Paddington to Penzance, then by bus to the fishing village of St Leonard's, where, as per her instructions, she'd headed to the harbour, looking for a postman, there to catch the same boat as him, on to Aoife's. It had been a relief when she'd spotted his uniform so easily on the small, drizzly quayside. She'd been fretting about missing him, missing the crossing. There were just three a week to the island, she'd been warned – Aoife's, with its less than twenty residents, apparently had no need for more. Small, and several nautical miles out to sea, it had never been a magnet for tourists like St Michael's Mount, or St Mary's. Violet herself hadn't even heard of it, until the headlines that had bellowed from the nation's broadsheets eighteen months before. Few had. Its isolation was, James Atherton had told her, the very quality that had most appealed to him when he'd built his now notoriously beautiful home into its cliffs.

The war made rather a bore of me, I'm afraid, he'd said, the first night they'd properly made one another's acquaintance, leaning across their table in Quaglino's, stubbing his cigarette into the tray. *When I came back, I craved silence, peace.* The lamplight had caught the glint in his dark eyes. His voice had been gravelly with irony. *I was utterly fixated on the idea of peace.*

It had been on a stormy October night in 1932 that his wife had disappeared. Violet had still been living with her father back then, the pair of them marooned in their own pocket of provincial obscurity, as they had been ever since Violet's mother had run off with an American serviceman, thirteen years before. Violet remembered how, sitting in her father's Oxfordshire kitchen, the news spread before her, reading the particulars of the final known movements of Elizabeth Atherton out for him, she'd stumbled over the pronunciation of Aoife.

'*Afe?*' she'd guessed. '*Oyfe?*'

Eee-fuh, she knew now.

Now, here she was, huddled into the cabin of a creaking tug, a battered lifebuoy knocking her shoulder, nothing but a stretch of churning water away from that infamous island becoming her home too.

On the floor, the postman crouched, his scuffed boots braced against the waves, sorting through his satchel of letters. The cabin air was stale, thick with the scent of petrol and rust. Every time the boat dipped, foam frisked the single porthole, dirtying it with salt. Violet stared at the keeling glass, her skin beading with the effort of

4

not regurgitating the bun she'd foolhardily consumed for breakfast. And the postman whistled, implausibly chipper. He'd told her at the quay that he'd been delivering to Aoife's since before Mr Atherton had lived there, back when its only building had been a lighthouse, its sole residents, the keepers. Clearly, he'd grown his sea legs.

He'd given up trying to make conversation now at least. Perhaps he'd realized how reckless further endeavours in that quarter would be.

He'd certainly been chatty enough when they'd met.

'A foreigner,' he'd declared once Violet had approached him on St Leonard's puddled harbour wall and they'd made their introductions. He'd crossed his arms, making a show of befuddlement as he'd looked her over, taking in her wide-legged trousers, belted winter coat and felt hat. 'Are you sure you're in the right place?'

'I hope so,' she'd said, absently, tired in that dizzy, queasy way. She'd barely slept on the train. Her dreams, when they had come, had been jerky disjointed affairs in which she'd already reached Aoife's Bay, and found James absent, his home an empty, windswept shell. It had been a relief, each time she'd woken, to discover none of it was real.

'You're here to visit?' the postman had asked.

'To work.'

'For Mr Atherton?'

'Yes.' She'd turned, looking out to sea, peering through the mist and drizzle. *You won't be able to see it*, he'd said. *It's too far away, below the earth's curvature.* 'Who else would it be, over there?'

There'd been a beat of silence.

She'd guessed the line the postman's thoughts had been taking.

To her mortification, she'd blushed.

They're all going to think you're there for Atherton's fun, you know, Mr Barlow had said, when she'd tendered her resignation back in London. *His wife barely cold in her grave.*

5

'I'm here as his new secretary,' she'd told the postman.

'Are you now?'

Her blush had deepened. 'Yes.'

'I had no idea he'd taken someone on.'

'No?'

'No. I normally know most things.'

'Right,' she'd said, and wished she could have thought of something cleverer to say.

He'd clicked his tongue. 'I wonder what Mrs Hamilton makes of it all.'

She'd heard his tone. His insinuation that she'd usurped Mrs Hamilton had been clear. But James had told her that Mrs Hamilton – his housekeeper, and the wife of his groundsman – had only ever been muddling along as his secretary. A stopgap after his old one had left, until he found someone permanent.

'She can't be happy,' the postman had persisted.

'I'm told she'll be relieved to have me there.'

'Well, if you'll believe that,' he'd said.

And she'd decided she really might not like him very much.

The boatman had arrived then at least, ordering them gruffly aboard, recommending they bunker down inside. 'Chop's up.' Whilst the postman had continued with Violet's interrogation as they'd set off into that undulating chop – asking about London, where Violet had worked, lived – she honestly couldn't vouch for how she'd responded. She wasn't even sure when he'd given up, switched to whistling instead.

And now they must be almost there. The boat's engine jolted, shifting in pitch as it slowed. Without the speed, the rocking became more pronounced. Feeling her stomach slosh, overcome by a suddenly urgent need to breathe fresh air, Violet clambered to her feet, and, bashing painfully against the boat's greasy wall, stumbled past the postman for the stairs.

The morning's chill struck her, biting and damp. Holding the doorway with one hand, and her hat to her head with the other, she filled her lungs, again, then again. Her eyes watered in the wind, the force of her nausea, so that her first sight of the island was taken in blurred snapshots, glimpses between heaves. The crescent of a deep, seaweed-strewn bay. A wooden jetty, washed by the waves, a boathouse beside it. Steep cliffs of rock, gorse and moss. Stairs, criss-crossing up them. A scattering of cottages at their head, a single chimney smoking. Then, away to her right, at the island's point, a distant lighthouse, stark against the slate sky.

And a white mansion, all glass, and light?

Where was that?

'You won't spot it from here.'

She started at the boatman's shout, and swivelled, jerkily, to face him. He was sitting at the tiller. He kept quite still as their eyes met, making no effort to conceal that he'd been staring, like a stranger normally would. He just kept on doing it.

'The big house is over the ledge,' he said. 'Nothing but the Atlantic between it and America.'

'I see.' The words, croaked from her too-tight throat, tasted of yeast, currants. She dipped her head, swallowing . . .

'You going to be sick?'

'No.'

'Sea doesn't suit you.' He stood, reaching for the mooring rope. 'You sure you're built for island life?'

It almost sounded like a warning.

She raised her eyes back to his, wondering if she'd imagined it. As she did, his attention shifted, caught by something on the shore, and she turned, following his stare, feeling the same stillness she'd observed in him take a hold of her. For he was there. James Atherton was there. Not absent from the island, as he'd been in her dreams, but jogging down the last of the cliff's steps, onto the jetty, come to meet her.

He had told her he'd come. *It's quite a hike to the house;*

I'll show you the way. His attention, his kindness, had ever felt unlikely, though.

She'd been so sure he'd send a member of staff in his place.

Distractedly, she pressed her hand to her clammy neck, eyeing him from beneath the brim of her hat. She hadn't seen him in weeks, not since the February morning he'd left London, when he'd startled her by proposing she take this position, and she'd startled him by accepting it. She'd pictured him often, after he'd gone – whilst in the office working out her notice; reading in her bedsit; walking away another weekend in Hyde Park – but memory, she realized now, made a sorry imitation of life. Somewhere along the way, she'd forgotten the subtleties, like his moderate height, and solid build; that air of understated assurance. He'd ceased to breathe, to move.

He moved now, towards the end of the jetty, his handsome face bowed against the wind. He breathed, deeply, his chest rising and falling beneath a thick cable-knitted jumper.

He'd always worn suits in London. Dark and expertly tailored, they'd been a breed apart from the sets her father had owned. (He had, for as long as she could recall, alternated between the same two ensembles – one brown, the other tweed – that by the end had been faded around the seams, their lining frayed.) She liked this jumper, the casual slacks and open jacket. Illusion it may be, but they made James seem more of this world.

He's a man mired in grief, Miss Ellis.

Out of nowhere, Mr Barlow's acerbic voice sounded again in her mind.

I never took you for a fool.

The boat chugged closer to the jetty, clunking alongside it.

The postman emerged, whistling from the cabin.

And James reached the jetty's edge, his dark eyes locking on Violet's.

You are swimming out of your depth. This decision, made in haste, will be one you regret.

'Welcome to Aoife's Bay,' James said, holding out his hand.

'Thank you,' Violet replied, taking it.

And, stealing one last moment to gather herself – tilting her head back, drawing another, deeper impression of the island, her eyes snagging on a figure that had appeared at the lighthouse – she climbed ashore.

Is it strange for you, seeing her there?

I expect it must be.

How do you feel about her, I wonder?

Or do you feel anything at all?

Are you capable of it?

Elizabeth certainly never believed you were.

I was at the funeral, you know. It was an interesting choice to hold it in St Leonard's rather than London. Oh, how funny! I was about to ask whether you agreed, but how could you possibly respond, when you have no idea who I am.

My word, how that must vex you.

But back to the funeral. Quite an impressive turnout, wasn't there? All those reporters, then so many of Elizabeth's crowd from London. Not quite as many as I'd expected. There were a few surprising faces missing.

I've marked them. I won't forget.

Still, it did amuse me, watching you. I have to applaud you, it really was such a compelling performance of shock, and sober reflection. I might almost have believed it, had I not been so certain of the relief coursing through your cold veins.

You thought it all over, didn't you?

All done with.

I want to believe you regret the torment you caused Elizabeth.
I want to think you might miss her.

I most certainly do. But I can't tell her that. There's nothing I can do for her at all, other than this one thing, which is to make sure that you do regret how you behaved, and that you are, however belatedly, served your just deserts.

I hope you have an appetite.
They're on their way.

Chapter Two

Violet

She hadn't told James who she really was, that first time they'd spoken, on a cold January night at the start of the year.

She hadn't needed to.

He, who'd attended her father's funeral the year prior, had already known that, before she'd taken her mother's maiden name of Ellis, she'd gone by her father's, Edevane. And that before her father had died, within months of Elizabeth, leaving Violet with nothing but a bar tally to settle, and a name too distinctive to use, he too had made it into the newspapers.

His funeral had been held in Pentonville Prison: a short, miserable affair. Violet, sitting alone in her front pew, had spent most of it furious, despising the intrusion of the reporters massed behind her, scribbling on their pads, and her father most of all, for so much: her childhood, the man he'd become, and the loneliness he'd inflicted on them; all he'd *done*. Locked in her own impotent rage, she hadn't noticed James, not until the end of the service, when – and she wasn't sure why: the weight of his attention? – she'd turned, and seen him, alone too, in the chapel's furthest most corner, looking right at her.

She'd never before met him, but had recognized him instantly from the papers' photographs. He'd known who she was, too, she'd been sure. What other reason could there have been for his interest in her? It had stunned her that he was there – her father had meant nothing but trouble to him, since they'd served together during the war – but what had surprised her more, had been the absence of any hostility in his stare. All she'd seen there was concern, warmth. And, for those few seconds that they'd held one another's eye, she'd felt strangely comforted: as though the reporters had disappeared, the indifferent chaplain too, taking her father's coffin with him, leaving just herself and James, and this utterly unexpected moment of compassion.

James hadn't approached her. Not that day. He'd slipped away as soon as the service had finished – anxious to avoid the notice of the reporters, she'd guessed – and she, full of shame, despite his silent kindness, certainly hadn't considered going after him.

She'd thought about him, though, afterwards. She'd done that often, reliving the fleeting sense of calm he'd given her; wondering, endlessly, how he'd done it.

She'd never imagined she'd see him again.

Never supposed their paths would cross.

But then they'd been thrown together, in January.

'Do you pity me?' she'd asked him, eyeing him across their lamplit table in Quagliono's: that haunt of London's bright and moneyed.

'Not now I've finally met you,' he'd said.

That night, the buzzing intimacy of the restaurant, felt a world away to her now, as, in Aoife's damp, swirling fog, with her hand slipping from James's, she drew another slow breath, her sickness still very much with her, an unsettling sense of disorientation too, because it was so odd to be here, on this island, living through this moment of her arrival, when she'd gone over it so many times in her imagination.

There were things she'd meant to say, she knew that there were, yet, for all her endless rehearsals, she couldn't recall them. All she could think of – as the wind gusted, stinging her face, and the postman remarked on how dark the sky had turned – was how strange it was to be seeing James again, seeing him at all, in the presence of an audience.

She looked to him, for a sign that he sensed the awkwardness too, but he was busy, catching the rope the boatman threw, crouching to tie it to the mooring.

'How was the journey?' he asked her, his voice raised above the weather.

'Fine,' she said, 'thank you.' That taste of currants again. 'Rather long.'

'I did warn you.'

'Yes,' she said, and managed if not a smile, then an approximation of one. 'You did.'

'Did you get any rest?' he asked, securing the knot.

'A little.'

'Well,' he stood, 'you must take it easy today. I hope the crossing wasn't too rough?'

'It was a bit choppy.'

'Been green as a cabbage,' said the boatman, dropping her case onto the wharf.

James raised a brow. 'A cabbage?'

'Not a cabbage,' said Violet. What an image.

'As the gills then,' volunteered the postman.

'It's at the gills,' she said, raising her hand against another blast of wind, 'green *at* the gills.'

'And how are you now?' asked James, studying her, not impatiently, nor unsympathetically – far from it – but nonetheless making her feel an idiot for being this cause for concern. 'Up to a walk, or need a rest?'

'Up to a walk,' she said, without hesitation, since it was either that, or stay on the wharf with him waiting for her to feel better.

'You're sure?'

'I'm sure.'

He scrutinised her a moment longer.

She held his stare.

Did he smile?

He turned away before she could be sure.

'All right,' he said, fetching her case. 'Then let's get on.'

The postman went with them.

The boatman, they left at the tug, setting a primus to boil, calling after the postman that he wasn't to be longer than he had to.

'I'll be long enough,' the postman called back, 'got something for everyone today.'

'No stopping for tea breaks.'

The postman didn't reply, just whistled.

'I mean it,' the boatman shouted.

He doesn't care, Violet silently told him, and wondered if it was Mrs Hamilton the postman was planning to have tea with.

She didn't ask.

But, as they neared the stairs, she did glance again at the lighthouse. There was no one there any more. Whomever it had been, up on that green elbow of land, had moved on. It was a relief, she realized.

She hadn't liked the way he'd stared.

'I'm glad you've come,' said James to her, bringing her attention back to the shore. He spoke with his voice lowered, out of earshot of the postman, forging ahead, letting her know that, for all his apparent oblivion on the wharf, he had indeed been conscious of their audience too. It struck her then that they'd both been acting. Putting on a show of comfort they neither of them felt. 'I'm not sure I believed you would.'

'I'm not sure I believed I would either,' she admitted.

She'd had to come, though.

It had been daunting uprooting her life yet again, and moving to this remote island of strangers – almost every one of whom had been a suspect, not so very long ago, in the death of a woman

15

who'd been a newcomer too, married to James for just four months. But she couldn't have borne to remain in London. Not once she'd grown to know James, and he'd offered her this escape from that deadening existence she'd believed herself so trapped in.

Ever since he had, she'd had not a moment's peace, taunting herself with the idea of passing such an opportunity up.

And she trusted James.

She looked at him sideways, then quickly away as his eyes moved, catching hers, and was almost convinced she could trust him.

She wanted to do that.

He, after all, had never been accused of anything, certainly not of murdering his wife.

No one had ever been formally accused of that.

Accidental death, the inquest had ruled, when Elizabeth's body had been discovered, a month after her disappearance, trapped in a mainland cave.

He surely wouldn't have invited her here, had he anything to hide.

It had been chance that had taken Violet to Quaglino's back in January, although James had told her that he'd have sought her out, had Nicholas Barlow not paid him the unintentional convenience of sending her his way.

It was on the last Wednesday of the month that it had happened.

Was there anything more insipid than a January Wednesday? Until that point, Violet hadn't believed there could be. She'd turned twenty-seven only the Wednesday before, and there'd been nothing but a couple of damp bus rides between her bedsit and the office, paste sandwiches for lunch, a jacket potato for dinner, and a single greeting card, to mark the day.

The card had been from her godfather: a solicitor cousin of her father with whom neither he nor she had ever been especially close (her father hadn't been the kind for *close*), but who'd nonetheless executed her father's will the June before. He'd also been the one to refer Violet for her post at Barlow Shipley, under the name of Ellis.

I doubt you'll warm to Nicholas, he'd cautioned, *but there are other things to recommend the position.*

He'd meant the wage, and the opportunity to strike a fresh start in a faceless new city. But the wage had barely covered Violet's rent, and, after so many years in a small town, where she hadn't been able to walk the length of the high street without bumping into someone she knew, she'd found London's sprawling vastness overwhelming, its indifference, oppressively lonely.

Her godfather's hunch about Nicholas Barlow had proven correct too; she hadn't warmed to him: not to his shouted commands, nor his allergy to the words please and thank you, nor his tendency to blink his eyes out of time when agitated. ('Nerve damage,' he'd told her, early on in her employment. 'The war, you know.' She'd felt almost sorry for him until his wife, cross about another missed dinner, had filled her in on the context: namely that he'd damaged the nerve when he'd fallen, drunk after enlisting, on a wine bottle at The Carlton Club, *so ensuring he never had to fight at all.*)

It was him who'd been meant to dine with James that icy Wednesday night. Violet had made the reservation herself, her mind a jangling confusion at the news that James Atherton was not only to be in town, come on a trip from the West Country, but was to be meeting her own employer, direct from his train.

He'd parted ways with his existing lawyer, Mr Barlow had smirkingly reported, and was looking for somebody new to manage his legal affairs. Violet had hardly needed it explaining what a windfall winning such a contract would be. There couldn't have been anyone left in England unaware of the scale of James's estate, when the newspapers had reported on it in such lascivious detail. On top of the vast swathes of landed wealth he'd inherited from his family, he had, since the end of the war, amassed his own personal fortune in cooperative retail, with stores spanning the country, selling the fruits of his tenant-farmers' labours. Managing the contracts of that business alone would have been more than enough to keep Mr Barlow's wife in pearls, his mistresses in diamonds. Given that – given Mr Barlow had only recently lost two important clients to a firm started by rivals of his, Edwin Firth and Patrick Knightley – it hadn't surprised Violet that he'd become so immediately fixated on winning James's business. It was why he'd had her reserve a table at Quaglino's.

'Let's see Firth Knightly top that,' he'd said.

What *had* surprised her was when, on that frozen Wednesday, he had, in his rush to return to the office from a court hearing, skidded his Aston on black ice, wrapping it around a Mayfair lamppost, and telephoned her from a paybox in the North London Hospital, ordering her to Quaglino's in his stead, there to apologise to James for his absence.

'Can't I just call?' she'd asked, unclear, in her sudden panic, whether that was what she even wanted to do. But she was to seek James out? *Talk* to him?

'Call and you're dismissed,' Mr Barlow had replied. 'Atherton's too important for a brush-off. And don't you dare tell him I crashed the motor. He might think me an idiot.'

'I absolutely think him an idiot,' James had said when, two hours later, they were eating the meal he'd insisted Violet share with him: a meltingly rare Steak Diane, creamy gratin dauphinoise, and a smoky merlot, that had all gone down so much better than any jacket potato. ('We'll have to tell the chef,' he'd said.) 'My only interest in meeting him was to find out how you are.'

By that point, she'd forgotten her nerves, and the inadequacy that had assailed her when she'd arrived at the packed restaurant. Forgotten that she was wearing a cheap blouse and skirt, her face make-up-less beneath hair she'd intended to wash that night, whilst every other woman around her wore silk dresses and feathered headbands, their rouged lips smoking cigarettes from opera-length holders. She'd almost forgotten her mortification, when, about to introduce herself to James, she'd only stared at him, crippled into silence by her uncertainty as to whether to go by Miss Ellis, or Miss Edevane.

'Which would you prefer?' he'd asked, guessing her dilemma.

'Miss Ellis, I think. It's what Mr Barlow knows me as. Please don't . . .'

'Tell him? I won't. Will you sit?'

So, she'd sat.

He'd tracked her down, he'd told her, care of her father's old landlord; the only person, other than her godfather, who'd known where she'd gone.

'Why go to the bother?' she'd asked, amazed that he had.

'Because I haven't been able to stop thinking about how alone you were at the funeral,' he'd said. 'I needed to know what had become of you. That you're all right.'

She'd flushed. 'I couldn't believe you were there.'

'I had to be.'

'To pay your respects?' she'd asked, dubiously.

'Say goodbye, anyway.'

'I would have thought you'd rather have forgotten all about my father.'

'He's not been an easy man to forget.'

'No,' she'd concurred. 'I don't suppose he can have been.'

The pair of them had met at the start of the war, in the same battalion from the off: Violet's father, a private, and James – more than fifteen years his junior – his officer. Whilst Violet's father had always remained in the ranks, James had been promoted quickly, becoming commander of the battalion in time for the Somme, where Violet's father had lost his foot. Enemy fire, he'd claimed, but had been court martialled for doing it to himself, got away with it somehow, and always blamed *Lieutenant Colonel Atherton* (the sneering way he'd said it) for his shame.

His resentment was why he'd become so morbidly fascinated with the news when Elizabeth Atherton had disappeared, having Violet buy all those newspapers, and read him every article, then writing his letters to the police, and the papers, full of his crackpot theories about the hand James had surely played in Elizabeth's fate.

The *Illustrated News* ran a piece on him in the end, far from kind, complete with a caricature of *our one-footed Sherlock Holmes*. Violet hadn't bought the edition, fearing her father's reaction, but he'd got wind of it at their local, and, that night, smashed a hole in their kitchen wall. Then, Elizabeth's body had been found, without any sign of struggle or injury, and, with the case closed, the journalist at the *Illustrated*, probably trying to fill column space, had written another jeering piece, pontificating on what new mystery Sherlock might turn his attention to next.

Perhaps he'll unmask Jack the Ripper. Or finally solve the murder of the princes in the tower. Oh, Private Nathan Edevane, do keep us posted.

Violet hadn't managed to keep that article from her father either. He hadn't smashed any more holes in their walls, though. Instead, he'd got himself very drunk (an art at which he'd had some considerable form), caught a train to London, and the *Illustrated News*'s office, where he'd set upon the wrong man – not a journalist, but a clerk – with a revolver he'd managed to hold on to when he'd been demobbed. It hadn't been loaded, but he'd cracked the poor man's skull with it anyway, and been hanged for his murder at Pentonville.

'Do you pity me?' Violet had asked James across their table, her chest tightening on the humiliating idea, when her father had been such an expert at pitying himself.

'Not now I've finally met you,' James had said. His expression had remained set, but his eyes had warmed. 'You don't warrant it.'

'Good.'

'I do however despise it for you.'

'I'm not your responsibility.'

'But your father was. Once, he was.'

'A very long time ago.'

'Perhaps I should have helped him more, though, after he came home.'

'Why?'

'Why not?'

'You must have had thousands under your command. Have you helped all of them?'

'A lot of them didn't come back.'

'But of those that did?'

'No . . . '

'Then why should you have helped my father?' She'd frowned, baffled. 'I could barely bring myself to keep doing it in the end, and I'm his daughter.' The words had been out before she'd known they were coming.

She'd bitten her lip, shocked at her own candour.

Never had she been so honest, with anyone. Thanks to her father, who'd guarded her movements so obsessively – setting his stopwatch to time her walks home from school, then work – she'd never really had anyone she could be honest with.

'Sorry,' she'd said, moving her eyes to her glass. 'I expect that must sound very selfish.'

'Not at all,' James had replied. 'He wasn't an easy man to help.'

And, at his understanding, she'd raised her gaze to his once more.

A short silence had followed. There were so many questions she could have filled it with. Such as, whether her father really had shot himself. And what hand he, James, had truly played in his court martial.

If it *had* been him who'd reported her father as a coward.

But she hadn't been able to bring herself to do it.

She hadn't wanted to know if James had done her father a disservice, because if he had, she'd have had to get up, leave the buzzing intimacy of the restaurant.

Leave him.

And honestly, in that moment, she hadn't believed he could have done her father wrong. Rather, as he'd continued to stare across at her, his strong face contemplative, seeming – however extraordinarily – to really *care*, about *her*, she'd felt how very nice it was to be cared about by anyone.

To be cared about by someone like him.

The novelty of the sensation had remained with her all through that evening, as, with the merlot softening her inhibitions, sip by sip, she'd found herself talking more – about London, the mundanity of her work, her motivation for qualifying as a secretary in the first place ('I needed to look after my father.' Truly, it worked as an explanation for almost every decision she'd made from the age of ten); even her mother, who'd endured just two more years of life with her footless father, before she'd fled to Boston with her American. *I can't bear the smallness of this life, Violet. Not even for you.*

'Why didn't she take you with her?' James had asked.

'I don't think her American wanted to be saddled with a stranger's child, who sucked her hair.'

'So, she left you alone with Nathan?'

'Yes.'

'How spectacularly selfish of her.'

'I don't know,' Violet had turned her glass, thinking of the countless times she'd yearned to run, 'I can see how life in America would have felt like a nicer adventure.'

She'd asked him questions too, not about Elizabeth, despite her curiosity – he hadn't mentioned her, and instinctively she'd sensed

22

she was off limits – but his home, and the fixation on peace that had led him to Aoife's; whether he'd ever had any intention of giving Mr Barlow his business.

'None whatsoever,' he'd said, with a laugh that was low, and complicit, and which had made her laugh too.

He hadn't let her catch the bus home, but had taken her in his motorcar. When they'd arrived, he'd got out to open her door, and, in the frozen, starlit night, turned to look up at the crumbling façade of her bedsit.

'It's nicer inside,' she'd lied.

'Is it?' he'd said, and she'd felt it again: the jolt of his concern.

She hadn't wanted to hope to see him again, fearing disappointment, but had hoped anyway, which had felt odd too, when normally she depended only on herself.

They'd met on four more occasions: twice for dinner, which he'd thrilled her by inviting her to with telephone calls at her desk ('Who was that?' Mr Barlow had barked from his office, and she'd fobbed him off with fibs about stationery suppliers, and his wife); once, for lunch ('Your paste sandwiches are preying on my mind.'); and then, at the very end of his fortnight-long trip, for a snowy Sunday morning stroll in St James's Park, the two of them wrapped in thick coats and scarves.

She'd felt horribly flat as they'd walked, discombobulated at the prospect of their looming goodbye – no more telephone calls to be poised for, nor meals to look forward to; those dinners that had lasted for hours, and passed in the blink of an eye. She'd glanced up at him, her gaze on his strong face, and – unable to bear, quite suddenly, that she might never see it, or him, again – had been on the verge of asking when he might return to the city. But then he'd stopped, turned to her; asked if she'd consider moving to Aoife's, working for him there.

'I've needed someone for a long time,' he'd said. 'Mrs Hamilton does her best, but she's had no training, she's not really up to it.

I think you would be.' His eyes had shone in the cold. When he'd spoken, he'd breathed fog. Behind him, framed by the white, leafless trees, the lake had looked like molten silver. 'This is not pity, you have to take my word on that. But Aoife's is a long way from anywhere. It's really not for everyone.' He'd paused. 'I think you'll find it's an improvement on your bedsit, though.'

'That sounds a little like pity,' she'd said, somehow sounding calm, despite the spin into which he'd just set her world.

'It's simple fact,' he'd replied.

She hadn't argued.

But nor had she really believed him.

I'm not your responsibility, she'd told him, back in Quaglino's.

But your father was, he'd replied. *Once, he was.*

Neither of them had raised the subject of her father again since that night. Painful and uncomfortable to speak about, she'd been glad of their silence on the matter.

But she'd thought about it.

Accepted, deep down, that guilt over her father's court martial, as well as pity for her, was, probably, what had motivated James to continue seeking her out as he had.

Rationally, she'd decided that she should probably refuse his offer.

Suspecting that part of him at least had been expecting her to do that, she'd even drawn breath to say the words.

Then she'd stopped.

She'd seen herself returning to her bedsit that afternoon, there to spend another evening all alone, hollow with melancholy that he was now gone.

She'd pictured the monotonous days, and weeks, and months lying ahead of her in London: full of nothing but paste sandwiches, solitary bus rides, and hours spent marking time, wondering whether life might, after all, have been different, if she'd just had the courage to seize this chance James was offering her.

She'd looked into his gaze – intent, steady, not rushing her – and wondered how it might feel to wake up tomorrow knowing that she *hadn't* said no to him.

That she had, in fact, said yes, and would be moving to his home.

To work for him.

Live with *him*.

She'd thought of how little there really was to keep her in London.

Then, of all the times James had made her smile, and laugh, and forget so much, over the fortnight just gone.

And, how miserable, how unutterably miserable, she'd been before it.

You can't do this, she'd tried again to insist to herself.

You can't.

Can you?

At the question, she'd felt a ballooning within her: part apprehension, but mostly adrenalin, at the decision she'd still been too confused to realize her heart had already reached, from the moment James had first spoken.

'I'd like to work for you,' she'd heard herself say. 'If you really do need me.'

'Yes?' He'd looked at her twice. 'That's a yes?'

'It's a yes,' she'd said, and in spite of her shock at what she'd just agreed to – or perhaps, because of it – she'd laughed. 'Yes, please.'

'Right,' he'd said, and expelled a laugh of his own. 'You'd better tell Nicholas Barlow.'

What a dark little horse you are, Mr Barlow had said, the following morning, as she'd stood before his desk. His stitches had puckered a livid welt across his forehead. His arm had been in a cast. In his bin, torn to clumsy chunks, had been the letter informing him that

James had appointed Firth Knightly as his new counsel. *Slick so-and-so hasn't even asked me for a reference. Although I suspect it's not your typing he's interested in.*

They're all going to think you're there for Atherton's fun, you know.

His wife barely cold in her grave.

MILLIONAIRE'S WIFE MISSING FROM
ATLANTIC ISLAND

It has been reported that the renowned society darling, Mrs Elizabeth Atherton, newly married to Mr James Atherton – himself a decorated war hero, and sole owner of the highly profitable Atherton Holdings Limited – has disappeared without explanation or trace from the West Country island of Aoife's Bay. Little is known about Aoife's Bay, other than that Mr Atherton, a notoriously private man, has used it as his main residence for some seven years. Reachable only by boat, the island was unusually full this weekend past, thanks to several guests invited by Mrs Atherton for a house party. These guests she left at six on Saturday night, venturing out into inclement weather for a walk from which she never returned.

At time of writing, the local police are in residence on Aoife's Bay, with an inspector from Scotland Yard to be despatched. All staff and guests have been detained indefinitely. An extensive search is being conducted of the island and neighbouring mainland coast. Furthermore, an appeal has been issued that anyone who may have seen or heard anything untoward in the surrounding area to come forward immediately.

Your sister was the reason you accepted that bribe to remain silent, wasn't it?

You could have told the police you'd done it. You really could have. You left it too long, I suppose. Became afraid of the conclusions they might draw.

Conclusions I can't help but come to, myself.

And now you're more frightened, aren't you?

How unbecoming fear is.

Almost as unbecoming as desperation.

Chapter Three

Violet

The sky had blackened even further by the time Violet, James and the postman reached the top of Aoife's cliff stairs. It felt more like nightfall than morning. Even the postman, staring upwards, paused his whistling, before making off for the cottages. Violet stopped where she was, catching her breath, and James set her case down, flexing his hand, narrowing his eyes at the leaden heavens.

'Will we make it?' she asked him, relieved to discover that, for the first time since leaving St Leonard's, her gullet hadn't opened when she'd spoken. At some point on their steep climb, the world had ceased to tilt.

'Possibly,' he said. 'Let's keep moving.'

They passed the postman at the first of the cottages, rifling through his satchel at its green front door. James offered to take the mail from him for his own house, but the postman refused, insisting it was more than his job was worth to delegate the servants' deliveries.

'It's the cake he cares about,' James said to Violet, as they continued on. 'He always calls in at the kitchen.'

This time she did ask. 'To see Mrs Hamilton?'

'To see anyone he can find.'

'Was that the Hamiltons' cottage?' she asked, glancing back at the green door, remembering he'd mentioned they didn't live with

29

the rest of the staff in the house.

'Yes,' he said, and told her about the other homes in the trio, each set in their own walled-off patch of land. One was empty, he said, and had been for years, no one on the island having any use for it. 'This one, however,' he went on, as they reached the final cottage, with the smoking chimney, 'belongs to our fire warden. Gareth Phillips.'

Violet's steps faltered at the name. She'd read it so often, it felt almost like hearing that of a film star. Gareth Phillips, variously painted as certain villain and innocent bystander by the papers, had been the last person to have seen Elizabeth, out walking Aoife's cliffs the October night she'd vanished. It had been James's thirty-seventh birthday; a celebratory dinner had been planned. Elizabeth, Gareth had claimed, had been wearing an evening gown and galoshes beneath a thick coat when he'd seen her. Violet, struck by the incongruity of that image, had wondered – as the papers had inevitably all come to wonder – what could have compelled Elizabeth to abandon her hostess duties and venture out into autumn winds that had sounded easily as bad as they were now.

She looked at the cottage, taking in its stone brickwork, climbing ivy, and murky salt-stained windows, catching the profile of a face at an upstairs one, peering down at her.

'Is that him there?' she asked James, raising her hand to point, but even as she did, the face retreated. 'Oh, he's gone,' she said, and thinking of that lone figure at the lighthouse, felt another shiver of discomfort.

All these silent observers.

'He keeps himself to himself,' said James. 'Don't worry about him.'

'All right,' she said.

But still . . .

Who else was watching, she wondered?

*

30

They saw no one at least on their walk to the house.

The first half-mile, they followed a narrow cliff pass away from the cottages, towards the lighthouse. They didn't talk; the gale was too loud, and the pass too treacherous for Violet to do anything but concentrate on each step she took. To her right, just a slip away, the ground disappeared in a drop to fifty feet below, where the waves crashed messily onto the shore. Every few seconds, Violet dared herself to look downwards, the gusts buffeting her, and each time she did, was struck by awful dread at how easily she might step sideways and fall. How silently one might tumble.

'Don't get too close,' called James over his shoulder, as though inside her mind.

It was a relief when, at length, they turned inland, veering onto another track, mown through high, wild grass. James slowed his pace to walk beside her – never less than a respectful distance away (was he as conscious of it as she?) – and, with the deluge still holding off, but the wind resisting every step they took, he told her about the room that had been prepared for her, not in the servants' quarters as she'd anticipated, but in the east wing of the house.

'Won't the other servants mind?' she said, squinting as the sun briefly pierced the clouds, then disappeared again.

'You're not a servant,' he said. 'And you'll be keeping very different hours.'

'I don't want to get off on the wrong foot . . . '

'You won't.'

'And where will I eat?'

'Wherever you like.'

'I'd better do it in the kitchen.'

'Whatever you want,' he said, 'really.'

He swapped her suitcase from hand to hand.

'I'm sorry,' she said, thinking of the items she'd packed. There really wasn't much, but she hadn't scrimped on the weight. She'd more dragged than lifted it through the various stages of her journey. 'I didn't think you'd have to carry it.'

'Who did you imagine would?'

'I don't know . . . a footman.'

'Let them do it, you mean?' He gave her a sideways look. 'And you worried about getting on with them all.'

She smiled.

'What do you have in here anyway?' he asked. 'Is it Nicholas Barlow?'

She burst out laughing. 'Not him.'

His eyes shone. 'Someone else then?'

'Just books. My favourite books.'

'Ah. And what are they, Miss Ellis?'

'No,' she said, her smile turning rueful, realizing it was an odd question to refuse. 'I'm not telling you that.'

'Whyever not?'

'Because you'll probably have a view on them.'

Another look. 'Well, of course I'll have a view.'

'Exactly. And then, whenever I read whichever of my books you had that view on, I'll think to myself, oh, this is the one that Mr Atherton,' (she still called him Mr Atherton), 'pulled an odd face at . . . '

'What book would I pull an odd face at?'

'I'm not telling you. Because if I did, and you did pull that face, then that book would cease to mean what it does to me now, and become something else instead.'

He thought about it.

And she replayed everything she'd just said, hearing it through his ears, cringing a little – because of course it *was* odd – but not too much, because it was also who she was, and if there was one thing living with an oxygen-stealing man like her father had taught her, it was to hold on tight to those parts of her that most mattered.

'You know there are such a thing as book clubs, don't you?' James said. 'They exist purely because people enjoy sharing what they read.'

'Yes, I do know that.'

'Oh, you do?'

'I do. And I enjoy sharing what I read too. With books like . . . Oh, I don't know, *The Great Gatsby*, or *The Mystery of the Blue Train* . . . '

'My God, Fitzgerald and Christie don't make your cut?'

She laughed again, relaxing more, but not so much that she wasn't conscious of him watching her do it; the curious slant to his smile.

'It's not that I don't admire those books. But these,' she gestured at her case, 'they're the ones that I've always turned to. They're mine. Just mine.'

'I wasn't even especially curious about them before. But now I am . . . '

'Then I'd definitely better not tell you. It's been built up too much.'

'Tell me one book, please.'

'No.'

The wind pelted them.

'Just one.'

'I shan't.'

'I like Maugham.'

'Good for you,' she said.

And this time, he was the one to laugh.

The house stopped her in her tracks when, at length, it came into view beneath them, on a plateau of land at the base of another steep set of stairs. She'd been braced for something incredible, something vast (*palatial*, the reporters had described it as; *magnificent*), but somehow nothing quite so elegant, so . . . modern. Running up to the glass-walled porch was a limestone path, rimmed by rectangular pools of water, and lush lawns, their calm symmetry a soothing contrast to the wilds of the waves, the cliffs and fields. The building itself spread across the entire width of the plateau; in the centre, it rose high, all glinting white paintwork, curved edges, and high windows; on either side spread two single-storied arms, hugging the drop to the water. It seemed to Violet – in the second before the heavens opened, compelling her to race after James down the stairs – that, with a single drawn breath, the house might raise those arms, and dive into the sea.

'Watch your step,' James warned, grabbing her hand at the base of the stairs, helping her across a muddy puddle, onto the limestone path. Rain drenched his face. His grasp, through her glove, was warm. 'Come on,' he said, and, as they ran, he held onto her hand for several seconds more, or she held onto his, the delay in them letting the other go too pronounced for her not to feel it.

It was only as they neared the house that they released one another. Trying to ignore the lingering sense of his touch, she followed him up the porch's front stairs, through the door, and into the entrance hall beyond, where they stepped apart, holding their arms wide, staring down at their soaked selves.

There was a fire crackling in a large, open grate. The relief of its heat struck, then oozed through Violet. Stepping towards the flames, she raised the hand that had just been in his up to them, studying her fingers as she curled them into a fist. Then, realizing what she was doing, she hurriedly reached for her sodden hat, removing it, and surveyed the room. It was more of an atrium than anything, with a cathedral-height ceiling, and expansive wooden floors, covered in rugs. Glowing lamps burned, lifting the gloom, and, on the far side of the room, the wall was entirely made of glass, with doors that opened onto a semi-circular veranda. Beyond that, there was only ocean. Violet could smell the salt, the smoke of the fire, and the oil from the lamps.

Then, a musky perfume.

This she attributed to the woman who appeared from a door behind her, the clip of her heels making her turn. She was older than Violet, but by no stretch old – in her mid-thirties, or thereabouts – and immaculately dressed in a pencil skirt and coral silk blouse, with tonged waves in her glossy black hair.

She glanced at Violet only briefly, before turning to James, holding out her hands to take his coat.

'I rather thought you'd have been caught in it,' she said, with a cutglass accent that wouldn't have sounded out of place on a wireless news broadcast. 'What a shame.'

'It's fine,' he said, handing her his coat.

'I told you Arnold could have gone . . . '

'It's fine,' he said again, 'just some rain.'

'Very heavy rain.'

'And I'll change. But first, meet Miss Ellis.'

The woman turned, her gaze settling on Violet longer this time.

'How do you do,' she said.

'This is Mrs Hamilton,' James told Violet, confirming what she'd already guessed, but which her mind had been fighting.

This smart, polished woman before her was just so very different to what she'd been expecting.

It was only now she saw her that she realized what a hackneyed bumpkin cliché she'd drawn in her imagination. She wasn't sure why she'd conjured someone so stout, and flush-skinned, and wispily white-haired. Perhaps it had been knowing that Mrs Hamilton was the groundsman's wife, with all the associations of wholesome country-romping and apple-pie baking that came with. She'd had little else to go on, after all. The newspapers had largely left the Hamiltons alone since the pair of them, with an alibi in the form of each other – they'd been at home, ready for bed, when James had sought them out that October night, enlisting their aid in tracking Elizabeth down – had been among the few unsuspected of foul play. Whilst foul play had still been suspected.

'It's a pleasure to meet you,' Violet said to her.

'You must be exhausted,' Mrs Hamilton replied, no allusion to pleasure or otherwise. 'I'll show you to your room directly.' She returned her attention to James. 'You have several letters to sign before the post goes. I've left them on your desk.' The corner of her rouged lips turned. 'My last little job.'

Her tone was amused. Violet might have believed her to be in jest. But it was the brevity with which she'd just addressed her – how she kept speaking to James as though she wasn't there; it was making her remember the postman's words earlier, when she'd said she thought Mrs Hamilton relieved that she was coming. *Well, if you'll believe that* . . .

'I'll fetch the letters once I have Miss Ellis settled,' Mrs Hamilton said to James, 'give you time to change.'

'Or I can fetch them,' Violet offered.

'Mrs Hamilton can manage this morning,' said James, and Violet didn't miss the glint of satisfaction in Mrs Hamilton's green eyes. 'I'll show you the ropes tomorrow.' He made for the stairs. 'Take the rest of the day to yourself, Miss Ellis. Get some rest.' He looked back at her. His hair was so wet it was black. Violet felt her own drip down her neck. 'If the rain stops, feel free to explore, but stick to the paths. Mrs Hamilton, please see to it that Miss Ellis gets some tea. Show her the kitchen too, please . . . '

'The kitchen, Mr Atherton?'

'Yes, she wants to eat down there.'

'Does she?'

'I thought that would be easiest,' said Violet.

Mrs Hamilton said nothing.

Instead, as James ran up the stairs, she flicked her chin at Violet's case, letting her know she expected her to pick it up, and set off across the atrium, compelling Violet to follow.

'I will show you the kitchen, once you're settled,' she said, as soon as they were out of James's hearing, 'but it would be better all round if you were to take your meals in your bedroom.' She made for a door midway down the atrium, opening it to reveal a wide, skylit corridor, on which the rain hammered a percussion. 'You've been given the best in the wing, so you may as well make use of it.'

April 1934

You're at sixes and sevens now, aren't you?
I would say I'm sorry.
But, I'm not sorry at all. Not about that.
Only that any of it happened.

Chapter Four

Violet

The room was beautiful. The most beautiful Violet had set foot in, by a long chalk, and well beyond what any secretary might, in their wildest dreams, hope to be given. It sat at the very end of the east wing, with windows on two sides, one looking towards the lighthouse, the other, out to sea. It had a bathroom ('Piped,' Mrs Hamilton supplied, gesturing at the bath's copper faucets, 'we have a hot water tank'), another blazing fire, and a set of French doors that opened to a smaller version of the veranda that ran off the atrium.

Violet crossed to those doors, looking out over the slate ocean. It was almost the same colour as the sky. She stared at the waves, her tired, gravelly eyes blurring on their rhythmic undulations, at once stunned by this luxury she found herself in – this was to be her home now, her *home* – and nettled by a growing conviction that James had been quite wrong on the fields, when he'd claimed the servants wouldn't mind her being given such quarters. Mrs Hamilton, cool and stiff behind her, undoubtedly did. As for the others . . . How could they not?

And if Violet wasn't to be accepted by them, then who exactly was she to belong with?

'The offices are in the west wing,' said Mrs Hamilton, slicing through her thoughts. 'Mr Atherton has his rooms in the main house.' She went to the bed, smoothing an invisible crease on its crisp, thick eiderdown. 'The kitchen, ground and house-servants have their rooms in the basement. You'll be all alone in this wing.' She raised her head. 'I trust you won't mind that.'

'Not at all,' said Violet.

Although actually . . . would she?

It was such a vast, silent house, after all.

On an island where women disappeared.

Accidental death, she reminded herself, *it was accidental death*.

Bloody rot, her father chimed in, *that woman was killed*.

'I'll leave you to unpack,' said Mrs Hamilton. 'I trust this is all to your liking?'

'Yes, of course,' said Violet, her mind still half with her father. 'Thank you.'

'I had very little time to prepare, you see.' Mrs Hamilton went to the door. 'Mr Atherton only let us know on Monday afternoon that you were to join us.'

That made Violet look at her twice.

'What, *this* Monday?' she said. 'As in, two days ago?'

'As in two days ago,' Mrs Hamilton confirmed. 'Peculiar that he didn't mention it before, isn't it?'

Violet couldn't think what to say.

Slowly, she turned the revelation over in her exhausted mind, making better sense now of why the postman had known nothing of her coming – his last round would have been Monday morning – but none at all of James keeping it hidden from his staff.

From the *woman* Violet was replacing.

You'll be doing us both a favour, he'd told her, back in London.

She'd simply supposed, when he'd left, that he'd have given Mrs Hamilton notice.

And whilst it now seemed painfully obvious that he must have known Mrs Hamilton wasn't going to be remotely relieved at this supposed favour Violet was doing her (and really, he might have warned Violet), he also hardly seemed the sort to let the potential sulks of an employee intimidate him. Violet could only assume, then, that he'd had another reason for keeping his business from his housekeeper.

But what?

'I've been helping in the office for almost two years,' said Mrs Hamilton, shedding no light. 'I wish I'd known I was falling short.' She rested her palm on the door's handle, her ivory brow pinching. 'I might have done something about it.'

'I'm sorry,' said Violet, the platitude empty to her own ears. 'It must have been difficult, juggling two positions.'

'I managed very well,' said Mrs Hamilton. 'I told Mr Atherton I would when his old secretary left.' She tapped the handle with her nail. 'She went just after he and Mrs Atherton married. She didn't want to be here any more. But then,' she paused, fixing Violet with a look, 'she didn't have this room.'

Violet stared.

So did Mrs Hamilton.

Below, the waves crashed.

They're all going to think you're there for Atherton's fun, you know.

For those few seconds, it was all Violet could hear.

She wanted to defend herself, to defend James – *he's never asked me for anything, certainly not that* – but how could she when nothing overt had been said?

The silence lengthened, straining the air with static.

And then Mrs Hamilton smiled, suddenly friendly, dizzying Violet with the switch.

'I'll send some elevenses up,' she said, and opened the door. 'In the meantime, why not have a nice long bath, find yourself some dry clothes and leave your wet ones in the basket for laundering. We don't want you catching cold.'

*

41

There was little risk of Violet catching anything that day, which, once she'd washed and changed, she spent almost exclusively in her room, curled up in the ocean-facing window seat, bathed in the heat of the fire. Mrs Hamilton didn't return to show her to the kitchen. James didn't call by to see how she'd settled in. The only person Violet saw was a maid called Diana: a pale girl in her late teens who appeared a half hour after Mrs Hamilton had left, bringing with her a tray of tea and lemon cake, setting it on the table by the hearth.

'You're welcome, ma'am,' she said, when Violet thanked her.

'No,' said Violet, appalled. 'You mustn't call me, ma'am.'

'But,' Diana froze, midway through transferring the water to the pot, 'Mrs Hamilton told me I should.'

'You don't need to . . . '

She frowned, warily. 'I think I'd best, ma'am.'

Unlike Mrs Hamilton, Diana's hair was lank and fair, and there was no trace of make-up on her round, scrubbed face. Nor was she dressed in smart, figure-hugging clothes. Rather, she wore a traditional uniform of black dress and white apron that hung loose on her thin shoulders, was too long to be a fashionable calf-length, too short to reach to her stockinged ankles, making her look at once gangly and stooped, and giving Violet – now in a pullover and woollen skirt – the quite novel sense of being the best-dressed person in the room.

She wasn't at all forthcoming. Violet managed to extract only the sparsest of information from her, discovering that she, like most of the house staff, was from St Leonard's – the daughter of a fisherman – and had come to Aoife's at the age of sixteen, at the start of September 1932.

'You were here at the same time as Mrs Atherton then?' said Violet, interest piqued.

For so long, she'd wondered about Elizabeth, probing at the little she knew of her like she might a sore tooth: this woman whom James had chosen as his wife and who had, from the day of her disappearance, altered the terms of Violet's own existence. Now she was here, though, she couldn't seem to stop thinking about her. Whether she'd walked the same paths Violet had. Warmed herself before the same fires. Sat in the same window seat . . .

She knew what she'd looked like. The broadsheets had reprinted all the old society photographs of her, taken back in the twenties, in the days before marriage had started the countdown to her death: black and white images of an effervescently beautiful woman who'd always looked direct at the camera, with diamonds at her throat, more hanging from her ears, and a smile that seemed so amused by the carnival of her life.

She'd had red hair, the descriptions had said. Blue eyes.

How ordinary Violet's brown and brown felt by comparison.

'Did you know her well?' she asked Diana.

'No, ma'am,' she replied, making a beeline for the door, 'I hardly spoke to her.'

'Really?' said Violet, disbelieving. 'But you must have been here together for weeks.' It had been right at the end of October that Elizabeth had gone. 'You must have got to know one another.'

'Not really,' said Diana, 'she wasn't the kind to chat,' and with that she went, leaving Violet even more disbelieving – Elizabeth had hardly looked the quiet type – and feeling somehow scolded, for her own chattiness.

Alone once more, she picked at her cake, drank her tea, then closed her eyes, replaying everything that had passed since she'd left St Leonard's, her time with James especially: that strange stillness that had coursed through her when she'd caught sight of him on the wharf; how long they'd held onto one another, running through the rain.

Had it been so very long, though?

Or had she exaggerated it in the hecticness of the moment?

Sighing on her own unanswerable question, she pulled *The Painted Veil* from her pile of books (she liked Maugham too), but, too tired to focus, quickly let it fall closed on her lap. Resting her head against the window, she watched the rain come down, and, resolving that she needed to move – but unable, in such a storm, to do as James had suggested and explore the island – decided to head out around the house instead.

Retracing her steps down the corridor, she eased open the doors of its other bedrooms, peeking inside. All of them were cold and unlit, with air so still, it seemed certain no one had disturbed it in months. It came to Violet, as she progressed, that these must have been the rooms given to James and Elizabeth's guests, when they'd arrived to celebrate James's fateful birthday. Caught by the idea, she lingered on the threshold of the final room, wondering who it had belonged to. Mentally, she sketched them: these six strangers she'd reluctantly learnt so much of.

Henry and Amy Astley.

Richard and Cressida Thompson.

Rupert Litchfield and Lady Laura Ratcliffe.

At the room's window, rain pelted, like gravel.

A flash of lightening electrified the walls.

Edgy, suddenly – overcome by a disconcerting sense that if she was to turn, she'd catch Elizabeth just behind her, watching her – Violet moved swiftly on.

It was only when she reached the atrium and found it empty that she realized how much she'd been hoping to come across James.

She felt idiotic in her dismay. Like an overeager schoolgirl.

What fun Mr Barlow would have had with her, had he been there to see.

She wasn't completely alone, though. There were voices, coming from not so far away, behind the door Mrs Hamilton had appeared through earlier. One was male, the other female, too muted to make out properly, although it sounded, from the urgent way they spoke, that they were arguing. Violet strained to hear, becoming surer, the longer she listened, that the woman embroiled in the exchange was

Mrs Hamilton. It was her clipped, careful tone. As for the man, he definitely wasn't James – his voice didn't have the same depth – nor the postman, who was reedier.

'We'll talk about this later,' he said, suddenly discernible.

Quickly, fearing he – whoever he was – might be about to appear, and not wanting to get caught eavesdropping, Violet turned, giving up on her doomed outing, retreating back into her wing and hastening to her room.

There she stayed until nightfall.

Diana came again, with her meals, speaking only when Violet spoke to her, revealing that Mrs Hamilton had returned home at lunchtime ('In this rain?' said Violet, taken aback. 'Yes, ma'am,' Diana replied), but refusing to show Violet to the kitchen in her stead.

'If you did, I could fetch my own food,' Violet persisted.

'It's not the way Mrs Hamilton wants it, ma'am.'

I don't care, Violet might have retorted. But she stopped herself, reluctant to make any more enemies than she apparently already had.

Silently, she smiled at Diana, nodding acceptance, and inwardly resolved that, however awkward, she'd simply have to speak to Mrs Hamilton, put a stop to all this special treatment and ma'am business, which really did seem designed to ostracize her.

Her opportunity to do so came just a few hours later, after she'd changed into her nightgown and robe, ready, at last, for bed. The fire in her room crackled greedily. Outside, the rain had finally ceased. The lighthouse's beam swooped over the waves, and a passenger ship rode them, ploughing towards the black horizon.

Drawn to it – feeling her isolation keenly enough by now to be lured by the thread that seemed to reach from its decks, connecting her to the heartbeats on board – Violet opened her terrace doors, heading outside.

The whip of fresh, salty air that greeted her stung her flushed skin, but did nothing to alleviate her exhaustion. She had, with the exception of her fractured naps on the train, now been awake for more than thirty-six hours. Her limbs felt weighted with fatigue; her face, as though it was hollow.

She studied the glowing liner, gliding through the night for America. As a child, she'd used to fixate on the idea of one day travelling on such a vessel, to Boston to find her mother. She wasn't sure when, exactly, she'd grown up sufficiently to realize what a foolish plan that was, and that her mother wouldn't thank her for invading whatever new life she'd created for herself. But, by the time she'd taken her secretarial diploma, she'd long since given up on it. She'd also accepted that, had she abandoned her father – whose gentler, softer, pre-war self she hadn't entirely forgotten – he'd undoubtedly have drunk himself to death.

In the end, it probably would have been a kinder way for him to go.

Violet pictured the people on the ship now, laughing, dancing, and felt such a yearning to be among their noise and company, rather than in this silent palace. It was like when she'd used to walk past the windows of cafés and pubs in London, observing the buzz within, knowing she was on her way back to her bedsit.

She really hadn't expected to be even more lonely here.

Hugging her robe closer, she let her eyes rove the blackness, first across the shadowy length of the house (which, of the countless windows, was James behind?), then out to the island's point, where the lighthouse stood, just visible: an inky silhouette against the inkier sky. Again, its beam swung across the water, catching the waves, the occasional late gull.

It had been Violet's mother who'd told her it was a keeper who turned the lamp. They'd been on holiday in Norfolk, in the early days of the war. Violet couldn't have been that little – no younger than eight – but she'd still sat on her mother's lap. Sucking her hair, probably.

What, all by themselves? she'd asked.

They're very strong, her mother had replied. *Although, lots use mercury to help. Makes the lamp lighter for them, you see.* She'd tickled Violet. *Turns some of them loopy too.*

'A penny for them.'

Violet jumped, spun around.

And there she was: Mrs Hamilton, stepping through the doors, shutting them behind her.

'You're letting the cold in.'

'My God.' Violet held her hand to her chest. 'You scared me.'

Mrs Hamilton's face, in the blackness, appeared unmoved. 'I did knock. I suppose you didn't hear me.'

'I suppose I didn't.' Her heart was still hammering. 'I thought you'd gone home.'

'I came back. I wanted to talk to you.'

'Yes.' Violet took a breath, her pulse normalising. 'I need to talk to you too . . . '

'Who knew you were coming here today?' Mrs Hamilton asked, cutting her off.

Violet frowned. 'Why?'

Mrs Hamilton studied her, not answering.

'What is it?' said Violet.

Still Mrs Hamilton said nothing. She tipped her head to one side, her green eyes sharp, evaluating.

Violet felt like she was being read.

'Mrs Hamilton?' she said, too tired for games. 'What's wrong?'

'The post came.'

'Yes, I know. I travelled over with the postman.'

Mrs Hamilton's eyes narrowed.

'What is this?' Violet asked, impatience growing.

For a beat, Mrs Hamilton remained silent.

Then she smiled, in the same jarringly amicable way as she

had when she'd left Violet's room earlier, and shook her head. 'It doesn't matter.'

'What doesn't matter?'

'A trifle, I shouldn't have worried you with it.'

Violet considered pushing her to say more. But only for a second. Mrs Hamilton, it was abundantly clear, was not the kind to be persuaded into something she didn't want to do. Even if she were, Violet really wasn't fit for the effort.

Deciding she wasn't fit to confront Mrs Hamilton on the rest of it either – quite glad, when it came to it, to put the uncomfortable conversation off – she said that she might turn in. 'It's been a long day.'

'I'm sure,' said Mrs Hamilton, and failed to leave.

Instead, she walked towards Violet, standing beside her at the balustrade, holding her hair back from her face as she too looked towards the ship, growing smaller, almost over the horizon.

Her curls were limper than they had been earlier, bedraggled. Her perfume had faded too. *That walk home in the rain*, Violet thought, and wondered if she'd discovered whatever this trifle in the mail had been there – the postman *had* stopped at her cottage – or if someone had brought it to her attention here. She hadn't specified after all that it was she who'd been the recipient. It could have been someone else.

That man, perhaps, who she'd been arguing with before?

Violet hadn't forgotten the heated exchange she'd heard in the atrium.

Who knew you were coming here today?

Now what possible reason could Mrs Hamilton have for being concerned with such a thing?

'I wonder,' said Mrs Hamilton, 'did Mr Atherton tell you how this island got its name?'

'No,' said Violet, absently. 'He didn't.'

'My husband told me when we moved here. We came in nineteen

twenty-five, as soon as the house had been built. I was twenty-five. As old as the century.' She smiled, slightly. 'Elizabeth was the same.'

Violet felt a jolt at the name, and the oddness of Mrs Hamilton using it, not, *Mrs Atherton*.

She turned, eyeing her, more interested suddenly in what she was saying.

'My husband served with Mr Atherton in France,' she went on. (*Him as well*, thought Violet, and didn't consider mentioning her father.) 'We got engaged when he was on leave in nineteen sixteen. I was a child really, but we wanted to make the promise, just in case.' Her eyes, staring into the wind, were glassy. 'Arnold struggled for work when he first came back. But then Mr Atherton gave him this opportunity. He was the one who told Arnold Aoife's legend.' A gust of wind blew. She raised her hand, wiping spray from her cheekbone. 'Aoife was the first young woman to come here, no one knows exactly how many centuries ago. A man brought her.' She paused. 'It was a man who decided she should come.'

'A knight?' guessed Violet, who knew how these legends went.

Another smile. 'There was a knight involved, certainly. A famous English knight. For years, he'd remained unvanquished, winning duel, after duel, appearing in the tournaments of every king, every lord. Wherever he went, women fell in love with him, giving him their favours, inviting him to play court, but he had no interest in any of them. Then he went to Ireland, and it was the same there. For so long, it was the same, and the knight felt terribly sad.' She gave a short laugh. 'Such a hardship for the poor man.'

'I suppose so.'

'But you see, *then*, just as he was about to return to England, he played in the tournament of a great king. He looked up into the stands and saw a woman more beautiful than he'd ever imagined possible.' She arched her brow. 'Can you guess who it was, Miss Ellis?'

49

'Oh, I don't know,' said Violet, pushing her own hair back. 'Aoife?'

'Yes, Aoife. But her father, the king, had already promised her in marriage to a cruel lord. One who she knew could never love anyone, and who she feared would make her life very, very unhappy. The knight couldn't bear it for her. He asked her to run away with him to England, but she was scared the lord would come after them. So, the knight challenged that lord to a duel.' She broke off. Her eyes glistened.

You just wait and hear what happens next, she seemed to say.

She was a good storyteller; Violet had to hand it to her.

She really did want to know what happened next.

'Did the knight win?' she asked.

'He did,' said Mrs Hamilton, 'and, according to the terms of the duel, the lord had to give him his blessing to take Aoife back to England. But the lord was terribly jealous, and humiliated. He couldn't allow the knight and Aoife to be happy. So, he stowed aboard their ship, and, when they were not so very far from these shores, he slayed the ship's captain, took the wheel, and slammed the ship against these rocks.' She pushed herself up on the balustrade, peering down.

Instinctively, Violet followed suit, watching foam shatter in the blackness below.

'Almost everyone on board perished,' said Mrs Hamilton. 'There was no lighthouse to guide them, no keepers to help. But Aoife survived, and climbed ashore, waiting here for her knight to find her. But the evil lord came instead. In his rage that Aoife had shunned him, he pushed her from the cliffs, then threw himself over too.' She returned her stare to Violet. 'Some say that, to this day, Aoife still roams our island, waiting for her knight, and seeking vengeance on her lord. When she sighs,' she sighed, 'the grass trembles. When she wails,' she raised her hand to the skies, 'the wind howls.'

Beneath her robe, Violet shivered.

Wrapping it around her tighter, she dragged her eyes from the grip of Mrs Hamilton's stare, tipping her head back, looking into the ink-velvet clouds, more disturbed than she wanted to be by such a dark, tragic story.

'Do you believe any of it?' she asked Mrs Hamilton.

'Thomas is the authority on that,' she said, not answering the question.

'Thomas?'

'One of the lighthouse keepers.'

'Right,' said Violet, thinking back to that figure who'd watched her get off the tug. His disconcerting stare. She tried to remember if she'd ever read mention of a Thomas in the newspapers.

She didn't think she had.

But then again, had she?

She did so need to sleep . . .

'He and Elizabeth became very close,' Mrs Hamilton said. 'He got her all riled up about Aoife. She'd walk for miles, back and forth across the island, and I used to wonder if she was looking for her.'

'She couldn't have thought she'd see her.'

'Maybe not. But it was as though she felt an affinity with her. Brought here, to this place that she sensed would be her end.'

Violet heard the words, then heard them again.

Felt them, like a cold breath brushing her skin.

Slowly, she turned to face Mrs Hamilton.

And Mrs Hamilton looked steadily back at her.

'How could she have sensed such a thing?' Violet asked, hating how shaken she sounded. 'How could she have known?'

'She couldn't, of course.'

'But you just said . . . '

'It's a myth, Miss Ellis.' She sounded almost rebuking. 'Just a myth.' She frowned, quite as though Violet had been the one to insinuate that Elizabeth had foretold her own death.

Violet tried to make sense, not so much of Mrs Hamilton's shift in tone, but, belatedly, of her coming to see her like this at all.

Speaking to her, so intimately, when before she'd been only hostile.

Walking all the way from her home just to do it.

I wanted to talk to you.

'What's this about?' she asked her, feeling, in her exhaustion and confusion, suddenly angry – at Mrs Hamilton, for her long, meandering tale, but even more at herself, for being sucked into it so trustingly. 'I think it must be to do with whatever the postman brought . . . '

Another frown.

Then, a laugh.

'What an odd suggestion.'

'Is it?'

'Yes. You really are tired, Miss Ellis. I've been selfish, keeping you up like this.' She turned to leave. 'I'm sorry.'

'No,' said Violet. 'Wait . . . '

'You need to rest. I'll say goodnight now.'

'Mrs Hamilton, stop . . . '

But she'd already gone, leaving the terrace doors she'd insisted on closing, open, swinging in the wind.

Reeling, Violet stared after her.

You sure you're built for island life? the boatman had asked her, on the tug.

Then, she'd wondered if she was being warned.

Now, abruptly alone on her dark, empty terrace, in her dark, empty wing – her robe no match for the chill she felt seeping through her – she felt the unease of his caution, all over again. Only this time, there was no James to distract her. There was nothing.

Just the haunting idea of Aoife and Elizabeth's sorry ends.

Mrs Hamilton had wanted to spook her, of course.

Probably, she'd thought she could intimidate Violet into turning tail and leaving Aoife's, giving her back the position she'd clearly been so vexed to lose.

Don't let her win, she told herself. *It's a foolish ghost story. Nothing to worry about.*

She almost managed to convince herself.

And yet, when she went inside, and the wind ripped the terrace doors from her grip, throwing them wide on their hinges, her hands shook as she reached for them, pulling them back.

They faltered as she locked them tight.

She found herself checking that lock, twice, before she went to bed.

She checked the door to her room too.

And, thinking of the emptiness in the corridor beyond – feeling her spine lengthen at another of Aoife's wails – she pulled her suitcase across the doorway.

Just for good measure.

Little bird,

I hope that this missive finds you in the throes of writing your first report. You know what to do with it. Don't fret, it will find me. I really am most eager to read it. I extend my thanks in advance. I'm sure your family are most grateful too. Simple people, I appreciate, but I trust they'll be grateful for your windfalls.

And have you been doing the chirping I asked of you?

I do hope so. It's terribly important that Miss Ellis receives the appropriate reception. You mustn't fail me on that. I'll find out if you fail me.

I really don't enjoy being disappointed.

Chapter Five

Elizabeth

January 1932

'God, *must* we go tonight?' Elizabeth asked of her dressing table mirror, and the reflection of Laura Ratcliffe, draped on the bed behind her.

'Inarguably,' said Laura, not glancing up from the copy of *Tatler* she'd been flicking through, an empty champagne glass held between two gloved fingers, her bilious fancy-dress costume frothing around her: a princess in a pea-green gown. 'It would be insufferably bad form not to, my snowiest of queens.'

They were expected at Dicky Thompson's engagement do. He was to marry a twelve-year-old. ('Eighteen,' he'd chided Elizabeth, in the same bed Laura was currently prostrated on, only the night before. 'Come now. Don't sulk.') The party was being held, unoriginally enough, at the Kit-Kat Club. The theme was Hans Christian Andersen. Another cliché. *A fairy tale for our fairy tale*, Elizabeth had read on the invitation, before lighting it with a match.

What a treat, she'd written, to Dicky's babe-in-arms, by way of acceptance. *Thank you, Cressida. I'm already planning my costume.*

She'd drawn a twisted kind of pleasure in commissioning the ivory silk dress she now wore, cut on the bias, and complemented by an ermine shawl, her diamond choker, clasped with its signature 'E', and a diamond headband that nestled in her dark red hair.

She'd wasted no time deliberating on any of it, as Laura had. She'd known, after all her years making herself into endless iterations of triumphs, just how to pull it off.

The weather might have been more cooperative, though.

There'd been such a cold snap, lately, she'd become rather taken with the idea of arriving at the Kit-Kat in a swirl of snow.

It irked her that it hadn't materialised.

'We may achieve sleet,' Laura had said, when she'd arrived at Elizabeth's Chelsea townhouse earlier, her skin flushed with the chill, her blonde hair beaded with drizzle. 'Really, though, Lizzie,' she'd shrugged off her coat, grimaced downwards at her gown, 'you might have talked me out of wearing green.'

'You look wonderful,' Elizabeth had said, without consideration, since Laura always looked the same to her no matter what she wore.

Rather like a strawberry, Dicky had once remarked, the two of them entwined on the sofa of Soho's Blue Lagoon, him whispering in Elizabeth's ear as Laura had been dancing, oblivious on the floor. *Sweet, juicy, and appealing enough. One could certainly sink one's teeth in. But nothing to make her stand out from the rest of the punnet.*

Elizabeth had laughed at the time.

But really, what an insufferable little cat he was.

Wanting Laura to despise him too, she'd flirted with the idea of telling her of his nastiness as, taking her hand, she'd pulled her up the stairs. But then she'd thought better of it, because of course she'd have become upset, and Elizabeth would have had to console her, which really would have been too tiresome.

Instead, she'd declared that what they both needed was a little pick-me-up. For the past couple of hours, they'd holed up in her bedroom, sinking their usual bottle of fizz, indulging in a little powder: a well-oiled routine that Elizabeth could usually depend upon to get her to just the right side of reckless before heading out, but which tonight had only dragged her down, leaving her with a pinching headache.

Placing a couple of pills on her tongue, she flicked them to the back of her throat, swallowing, then examined her face, cocking her head from left to right, pressing her fingertips to her temples, pushing the skin back. Carefully, she adjusted her headband, tucking a loose wave in, moving the headband again.

'Leave it,' said Laura, still not looking up from her magazine. 'You need do nothing more. I assure you, Cressida's going to despise you.'

'Good.'

'I really must say, I can't see what all this fuss is about.'

'I know you can't.' They'd already had the conversation too many times to bear repeating. From Laura's tone, she was growing even more fed up with it than Elizabeth.

'You've never wanted to get married.' Laura turned the page. 'Or have you been fibbing all these years?'

'No,' said Elizabeth, which she hadn't.

It was, in fact, the very matter that she and Laura had had their first ever meeting of minds over, at the start of their deb season in 1919: how immensely satisfying it was going to be, flouting society's assumption that they must be in want of a husband. They'd been in the ladies' room at the Savoy. Laura had said something nice about Elizabeth's gown, Elizabeth had thanked her, remembered that she'd better say something nice about Laura's too, then, spotting the cigarettes in Laura's purse, asked if one might have a try, and that had been that.

Laura had already been a wealthy orphan by then, her parents having succumbed to the influenza the winter before – a matter on which she'd always insisted it was better not to dwell. Elizabeth had joined her ranks the following year – a motoring accident, she didn't much like to dwell on it either – inheriting the kind of fortune that meant she'd never have any material need to wed. She'd long believed that she'd have no emotional one to either. Why would she, with Laura in her own Chelsea bolthole, just down the river, too many other friends to remember, and her pick of London's eligibles for a bit of fun?

Dicky had been her most recent, and durable, of those. For the past two years, they'd been sidling home from nights out together, keeping each other's beds warm. Whilst they'd been at it, others in their circle had started to drop off, slowly at first, then like veritable flies, shackling themselves to one another with bands of gold.

Maybe one should join them, Dicky had said, on the morning of Elizabeth's thirty-first birthday, back in May.

She'd smiled. She'd thought he'd meant the two of them.

Ever since, she'd been anticipating his proposal. Even toyed with the idea of saying yes. For mightn't it be nice to have someone sworn to care for you, in health, sickness, all of that? Plus, it had dawned on her, sitting in the congregation at all those weddings, that, with the exception of Laura, she was in danger of being the last unattached left.

She abhorred being last at anything.

And being single really had felt rather more like fun, and rather less like on the shelf, whilst she'd still been in her carefree twenties, and everyone else had been single too.

So yes, she'd considered accepting Dicky's proposal.

Pretty much resolved that she would.

He hadn't told her that he was courting anyone. Certainly not a child called Cressida, whose existence Elizabeth hadn't even known of, until she'd read the announcement of their engagement in *The Times*.

The first she'd seen of Dicky since had been when he'd called by the night before, without warning, come to make sure Elizabeth intended to behave herself at the party.

'Do you love her?' she'd asked him, when, out of spite – to him, to Cressida – she'd taken him to bed.

'You know, I think I might. She's very loveable. Much more so than you. And she does adore one so.'

'What on earth does she see in you?'

'Everything you've seen, I expect.' He'd traced a finger around her face. 'Plus, babies. All the beautiful babies we'll make. Oh,' he'd given her a sorry look as she'd pulled away, 'come now, Lizzie, don't be cross.' He'd taken her hand, kissed it. 'The thing of it is, you're just not the sort a fellow marries. Not any more. You've been around too much. No one wants to bump into one's wife's old lovers at the club.'

Her pale skin flamed, remembering.

She watched it happen in the mirror, her eyes blue and hard.

'And besides,' Dicky had gone on, with another kiss, 'you're too damned old.'

That had been when Elizabeth had booted him out, throwing his clothes into the street below.

It *had* been entertaining, watching him dress in the icy January drizzle.

But not enough, not nearly enough, to show him how wrong he'd been, passing her up like this.

'Who was it who said that thing about a good life and revenge?' Elizabeth asked of Laura. 'I can't remember.'

'Did you ever know?'

'Possibly not.'

Laura set the magazine aside. 'It was a poet, I think. George someone or other . . . ' She leant down, rolling her empty glass onto the carpet. '*Living well is the best revenge.*'

'That's it.'

'But you do live well, Lizzie.' She stood, brushing out the creases in her gown. 'Why can't you be content with all you already have?'

'Because it's not enough.' Elizabeth got up too, adjusting her gloves. 'And I can't bear the thought of Dicky Thompson believing he might be happier than me.'

Laura studied her, contemplative.

Then, infuriatingly, she smiled.

'What?' said Elizabeth.

'I think it might be simpler than that.'

'Oh, really?'

'Really.' Her smile broadened. 'I think, that after a lifetime of getting whatever you want, it's shocked you that you can't have this. I think . . . ' She laughed.

Elizabeth didn't.

Laura was high, it was clear.

It grated that she'd managed it, when Elizabeth hadn't.

'You think what?' she asked her, coldly.

Laura laughed more, unperturbed. 'I *think*, dearest, that you simply detest being told no.'

Cressida had dressed as the ugly duckling, in an ebony dress that hugged her petite, curvy frame and plunged at the back to a little feathered tail which bobbed on her pert, eighteen-year-old bottom. She wore more feathers in her black, crimped hair, thick kohl around her dark eyes, and a coy smile on her plump rouged lips, with the effect that all anyone could talk about, in the packed, smoky, glitz of the Kit-Kat Club's ballroom, was what a beauty she was, and clearly *such a darling* for being so self-effacing as to come as the duck.

Elizabeth hated her.

'He'll have cheated on her before their first anniversary,' said Amy Astley at the bar, clinking her champagne coupe with first Elizabeth's, then her husband, Henry's. The two of them had dressed, like almost every other couple present, as Thumbelina and Cornelius. 'Sooner, even . . . '

'He's cheated on her already,' said Elizabeth.

'Oh, *ouch*,' said Henry. 'What a cad.'

'You might try to conceal your approval, darling,' said Amy. 'One is standing *right here*.'

'Oh, is that *you*?' said Henry, embracing her. 'Well, *hello* . . . '

As they kissed, Elizabeth angled herself away, surveying the crush of the room. At the far end, a jazz band was in full swing. On the floor, so many little mermaids and matchstick girls danced. There were several other snow queens, none in a dress as elegant as the one Elizabeth wore, but still . . .

It was annoying that no one else had come ugly.

She caught Dicky looking at her from across the room. He was at Cressida's side, his arm slung proprietorially over her shoulder. He held Elizabeth's eye for no more than a second before returning his attention to his intended, but Elizabeth saw his self-satisfied smirk. She guessed, from his white feathers, that he was supposed to be the swan of Cressida's future. It was a tenuous kind of pairing, but he at least looked preposterous, so Elizabeth would forgive it.

She settled her attention on Laura, huddled with Rupert Litchfield by the entrance. They were out of the reach of lamps, more shadows than people. Laura, blonde head tipped downwards, was pulling at her green skirt, and Rupert, holding a trident, appeared to be laughing, shaking his own floppy blonde locks, doubtless trying to reassure Laura how well she looked, dear man that he was.

He'd been there too, that night that Elizabeth and Laura had met at the Savoy. He'd still been rather twitchy in those days, only recently released from convalescence after a run-in with some shrapnel in Ypres. Elizabeth had been a little twitchy herself, at not having done more, or really anything at all, to support the war effort – unlike Laura, who'd *nursed*. When Rupert had asked her to dance, she'd decided to make herself feel better by doing her bit for Blighty belatedly and indulging him. She'd danced with him several times, even let him kiss her: just a brush of the lips, but from that evening on, he'd been hers, ready to drop any plan to join her for lunch, or tea, or a walk, always on standby as a dance partner on the rare occasions she found herself without one.

Really, Dicky had been entirely wrong when he'd said she wasn't the kind that men married. Elizabeth could marry Rupert tomorrow if she wanted. Could have married him a hundred times over by now. How many glorious summer Saturdays had there been since that night in 1919? She had no idea, no interest in mathematics. It bored her, utterly. But there'd been legion, and on any one of them, if she'd just said the word, Rupert would have waited for her at any altar, ready to vow to cherish her forever.

And therein lay the problem. Dicky knew that. Elizabeth had *joked* with him about it. If she were to become suddenly engaged to Rupert now, he'd see right through it, and probably feel even more superior.

Besides, she didn't want to marry Rupert. It would be like marrying one's pet puppy. As for going to bed with him . . .

'Top-up?' said Henry, detaching himself from Amy, swiping a bottle from the bar.

'Yes, I think so,' said Elizabeth, holding out her glass, 'keep it flowing.'

Her headache was no better, the diamonds weighing on her skull felt like a vice, but she fished another pill from inside the hem of her glove (third's a charm) and resolved to drink through it.

It really did feel the only way to survive the night.

But even with the pill, and the champagne – neither of which touched her pain, and certainly not her mood – the party became less bearable by progression. Dicky and Cressida wrapped themselves around one another on the dance floor, and everyone else grew louder, looser, their costumes slipping and tearing as they collided in clumsy shimmies and Charlestons, out of step with each other, out of rhythm with the band.

By two, the smoky air had grown stale, the club's floor sticky with spilt liquor, and Elizabeth – ensconced with the Astleys, Laura and Rupert at a bottle-strewn table – had had enough.

'Time for me to climb into my pumpkin,' she announced, getting unsteadily to her feet.

'Wrong fairy tale, darling,' said Henry. 'I think you mean a sled.'

'I mean a taxicab actually. And I'm off to catch one now.'

'I'll hail you one,' offered Rupert, predictably. 'You wait in the warm.'

'I'll come with you, Lizzie,' said Laura, as he headed off. 'I'm beside myself to consign this dress to the bin.'

It was after the two of them had said their goodbyes to Henry and Amy, and were following Rupert out, that they approached Cressida and Dicky, standing at the ballroom door. Elizabeth, who'd had no intention of thanking either of them for the hideous night, nonetheless paused, seeing that they were greeting a man who'd apparently just arrived. He wasn't in costume, but a dinner suit. Clearly, this party was no more than a postscript to his night. One he wasn't particularly enthused about, from the set of his shoulders as he kissed Cressida on the cheek.

His coolness was the first thing that intrigued Elizabeth about him.

The second, as he moved, revealing his profile, was the jolting realization that she knew him, had met him before, on a train from Oxford to Paddington.

The one that got away, she'd often thought of him as, rather enjoying the idea of him thinking of her, just the same way.

It had been in the April of 1929 that they'd met. Elizabeth hadn't forgotten the date, for more reasons than just him. But the two of them had shared an otherwise empty first-class cabin out of the city. He'd been there visiting a friend, he'd told her.

'So have I,' she'd lied. 'What a coincidence.'

Their train had got stuck at a signal. For *hours*. He'd tried to work, but she, reluctant to be left alone with her thoughts – and rather keen to invade his – had persuaded him into conversation, entertaining him with stories, watching the enjoyment in his face (that face!), but actually learning not much at all about him.

Wanting to fix that – wanting rather a lot more, actually – she'd invited him home with her when they'd finally reached London.

'I can't I'm afraid,' he'd said, regretfully. 'I'm extremely late for a meeting.'

James, he'd told her he was called.

She hadn't thought to ask his surname, not until he'd gone.

She'd been certain that she'd see him again, though. How could she *not*, when they'd shared such a connection?

And she had seen him again, the *very next day*, on Regent's Street. She'd been in rather a foul mood, but had felt that change the instant she'd spotted him on the opposite side of the road. Heart catapulting, she'd called his name and waited for a break in the traffic so that she might cross over to him. But the traffic had been heavy, the pavements busy, and James hadn't heard her when she'd called.

By the time she'd reached where he'd been, he'd disappeared.

Was it fate that had brought him back to her again, now?

Maybe so, she thought, and felt intrigued by that, too.

The next thing – the third thing – that caught her attention, was the way James stepped away from Cressida, as soon as he'd kissed her, and, ignoring Dicky's proffered hand, reached for his cigarettes, dipping his head to light one.

It was a delight, it truly was, seeing Dicky's smile falter; then, the uncharacteristic awkwardness in him as he withdrew his hand, placing it first on Cressida's back, then, seeming to think better of that, in his pocket.

The fourth thing that struck Elizabeth, as she and Laura drew closer to the trio, was how unremarkable and juvenile Dicky – who Elizabeth had always thought rather pretty – looked suddenly, beside James: his jaw slack from too much drink, his features, soft and ill-defined.

Her fifth, jarring, realization was that James didn't recognize her. He glanced her way, as she and Laura passed, but his eyes did no more than flit across hers, before settling on Laura, at which point they warmed momentarily, the skin around them creasing in a brief smile.

He had such a delicious smile.

And that was the sixth thing that came to Elizabeth: how little she enjoyed that he'd given it to Laura rather than herself.

'You know him?' she asked Laura, once they were through the door, and safely out of hearing.

'James? Yes. He's Cressida's older brother.'

'What?' How interesting. 'Dicky didn't mention any family.'

'There's only the two of them. More orphans, I'm afraid.'

'I didn't think you knew Cressida.'

'I don't.'

They reached the cloakroom, and handed over their tickets.

'Then how do you know her brother?' Elizabeth asked, as the attendant went off.

'We were children together. I haven't seen him in years.'

Elizabeth waited for her to go on.

When she didn't, she said, 'You're not being very forthcoming. Did the two of you have some secret dalliance you've never told me about?' The idea appalled her.

'Nothing like that,' said Laura. 'Our parents were friends, that's all. I used to see James at various get-togethers. Tennis matches and so on. You know, before the war, and all that. Cressida wasn't even born.' She took her coat from the returning attendant. 'God, how depressing.'

She set off for the door.

Shrugging on her shawl, Elizabeth followed. 'You played tennis with James?'

'Once or twice. He's a few years older than us. I'm not sure he ever paid much attention to me.'

65

'Like a strawberry.'

'What?'

'Never mind,' said Elizabeth. 'He seemed to remember you now, anyway.'

'He did, yes.'

'So?'

'So?'

'Why are you being so cagey?'

'I'm not.'

'Yes, you are,' said Elizabeth. 'When was the last time you saw him?'

'At my parents' funeral, if you must know. He was just back from France.'

'And?'

She sighed. 'And I couldn't bring myself to throw earth on their coffins. I was in a horrible state actually. All on my own, snotty and undignified . . . '

Elizabeth could picture it.

The image made her feel a bit better.

'He came and stood with me,' said Laura. 'He was the only one who did. Everyone else was just . . . mortified, I think. He said I should leave the earth where it was and give my parents something of mine to keep with them instead. So, I threw them my scarf.'

'That was rather sweet of him,' said Elizabeth, liking him even more.

'It was,' said Laura.

'Why have you never mentioned it before?'

'Well, we've discussed this, Lizzie. We don't normally talk about such things, do we?'

They'd reached the street door. As the attendant held it open, letting a rush of freezing night air in, Elizabeth paused, looking back towards the ballroom they'd left.

'I shared a train cabin with him, from Oxford. You remember

that man I used to talk about . . . ?'

Laura stopped. 'That was him?'

She didn't sound especially happy about it.

It was rather satisfying, confirming to her.

'Yes, it was.'

No reply.

Narrowing her eyes, Elizabeth asked, 'Why is he never around?'

'He rarely comes to London,' said Laura, continuing outside. 'He lives as a bit of a recluse.'

'He's in London now,' said Elizabeth, following. They had indeed achieved sleet. It was coming down thick and wet, melting the instant it hit the grubby pavement. 'I expect he will be until the wedding. Gosh, just imagine how furious Dicky would be if —'

'Lizzie, no.' Laura stopped, turning to face her, surprisingly firm. 'Leave James alone.'

'Why? Do you like him? You do, don't you?'

'Not like that,' said Laura, wiping a soggy flake from her nose. Behind her, beneath the sickly glow of a streetlamp, stood Rupert, shivering in his merman costume, holding a cab. 'But yes, I like him. He was kind to me. Incredibly kind, when no one else was. And I heard he had a horrible war . . . '

'Did anyone have a pleasant one?'

'You,' said Laura, taking Elizabeth aback again, with the barb.

'That wasn't very nice, Laura.'

'I'm sorry,' Laura said, not especially apologetically. Over-tired, probably. Annoyed about her dress.

Elizabeth decided to let it go.

'Surely you want me to be happy?' she said.

'This isn't about you being happy,' said Laura. 'It's about some . . . fixation . . . you developed after, what . . . ? A couple of hours on a train?'

'It was at least five.'

'And you winning,' Laura continued, ignoring her. 'Over Dicky.'

'What's wrong with winning?'

'Nothing, normally. But I can't bear you trying to drag James into one of your dramas.'

'Who says it would be a drama?'

'It always is with you.'

'*Laura*,' said Elizabeth, pouting, feigning indignation.

But Laura didn't smile, like she'd intended.

Or laugh, as she had back in Elizabeth's room.

On the contrary, she sighed again.

When had she become so tiresomely sober?

'Put James from your mind,' she said, 'really. Pursuing him will make you both miserable, and he's already told you no once. He won't give you what you want.'

'He might,' said Elizabeth, forgetting his earlier indifference, which she'd in any case already put down to the dark. 'Men tend to.'

Laura did laugh at that. 'He's no Dicky, Lizzie. He hasn't wasted his life dandying around town. He's made himself into one of the richest men in England, and chosen to live in the type of place I know you hate . . . '

'So?'

'So, he's not the kind to let someone like you manipulate him.' She wiped more sleet from her face. 'And I don't expect he'll thank you for trying.'

'I expect he will.'

'I expect you'll be disappointed.'

'Girls.' Rupert. He sounded hypothermic. 'Are you coming?'

Elizabeth didn't move.

'I like him,' she said to Laura.

'You don't know him,' said Laura, who did then go.

'You're wrong,' Elizabeth called after her. 'I do.'

'No, you don't.'

'I'm not getting into that cab,' Elizabeth said, deciding, as she spoke, that she wouldn't. 'I'm going back in. I want to talk to him.'

She expected Laura to turn around.

She assumed she'd go with her.

That was the kind of thing Laura *did*.

But Laura didn't so much as slow her steps.

'Fine,' she threw back wearily, over her shoulder, 'do as you please. You always do anyway.'

'Yes, I do.'

'Just don't expect me to cheer you on.'

'I won't.' Elizabeth felt like stamping her foot. 'I don't need you to.'

'Good,' said Laura, infuriating Elizabeth more by carrying on walking, towards Rupert.

'You're really going?' she called after her. '*Laura* . . . '

'I'm really going,' Laura replied. 'I want no part of it. And don't you dare come crying to me when it all ends in tears.'

This time, Elizabeth didn't respond.

She, who really did despise being told no, had already stopped listening.

Turning on her heel – leaving Laura to sulk her way home alone – she adjusted her diamond headband, rearranged her face into a smile, and, more determined than ever to take what she wanted, headed back into the club.

SEARCH FOR ELIZABETH ATHERTON
ONGOING

It has now been five days since Elizabeth Atherton disappeared, on Saturday 29th October, and this reporter has it from his exclusive source that investigations on the island have so far uncovered few clues as to her whereabouts.

What has now been confirmed is that Mrs Atherton took nothing with her when she left the house for her walk: no money, nor personal items. Since she left no note either, the police have ruled out the possibility that her disappearance was intentional.

Furthermore, they are no longer considering that she might have fallen. Might it be hazarded that additional evidence, as yet undisclosed, has been uncovered to sustain this conclusion?

And if so, who, of those under question, has this evidence come from?

Chapter Six

Violet

April 1934

It was raining again by the time Violet rose from her first, fitful night on the island, jerking awake at every blast of wind, her mind replaying Mrs Hamilton's voice over and again. *When she sighs, the grass trembles. When she wails, the wind howls.* She felt marginally easier, in the watery light of dawn – ridiculous, even, at the sight of her case pulled across her door – but still, not so easy that she didn't dress as quickly as she might, faltering over her skirt's buttons, and the fastenings on her stockings, desperate to escape the unnerving solitude of her room.

She made her way to the atrium, not stopping this time at the other bedrooms, not wanting to remind herself of their abandonment. But she thought again of their previous occupants as she passed.

Henry and Amy Astley, her mind sounded, in rhythm with her steps. *Richard and Cressida Thompson. Rupert Litchfield and Lady Laura Ratcliffe.*

The atrium was empty when she got there, its lamps all extinguished, the grate cold. The wall of glass tremored, its panes braced against the wind; Violet watched them shift in their frames, then turned away, nauseated by the same vertigo she'd been struck by the morning before on the cliffs, only worse, because now it was the house that felt as though it might tumble; its glasswork

71

too delicate, its setting too precarious to withstand such violent elements.

Distracting herself from the idea, she set to browsing the collection of photographs adorning the room's tables. Several were landscapes – a trio of the house, chronicling its construction, then a shot of an older manor set in parkland – and many more were of people.

The first that drew Violet's eye, beside a vase of wildflowers, was a studio portrait of a man in army uniform, his hand resting on the shoulder of a dark-haired woman in a lace gown: James's parents, she guessed, from the similarity of the man's features, and the woman's colouring; that unabashed gaze.

She became surer of it when she reached another, less formal, photograph of the same woman, on a rug beneath a willow tree, her arms wrapped around a little boy who could only be James. Violet leant closer, getting a better look at the dimples in his chubby cheeks, the sweetness of his grin.

So, this is what he used to be like, she thought, and – recalling that he'd lost this mother who held him, only months before he'd been dragged into the same trenches that had ruined her own father – she felt an ache in her chest. *How happy he was.*

He hadn't talked of his family, not to her. She knew only what the papers had reported: that his mother had died in childbirth with his sister in 1914, and that his father had followed before the armistice, leaving James, then twenty-three, with four-year-old Cressida to raise.

There were photographs of her too, ebony-haired and strikingly pretty, and too much of a mix of her mother and brother for there to be any question of who she was. All were of her as a child: beaming stills that had her variously on a pony, building a sandcastle, then in uniform on the steps of a grand-looking school. In the latter, she was sticking her tongue out – at James, Violet presumed, and found herself smiling, imagining him behind the lens. He'd looked after his sister well, it was clear.

Loved her, obviously.

Violet waited to come across a picture of her on her wedding day. She could only imagine it had been quite a do – Richard Thompson, *Dicky*, was, after all, the younger son of some lord or other. Portraits must have been taken at the ceremony.

There were none on display, though.

None of James's own nuptials, either.

It took Violet several minutes to be certain of that. As she rotated the room, she found other bucolic pre-war images – a cricket match on a village green; a couple in a riverboat – even a shot from the war itself, of a group of soldiers clustered in a clearing (Violet's father wasn't there; she searched for him), but there were no photographs of Elizabeth to be seen.

Violet walked the room another time, looking for any trace of Elizabeth at all. A lady's coat hanging on a hook. Or a hat left in the porch.

But she found nothing.

Elizabeth had only lived there such a few months of course. It had been many more since her death.

Still . . .

How completely the memory of her had been wiped clean.

It was a pair of scullery maids who finally penetrated her solitude that morning, appearing just as the atrium clock struck a quarter past six. They came with baskets of kindling, through the same door Violet had heard Mrs Hamilton arguing behind, making Violet – once again at the picture of the soldiers (had James taken it? Was that why he wasn't in it either?) – start and twist.

'Good morning,' she said to them.

'Good morning, ma'am,' they chorused, after a discomforting pause, through which they both gawped.

Another protracted silence followed. Violet tried to think of something else to say, her mind simultaneously throwing up, and discounting, inane possibilities, while the girls continued to take her measure.

'Isn't this weather terrible?' she finally forced out, and immediately wished she hadn't, because of course it was.

One of the girls nodded. The other bit away a smirk. Then they did at least move, setting off to light the lamps and lay the fire.

Unable to bear the awkwardness of standing idly by whilst they worked, Violet moved too, heading for the door that she guessed would lead to the west wing, and the offices Mrs Hamilton had said were situated there.

The unlit corridor she found herself in was indeed a mirror-image of the one that ran to her own bedroom. Here, though, all the doors had been left ajar, and Violet, walking the corridor's length, could see easily into the rooms behind them, with their panelled walls and ocean views. The first three were full of filing cabinets; the fourth had a conference table within it. The fifth, at the end of the corridor, was, with its large desk, obviously James's. There was a fireplace with armchairs flanking it, and, opposite that fireplace, an archway leading to an adjoining office: smaller, with a desk of its own, atop of which sat a typewriter.

Supposing that typewriter was to be hers, Violet crossed to it, lowering herself into the desk's leather chair, which, she couldn't fail to appreciate, was a different beast entirely to the creaking, sprung affair that had made her coccyx ache at Barlow Shipley. Quickly, she tapped her name on the typewriter keys, enjoying that there was no stuck 't'.

Turning, she peered out through the drenched window behind her, finding an inverse of the view from her bedroom. She couldn't see much detail of the house – the rain and mist were too heavy for that – more a blurred shape, and the glow of windows where lights were burning. The atrium itself was all lit up now, as were the servants' quarters, built into the cliffs below. Letting her eyes rest on those windows, she imagined the steam and bustle behind them, and, in the cold silence surrounding her, thought she should probably have gone in search of the elusive kitchen rather than coming alone to this empty wing. One of the maids could surely have directed her.

But then again, maybe everyone down there would have stared at her, too.

They're all going to think you're there for Atherton's fun, you know.

If only she could forget the jibe.

She moved her focus to the east wing, then stopped, brow creasing, seeing the light coming from her bedroom.

Hadn't she extinguished her lamps before she'd left?

She was sure she had . . .

A sound behind distracted her: the click of the wing door opening, then the careless swoosh of it falling shut.

Footsteps followed, brisk and purposeful.

Forgetting who might or might not be in her room – feeling her heart quicken at who was about to be with her now – Violet got up, returning to the corridor.

Then stalled, seeing that it really was James who'd come.

He stopped too, seeing her.

She watched how his eyes widened in surprise.

Felt her own do the same, taking in his soaked state. His hair was tousled and dripping, his face, beaded with rain. He wore no coat, which she deduced he'd removed, but a grey knitted jumper, and drenched waterproofed trousers. On his feet, he had only socks.

Violet found herself staring at those socks.

She'd never seen him without shoes before.

'Miss Ellis,' he said, bringing her attention back to his face. 'You're up early.'

'Yes.' (Why had she looked at his socks for so long?) 'I hope you

75

don't mind me being here.'

'Not at all. I was just coming to check your office was ready for you.'

'It looks to be.'

'Good.'

She couldn't not ask. 'Have you been out walking?'

'Sailing.'

'*Sailing?*'

'I was in Penzance. Some unexpected business. I needed to make a call, send a wire, wait for a reply.' He sighed, clearly unwilling to talk about it. 'I ended up staying, but wanted to get back before the sea got worse.'

'I can't believe you went anywhere the way it is,' she said, and, as though on cue, thunder rumbled.

She had known he kept his own boats at Aoife's, a motor in St Leonard's, too. He had, when they'd first been making her travel arrangements, tried to insist on having someone meet her from her train, but she'd been adamant it was too much trouble.

What kind of unexpected business had compelled him to risk such wild conditions now?

She wanted to ask, but didn't know how to when he'd been so obviously reluctant to discuss it.

Her mind moved to Mrs Hamilton.

The post came, she'd said the night before.

Was that what this was all about?

Had James some interest in whatever trifle had arrived, too?

'I thought of you on the crossing, actually,' he said, diverting her.

'Did you?' she said. 'Why?'

'It was so rough, I felt awful for you. Green as a cabbage . . . '

She had to smile.

'I trust you're recovered now?'

'I am.'

'Mrs Hamilton showed you the kitchens?'

'No. Not yet.'

'Well, that's no good.' He frowned. 'Where have you been eating?'

'In my room.'

'Your *room*?' His frown deepened. 'You're not a prisoner, Miss Ellis. You must be crawling up the walls.'

'I'm fine . . .'

'You can't be.'

'Well . . .'

'Yes, exactly.' He turned, looking over his shoulder, like he was thinking about something there. 'Come on, let's go for a walk.'

'A walk?' She laughed. 'But it's pouring.'

'Is it?' He glanced upwards, at the bouncing puddles in the skylights above, then back at her. 'So it is.' His face was all seriousness, but there was amusement in his dark eyes. 'Come with me anyway. I promise you won't get wet.'

She wasn't unconscious of the impression the scullery maids might draw of them as, together, they returned to the now much warmer atrium, so she was relieved when neither of the girls were there. The entire room was empty, its silence fractured only by the crackling of flames, the drumming of rain, and the ever-present crashing of waves below.

Telling her he'd be a moment, James went to the porch, and returned with boots on his feet, carrying the jacket he'd worn to collect her from the wharf the day before.

'Here,' he said, holding it up, 'put this on. You'll freeze otherwise.'

'I'm intrigued,' she said, pushing first one arm, then the other, into its sleeves, and shrugging it onto her shoulders. It was far too big, but comfortingly heavy. She could smell fresh air, and the faint trace of his soap. 'Have you a woodland hidden somewhere in these cliffs?'

'I'm afraid not,' he said, and, raising his hand, flicked the coat's collar out from where it had been tucked in at her neck. She felt the movement in the fabric, a sudden heat in her skin. 'But I think you'll like this more. Now come on. This way.'

He led her to the door the scullery maids had appeared from. Thinking not so much of them any more, or even of Mrs Hamilton and her cross words, but only of where they could possibly be going, Violet followed him through it, onto a stone landing, which itself gave way to a wide staircase, lit by burning wall lamps.

'The servants' quarters are down this way,' said James, descending the stairs at a jog. His hair was drying, Violet observed, curling at his broad neck. His trousers crackled as he moved. 'I can take you now to see the kitchen if you'd like. Everyone will be at breakfast . . . '

'No, that's fine,' said Violet, too quickly, but she couldn't meet them all for the first time like that, with him. 'I can go another time.'

'All right,' he said, as they reached the base of the stairs, and a tiled hallway, off of which ran three doors. 'But, so you know, this,' he gestured at the first of the doors, 'runs to the staff bedrooms. Then this,' he pointed at the second, 'to the storerooms and kitchen, for when you are ready to brave it . . . '

'I didn't say anything about braving it.'

'You didn't need to,' he fixed her with a wry look, 'but we'll get to the bottom of that later.' He opened the third door, into darkness. 'Because this is where we're going.'

Her curiosity thoroughly piqued, she stepped in behind him, waiting as he lit the lantern that had been left on a small table. The flame's glow sprung to life, playing on his face, accentuating his jaw and cheekbones.

'Ready?' he said, raising his eyes back to hers, more gold now than brown.

'Ready.'

They continued along what turned out to be a very narrow, very cold corridor, which ended in an even narrower, even more frigid, staircase. It was again made of stone, but the steps weren't neatly cut, as those to the servants' quarters had been; rather, they were crooked, worn smooth from age, and chipped in parts.

'Was this here before the house?' she asked, following James downwards, hearing her voice resound into the blackness. 'It feels medieval.'

'Not quite medieval,' he said. 'Victorian actually.'

'Oh, close then,' she said, and more sensed than saw his smile.

'It was going to be the entrance up to the lighthouse, before someone thought better of the location,' he said. 'I didn't want to knock it down. You'll see why. Now, watch yourself on this last step.' He turned, lighting her way onto a craggy platform. 'It gets quite low here. Are you all right?'

'I'm fine.'

'Good,' he said, and, crouching, holding the lantern steady, he led her on, down a declining tunnel that some hapless Victorian labourers must have spent months, chiselling into the rock.

Later, Violet would think of her father, and how incandescent he'd have been – if he had been looking down at her (or indeed, up at her) – seeing her going so willingly into this hidden tunnel, on this remote, hidden island, with this man he'd so despised.

But, for the present, she didn't spare him a moment's consideration.

She focused solely on James's knitted back, her footing as she followed him, and the jolt of his eyes connecting with hers each time he glanced backwards, checking that she was keeping up, warning her of places where she should mind her head, watch her step.

'You're not claustrophobic then,' he said.

'It would seem not,' she replied.

'Well, thank God,' he said, making her laugh.

And then they were climbing down a final set of steps, carved into a sheer drop in the tunnel's floor, and stepping into a rush of sudden light, and the salty thrust of chill air gusting through an opening in the rockface.

An opening that, to Violet's amazement, had a drop of several feet below it, down onto a vast flat of rock, half of which was more like a room than anything, dry and sheltered by the jutting ceiling of the cliffs. The other half was exposed to the gale and rain, and the rolling Atlantic waves crashing onto its edge.

'It's almost the same size as the atrium,' she said, holding her hair back.

'The what?' said James.

'The atrium,' she said. 'You know, upstairs.'

'You mean the entrance hall?'

'If you like,' she said, and laughed, covering her embarrassment that she'd renamed it.

'You want to go down?'

'Yes, please.'

'All right,' he said, and, first setting the lamp aside, jumped onto the shelf below, then turned, holding his arms up to her. Behind him, the ocean threw up spray. 'Come on.'

With little else for it, she placed her hands on his shoulders, and felt his close around her waist.

She held her breath. Dimly, she was conscious that she did it.

And of the barely there pause before his arms tensed, his hands tightened, and he swung her down, setting her on her feet.

'Thank you,' she said, stepping away as he released her, then walking forwards, into the wind, thinking a little of Aoife – for how could she not, in the face of such furious gusts? – but mainly the relief of the fresh air on her hot skin. 'Is it ever calm?' she called back, needing to say something. 'I can't imagine it.'

'Sometimes it is,' he said, coming to stand beside her. He pushed his hands into his pockets, staring outwards. She looked up, watching him; how the muscles in his cheeks moved in a smile of recollection. 'Sometimes it's so still and clear, you can see all the way to the bottom.'

'That must be beautiful.'

'It's pretty spectacular.'

Another thunderclap sounded, making her start, and then smile too, noticing that he saw her do it.

'It was quite loud.'

'It was,' he agreed.

'It's always made me uneasy,' she confessed, and did then recall her father (looking down? Looking up?), who'd always used to don a tin hat in storms.

To her surprise, she found herself telling James about the habit – wondering, even as she spoke, why she was doing it. They'd talked so little of her father that he'd started to feel almost as unmentionable as Elizabeth.

But if James was shocked that she'd brought him up, he gave no sign of it.

'His hat from France?' he asked.

'From the army surplus,' she said, raising her voice against a stronger surge of wind.

'And did he get you one to wear?'

'No. But when I was littler and the weather turned, he did make dens for us both under the stairs.' She broke off, remembering the rations he'd used to have her pack for sustenance. *Lots of biscuits, Vi. Don't scrimp on the nice stuff.* 'That actually wasn't always bad.'

'It wasn't?' said James, disbelieving.

'Not really.'

'Christ.' He shook his head, returning his stare to the churning ocean. 'What a damnable war.'

Violet stared at the ocean too, her mind abruptly alive with that question she'd been too afraid to ask him, ever since they'd met, and which had haunted her now for almost eighteen years. *Did he do it? Did he shoot himself?* She felt the words rising in her throat, pulling on her cheeks . . .

Until, heart racing in sudden adrenalin, she let them go.

She took a breath, realizing what she'd done.

She had no idea what had made it seem so suddenly possible – the regret in James's voice just now, maybe – but the relief of it filled her. The *release*.

For a second, that was all she knew.

Then she registered how silent he was.

Saw the sobriety in his frown.

'He did do it then,' she said, and was glad of the storm's noise, because, to her mortification, her voice shook.

She truly hadn't thought, until that moment, that there could be any part of her left hoping her father had been telling the truth all these years.

With a sigh, James turned to her. 'I don't know. It was another man who reported him.' His frown deepened. 'Honestly, I've been wondering if he ever told you.'

'He always insisted it was an accident.'

'Maybe it was.'

'You don't think so, though?'

'Does it matter what I think?'

'Yes,' she said. 'It does.'

'I wasn't even there. I was in another part of the line. The first I heard of it, your father was already at a clearing station.' His eyes held her. 'But if he did do it, I've never blamed him.'

'Really?'

'Really.'

The honesty in his stare was too sincere for her to doubt it.

'I'm not sure that's the impression he had,' she said.

'No,' he said. 'He knew.' And again, there was such conviction in his tone.

'But . . . ?' she began, and broke off, unclear how to put words to the hideous question, *Then why did he loathe you so?*

Saving her the discomfort, James said, 'He wanted me to stop the trial.'

'You could have done that?'

'No, but he thought I could.' He filled his cheeks with a long breath, then expelled it. 'He thought I should have put a stop to a lot of things I couldn't.'

'The war, you mean?' she said, incredulous.

'The death, anyway. His CO sent him on a patrol the night before . . . what happened. He was the only one who came back.' His face darkened. 'He was very afraid. Everyone was.'

'But not everyone shot themselves.'

'No,' he acknowledged. 'They didn't.'

'How did he get away with it?'

For a beat, James was silent, his eyes moving to a passing gull.

'Who knows,' he said. 'Luck, I suppose. A judge willing to give him the benefit of the doubt.'

'And then he ended up before another one,' said Violet, recalling, before she could stop herself, the moment of his sentencing at The Old Bailey: the steadiness in that judge's cold stare as he'd placed the black cap on his head; the taste of blood in her mouth from where she'd bitten her cheeks to stop herself screaming. 'I can't imagine there are many who run that gauntlet twice.'

'No,' said James again.

She sighed. 'What a waste of a second chance.'

Another punch of wind came, spraying them with rain.

'Come on,' said James, and they retreated, further into the shelter of the cliff, sitting on a ledge – lingering, by unspoken agreement.

He doesn't want to go back either, Violet thought, and in spite of the sadness hanging between them, was glad of that.

Hugging his jacket around her, she settled her eyes on the sea.

The waves rolled in, rolled out, and the gull swooped, fishing for its breakfast, then rose, buffeted by the wind. She watched it move, like a puppet on strings, and found herself reflecting yet again on Aoife; picturing her drifting spirit, conducting this gull with her despair.

It was nonsense. Rationally, she knew it was.

And yet, how compelling this weather made such nonsense feel.

'Can I ask you something?' James said, his deep voice echoing from the cold rocks.

'Of course.'

'Your father hated me. Abhorred me. But you still came here.'

'Yes.'

'Why?'

'Because I wanted to,' she said, more honest than she might have been, had it not been for the openness they'd just shared. 'And my father despised the world.' She watched the gull rise, circling, ready to dive again. 'One winter, we lost a tile from our roof. Just a tile, but he went up and down our road, shouting, accusing our neighbours of stealing it.' Even now, years on, the humiliation still stung. 'Another time, my lunch box got broken at school. I don't know how, one of the other children probably, but he wouldn't let me go back for the rest of the term, convinced the teacher had done it to spite him.'

'I'm sorry.'

'You don't need to be. It's done with, gone.' Looking away from the gull, she turned back to him. 'The point is, our neighbours weren't bad people. My teacher was actually very nice. My father, though, who married my mother,' she gave a short laugh, 'well, he was an appalling judge of character.'

James didn't laugh.

'You're not pitying me, are you?' she said.

'I'm pitying the child you were,' he said, without apology. 'Why

84

did no one help?'

'I suppose everyone had their own troubles.'

His brow knitted. 'I feel like it might have been better for you if he hadn't come back.'

'No, I never wished for that. And,' she hesitated, then decided to say it. 'I am glad that it wasn't you who reported him.'

'Good,' he replied. 'Although I'm not particularly glad you've been thinking it might have been me all this time.'

She laughed again, more freely this time.

He smiled, shook his head.

For a few moments after that, they were silent.

Still, neither of them made to move.

She wondered if she really had heard everything now that had gone on between him and her father.

She wasn't sure.

It all felt a little too neat; too easily explained. She thought she might still be missing something, but didn't want to labour it . . .

'So,' he said, 'about the kitchen.'

'Oh, no,' she said, pulling a face. 'Let's not, really.'

'Oh, yes,' he said, raising a brow. 'Let's, please.'

And somehow – mainly because he wouldn't let it go – they did.

She didn't tell him everything, sitting there on that ledge.

She said nothing, for instance, of Mrs Hamilton's strange visit the night before, or how Aoife's myth kept nagging at her, because she honestly wasn't sure where to start with that. But she told him enough.

Like, how worried she was at the resentment her room might be causing.

And, how everyone kept calling her ma'am.

The stares of those scullery maids . . .

'I feel like they're all wondering what I'm really doing here,' she said, her cheeks on fire at her own unspoken implication. 'Mrs Hamilton said you only told them on Monday that I was coming . . . '

'Oh, she did, did she?'

'Yes. And I'm sure they've all been talking about me since.'

'Then let them talk.'

'It's not that simple.'

'Of course it is. No,' he said, as she opened her mouth to protest, 'you won't be able to stop them, so let them at it. They'll get bored and move on to something else, very quickly, I assure you.'

'But why didn't you tell them I was coming?'

'I did tell them. When they needed to know.'

'And what about Mrs Hamilton?'

'What about her?' He seemed genuinely bemused. 'She didn't lose her job, had no adjustment in her income, so required no notice. She's certainly not someone I've ever consulted on my private business affairs.'

Put like that, she couldn't think how to argue with it.

'As for your room,' he said. 'Do you not like it?'

'Of course I *like* it.'

'But you'd rather it sat empty, whilst you had something less nice?'

'No . . . '

'Then why shouldn't you have it?'

Again, she couldn't think of a good answer.

'I hated it when I saw your bedsit,' he said. 'I've hated thinking of you there, ever since.'

'Because of my father?'

'No, Miss Ellis.' He gave an exasperated laugh. 'Because of you.'

She stared.

She didn't know what to say.

She wasn't even sure of what he meant, only that she was suddenly very aware of how close they were sitting to one another, and the pull of his eyes.

'You can change room if you want to,' he said, softer now, 'but

86

I hope you won't. I hope you'll be comfortable.' His eyes narrowed in question. 'What do you think?'

Slowly, she nodded.

'Good,' he said. 'That's agreed then.'

'You're quite persuasive,' she observed.

'Oh, I don't know,' he said. 'You wouldn't tell me what those books were in your trunk yesterday, would you?'

'No,' she said, and found herself laughing again, amazed that he'd cared enough to remember. 'I have been feeling awful, you know . . .'

'About not telling me?'

'No. About you carrying them all that way.'

'Yes,' he said. 'I've been feeling awful about that too.'

She laughed more.

Then, feeling her stomach rumble, she pressed her hand to it, as though such a gesture ever worked at quietening the noise.

'Hungry?' he said.

'Apparently so.'

He smiled.

How she liked his smile.

'Come on,' he said, getting up. 'Let's get you some breakfast.'

She didn't dine in her bedroom that morning.

When they returned to the house, James insisted on calling by at the kitchen himself to tell them there'd be no more of that.

'Why not eat in the atrium?' he suggested to Violet, before sending her on ahead.

She did eat in the atrium, by the fireside.

She ate there alone.

Served by Diana, who called her, Miss Ellis.

James had disappeared upstairs. He needed to bathe and change, of course.

Violet thought he was probably also keeping his distance whilst they were in the house because of everything she'd said.

She was grateful for that.

She was.

But, as she sipped her coffee, staring into the fire, she kept one ear out for him returning.

Mesmerised by the crackling flames, she relived the hour they'd passed, moment by moment – just as she'd replayed their walk from the wharf the day before – and picked over those words of his, again and again.

No, Miss Ellis. Because of you.

She still couldn't be confident of how he'd meant it.

She only knew that, when his footfall did finally sound on the stairs, jogging down them, towards her, she was quick to get up, setting her coffee aside and straightening her skirt with an eagerness she'd never felt starting any morning at Barlow Shipley.

When she saw him, turning to face her at the bottom of the stairs – much tidier now, his face cleanly shaven above a fresh jumper, a pair of slacks in place of his waterproofs – she smiled, instinctively.

And felt her smile grow, when he smiled too.

'Ready, Miss Ellis?' he said.

'Ready, Mr Atherton,' she replied.

Chapter Seven

Violet

They spent the entire of that stormy, grey day together in the offices, James showing Violet his promised ropes.

Violet didn't see Mrs Hamilton.

She didn't see many people at all, besides him.

Only Diana – who appeared intermittently, bringing and clearing refreshments – and Mr Hamilton, *Arnold*, who called by mid-morning, introducing himself to Violet, astounding her every bit as much as his wife had, by once again being entirely different to the gruff, wizened groundsman she'd cultivated in her mind (really, how formulaic her imagination was), and, actually, rather likeable.

He was a great bear of a man, much taller than herself, and a head taller than James, with solid shoulders and giant paws of hands, both of which he used to grasp Violet's as, at James's fireside, he bade Violet welcome. When he spoke, he did so with a London accent, no trace of his wife's clipped RP. His pitch was a different one entirely to that of the man Violet had heard Mrs Hamilton arguing with the day before, too. He had grey-green eyes that disappeared into creases when he smiled, curled blond hair, and he wore a chequered shirt, thick utility trousers, and a pair of slippers on his feet. All of these things Violet noted, in those first seconds of their acquaintance, but mainly, and to her shame, it was his painted mask that drew her eye.

Moulded to his face, and covering almost the entire bottom third of it, it was no different to many others she'd seen before, out on London's streets, and buses. She knew what it meant, and that Mr Hamilton – gentle, indestructible giant that he seemed – had, like her father, returned from the trenches minus a part of himself. She remembered (as she replied to his polite enquiries, into her journey down; how she liked the island; the house; the weather), that Mrs Hamilton had told her he'd struggled for work when he'd first come back.

She supposed his injuries must have been why.

How relieved they must both have been when James had offered them employment, here.

She wondered (as Mr Hamilton recommended to her walks she should go on, once the rain cleared; a colony of seals she might be lucky enough to spot), if he'd bring his wife up.

Perhaps even allude to knowing of Violet's conversation with her.

Or, if Mrs Hamilton had even spoken of that bizarre encounter, to him.

If she had, he gave no hint of it.

Saying nothing whatsoever of his wife, he turned to James, mentioning a problematic drain he needed to clear, then, a concern about the weather, and some subsidence on the other side of the island that he wanted them both to look at, and – with a warm nod to Violet, a jest that she wasn't to let James work her too hard – he went.

'You can say it,' said James, once he had.

So Violet did.

'He's nothing like her.'

'No,' said James, picking up the office diary from the table before them, 'he isn't.'

'I can't imagine them together.'

'And yet, he worships her.' He raised a brow. 'Make no mistake about that, Miss Ellis. There is nothing that man would not do for his wife.' He sounded almost weary. 'Now,' he flicked open the diary, 'dates for invoicing . . . '

It was a very long day.

They didn't finish until dusk, and broke only briefly for lunch – which Violet once again ate in the atrium, whilst James headed back out into the rain, with Mr Hamilton, checking on that subsiding cliff. Other than that, they remained in James's office, by James's fire – where, as the meagre light outside faded, the lighthouse's beam flickering on, James took Violet through everything she'd need to know to become proficient in her new role: moving from his calendar, to the handling of the thrice-weekly post, to the meetings he travelled for throughout the year, to the names of all his key accounting, procurement, and management personnel in London. They had a number of secretaries there, he said, including Miss Phillips: the same secretary who'd once worked for him here on Aoife's, and now supported the executive office. It had been she who Mrs Hamilton had stepped in to replace in 1932, and who had, for the duration of Mrs Hamilton's tenure, continued with many of the responsibilities she'd used to hold here on the island – most notably, taking charge of the correspondence that came from the company's several hundred foremen.

'There's a lot,' James said. 'All manner of requests arrive, from all over the country, for resource, guidance . . . you can imagine the thing. It all needs to be prioritised, directed to the right department. Mrs Hamilton couldn't have coped, not with the house to manage as well. And she hasn't had the training, or the experience. But,' he got up, stoking the fire, 'I've been unfair to Miss Phillips, asking her to bear so much. It's gone on far too long, and I've become too distanced from what's happening on the ground. So, from Monday, you, Miss Ellis,' he sat back down, 'will be getting rather a lot of post.'

'All right,' she said, and wasn't concerned. For the six years before she'd moved to London, she'd been employed at the head office of a large confectionary company in Banbury. She was well-used to such work.

She wasn't fazed by anything else that James had briefed her on either – not the calendar management, nor the filing, nor the typing. It would take her some time to get her head around everything, of course, but it was hardly Astrophysics.

She'd manage.

What did, however, give her pause was when, in response to her asking whether Miss Phillips ever returned to Aoife's, James said that yes, she did, from time to time, mainly to visit her father.

'Her father?'

'Yes, I should have said. Gareth.'

'Gareth Phillips?' said Violet, stupidly. 'The fire warden?'

'The very same.'

'So, she used to live in his cottage?'

'Yes, of course. Where else would she have lived?'

'I don't know,' said Violet, through set teeth.

She didn't want to be here any more, Mrs Hamilton had said, *but then she didn't have this room.*

Had it not occurred to her that Violet would find out what room she *had* had?

Or had she been too concerned with jabbing Violet with whatever discomfort she could, to care?

Undoubtedly so.

'The isolation here got too much for her in the end,' said James, talking on. 'There were other things too.' He didn't go into them. 'She was pleased at any rate to know that you'd accepted this position. She'd heard of you . . . '

'Heard of me?' Violet frowned. 'How?'

'Oh, I don't know. Some friend of a friend who knew you were working for Barlow.' It was clear he hadn't spared it much thought.

'She said you must be a saint, anyway, for putting up with him.'

'Not a saint,' Violet said.

'Good,' he replied.

And she wondered what he could mean by that.

Despite such conundrums, and despite her growing tiredness, it was so very comfortable, spending those hours with him, sitting by his fire. Incredibly snug, with the lamps flickering, the flames crackling, and the weather raging outside. He talked, she scribbled notes, asked countless questions, he talked more, and so they went on.

Their conversation wasn't all work. After Diana had brought their afternoon tea, they stopped and spoke of other things – like the globe that sat in the corner of the office, by James's desk, and which had once belonged to his father.

'When I was a child, he'd used to spin it for stories,' said James. 'He'd swear blind he was closing his eyes, then place his finger on the globe, and make up a tale for whatever country he happened to land on.' He gave a short laugh. 'It was almost always Africa. He travelled there, you see. Fought there a bit, too.'

'Have you been?' Violet asked.

'Once, with my parents. A long time ago.'

'You liked it?' She could tell he had, from the way he'd spoken.

'Loved it.'

'I'd love to go,' she said, picturing the plains, the animals. 'There are so many places I'd love to go, actually.' She leant forward, breaking her scone into two. 'I'd start in Europe . . . '

'With your suitcase of books.'

'With my suitcase of books.'

'And where would you head to first?'

'Italy,' she said, without hesitation.

'Which part?'

'Tuscany, obviously.'

'Obviously,' he said. 'I have a villa there actually.'

'Of course you do,' she replied, and grinned, enjoying it when he laughed.

She asked him where he'd grown up, he said, 'Kent,' and she mentioned the photograph of the house she'd seen earlier. 'Next to the ones of all this being built . . . '

'Yes, that's it,' he said. 'Harbury. My sister lives there now. I expect you've heard of her.'

'Yes,' she said, since it would have felt ridiculous to deny it.

The papers had rather gone to town on her, after Elizabeth's disappearance, not at all pleasantly.

'No doubt you'll meet her at some point,' James said. 'One way or another.' He eyed her scone. 'Why aren't you having any cream?'

'What?'

'You have no cream on your scone.'

She looked down at her scone, then back at him. 'I don't like it.'

'You don't like cream?'

'No, I never have.'

'Well, aren't you full of surprises,' he said.

Was she full of surprises?

She mulled the question over, for the remainder of their time together that afternoon, taking James's dictation for several letters he needed sent, then typing them up, her fingers racing over the keys. (No stuck 't'; how *nice* it was.)

She kept mulling it as she addressed the envelopes, ready for collection in the morning.

She mulled it still as she asked James if he needed anything else from her, and he – behind his own desk, working through a stack of papers in the lamplight – told her no, thank you, she'd done more than enough. 'Go, please, get some rest before dinner.' He smiled, tiredly. 'Read a book.'

'You're sure?'

'Quite sure.'

'All right,' she said, reluctantly. 'Well, goodnight then.'

'Goodnight, Miss Ellis.'

And, slowly, she went.

Aren't you full of surprises.

Her father wouldn't have thought so, she felt sure, walking back to the atrium.

Steady, he'd used to call her.

A rock, had been his preferred term of endearment, on the scarce occasions he'd used one.

Not like that mother of yours, he'd say. *I always know where you are, and what you're up to, don't I? You're a good girl, Vi.*

Violet's classmates at school, and college, hadn't found her surprising either. They, she had no doubt, had only ever considered her tiresomely predictable – always ready with an, 'I'm afraid not,' to any invitation to a dance, or trip to the pictures, until, eventually, she'd stopped having to say it, because no one had asked her anywhere any more.

It had been the same with her handful of beaus, over the years: boys she'd met at the office, or eating her sandwiches on her lunchbreak in the park. None of them had lasted more than a few weeks, tiring, so quickly, of her insistence that she had to be home by dark.

And she had had to be.

Whilst there'd been nights when her father might have been fine if she hadn't, they'd been few and far between. Much more often, he'd used to panic, terribly, if she wasn't in, with all the doors and windows locked, by the time his stopwatch alarm rang. Grown angry too.

In fairness to those fair-weather beaus, Violet had never explained any of that to them.

She'd always been too embarrassed to get into it.

And truly none of them – with their cocky smiles, and faux-leather briefcases full of nothing but their mum's homemade sandwiches – had felt worth the effort.

And she, without doubt, had only ever felt frustrating to them.

Disappointing and dull.

Not surprising.

Never surprising.

Aren't you full of surprises.

It was rather nice, thinking that she'd had that in her, all this time.

Absently, she opened the atrium door.

It really was rather nice.

The east wing felt very empty when she reached it, without him there, and too dark: only a single lamp burned, halfway down the corridor. Draughts blew beneath the seams of the closed bedroom doors, bringing Aoife once again to the forefront of her thoughts. *When she wails, the wind howls.* Clenching her fists, she hurried on, letting herself in, quickly, to her bedroom.

To her surprise, Diana was there, dropping off some fresh towels, and Violet's laundry. The fire was ablaze, which Violet might have found more reassuring, had it not reminded her of the light she'd seen burning in her window earlier that morning.

Nothing to worry about, she resolved.

It would have been one of the scullery maids who'd lit it.

Nothing more sinister than that.

There was nothing sinister in anything.

And there was no Aoife.

A ghost story, she repeated to herself. *A foolish myth.*

Still, she decided she'd rather not venture back out again to the atrium for dinner. Childish it might be, but she felt more comfortable remaining in the cocoon of her room. She was full, anyway, from her afternoon tea.

Thanking Diana for her laundry, she told her that she needn't worry about bringing her a tray.

'But there's treacle surprise for pudding,' replied Diana.

It was the most Violet had heard her voluntarily say.

'You can have my portion,' she replied.

And was Diana happy about it?

She made no mention of it if she was.

Her expressionless face didn't move as she turned to go.

Following her to the door, Violet locked it, twice, then, fetching a towel, went into her washroom, ran a hot, steamy bath, and – undressing, dropping her clothes to the floor – gratefully sank into it.

She didn't know how long she lay there.

It was a long time, though. The water cooled around her, and she ran the taps, twice, warming it back up.

It was still raining when, at length, dry and dressed in her nightrobe, she returned to her bedroom.

Picking up Maugham, she went to her window seat, and rested her head against the cold, black glass. Through the rivulets of water, she looked past the lights spilling from the main house, to the lone golden glow at the end of the west wing.

He was still working, then.

She felt guilty, seeing it, thinking of how much of his time she'd taken up all day.

Resting her book in her lap, she stared at his window, just as she'd stared at that ship the night before.

She felt a thread reaching not out to sea, but to him.

She didn't question whether he was there at his window, looking back at her.

In that moment, she knew, with a surety that grew in her chest, moving through her tingling skin, that he was.

Aren't you full of surprises.

Biting her lip, opening her book, she smiled.

ATHERTON'S SISTER IN POLICE CUSTODY

In an exclusive report, we here reveal that Cressida Thompson, only sister of James Atherton, and wife of Mr Richard Thompson ('Dicky' to friends), has been arrested and taken to Scotland Yard for formal questioning. It is not known what charges have been brought against her, or indeed what evidence has led to her removal from Aoife's Bay, but it is to be presumed that the police are now officially treating Elizabeth Atherton's disappearance as sinister.

Cressida, born in August 1914, and an orphan by 1918, has been raised as the ward of her older brother. Described by an undisclosed source as someone who has always guarded his affection jealously, one can but assume the view she took of his marriage. As a child, she lived solely with him, under the care of a governess, and then, at eleven, attended the prestigious girls boarding school of Chargrove Abbey. There, according to our same source, she allied herself with a disreputable crowd, before securing middling results in her final exams last year. Disruptive, and over-indulged – born with a silver spoon in her mouth, but purportedly no moral compass – Cressida Thompson is certainly not a young woman one might expect to respect the rule of law.

Chapter Eight

Elizabeth

April 1932

Dicky and Cressida's wedding was held the weekend after Easter, on the first Saturday of April, at All Saints Church in Fitzrovia. The sun, gallingly, shone, and a dappled breeze blew, sweet with the scent of cherry blossom, which, over the past weeks, had bloomed in abundance, festooning the city's parks and avenues with clouds of pink.

The church itself had been garlanded in hothouse jasmine and tuberose. To the left of the altar, a string quartet played Vivaldi (was there to be no respite from these banalities?), and, at the altar itself, stood Dicky, all puffed-up swagger in his morning coat, affecting faux-nervous smiles for the benefit of various of the congregation; studiously avoiding catching Elizabeth's eye. Henry Astley stood next to him as best man, rather green from celebrating Dicky's final night of bachelordom, and sporting an expression of rather more convincing apprehension, as well he might. Amy had told him, that very morning, that he was going to be a papa in November.

'I suppose one might have waited,' Amy had said to Elizabeth, as, together, they'd slid into their pew, amusement dimpling her cheeks. 'Granted him this last day of carefree boyhood. But honestly, he woke me up at three, then again at four to be sick. He'll be thirty-six next month; high time he grew up.' She'd swallowed a burp, as though trying not to be sick herself. 'He'll be happy once he gets used to the idea. His mother will anyway.' She'd placed her fingers to her lips. 'She has kept *on* about us producing another little Henry.'

'Better a little Amy,' Elizabeth had replied. One big Henry really was more than enough. 'Congratulations, though, darling. Clever old you.'

Amy had grimaced. 'I promise not to become a terrible bore.'

'You won't be able to help it,' Elizabeth had replied.

And Amy wouldn't. They both knew it, had rolled their eyes at countless others of their friends who'd swapped their heels and feathers for brogues and perambulators, and become so utterly, tiresomely obsessed with nannies and routines and *sleep*. Elizabeth might have minded more that Amy – wicked, fun Amy – was about to join their ranks, had she not been so preoccupied with the day at hand.

Looking past her, along the pew, she tried to catch Laura's attention, wanting to make sure she'd noticed Dicky's theatricalities. But Laura had her cloche-hatted head turned away from her, and was chatting with Rupert, their voices dropped to a congregationally appropriate hush.

Elizabeth and Laura hadn't argued again since their cross words at the Kit-Kat Club. There'd been a few days afterwards when they hadn't spoken, and that had been strange and strained – no gossipy strolls along the riverside to break the morning up, nor afternoon trips in Laura's motor to the King's Road to eat pastries – but then, inevitably, they'd crossed paths, arriving for an art exhibition in Kensington at the same time, and, without ever really addressing what had happened, slipped into a truce of sorts. It wasn't an entirely easy one – Laura really had grown perplexingly prone to the odd barb – but infinitely better than not speaking at all. Everyone else was so busy, with their husbands, and children, and *jobs*; the hours really had been horribly long, without Laura in them.

The string quartet fell silent.

In the void, whispers and shuffling took over.

Then, the organ set in, filling the church with Mendelssohn (naturally).

Standing, Elizabeth turned, along with everyone else, looking back along the aisle towards the doors of the knave, curling her fingers into fists as she watched them open, and Cressida and James come in.

James hadn't worn uniform, which struck her as a shame. It would have become him, really very nicely, and he'd more than earnt the right to bring it out on an occasion such as this. Elizabeth had done plenty of digging into his past by now, and knew that he'd remained in the reserves after the armistice, amassed quite a number of medals in action, too.

How impressive they'd have looked, across his chest. And what a serve they'd have been to Dicky – who, as everyone knew, had never won one.

Still, James's morning suit *did* look well on him.

But then, everything looked well on him.

Especially his seriousness; that grim resolve in his set jaw.

Cressida, beside him, looked pretty resolved herself, with her dark, slanted eyes fixed on Dicky, her every step steady, sure. Her dress was pure silk. Her veil, Chantilly lace.

All white.

'To which she has every right,' Dicky had said, tracing circles on Elizabeth's bare back, in Elizabeth's bed, at the start of the week.

'Or so she tells you,' Elizabeth had riposted.

But he hadn't risen.

He'd laughed, kissed her shoulder.

'She's no liar, Lizzie,' he'd said. 'Not everyone lies.'

'Of course they do,' Elizabeth had replied, getting up, pulling on her robe. 'Some people are just more accomplished at it than others.'

She felt she knew Cressida better now.

She'd moved to London after the engagement, swapping the Atherton family estate of Harbury for her brother's Fitzrovia pile, and James – temporarily abandoning his Atlantic island – had moved there too.

'Bastard doesn't trust me,' Dicky had whinged to Elizabeth, often.

Certainly, James had never let Dicky escort Cressida anywhere alone, but had had one of his own drivers courier her to and from whichever party, show, or meal Dicky had asked her along to. And Cressida had come, chatting and laughing with the crowd – all the while Dicky sticking to her side; watching her, much as a jealous child might guard his new favourite toy.

Elizabeth hadn't really spoken much to her.

She couldn't be *that* duplicitous.

Besides, now that she knew who her brother was, she'd grown more mindful of the impression she might cast and, bluntly, didn't want to give her reason to say anything unkind about her behind her back.

'Best steer a wide berth then,' Laura had advised, not kindly.

Elizabeth had heeded her advice, though, and, from a distance, had observed Cressida, listened to her; *taken her measure*, learning, in the process, all sorts of interesting things – such as, that Dicky had been at school with James, and had first met Cressida when, on calling by at Harbury, intent on catching up with his old classmate, he'd found Cressida at home instead.

'What were you even doing in Kent in the first place?' Elizabeth had asked him.

'I was out for a drive, you know.'

'I'm not sure I do,' she'd said, appraising his soft, pretty face, which really was at risk of running to podge, and would, if he didn't rein in his high living, almost certainly soon become fat. (She might have bothered to warn him of it, if she'd been the one marrying him.) 'I had no idea you liked taking long drives.'

'Well, there you have it.'

'Did you not know James no longer lived there?'

'I forgot,' he'd claimed.

'And about her brother's many millions too, I expect,' Elizabeth had said.

'I really do love her, you know,' he'd insisted, and, at the sudden earnestness in his bloodshot stare, she'd almost believed him.

Then she'd remembered that he was the fifth son of a man whose dwindling fortune was entailed to his eldest heir.

She'd thought about the fact that the two of them were entwined, naked, in her bed.

And reminded herself of how often he, Dicky, in his impatience to wait for anything, even his own wedding night, had come knocking on the door of Cheyne Walk since January – swearing blind, each time he left, that it would be the last, only it never was.

He wanted to be a better man for Cressida, Elizabeth did acknowledge that.

He disgusted himself with his faithlessness, she knew.

It was why she'd kept letting him return as she had, even though his touch now left her cold.

Cressida, though.

Cressida really did seem to love him.

Elizabeth had heard her talk too often, too dotingly, of his jokes, and funny stories, and their walks and rides together around Harbury – the hilarity of Dicky splashing around on boating trips across its lake – to doubt it. Seen far too many of the doe-eyed looks Cressida had cast him when she'd believed no one else watching, to consider them a pretence.

Mostly, Elizabeth had disliked her more, for being so easily taken in. Because, really, what a silly little fool.

But sometimes, *sometimes*, she'd been of a mind to remember that she herself had, not too very long ago, thought better of Dicky, for rather a long time. She'd felt able to acknowledge that, for all his narcissism, he could be undeniably charismatic too, with his quips, and wit, and clever teases; that winning smile.

And Cressida was such a baby still, with no experience to guide her.

Was it any wonder she'd fallen under his spell?

And perhaps she hadn't been fibbing when it came to her past.

Perhaps she did truly belong in virginal white.

She was only eighteen, after all, nearly twenty years younger than Dicky, and had lived all her days within the walls of a boarding school, or at home with a governess, and her brother.

What opportunity had she to get up to any serious kind of mischief?

None, really.

But it didn't follow that she didn't have such mischief in her.

On the contrary, Elizabeth had become quite certain that she had it in her in spades.

First, there was the way she dressed, with her black hair bobbed around her elfin face, and her calves always on show – a great deal of her skin too – her lithe, young body poured into gowns that only didn't look scandalous because they were so obviously expensive.

Then, there was her smile, which was slow, and sultry, and far too seductive, frankly, to belong to an innocent heart.

Mainly, though, it was the fact that she was marrying Dicky, when her brother was so against the match. Not only against it, but out and out hostile about it, refusing – as everyone who was anyone now knew – to give Cressida any kind of dowry, or leave anything in her name that Dicky might take. Whilst he'd agreed to pay for the wedding, and would give Cressida an allowance afterwards, the London house to live in too, that was to be it.

'It's all *very* tightly tied up, legally,' said Amy, who'd had it from her brother, Edwin Firth: a partner at the legal firm James used. 'One suspects Dicky's rather relying on James dying, so Cressida will inherit it all.'

Elizabeth wouldn't put it past him.

And she would have liked to have enjoyed Dicky's frustrated ambitions more, she really would.

She might have, had James been a little friendlier to her, in the weeks since they'd been reunited.

But when she'd gone back into the Kit-Kat Club that sleety January night, and re-introduced herself to him, he'd acted as though he truly didn't recall her.

'We were stuck together on the train for hours,' she'd said, her smile straining, making her head hurt all the more. 'I rather got in the way of your work . . . '

'Oh, yes,' he'd said. 'Of course.'

She'd touched his arm, and felt a jolt of heat, all through her own. 'It's lovely to see you again.'

'And you.'

She'd smiled, less painfully this time. 'Yes?'

'Yes.'

'I've thought of you, you know.'

'I'm afraid I'm on my way out,' he'd said, at the same time, setting off for the door. 'I only came to show my face. It was a pleasure to run into you, Emily.'

'Elizabeth,' she'd said, the burn of his mistake seeping through her skin.

He hadn't even replied.

Furious, yet somehow more drawn to him than ever, she'd waited to meet him again, so that she might compel him to rediscover the magnetism that had pulsed between them, on that Oxford train.

But he'd never been anywhere that his sister was, so, in the end, Elizabeth had conspired to be where he was instead, listening for clues dropped by Cressida as to his movements, and using those of their mutual acquaintance to ferret out word of business luncheons he was to be at. She hadn't appeared at all of them (that would have looked quite mad); rather, she'd crossed his path just often enough for it to seem as though serendipity was at work, him to start invading her every waking and sleeping thought, and for him to remember her goddamn name.

Laura had persisted in her refusal to be of any help at all, but Amy had been more useful, arranging, with the aid of her lawyer brother, Edwin, a dinner party, just the week before, at which she'd placed Elizabeth and James side by side.

'So, we meet again,' he'd said to her, as he'd sat.

'Indeed we do,' she'd replied with a smile, only to feel it stick when Laura had arrived on his other side, and he'd turned to greet her.

He had *talked* to Elizabeth through the meal, and been perfectly civil, just not nearly as relaxed as he'd been with Laura, with whom he'd chatted so much more, about what, Elizabeth couldn't say, because, with little choice, she'd spent most of her time talking to Rupert, on her right.

'Have you said something to him about me?' she'd challenged Laura when, after the main course had been cleared, and she'd retreated to Amy's bathroom to pop a pill, Laura had followed her in, to powder her nose. 'Put him off?'

'Of course not,' Laura had said, adjusting her hair in the mirror. 'Anything I have to say about you, I say to your face.' She'd frowned. 'I would have hoped you know me well enough to trust that, by now.'

'Then why is he being so . . . ?' Elizabeth had left the sentence hanging, unwilling to give his disinterest a name.

Laura had sighed. 'I did try to warn you.'

'No one likes an I-told-you-so, Laura.'

'But I *did* tell you so.' She hadn't looked gleeful, or victorious about it, rather sympathetic, over which irritation Elizabeth was still smarting.

Really, how had she, Laura, *dared* to feel sorry for her, Elizabeth?

Elizabeth was the one who felt sorry for Laura.

'I'm honestly not sure what you even think you're chasing after,' Laura had gone on.

'I'm not *chasing*.'

'You are. You've become obsessed with this idea that the two of you are meant to be, because of some stupid train journey —'

'It wasn't stupid —'

'It was a *train journey*, Lizzie. And now you've created this . . . fantasy . . . in your mind.'

'James is no fantasy, Laura.' He was real. So very real. 'And I'm *not* chasing.'

'Then what do you call it?'

Elizabeth hadn't had a good reply for that.

'Let it go,' Laura had told her. 'And leave Dicky be too.'

'Why should I?'

'Because,' and at this, Laura's voice had hardened, 'you're stringing him along to be cruel.'

'I'm not cruel.'

'At the moment you are. And it's making you miserable, so please, give it up, because really, James has made it abundantly clear he's in no mind to take you on.'

'We'll see about that,' Elizabeth had replied, whipping from the room, her head splitting in anger and frustration, resolving there and then that she'd prove Laura wrong, that very same night, and not leave the Astleys' without taking James with her.

For the rest of the evening, she'd applied herself to charming him like she'd never had to apply herself to charming anyone before: quizzing him, as dessert was served, on everything from his tastes in music, to the size of his business, to the people who worked for him, to his time in the trenches.

'Well, let's not talk about that,' he'd said, setting his fork down.

'You're too modest,' she'd replied, touching her hand to his. 'I've heard you were rather a hero.'

Afterwards, in the drawing room for coffee, she'd perched next to him on the settee, letting her leg rest against his (the firmness in his thigh; the strength . . .), smiling, laughing at everyone's chatter, and arching her brows at him, just for him, when somebody had cracked a bawdy joke, until neither he, nor anyone else there, could have been left in any doubt of what she was offering.

She'd started to believe him receptive.

He hadn't got up and moved from her side, after all.

And when she'd yawned and leant towards him, telling him that it was high time she got home to bed, he'd offered to see her out, and hail her a cab.

She'd hung back, her heart pumping in triumph as he'd bid Henry and Amy goodbye. He'd placed his hand in the small of her back, and she, shooting a smirk of triumph at Laura, had let him steer her from the hot, chaotic room, down the stairs, out into the silent, cold night.

But then, on the street, he'd removed his hand from her back.

Together, they'd walked to the corner of the main road, and he'd said nothing.

Then he'd stopped, turning to face her.

'Don't imagine me a fool,' he'd said, 'and don't ever treat me like you believe me one again.' His eyes had flashed, hard with fury. 'I know all about you, Elizabeth. I know the company you keep, and have kept. I know what Dicky Thompson was to you, for a very long time, and make no mistake, my sister knows what you were to him, too.'

Elizabeth had stared, too stunned to correct him on his past tense.

Raising his hand, he'd flagged a passing cab, stepping back as it had come to a halt.

'Find some other way to punish him,' he'd said, opening its door.

'Please, do. Ideally, open Cressida's eyes to the man she's marrying whilst you're at it.'

'This isn't about punishing—'

'Stop. Tell it to someone who wants to listen.' Impatiently, he'd flicked his hand, gesturing her inside the motor. 'And leave me the hell alone.'

Elizabeth watched him now, walking Cressida down the aisle.

His spine was straight, his face, statuesque. Really, he gave away no emotion at all, and yet it could not have been more obvious how much he despised what he was doing.

And Elizabeth hated him.

She hated him so much, for not wanting her more.

For not wanting her at all.

She wanted to punish him for it.

But she did, also, want *him*. She wanted him so much. That hadn't changed.

Or rather it had, because, after his rejection, she only wanted him more.

All week, she'd stewed over it, turning herself in head-splitting circles, trying to devise how she might go about getting her way.

And, at last, it had come to her.

Now, finally, she knew exactly what she needed to do.

The wedding breakfast was held in the ballroom of Claridge's, in predictably formulaic style, with everyone seated at white-clothed tables with floral centrepieces, drinking champagne, eating oysters followed by salmon, and raising their glasses to speeches before cake.

Elizabeth paid scant attention to the speeches, other than to note that James's was short, Henry's amusing, and Dicky's far too long. She picked at her food, hardly drank or smoked, and powdered not a single part of her.

'You're rather muted,' Amy observed, 'what's your excuse?'

'I have none,' said Elizabeth, and took a sip of her champagne to placate her, then put it back down, wanting to keep a clear mind.

After the meal was cleared, the lights were dimmed, a band set up, and there was dancing.

Elizabeth eyed James, standing by the ballroom's doorway, talking to some men she didn't know. Business associates, she supposed, and, thinking no further of it, but feeling an unfamiliar fluttering of nerves, now that her moment was finally at hand, she crossed the room, towards them.

James saw her coming.

She could tell from the hardening in his face.

Finishing his conversation, he detached himself from the men, and began to walk towards her.

He stopped several feet away.

Holding his gaze, she continued walking towards him until there was little more than a breath of air separating them.

She raised her face to his, inviting his kiss, knowing he wouldn't give it to her, but taunting him – and Cressida and Dicky, who she hadn't failed to notice were watching – anyway.

'I'm in no mood for any more of your games, Elizabeth,' he said. 'Run along and find someone else to play with.'

'But I want to play with you.'

'You can't.'

'Are you sure about that?' she said, and leant closer, whispering in his ear.

Then leant back, just far enough, to watch his face pale.

You told her that she'd known what she was getting herself into, didn't you?
You insisted that she must have realized.
You made your bed, you said to her.
Honestly, how little compassion you had.

Chapter Nine

Violet

April 1934

Violet wasn't aware of the postman's call when he returned to Aoife's, that first Friday she spent on the island. She rather expected he wouldn't come; the weather was no better, and James had told her the tug's crossings were cancelled if the conditions became bad enough.

She assumed, when no one appeared in the office to fetch the letters she'd prepared the evening before, that that's what had happened. The envelopes sat in their tray on her desk, and she got on with reorganising Mrs Hamilton's filing systems. As she worked, she kept stealing glances at the door – waiting for James, who'd yet to appear, hoping it wouldn't matter that his letters now wouldn't be sent until Monday.

It was only when a tall, skinny man in footman's livery arrived at her door, bearing a basket brimful of neatly sorted mail, that it came to her, with a sickening thud, that the postman had not only come, but that she'd missed him.

'Or is he having cake?' she asked the footman, hopefully.

'No cake today,' the footman said, gloomily.

'So, he's gone?'

'He's gone.'

'But why didn't anyone come for these?' she said, gesturing at the letters, her heart pumping in panic, for how could she have failed at something so simple? And so early on? 'They were meant to go.'

'Why didn't you bring them down?'

'I didn't know I was *meant* to.'

'Well, it's not *my* job to see to your mail.'

'But Mr Atherton said someone would come.'

'Mrs Hamilton normally takes care of it.'

'Where is she?'

'In the kitchen.'

'Oh, God.' Violet placed her hands to her face, staring at the letters, not wasting her breath asking why Mrs Hamilton hadn't been more helpful – it was hardly a conundrum, and how churlish of her, really – rather, moving to her desk, gathering the letters up and stuffing them into her handbag. 'Was this the postman's last stop?' she asked the footman.

'It won't have been if he has something for Thomas and Francis up at the lighthouse. But I don't think they get much there.'

'Well, let's hope today's an exception.' She made for her door. 'I might just catch him before he leaves.'

She didn't want to waste time returning to her room for her coat, and didn't feel right borrowing another of James's without his knowledge. She did grab an umbrella, though, as she ran from the porch, but it wasn't much use to her up on the exposed fields, where the wind was blowing in such a frenzy that she had to hold the umbrella out before her, just to stop it whipping inside out. Her every step was an effort, pushing into invisible resistance. She might have imagined Aoife herself was in front of her, blowing her backwards, had she not resolved once and for all, that very morning, that she simply couldn't let herself think about her any more.

She hadn't slept well again the night before.

After James's office light had gone out, she'd climbed into bed, and fallen off easily enough, but then been woken in the small hours by a sound beyond her door: one which she was sure now, in the light of day, she must have dreamt, only in the darkness it had felt all too real.

Shakily, she'd lit her lamp, and gone to her door, listening for another noise beyond it. She'd heard nothing. Eventually, she'd returned to her bed, and tried to push thoughts of the large house, and rugged, spirit-shrouded island outside, from her mind. But every time she'd felt herself slipping towards unconsciousness, she'd started awake at the creak of a beam, or the rattle of a window – or simple panic, that her lamp, which she'd been too afraid to extinguish, might burn the house down.

That she'd let herself get into such a state felt incomprehensible to her now, ploughing into the rain. All she wanted to do was climb back into the warmth of her bed and sleep. How could she have wasted so many hours *not* doing that?

At length, she reached the other side of the coast. To her left, loomed the lighthouse, its white walls piercing the heavy grey sky. To her right, high above the boatman's tug and the wave-battered wharf, sat the three cottages, shrouded by fog. And much closer by, just a few yards from where Violet stood – at the point where the lighthouse's peninsula joined the main body of the island – was a horseshoe of wooden posts joined together by wire: the fencing, she realized, that James had told her would be built to cordon off the subsiding cliffs. Seeing it, feeling her legs turn liquid at the idea of the solid ground beneath her dissolving – a sudden, overwhelming sense of foreboding – she stepped away from the plummet, and moved her focus to the peninsula itself.

Where, to her sincere relief, the postman was, walking away from the lighthouse, towards her.

He had had something to deliver to the keepers after all.

Thank God, Violet thought, but didn't set off to meet him.

Instead, she remained where she was, her attention caught – just as it had been on the morning of her arrival – by the other man she'd seen then: the one who'd been watching her disembark the tug, and who was standing outside the lighthouse again, heedless of the rain, watching her now.

For a few seconds, she watched him too, and, in spite of the cold, felt heat creep through her skin. Not a welcome kind. Not a comforting kind. Rather, prickling.

Deeply unpleasant.

'Here's our foreigner,' called the postman, and she turned to him. He wore a raincoat and sou'wester, the rim of which had a river of rain pouring from it. Beneath it, his ruddy, ferrety face was drenched, but smiling. 'I thought you might have forgotten your post.'

'I didn't forget.' She wasn't sure why she bothered to defend herself.

Or why indeed, if he *had* thought such a thing, he hadn't said something about it to someone back at the house, and saved her this race to find him.

But then, that would rather have ruined his obvious enjoyment.

'Three times a week.' He raised his gloved finger to her, wagging it. 'You must be ready for me, three times a week. Monday, Wednesday, Friday. Repeat that, please.'

'I don't need to.'

'*Miss Ellis . . .*'

'Fine. Monday, Wednesday, Friday.'

'Good girl.' He opened his bag. 'Let's have it then. Quick now, I need to be getting on before this weather turns worse and we get marooned.'

'Thank you.' Holding her umbrella fast, she reached into her own bag with her free hand and, bringing out her letters, bundled them into his satchel before they could get too wet. 'Have a safe trip back.'

'You'd be no good for it.'

'I'm sure I wouldn't.'

'Green as the gills,' he said, and, chuckling, strode off.

At the gills, she thought, but didn't say.

Not this time.

She was looking again at the man at the lighthouse, wondering if he was the Thomas Mrs Hamilton had spoken of. *He and Elizabeth became very close.* Or the Francis that footman had mentioned.

Whatever the case, he'd moved several paces closer to Violet, like he was trying to get a better look at her.

Loath, instinctively, to let him do that, Violet turned from him, ready to hasten away.

And the wind gusted, almost as though in a fit of Aoife's pique, cracking her umbrella's frame, rendering it useless.

She ran back across the fields, as anxious to escape the keeper's sight as she was to get out of the rain. She didn't expect to see anyone else on her way, not in such weather, and she didn't, not until she reached the house itself, when, on entering the atrium – sopping wet, for the second time that week – she found Mrs Hamilton there once more, pristine in another silk blouse and smart skirt, standing alone before the fire, staring into it.

Her head snapped up as Violet came into the room, but not before Violet had noticed how deep in thought she'd seemed. And how perfectly warm and dry she looked.

'You're extremely wet, Miss Ellis.'

'That's because I had to go for a walk, Mrs Hamilton,' said Violet, too cross to consider hiding it.

'Without a coat?'

'I was in a rush. You must have known I'd have letters that needed sending.'

She frowned. 'Letters?'

'Yes, *letters*. Mr Atherton's letters.'

'No, I didn't know that.'

'Of course you did.'

'No, Miss Ellis. I didn't imagine you'd have had time to get to anything like that yesterday.'

Was she telling the truth?

She seemed in earnest.

It was so hard to tell with her, though.

'You might have checked,' Violet said. 'I would have checked.'

'Then perhaps you'd like to take the role of housekeeper too.'

'That's not what I meant.'

'Wasn't it?'

'No.'

Mrs Hamilton touched her fingertips to the bridge of her nose. 'It's been a very difficult morning, Miss Ellis. I'd appreciate you not adding to it further.'

Why, difficult? Violet might have asked.

Did another trifle come in the postman's sack?

For the present, she was too cold, and too indignant at Mrs Hamilton's insinuation that she was the one who was behaving badly, to think clearly enough for it to occur to her.

Instead, she voiced the concern most pressing in her mind.

'There's a man at the lighthouse who watches me.'

Mrs Hamilton didn't seem surprised.

'Would it be Thomas?' Violet asked.

No reply.

'Perhaps I should go and ask him,' said Violet, in exasperation.

And, slowly, Mrs Hamilton raised her green eyes back to hers.

Then, they both started at the sound of the porch door opening, bringing more damp air into the room, and Mr Hamilton; James, too.

In spite of everything, Violet felt her heart lift, seeing him.

He in turn appeared somewhat perplexed, seeing her.

'Where have you been?' Mrs Hamilton asked, crossing to her

117

husband. Her voice was different when she spoke to him. Softer. When she pulled a kerchief from her sleeve, wiping the rain from his mask, she did it with almost shocking gentleness. 'I've been looking for you.'

'We were at the dairy,' Mr Hamilton said, letting Violet know that the island had one. 'Vet's been. For the inoculations, remember?'

'Of course.' She shook her head. 'How foolish of me.'

'Miss Ellis,' said James, removing his jacket, 'you appear to be standing in a puddle.'

'Yes,' Violet said, glancing at her feet. 'I'm sorry.'

'What for?'

'The puddle.'

'I'm not worried about the puddle.'

'I'm afraid I broke an umbrella, too.'

'I'm not worried about that either.'

She smiled, then stopped herself, conscious of how the Hamiltons had both turned to look. 'I'm still sorry.'

'What on earth took you out?'

'I needed to go after the postman,' said Violet, and could have told him the truth as to why. Could probably have made Mrs Hamilton rather uncomfortable.

Embarrassed her, in front of her husband.

But for what purpose, other than to make Mrs Hamilton resent her more?

She didn't want to do that.

So, she fibbed.

'I forgot to pass on one of your letters. I didn't want it to have to wait until after the weekend.'

'It easily could have.'

'I thought it might be urgent.'

'Miss Ellis, there's nothing so urgent that you should ever feel compelled to go out in weather like this.'

'All right.' She nodded, smiled again, then, to her embarrassment, coloured, because the Hamiltons really were so silent, watching them both. 'I'd better change.'

'You better had,' James agreed.

'I won't be long.'

'No rush.'

She glanced Mrs Hamilton's way as she went.

Expecting what?

A smile?

Gratitude, that she'd protected her.

She got neither.

Just a small tilt of her head in what might have been acknowledgement.

But could just as easily been a figment of Violet's imagination.

Later, though, much later, after she returned to her room at nightfall, Mrs Hamilton paid her another visit.

She knocked this time.

An olive branch?

Violet considered the possibility as Mrs Hamilton stepped into her room, pulling the door softly shut behind her. But Mrs Hamilton's composed expression gave nothing away.

As ever, Violet struggled to be sure what was going through her mind.

She waited for her to speak.

When she didn't, Violet asked her how the rest of her day had been. 'It improved, I hope.' *It's been a very difficult morning.*

'Certainly, it got no worse. And yours?'

'No worse either,' said Violet, thinking of the afternoon tea that she and James had once again shared by his fire; her amusement, listening to him recount his own ridiculous morning helping the vet and Mr Hamilton with the cows' inoculations, his dairy farmer

119

having come down with a bad cold.

'Could no one else have done it?' she'd asked, picturing him, knee-deep in mud, holding a calf called Lettice steady.

'Probably . . . '

'But you didn't ask them?' She'd leant towards him. 'Did you *want* to do it, Mr Atherton?'

He'd laughed. 'I didn't mind. I've always liked that kind of work.'

'A frustrated farmer,' she'd said, and loved it when he'd grinned, found out.

'I can't be long,' Mrs Hamilton said, drawing her back to the infinitely less convivial atmosphere of her bedroom. 'Arnold's waiting to go home. But you did me a kindness earlier.' (So, she had been grateful for Violet's lie.) 'Would you permit me to offer you some advice in return?'

'All right,' said Violet, cautiously now, thinking of the interested way that she and Mr Hamilton had been observing her and James earlier; fearing, suddenly, that a lecture on professional distance might be about to come her way.

But it wasn't James whom Mrs Hamilton wanted to talk about.

It was the keepers, up at the lighthouse.

'You worried me earlier when you talked about going there. They don't welcome visitors, Miss Ellis.'

'They don't?'

'No.'

'What about Mrs Atherton?' Violet asked, daring herself to do so. 'You told me that she and Thomas were—'

'Yes,' said Mrs Hamilton, cutting Violet off before she could say *close*. 'And look how that ended for her.' She frowned the instant she'd let the words go, like she'd already thought better of them.

But it was too late.

She *had* let the words go.

They were spoken, reverberating in the air.

Look how that ended for her.

'You mean her accident?' said Violet, and somehow kept her tone level, despite the chaos that had, quite abruptly, erupted in her chest. 'Or are you suggesting—'

'I'm not suggesting anything,' Mrs Hamilton interrupted, frown deepening, her eyes moving – whether consciously, or subconsciously – to the window facing the lighthouse. 'I wouldn't presume to.'

'Are you sure?' asked Violet, following her gaze, a chill snaking her spine.

'Quite sure, thank you.'

'I'm not,' said Violet, and wasn't. Not at all. *Look how that ended for her.* 'I think you might have been implying that Mrs Atherton was hurt.'

And back Mrs Hamilton's green stare came to her.

'She died, Miss Ellis.'

'I know that. I meant, deliberately.'

Mrs Hamilton said nothing.

'Do you know something?' Violet pushed her, unease deepening.

'Of course not.'

'I think you might.'

'No . . . '

'Yes . . . '

'For heaven's sake.' Mrs Hamilton snapped. 'What would I know? I have no idea what happened that night. No one does.'

'What about the police?'

'What about them?'

'Well, they knew.' Violet wasn't sure who she was trying hardest to convince. 'They closed the case.'

'They did,' agreed Mrs Hamilton, too readily, wanting, very obviously, to end the conversation.

Violet rather wanted to do that too.

And yet,

121

'You don't think they really knew what happened?' she persisted.

'That's not what I said.'

'No, you said, look how that ended for her.'

'I know what I said.'

'Then you must realize how it sounded.'

'Miss Ellis, please.' Mrs Hamilton dipped her head, eyelids flickering shut: tired, it was clear; extremely tired, like she hadn't slept much the night before, either. 'You're making something out of nothing, twisting my words . . . '

'I'm not twisting anything,' said Violet, stung. 'Or, if I am, then what *did* you mean, when you said that nobody knows what happened to Mrs Atherton?'

'I meant nothing.'

'Of course you did.'

'You're behaving like a dog with a bone . . . '

'Just tell me what you meant.'

'That certain things were brushed over, that's all. Not everything made complete sense.'

'Such as?'

'*Miss Ellis*.' The words cracked. 'I won't discuss this more. And I really do need to get on. I wish now that I'd never come . . . '

'Why *did* you?'

'To settle our account.' She sounded indignant, as though Violet had been horribly ungrateful. 'Tell you that you need to take care who you form your friendships with. Francis and Thomas Browning prefer their own company.' She reached for the door handle. 'If you heed what I say, you'll leave them to it.'

And with that, she went.

For several moments, Violet remained still, staring into the static air she'd left – just as she had out on her balcony, when Mrs Hamilton had chilled her to the bone with her story of Aoife – wondering whether she'd been trying to scare her again now.

She didn't think so.

Jarring as it felt, it really did seem that she'd genuinely intended to do Violet a favour in coming to see her.

Only for the conversation to have run out of her control.

Violet drew no satisfaction from having wrested it from her.

Rather, as she turned back towards the dark, rain-spattered window facing the lighthouse, she felt another shudder.

Slowly, she walked to the window, following the all-seeing beam with her eyes.

Look how that ended for her.

Coming to a halt, she pictured the brooding man behind the lamp.

Then, jumped, startled by the sudden white of a gull, swooping towards her out of the night, its beady eyes manic; its squawk, petrified.

Hand to her hammering heart, she took a breath, trying to calm herself, but her imagination took over, taunting her with the idea that Aoife had sent that gull hurtling her way.

Stop, she ordered herself, *Just stop*.

The beam swung.

The black waves rolled.

Jerkily, she tested the windows' fastenings, tugging them to be sure, and, quickly, resolutely, wrenched the drapes shut.

SAILING BOAT MISSING FROM ISLAND

Whilst still refusing comment on the matter of Cressida Thompson's ongoing questioning, a source at Scotland Yard has now disclosed that a one-man dinghy also vanished from Aoife's Bay on the night of Elizabeth Atherton's disappearance.

Small, and unrobust, the dinghy is said to be the kind used for recreational sailing rather than navigating treacherous winter seas. The police haven't confirmed whether they believe Mrs Atherton left the island in this dinghy willingly, or otherwise, but have stated that they are working under the assumption that leave the island on it, Mrs Atherton did.

Without wishing to speculate, it is this reporter's view that, given the storm raging on the night in question – and given the party Mrs Atherton was imminently to hold – her departure in such an unsafe vessel could have been no intentional thing.

And was Mrs Atherton a sailor?

No, she was not.

According to our source, she was never known to go near the sea . . .

How are you, old thing?

And how is she? Our sweet Violet. Missing home? The big smoke. Or has she warmed to her new reclusive abode, breathing that fresh, salty air?

You love that air, I know.

Nectar, Elizabeth once told me you called it.

You must be very afraid of being taken away from it. Terrified of being denied the freedom of your island.

Elizabeth never really got on with it, did she?

That infuriated you, I'm sure. But she didn't used to be so miserable.

She had a life full of happiness, and you took that from her. You took that, and everything else too, and honestly, when I let myself reflect on your thievery for too long, I grow so consumingly angry, until I can focus on nothing else, and it makes me dizzy with hate.

But then, I remember that what goes around always, always, comes around.

I take heart from that.

Chapter Ten

Violet

April–May 1934

Violet did steer clear of the lighthouse, in the wake of Mrs Hamilton's visit. Even had she felt tempted to ignore her advice – which she honestly didn't – the weather would have prevented her from doing so. The stormy conditions persisted throughout her first fortnight on the island, the rain falling, the wind blowing, until the house felt an island in itself, the idea of venturing beyond its walls too off-putting to be considered for anything beyond necessity. The Hamiltons continued to come and go, Mr Hamilton's ground staff did too, but few else. Whilst the seas calmed just enough each weekend for Mr Hamilton to ferry the islanders over to St Leonard's for Sunday morning visits to their families, and church, they quickly worsened again. Twice the mail boat really did have to be cancelled, so that when the postman appeared, he did so with his soggy satchel stuffed.

The days, though, which might have felt very long to Violet under such confinement, passed with strange speed. She was busy in the office, of course – especially once the inundation of foremen correspondence began to arrive (when the post ran) – and the work was more than novel and copious enough to make the hours fly.

There was so much else that was new too. The house, obviously, which she gradually found her way around, growing more accustomed to its proportions, if not at all to its silent splendour. There was one area in which she never strayed – up on the second floor of the main house, where James's room was – but she did come to spend more time on the first floor, which housed the dining room, drawing room, and a large library.

'You must come whenever you like,' James said, showing her that library, on the Saturday of her first weekend. 'You have my word I'll make no attempt to decipher what you read whilst you're here.'

'It's not always a secret,' she reminded him, taking in the room's shelves upon shelves of books, its roaring fire and sumptuous settees. 'Not even mostly.'

'Well, then keep me posted,' he said, leaving her to it. 'We can exchange critiques.'

And they did.

When he came by, later that afternoon, to see how she was, they shared tea by the library's fire, and discussed Leopold Bloom, for a few minutes, but mainly (and Violet wasn't sure how they got on to the subject) the zoo at Regent's Park, and the fact that James had never visited.

'What, never?' Violet said.

'No, never,' he replied.

She stared across at him.

He stared back at her.

'I don't know what I'm more shocked about,' she said, at length. 'That you haven't been, or that I've done something you haven't.'

He laughed.

'No, seriously.'

'How many times have you been?' he asked.

'I've no idea,' she said, 'many,' and went on, telling him how her parents had taken her for her first visit, before the war. 'My mother took me again, just before she left. I think she was probably feeling guilty. We had a ride in a carriage pulled by zebras.' She thought back to it, remembering the twist of sherbet her mother had bought for her afterwards. *You enjoy that, Violet. Make it last now.* Really, how long had she imagined such a tiny thing *could* last? 'I was excited. It all felt such a treat ... Anyway,' she expelled a quick breath, 'I got into the habit of going again, this past year. It's obviously not far from Lancaster Gate ...'

'What do you like about it?'

'Well,' she found a smile, 'they have all these *animals*.'

He smiled too.

'It's not actually just the animals,' she admitted. 'Not even really them. I liked being where my mother was. And my father, when he was different.'

'You remember much of him, then?'

'Enough.'

'Tell me about him,' he said.

So she did, talking of all the little things that had remained with her – like, the foam he'd used to dot on her nose when she'd watched him shave; the feel of his hair beneath her cheek on shoulder rides; how he'd pretend to fall asleep next to her after bedtime stories, then make her hysterical by starting awake – realizing, as she spoke, how much she'd wanted James to know this version of her father too.

How glad she was that he'd asked.

They took a long time about their tea, that afternoon.

Then, with the rest of the household gone to St Leonard's for church the next morning, shared it again, back in the library, playing a hand of cards.

'Do you ever go to church?' Violet asked James.

'Rarely since my mother died,' he said, mentioning her for the first time. 'And you?'

'Much the same since my father.'

He reached for a card. 'Why were you alone at the funeral?'

'I wasn't meant to be. My godfather couldn't come, though.'

'Why not?'

'He was indisposed.'

'How, indisposed?'

'He ate a bad oyster.'

'A bad oyster?'

It was the way he said it.

Out of nowhere, laughter burst from her.

Immediately, she placed her hand to her mouth to stop it, but it wasn't much use. Then he told her how inappropriate she was being, really, which made her dissolve all over again.

Cheeks pulling, he moved his cards.

Getting her hilarity under control, she examined her own.

'I think I've probably won, actually,' she said, laying them down.

He looked at them.

Then back at her.

'Yes,' he said, 'I think you probably have.'

And she was laughing again.

He leant forward, gathering the pack to reshuffle.

'For what it's worth,' he said, 'I wish now that I hadn't left you alone in Pentonville.'

'I wish you hadn't either.'

He raised his gaze back to hers. And, in the ensuing silence, that was all there was: him looking at her, and her looking at him.

Thinking to herself how very different it all might have been if he *had* come forward and been by her side, that bleak, hideous day.

She would have liked to eat dinner with him that night.

Truly, she would have liked to do that with him every night.

But he ate his meals alone in the dining room, or the office, and she had hers alone in the atrium, with the exception of dinner itself, which, giving into her fears (she wasn't proud of it), she took in her bedroom, so avoiding a dark walk alone back through the empty east wing afterwards.

Perhaps it would have been nice, once in a while, to have joined the servants in the kitchen for a meal, but no one ever invited her to do that, so she never found out.

It really was a strained kind of limbo that she inhabited, belonging neither below, nor entirely above, stairs. She didn't mention her discomfort to James, fearing she'd come across as asking him for something she was herself only slowly becoming able to acknowledge wanting. (And how smug Mr Barlow would be, to know it. *He's a man mired in grief, Miss Ellis. I never took you for a fool.*) She didn't speak to him about the Brownings either, or the things Mrs Hamilton had said, fearing it would only cause him pain.

But she did try to befriend the servants, forcing herself to venture into their domain at least once per day – either to fetch her linen, or drop the office mail for collection herself, or return her meal trays. Gradually, she made everyone's acquaintance.

There were eight house servants in total: two footmen, one called Simon – who'd she met in the office – and the other, Alan; then there was Diana, of course, another housemaid called Nelle, the two scullery maids, and, finally, a young kitchenhand who was apprenticed to Chef – himself a middle-aged Parisian who everyone called simply, *Chef*.

Chef, and everyone else, called Violet, *Miss Ellis*, and although Violet always greeted each of them warmly, she never got much beyond mutters by way of a response. Mrs Hamilton, meanwhile, seemed to be avoiding spending any more time with her than was absolutely necessary – pausing to enquire into how she was, whenever they ran up against one another, but never delving further than that, and certainly not ever lingering long enough to offer Violet the opportunity to do so. Whether she acted out of simple dislike, or fear that Violet might push her into further discussion on the subject of Elizabeth – or both – Violet didn't know. But so often she seemed distracted, with an air of pensive contemplation about her that Violet had first been conscious of when she'd seen her staring into the atrium fire, but realized in retrospect had been there in her manner the first night she'd come to her room, too.

The post came, she'd said, mere hours after Violet had overheard her locked in that furious exchange, with a man whose voice Violet still hadn't recognized among any of the servants. *A trifle, I shouldn't have worried you with it.*

Had she worried anyone else?

Violet couldn't imagine her confiding in any of the staff, with whom she appeared almost as distant as she was with Violet, speaking to them only to issue clipped instruction.

Maybe she'd talked to Mr Hamilton, though.

Arnold.

He seemed to be her only real friend on the island, and, really, how lonely that must have been for her, all these years.

Occasionally, Violet would catch sight of them together, walking to and from the house. Always, they were holding hands. Seeing that – seeing the way Mrs Hamilton leant into her husband's giant body with her slight one – Violet would recall the tender way she'd brushed rain from his mask, and find herself wondering what version of herself she revealed to him, when it was just the two of them.

A warmer one than the rest of them were treated to, undoubtedly.

Mr Hamilton at least, Violet really did like – more every time he visited the office – but his ground staff were as withdrawn as the house servants, responding to Violet's hellos with curt nods whenever she saw them in the kitchen, then turning back to whatever they might have been talking about, shutting her out.

She was still a newcomer, she did realize that.

A *foreigner*, as the postman had said.

It was natural that everyone should take time to warm up to her. Especially on this island, which, less than two years before, had had its business laid bare for all to read.

Still, their reticence felt deeper, more personal, than simple reserve.

On bad days, it really felt like some of them might hate her.

And Diana thawed not at all. Although she did, gradually, enlighten Violet as to her age (seventeen), names of her parents (John and Melder), and the fact that she didn't go with the others in Mr Hamilton's ferry on a Sunday morning, because John, her fisherman father, collected her for dinner at home every Saturday night, her monosyllabic revelations – let go, much as a stone might release blood – could hardly be called the starting of a friendship.

Violet wasn't entirely sure what they should be called.

Torture, perhaps.

She didn't want to be hurt: not by Diana's detachedness, nor the others' chill, nor her absolute conviction that they were all just waiting for her back to be turned to begin talking about her again.

But she *was* hurt.

She couldn't help it.

Nor did she believe that anyone was going to get bored of their hostility. Certainly not soon. She, who'd been gossiped about for almost her entire living memory, knew full well how long these things could run for. And whilst she was sure she should have grown a thicker skin by now, that trick of evolution seemed to have eluded her, because the idea of the whispers surrounding her now taunted her, every bit as sorely as those of the neighbours had, back when her mother had run off, and after every one of her father's indiscretions since.

Yet, she still took tea with James: at weekends in the library, and during the week, by his office fire.

Whenever she beat him at cards, she'd clap her hands, noisily victorious.

Whenever she lost, she'd congratulate him on his luck, just to hear him laugh.

And, whenever he asked her if she could do with a break – from her typing, or his dictation, or filing – and some fresh air, she'd always say yes. Grabbing her coat, which she got into the habit of bringing with her to the office each morning, she'd walk with him again, down to the rocky ledge at the foot of those old lighthouse stairs.

Almost always, they passed someone on the way – Nelle or Diana in the atrium; Simon or Alan on the servants' stairs – and, for their benefit, Violet would talk to James about work, telling him of a signature she needed, or a query that she had on some contract or other. He'd play along, never embarrassing her by calling her out on the pretence, but she knew he knew that's what it was.

She doubted the servants were fooled, either.

But reluctant as she was to give them more fuel for their gossip, she couldn't *not* go on those walks with James.

Those hours they amassed together, huddled beneath the shelter of the cliffs, the sheeting rain falling, and the waves rolling on, became, very quickly, far too quickly really, the highlight of her every day.

They talked about so much – his family, her family, books, friends, childhoods – she could quite easily have lost track of what they talked of.

Yet, she lost track of nothing.

Each evening, back in her solitary east wing, she'd close the drapes of her window facing the lighthouse, and sit at the one facing his, going over it all again: smiling, recalling a tease, or a quip, or a moment when they'd stopped talking, saying nothing at all. She'd stare across at the light burning in his office, and wish she was back down on that rock with him again.

She'd remain at her window, watching his light, as, one by one, all the other lamps in the house were extinguished, not moving until his went out too, breaking that thread between them.

At which point she'd reluctantly rise, and get into her bed.

133

Those nights alone in her bed were much harder than the days.

Longer.

With just the wind for company, her worries, kept in the wings of her mind all day, would grow louder, elbowing all else out, gradually becoming all she could hear. And there was so much to worry her, well beyond the animosity of the staff.

The post, for example.

It really did come to feel that there might be something strange going on with Aoife's post.

At first, she thought she must be imagining the tension that descended on the house every Monday, Wednesday, and Friday, when the postman was due. She decided it most likely a coincidence that, when she went down to the kitchen to drop the office mail, it was always so full: Mrs Hamilton checking the larder, or counting the silverware; Diana perched at the long dining table, absently stitching stockings, and napkins; Nelle beside her, polishing cutlery; Alan the footman, polishing shoes . . .

But then she realized that, on the mornings when the postman wasn't expected, rather than being in the kitchen, they were all largely elsewhere.

She observed, a palpable easing in the house's strained silence.

More chatter.

And, on the two Mondays that the mail boat was cancelled, even the odd laugh.

Another thing that she couldn't fail to notice was the bizarre manner in which the office mail arrived on her desk, always brought in a basket by Simon, with the envelopes sorted, quite forensically, by postmark, and bearing the unmistakeable trace of Mrs Hamilton's scent.

Violet couldn't think what Mrs Hamilton might possibly be looking for, in those stacks of meeting minutes, and invoices, and contract enquiries, and yield reports. But, by the final Friday of the month, she'd become baffled enough to corner her in the larder and ask.

And was rewarded with a long, cool stare.

'I'm not looking for anything,' Mrs Hamilton said. 'I've always sorted the post. But if you think you can enlighten me on how to do it better, perhaps you'd like to train me.'

Violet didn't want to do any such thing.

But nor did she take Mrs Hamilton at her word, because she wasn't an idiot.

No one sorted mail by postmark.

Of course she was searching for something.

And Violet had a hunch that, whatever it was, two letters in particular caught her eye.

They arrived for James a week apart, from London, and were addressed to him personally. Violet didn't open either of them – they were labelled Private & Confidential – but she watched James when he read those letters.

Saw his expression darken in a furious frown.

He didn't dictate his replies to her. Instead, he placed those letters in his locked bottom drawer and handwrote his own responses, sealing them in envelopes which he asked Violet to send on to his solicitors, Firth Knightley, in town.

Tempted as Violet was, she didn't ask him what any of it was about.

He, increasingly open with her about so much, hadn't told her, and it wasn't her business to pry.

She didn't *want* to pry.

Not with him.

But she had no such qualms with Mrs Hamilton.

Rather, once she'd got her in the larder, she finally raised the matter of the supposed trifle that had come in the mail, enquiring if there'd been any more.

'Now, why would you ask me a thing like that?' Mrs Hamilton said.

'Wouldn't you in my shoes?'

'I'm not in your shoes, Miss Ellis. And I haven't given the matter another thought. Really,' a rictus smile, 'you mustn't concern yourself either.'

But Violet did concern herself.

She was *concerned*.

More and more about Elizabeth too.

Because no one ever talked about her.

Not ever.

Which was strange, wasn't it?

She'd been the mistress of the house. James's wife.

Even if he was too traumatised, too *mired in grief*, for recollection, surely her name should come up with the others once in a while.

Violet was certain they must all think about her.

How could they not?

She knew she did.

She thought about her every night.

Quite as much as she thought about Aoife. Because she couldn't forget her either, no matter how determinedly she tried to.

Rather, in the gusting wind and rain, she'd lie in her bed, hearing her centuries-old wails of sorrow, imagining her plummet to her death.

Throwing her blankets off, shivering in the cold, she'd get up, moving around her room, infuriating herself with her own irrationality, but nonetheless needing to check her locks, and pull her suitcase into position across her door.

It didn't reassure her, though.

Nothing reassured her.

Back in bed, she'd find herself picturing that doomed princess again, out roaming the island, Elizabeth with her, still at large in the darkness, dressed now for eternity in an evening gown and galoshes.

Eventually, she'd fall asleep, but she'd always jerk back awake at some point, her body slick with sweat beneath her nightdress, her heart hammering a hectic accompaniment to the footsteps she'd imagined, walking past her door.

It was at the start of May that James left for meetings in London, and the clouds shrouding Aoife's finally fragmented, opening blinding gateways into the boundless sky above. The sea stilled, glistening beatifically, and all over the island, an abundance of blooms sprung – as Violet discovered when, with less work to do, now James wasn't there, and finding the days suddenly endless without him, she got into the habit of taking morning and afternoon walks.

She went for miles, exploring the island's craggy ups and downs, discovering the dairy in the fields behind the cottages – patting the calf, Lettice's head – and occasionally spotting Mr Hamilton's seals, bobbing beneath the cliffs. Often, she ended up passing the cottages, one time seeing Gareth Phillips, the fire warden, out in his garden, weeding ('I gather I've stepped into your daughter's shoes,' she said. 'I gather you have,' he replied, still weeding), and always carrying on down the cliff stairs to the beach, where she'd wander the lapping shore, skimming stones, fighting to ignore the spectre of the man who'd inevitably appear outside the lighthouse, watching her every movement.

Even without Mrs Hamilton's warning, she'd have known to continue keeping well away from him.

Each time she saw him, she trusted him less.

And she didn't trust the weather's change.

She waited for it to turn once more, whisking them all back to winter.

But the days only grew warmer, until, by the first Sunday of that May, when everyone once again headed off to church, the men did so in shirtsleeves, and the women in cotton dresses. It felt almost impossible to believe that, just the week before, they'd made the same journey in thick scarves and waterproofs. The calm, the golden warmth, was such a stark difference to what had been, that it made Violet think of the nursery rhyme about the child who when nice, was very, very nice, and when bad, horrid.

Making the most of having the house to herself that morning, she washed her hair, wrote to her godfather, and went down to the kitchen, where she luxuriated in the freedom of making herself lunch, then eating it at that table she'd never been invited to sit at.

Afterwards – and much to her shame – she flirted with the idea of going up to the second floor of the house. Just for a peek.

A quick peek to see if she could find anything of Elizabeth there.

She stood at the bottom of the stairs, looking upwards, considering doing that for quite some time.

But then she imagined James appearing behind her.

She heard his low voice.

How inappropriate of you, Miss Ellis.

She knew she couldn't do it. Just as she hadn't been able to ask him about those letters.

She wouldn't become another person in his life who snooped.

Taking herself away from temptation, she buckled on her sandals and headed out for another walk, thinking to go to the wharf to keep an eye out for the others coming back.

But, when she reached that other side of the island, she turned left instead of right, deciding on an impulse to make the most of the island's emptiness by finally having a look around the lighthouse.

She'd long since asked Diana what she knew of the two keepers. Diana, unsurprisingly, hadn't volunteered much: only that Francis Browning was Thomas's father, and that they'd both worked on the island for as long as she could remember.

Violet had become quite certain by now that she hadn't read either of their names in the newspapers. She would have recalled. Other than Gareth Phillips, the reporters hadn't much focused on any of those in service on the island, other than to allude to them as a collective of suspects, and publishing the odd defamatory remark made by some local or other. Mainly, they'd kept their ink for James, and his and Elizabeth's six guests; Cressida especially.

It struck Violet as odd, now that she knew what Mrs Hamilton had told her about Thomas and Elizabeth being close, that no one had made more of him.

Hadn't anyone mentioned their friendship to the press, or the police?

Had James even known about it?

Or had it been an illicit thing?

It was curiosity that propelled Violet all the way to the lighthouse's door.

That, and her confidence that the Brownings really had, along with everyone else, gone to St Leonard's.

Which Francis Browning had.

He never missed church.

But Thomas did.

As Violet discovered when she met him for the first time that afternoon.

And knew, the instant he spoke, in his flat, Cornish burr, that he was, at last, without doubt, the man she'd heard Mrs Hamilton arguing with, back on the day she'd arrived, behind the closed atrium door.

Chapter Eleven

Violet

She was out of breath by the time she reached the lighthouse. The ground leading up to it wasn't as flat as it had appeared from below, and the track was overgrown with nettles, more churned mud than path, much of it still soft, boggy in parts, from the storms. She hadn't worn stockings – who was there to see her? – and her skin quickly began to smart from the sting of nettles she didn't manage to avoid.

Cursing, she crouched beside the lighthouse, searching for a dock leaf and rubbing it, without much effect, on her calves. On her hatless head, the sun beat down. Beneath the collar of her blouse, she felt sweat beading.

Letting the leaf fall, she looked upwards, squinting, taking in the length of the lighthouse, which, against the sun's blaze, formed a conical silhouette. It looked taller up close, wider, and sturdier. And, when she got up, walking around it, she discovered a small house: the Brownings' home, obviously. It wasn't nearly as charming as the cottages near the wharf. There were no lace curtains at its windows, nor paint on its front door. The front door was stripped wood. The walls were plain cement. There wasn't even a proper chimney, just a steel tube that jutted from the tin roof. To its right, a washing line had been strung, and there were several pairs of long-johns hanging to dry.

It was those long johns that Violet was looking at when, hearing the slam of the lighthouse door behind her, she realized she wasn't alone.

Heart hammering, she span around, then froze, seeing the stranger before her.

He, appraising her, didn't seem nearly so surprised by her own presence.

Clearly, he'd seen her coming.

'You seem to have lost your way, Miss Ellis.'

He knew her name.

Violet registered that, in the same split second that she made the connection between his voice, and that of the man who'd rowed with Mrs Hamilton.

Struck dumb by the unexpectedness of both, not to mention the fact that anyone was there at all, it took her a second to realize she should respond.

Just a second, but it was enough for her to absorb plenty else about him.

He was Thomas, she was certain. He wasn't old enough to have an adult son who'd worked here since before Diana could remember.

He wasn't particularly young either. In his mid-forties, perhaps.

Older than James, at any rate.

His hair, dusty brown to James's dark, was shorn short. A close-cropped beard framed his rigid jaw. Tall and lean, he lacked James's solid strength, his body swimming in a baggy shirt and faded corduroy trousers that he'd belted, tight, at the waist. His face was striking, undeniably, but it wasn't one she felt at ease looking at. There was a gauntness to his cheeks, a hollowness to his hooded grey eyes which made them impossible to hold. He stood very still, a barely contained energy to him, his booted feet apart, and his hands held rigid, his fingers spread out, as though he was resisting the urge to clench them.

141

Looking at those fingers, then back at his eyes, Violet recalled what her mother had used to tell her, about mercury sending lighthouse keepers mad. Remembering too, quite abruptly, that the two of them were alone on the island, she felt an overwhelming urge to run.

Then it came to her that he, staring at her so intently, might be waiting for her to do that very thing.

That he wanted her to run.

Wanted to intimidate her.

Just as Mrs Hamilton had assuredly wanted to intimidate her – whatever her more recent motivations – when she'd told her that damnable tale of Aoife.

She saw herself through Thomas's eyes: hot, sweaty, her bare legs covered in stings, looking up at him like a deer caught in a fox's sights. Then she saw herself again as she must have looked to Mrs Hamilton, fresh off the boatman's tug: soaking wet in her best clothes, her hair bedraggled, her skin pasty and pale; *green as a cabbage* and easy pickings.

A pushover.

Was that how the staff saw her, as well?

Were they all just waiting for her to run too?

She thought they probably were, and it made her angry.

It made her furious.

What was it about her that made all these people – not only here, but Mr Barlow in London, her own father before him; even her mother – believe they could treat her however they damn well pleased?

That she'd *let* them.

She'd done that too often with her parents, Mr Barlow as well.

But no more.

She'd had enough.

She'd had her *fill*.

'I haven't lost my way,' she said. 'I assume you're Thomas

142

Browning?'

'I am.'

'Why have you been watching me?'

That surprised him.

She saw it in his face.

Aren't you full of surprises?

Yes, she thought, *yes, I am.*

She waited for Thomas to deny that he had been watching her. But he simply folded his arms, and watched her still.

'Why are you here?' he asked her.

'I came for a walk,' she said, tipping her chin against the discomfort of his stare.

'Not *here*,' he said. 'Here.' He stamped his foot twice. 'On Aoife's.'

She frowned. 'I work here. The same as you.'

'No.' He shook his head. 'Not the same as me. I was born here. I belong here. But you,' he sucked in a breath, 'I don't think you do.'

She couldn't argue with that.

She wasn't at all sure she belonged either.

Still,

'Why should I need to?' she asked. 'I'm here to type, and file. Not lay down roots . . .'

He narrowed his eyes. 'Is that right?'

'It is.'

'Question for you. Do you like typing?'

'I don't mind it. It's my job. It's what I know how to do.'

'Learnt it did you?'

'Yes.'

'Went to a college?'

'I did.'

'I didn't.'

'Oh.' She wasn't sure why they were talking about this. 'Did you want to?'

'Never had the choice, did I? I barely went to school. I was set to be a keeper from the day I was born.'

'Do you like it?'

'What?'

'Being a lighthouse keeper.'

'Oh, yes, I love it. I breathe for it. It's what gets me up, every single day.'

Was he in earnest?

He spoke in such a monotone, it was impossible to be sure.

'What do you love about it?' she asked.

His stare hardened.

'You were being sarcastic,' she said.

'I was, Miss Ellis. I love this island, but I don't love my job. It's very, very, boring.'

'Is that why you've been watching me? For a diversion?'

He said nothing.

His expression didn't move.

Violet, feeling ever hotter, shifted on her feet.

She wished she hadn't stayed, after all.

She could have made her excuses and walked calmly away.

Why had she stayed?

Mrs Hamilton, she thought. *Ask him about his argument with Mrs Hamilton.*

But he brought her up first.

'She doesn't want you here,' he said.

It was hardly news.

Still, it wasn't a pleasant thing to have to hear.

'Well, I am here,' said Violet. 'I'm not leaving.'

'No?'

'No.'

'Another question then. Why not?'

'Because I've got nowhere else to go.'

It was part of the truth at least.

144

And it seemed to satisfy him.

He didn't press her on it, anyway.

He once again didn't say anything at all.

'I heard you rowing with her,' Violet said to him, finally getting to it.

He looked at her blankly. 'Who?'

'Mrs Hamilton.'

'When?'

'The day I arrived.' She glanced down at her legs. They were stinging so much. 'You came to the house.'

He scowled.

Trying to remember?

'You were on the servants' stairs,' she said, to help him.

Still, he frowned, either truly confused, or making a very good pretence of it.

But why would he pretend?

'I heard you,' she repeated.

'Did you?'

'Yes.'

'Enjoy nosing around other people's business, do you?'

She flushed. 'Not especially.'

'You sure about that?'

'Yes.' She batted a fly from her face. 'Quite sure.'

She really wanted to go.

She looked past him, out across the gorse to the glistening sea, and, catching sight of Mr Hamilton's boat returning from St Leonard's, decided it would do as an excuse.

'Everyone's coming back,' she said, setting off. 'I'd better get on.'

'Another question for you first, Miss Ellis,' he said, stopping her. 'If you're not one for nosing, then what were you hoping for, coming all the way up here today?'

He spoke conversationally, much as he might have enquired about her views on the weather, or what she'd had for lunch.

But his eyes, unblinking, were cold.

'I wasn't hoping for anything,' she said, fighting to keep her own tone light. 'I came on a walk. I walk a lot.'

'Yes. And always on your own.'

'That's right,' she said, and began walking again.

'Got a regard for Mr Atherton, have you?' Thomas called after her. 'Trust him, do you?'

This time, she didn't stop.

And she didn't answer.

'She doesn't want you here, Miss Ellis,' Thomas repeated. 'She doesn't.'

'Yes, thank you,' she replied, and, in her distraction, stumbled against more nettles, their stings catching her already throbbing skin.

'Watch how you go,' he called. 'Mind those loose rocks by the fence too.'

'I've seen them.'

'Good,' he said. 'Good. I wouldn't want you to take a slip.'

She didn't slip.

Circumnavigating the fencing, she headed at pace across the fields, her eyes smarting at the friction of the long grass on her swollen skin, intent on reaching the house before everyone from the boat caught up with her. She didn't want to have to talk to anyone.

She wanted to think.

She tried to do that all the way back, growing sweatier, the faster she moved.

She supposed she did at least now know for certain that Mrs Hamilton didn't like her.

She doesn't want you here.

And that Thomas really had been watching her.

She hadn't been imagining any of it.

She took some cold comfort from that.

But none whatsoever from the fact that Thomas clearly didn't want her on the island either.

Because why shouldn't he?

Why did everyone here, except for James, and perhaps Mr Hamilton, seem to want her gone?

She no longer believed it could just be about them thinking her a piece of James's fun. That was part of it, undoubtedly. But there had to be more to it.

She was sure there was more to it.

Something they all knew, and weren't saying.

At least, not to her.

What, though?

Reaching the stairs to the house, she ran down them, combing over every strange thing that had happened since she'd moved to the island, starting with the boatman's veiled words of caution at her having come. *Are you sure you're built for island life?* She recalled Thomas and Gareth Phillips' stares when she'd arrived, Mrs Hamilton's angry exchange with Thomas, and her visit to Violet afterwards.

Who knew you were coming here today?

Opening the porch door, Violet thought of everyone's pensiveness on the post days, and their stubborn chill towards her, always. She pictured the office mail, sorted by postmark, then, Mrs Hamilton's affronted expression when she'd asked her what it was all about.

Finally, she relived, in high speed, every second that had just passed between herself and Thomas, feeling again that overwhelming instinct she'd been struck by to run.

It was all connected. She was certain of it.

Disparate and lunatic as everything seemed, she felt in her bones that it fitted together. Fitted with Elizabeth too.

She just couldn't grasp how.

147

She continued to pick at it as she crossed the atrium, making for her bedroom.

She kept on picking at it as she kicked off her sandals, hitched up her skirt, and sitting on her bath's edge, ran the tap. Stretching her legs out beneath it, she exhaled at the relief of the cold water drenching her burning skin, and, starting back at the beginning, went over everything again.

But try as she might, she couldn't make the dots join.

With her legs numbing, her muddled thoughts moved, back to that final question Thomas had posed, about James.

Trust him, do you?

That at least she didn't have to consider.

She and James had spent too much time together now, and shared far too much, for her to have to give the matter any thought.

He was the person who'd carried her suitcase full of books across the fields, and who, after he'd returned from a dawn journey through a gale from Penzance, had taken her for a walk, just to stop her crawling up the walls.

He was the person who'd never blamed her father for cowardice in France, but had shown him enough compassion to attend his funeral, in spite of all the venom her father had poured on him. The person who'd shown *her* enough compassion to listen to her stories of her father as a better man.

He was the person who, at the age of twenty-three, had come home from the front to bury his own father, and become one to his tiny sister.

The person who she could listen to talk, all day long, and who, in a hundred different ways, had reminded her of what it was to not be alone.

The person whose lamp she watched, every night, just to feel anchored.

Trust him, do you?

In all the unknowns here on Aoife's, amid all the strangeness and strangers, the people who whispered, and watched, it was the sole matter on which she had not a single doubt: James was the one person she did trust.

She trusted him entirely.

And wanted, very much now, for him to come home.

May 1934

*Are you aware of the gossip that's begun to circulate about
you?*

The rumours about the part you played in Elizabeth's end.

*One assumes that you swore your pal, your brother-in-arms,
to secrecy, and yet I think he might have let something slip.*

Simon says!

*A little bird tells me he's been chatting about all sorts of
things . . .*

Chapter Twelve

Violet

Violet didn't have to wait too long for James, at least. He was due to return the Tuesday evening following, and she, in the meantime, endeavoured to carry on in much the same solitary routine she'd become used to: meals; teas; walks; work. She did at least have more to occupy her in the office, thanks to a weighty sack of handwritten minutes that arrived on Monday morning, all from monthly reviews that had been held across the country, and all of which needed typing up before they could be passed to James. It was a dry, repetitive job though. Quickly, it became monotonous.

That Monday, hot and sunny, and empty of him, might very easily have become monotonous.

There were, however, a couple of distractions.

The first, which happened not long after the postman's call, wasn't a huge one. A storm in a teacup, really. It involved the footmen, Alan and Simon, who, having always appeared very tight to Violet in the past, came to blows, proper actual fisticuffs, in their shared bedroom. Whilst Violet didn't witness the incident, she was in the kitchen for the aftermath, arriving there with her finished luncheon tray to discover the rest of the staff congregated, hushed at its door, staring at Simon and Alan, perched like scolded schoolchildren at the dining table: Simon clutching a piece of raw steak to his eye, Alan another piece to his nose, and Mrs Hamilton standing over them both, composedly informing them that their behaviour would be relayed to Mr Atherton, directly he was home, and that they had better hope he wasn't in a mind for dismissals.

'What has come over you?' she asked, with quiet control.

'Ask Alan,' Simon said.

'You're the one with the big mouth,' Alan snapped, then immediately clamped his own shut, like he wished he hadn't spoken.

'What's that supposed to mean?' said Mrs Hamilton.

Silence.

'Alan,' Mrs Hamilton said. 'Are you suggesting Simon's been saying something he shouldn't?'

'I've been saying nothing,' Simon said.

'Alan?' Mrs Hamilton persisted.

'It's fine,' Alan muttered. 'It was nothing.'

'I don't believe you,' Mrs Hamilton told him.

And really, it was such an obvious lie, that Violet found herself feeling almost sorry for her.

'Do you know what it was about?' she asked Diana in the office, at afternoon teatime, with little hope of Diana offering an answer.

Which Diana didn't.

With a silent shrug, she dipped her head and left.

Resignedly, Violet resumed her typing, learning more than she'd ever wanted to know about the potential implications of a failing cog in a Lancashire mill, and letting Simon and Alan's squabble slip to the back of her mind.

By the time she decided to finally call a day to her typing, much later that afternoon, she'd all but forgotten about it.

Peeling her sweaty legs from her chair, she headed out into the fresh air and sunshine, more than ready for a walk.

What happened next was different.

The turn her walk took, little more than a quarter hour later, didn't feel like anything in a teacup.

It wasn't forgettable.

She didn't return to the lighthouse. Thomas for once wasn't there, watching her as she crossed the fields, and, feeling no temptation whatsoever to risk another run in with him, she veered away from his home, along the coast to the cottages, aiming for the beach. Her nettle stings had long since eased, but she was so hot and sticky. She wanted to remove her shoes and stockings and get up to her knees, at the very least, in the Atlantic's chill.

The cottages were quiet when she reached them. Gareth Phillips wasn't in his garden. Mrs Hamilton, Violet knew, was still back at the house; she'd passed her, checking on Diana and Nelle's dusting in the atrium, when she'd left. She'd said nothing to Violet, preoccupied, Violet had assumed, by the earlier scene in the kitchen. Mr Hamilton was doubtless still there now, waiting to escort her home. *There is nothing that man would not do for his wife.* He really did seem to dote on her. Again, Violet thought how different she must be, behind their closed doors.

'Or perhaps he feels indebted,' James had said, when Violet had hazarded as much to him, down at the bottom of the old lighthouse stairs, before he'd left. 'He was terrified she wouldn't want anything to do with him after he was injured.'

'When did it happen?' she'd asked.

'Right at the end, if you'll believe it.' He'd shaken his head. 'Four years he was in the trenches, barely a scratch, then that, two days before the armistice.' He'd picked up a loose stone, flicking it into the waves. 'He was at a plastics hospital in Suffolk for a long time. At first, he wouldn't let her visit. To her credit, she never gave up. I was at their wedding.' He'd frowned, remembering. 'He was so damned grateful.'

'You don't like her, do you?'

'I don't know enough about her to like. I've lived on the same island as her for nearly a decade, and she's never volunteered a thing about herself.'

'Have you asked?' she'd said, playing devil's advocate. 'Tried to get to know her?'

'She's my housekeeper, Miss Ellis.'

'I'm your secretary.'

'Are you?' he'd said, flicking another stone, his frown turning to a smile. 'I'd quite forgotten.'

It was his smile Violet was remembering, when, at the sound of her name being shouted, she stopped, and turned.

To her amazement, it was Gareth Phillips who'd yelled, from his top window.

Violet, he'd called her.

'Wait there,' he said, and disappearing back inside his window, appeared a few seconds later at his front door. 'Do you like elderflower wine?'

'I'm not sure,' said Violet, nonplussed. 'I've never tried it.'

'Right,' he said, and beckoned her towards him. 'Better come in then, hadn't you.'

She did go in.

She was too intrigued not to.

Besides, the way he'd posed the invitation really hadn't brooked a refusal. And she'd felt no real compulsion to refuse it, not like she'd felt to run from Thomas the day before. Nor was she particularly uneasy, following Gareth through his ivy-bordered front door. Certainly no more than she might have been with any stranger, going into their home for the first time. Gareth had given her plenty of reasons to be, with his stares and standoffishness. But now that she was actually with him – wiping her sandals on his mat, as per his instruction – they faded to nothingness.

Don't worry about him, James had said.

Instinctively, she didn't.

Instinctively, she sensed that here, at last, was someone who bore her no ill-will.

'That'll do,' he said, with a satisfied nod at her sandals, 'that'll do,' and, with his broad shoulders hunched beneath a creased linen shirt, he turned, leading her along a narrow corridor, into a square kitchen that was filled with sunshine, and overlooked the garden on one side, the sun-sheened sea on the other.

It smelt of soap, and lavender; there must be a bush, Violet guessed, beneath the open window. The worktops were stacked with tinned goods: beans; soups; beef; tongue (she felt her own curl, reading the label), and the shelves, with crockery. There was a wooden table, at which there were two chairs, and atop it was a mess of papers, pencils, and charcoal.

As Gareth crossed to the larder, pulling out a glass bottle, Violet cast her eye over his sketches, recognizing the dairy, the wharf, and a number of coves she'd come across on her own ramblings. There were several portraits as well: some of a young man, others of a young woman.

'That's the face that belongs to the shoes you've stepped into,' said Gareth, noticing her looking at the woman. 'My Delen.' He crossed to the shelves of crockery. 'I draw her so I have her with me.'

'When did she last visit?'

'End of November.' His brow knitted. 'Or was it the start of December?' He shook his head. 'I lose track of time.' Fetching two tumblers, he returned to the table. 'Don't mind me calling you Violet, do you?'

'Not at all.'

'You've made me think of my Delen, you see. Felt a bit strange calling you miss anything. You can call me Gareth.'

'Thank you.'

'Welcome. Here,' he jerked out one of the chairs, 'Delen's seat.

It could do with some use.'

'Thank you,' repeated Violet, and, as she sat, she mused on his stilted manner of speaking; the discordant rhythm to his words. He was out of practice, she could tell, yet obviously determined to force himself on.

Why, though?

What had he asked her in here for?

It felt too rude to ask.

Instead, she said, 'How long did Delen work here for?'

'Six years. Came a few months after me. Got here in nineteen twenty-six. Needed to finish her training first.'

'You're from St Leonard's?'

'Not far away. A village called St Just. Near the tin mines. My wife's still there, won't leave.' He unstopped the bottle. 'I had to. I couldn't go on mining.' His eyes moved to the pictures on the table of the young man. 'That was our son, he worked in the mines too. Lost him, though, didn't we?' He stared at the sketches, abruptly motionless. His weathered face slackened. His gaze seemed to empty. Really, in that moment, he looked so sad, so lost himself, that Violet very nearly reached out and touched his hand.

Then he blinked, and, placing the tumblers side by side, poured the wine.

'I couldn't stay after that,' he said, pushing a tumbler towards Violet. 'Delen didn't want to either. She needed to be with her old dad, didn't she? Until she didn't.' He picked his own glass up, and, tapping it to Violet's, sunk it in one, then nodded at her, letting her know she was to do the same.

So she did.

'Like it?' he asked.

'It's delicious,' she gasped, and wondered if she might actually have just lost the lining of her throat.

Refilling their tumblers, he said, 'You must be thinking, what's this old man who's hardly said two words to me brought me in here for.'

It was so exactly to the point of what she had been thinking, it was impossible not to smile.

He made a short, wheezing sound.

It took her a second to realize he was laughing.

Then he stopped.

'I told you just now that you've made me think of my Delen. The day you came, I saw you . . . '

'I know. I saw you see me.'

'Yes, I saw you see me saw you.'

She smiled again.

'Felt an idiot, didn't I? Wished you were her, if I'm being honest. You're around the same age. She's just turned twenty-eight . . . '

'I'm twenty-seven.'

'Well, there we go.' He picked up his glass and took another drink. 'I wasn't at church on Sunday. I don't go. I prefer to get out, drawing, with the rest of them all gone. I saw you heading up to the lighthouse to talk to Thomas . . . '

'I didn't *want* to talk to him. I didn't think he'd be there.'

'He's always there, Violet. Always. Always. In nearly ten years, I have never seen him leave this island. That's not natural. It's not.'

'No,' Violet agreed.

'I can't claim to know him. But there's something not right about him. You live long enough, spend half your years down the mines, you get a sense for that kind of thing. I always told my Delen to keep away from him. I thought to myself, when I saw you up there with him, I'm glad that's not my Delen. Then I thought, what if it was my Delen? What if someone else's dad was standing here, looking up at her there? Wouldn't I want them to have a word?' His eyes, set deep in his wrinkled face, bore into Violet's. 'I would, Violet. I would want them to have a word. I'm not one for chat, not at all, but I needed to have this word with you now.'

157

'Thank you,' said Violet, and didn't add that Mrs Hamilton had beaten him to it, or that she was already well resolved on avoiding Thomas anyway. It touched her that Gareth had put himself out like this, for her. Moved her, that he'd likened her to his daughter. 'I'll keep away.'

'Right. Good.' He stood up. 'I'll show you out then.'

'Oh,' said Violet, too startled by the abrupt dismissal to conceal her surprise. 'Yes.' She stood as well. 'Thank you for the wine.'

'Welcome.' He headed back to the corridor.

Violet, realizing she was meant to follow, nonetheless lingered. Now that Gareth was ejecting her, her head filled with questions she wanted to ask him: about Delen, and why she'd left; whether it had anything to do with Elizabeth who, after all, had arrived on the island not long before Delen had ended her six years of service.

She wanted to ask him about Elizabeth too, and where he'd seen her out walking in her evening gown and galoshes. The papers had never specified.

Had she been up at the lighthouse, too?

Violet felt her skin prickle at the possibility.

She couldn't waste this opportunity to ask about it.

'Mrs Hamilton told me that Thomas and Mrs Atherton were close,' she said, and felt her throat stick on those words. *Mrs Atherton*. It had been so long since she'd last said them aloud.

'They were that,' said Gareth, carrying on towards the front door. If he was taken aback that she'd mentioned Elizabeth, he gave no hint of it. There was no change to his tone at all. Really, he didn't seem to very much care. 'She was up there a lot.'

'Didn't you warn her not to go?' said Violet, moving too now, to catch him up.

'Warn her?' He let go another wheezing laugh. 'Wouldn't have wasted my time.'

'Did you talk to her much?'

'Not if I could help it.'

'What about Delen?'

'Not if she could help it.'

Clearly no love lost there, then.

The realization only added to Violet's impatience to know more.

They reached the front door.

'But you saw her,' she persisted, 'before she disappeared.'

'I did.'

'Was she with Thomas then?'

He set his hand on the door handle, studied it, then raised a perplexed frown to her.

'Why are you fretting over this? It's done with. Gone.'

'I just want to know.'

'Why?'

She considered fudging a reply. Concocting something about the papers, and her curiosity.

Then she decided that, since she was asking him to be open with her, she should probably be open with him.

Plus, he struck her as the sort who'd see straight through a lie anyway.

'Mrs Hamilton told me she thought something might have been hidden back then. She said not enough made sense.'

'She shouldn't have.' He pushed the door wide, bathing them both in light. 'I don't know what she's dredging it all up for.'

'I didn't really give her much choice.'

'Can't imagine she thanked you for that.'

'No. But do you think it was an accident?'

'God knows. There were certainly enough of us here who wanted her gone, Sarah Hamilton included.'

That threw Violet. 'Weren't she and Mrs Atherton friends?'

Elizabeth, Mrs Hamilton had called her.

'Friends? Them two?' Another barked laugh. 'They loathed each other.'

Silently, Violet absorbed it.

'We all loathed her,' Gareth went on. 'Thomas was her only friend.'

'What?' Her brow creased. 'But what about . . . ?'

'Your Mr Atherton?'

'He's not mine,' she said, automatically, giddy now with confusion.

'Well, he wasn't hers either, I'll tell you that. No idea why he wed her. My Delen said there was nothing but fighting between them. Upset her, didn't it? Thinks the world of Mr Atherton, she does. He's been good to her. Good to us both.'

'I . . . ' Violet began, then stopped.

What did she even want to say?

'No one talks about her,' she settled on. 'Ever.'

'Because she's best forgotten. Now come on,' he nodded towards his front gate, 'off you go. Put this from your mind. They were bad times. Bad, bad times. Leave them in the past. There were many, far more qualified than you, who couldn't get to the bottom of what happened . . . '

Violet jumped on that. 'So you *do* think something happened?'

He sighed, deeply.

'That's a yes,' she said. 'Isn't it?'

'It's an I really don't know.'

'Will you please just tell me where Mrs Atherton was walking when you saw her?' she entreated. 'Was it up to the lighthouse?'

'No good'll come of these questions . . . '

'Just answer this one. Please. I'll only keep asking otherwise.'

He shot her a weary look. 'Will you now?'

'I will.'

'You really are like my Delen.' He reached up, scratching the thatch of grey hair above his ear. 'If you must know, she was coming back down from seeing Thomas. I told the police that, and they found nothing in it. Thomas was the one on shift that night, watching

160

the lamp. He couldn't have done anything. He wouldn't have. Like I said, he was pretty much Mrs Atherton's only friend here.'

'But where was she going when she left him?'

'I didn't stop to look. That woman caused nothing but trouble, from the day she arrived, and drove my Delen away to boot.' His voice toughened. 'I didn't give a damn then what she was up to, storming around in her fancy dress, and I don't give a damn now. She can rot in hell, for all I care.'

Violet wasn't in much of a mood for the beach, after that.

She wasn't in much of a mood for returning to her silent bedroom either, but with nothing but silence waiting for her wherever she went, to her bedroom she returned. There, she ran her bath, unpinned her hair, and, in looking for her comb in her washbag, discovered the zip fully fastened, which was strange, because she always left it open.

Had she absent-mindedly closed it that morning?

Or had someone been going through her things?

The question wasn't a new one.

Ever since her first morning on Aoife's, when, from her office, she'd noticed that light burning in her bedroom window, she'd been plagued by a sense that her room wasn't always exactly as she'd left it. It was the tiniest things: a stocking folded instead of rolled; a book left on her side table closed instead of open; this zip now. Normally, she put the anomalies down to the maids, just as she had that light in her window. Them, or her own tiredness: a paranoia born of insomnia.

But that evening, in the wake of all Gareth had just said, they nagged at her.

Everything nagged at her.

Sinking into her bath, she filled her lungs with a long, ragged breath, closed her eyes, and tried to clear her mind.

But she heard her father's voice instead.

This isn't as simple as they want us to believe, he'd always said. *There's mischief at work here, Vi. You mark my words.*

She was marking them now.

And, for the first time since his death, she wished he was still with her.

She missed him. Wanted to talk to him.

Not about James. Reeling she still might be from Gareth's revelation that his and Elizabeth's marriage hadn't been the love story she'd long been torturing herself with (and did her heart pummel faster, in spite of everything, to know it? Of course it did), but she couldn't believe him capable of harming anyone.

She didn't.

Her father had been very wrong about that.

But if he'd been right about the rest of it, if Elizabeth's death really hadn't been an accident, then whoever *had* hurt her, had got away with it.

They were still getting away with it.

Haunted by the idea, Violet locked and double-locked her windows and doors before she got into bed that night. She rammed her bureau chair against her suitcase to secure it, and twice got up to check behind her drapes, certain she'd heard a noise outside.

There was nothing there, though.

There was never anything there. Just the roving lighthouse beam, sweeping across the black water.

Back in bed, she couldn't stop picturing that beam, whenever she closed her eyes.

Elizabeth must have seen it too, that night she'd gone.

Had she been thinking about Thomas behind it, Violet wondered?

Had she still been thinking about him when whatever happened, had happened, taking her to her end?

Violet didn't know.

How could she possibly ever know?

But of all the sleepless nights she'd known since arriving on the island, that night, twitching, and tossing, frustratedly kicking off her hot sheets, was her most sleepless yet.

The breaking sun, though, worked its usual magic, shrinking, if not entirely dissipating, the anxieties that became so overwhelming to her in darkness, and the hours that followed, taking her, too slowly, towards James's return, brought no further surprises: no fights among the staff, nor declarations that Elizabeth could rot in hell, nor unsettling revelations of any kind.

Mrs Hamilton kept everyone busy in anticipation of James's arrival – dusting, mopping, making sure everything was just so – and remained late at the house, Mr Hamilton with her, to welcome him home. Violet had intended to wait for him there herself. Whilst she knew that his train was due to reach Penzance at a quarter to six, and that he'd reach Aoife's by seven – speeding over from St Leonard's in the same motorised runabout he'd left in, and which had been moored there ever since – she hadn't thought to go to the wharf to meet him. No, she'd planned to be in the atrium, reading, when he came through the front door.

But that had been before Gareth had said all he'd said to her.

Before she'd made new sense of the absence of photographs of Elizabeth, anywhere in the house, and, through that different lens, replayed every look, and word, and touch that she and James had shared since the June day he'd caught her eye in Pentonville, giving her that precious moment of peace, so showing her the first of the countless kindnesses he'd by now sent her way.

Because of my father? she'd asked him.

No, Miss Ellis, he'd said. *Because of you.*

She'd listened to those words convinced of the love he'd still borne for Elizabeth.

Listened to him saying he'd forgotten she was his secretary, that day before he'd left, convinced of that love.

She'd convinced herself those words had been a simple tease. Nothing more.

Now, though . . .

Now it had started to occur to her that perhaps the two of them had been locked in a dance of misunderstanding, all this time: one in which she'd assumed she could never be anything to him beyond an inconsequential pretender to his lost, glittering wife, and in which he, her employer, with whom she'd been so fiercely adamant about remaining ever-proper, had been waiting for her to give him a sign, any sign, that she might after all, be quite happy, really very happy, to not be proper at all.

They're all going to think you're there for Atherton's fun, you know.

She didn't care any more.

She truly didn't care.

Because even if she was wrong about this dance – even if she was about to humiliate herself, and embarrass him, by going to the wharf to meet him rather than remain at the house, feigning indifference – she'd missed him too much, and far too impatiently, to wait a moment longer than she had to, to see him.

Chapter Thirteen

Violet

She felt drunk, heady with anticipation, as she set off that evening, just as the sky was paling into early dusk. This time, Thomas was out, watching her as she crossed the fields, but, determinedly, she ignored him, picking up her pace towards the cottages. When she passed Gareth's kitchen window, he nodded a greeting, but didn't stop her. The Hamiltons, of course, weren't home. She reached the cliff stairs without interruption, just as James's runabout came into view, scudding across the shimmering ocean for the shore.

Pausing at the top of the stairs, Violet watched the boat glide effortlessly towards her, its sleek wooden façade glinting gold under the sinking sun. The engine grew louder, a throaty growl. Already, she could make out James: the darkness of his hair; the blinding white of his shirt. Tapping her hand to the stair's rail, willing herself back into motion, *come on, come on*, she drew a steadying breath and carried on downwards.

Thomas hadn't moved from the lighthouse. She saw him from the corner of her eye, but didn't know if he was still watching her, or James, because she didn't want to give him the satisfaction of checking. If he *was* watching her, she'd rather he believed she didn't care.

She reached the wharf, and oh God, James, at the boat's wheel, had seen her. He'd seen her and raised his hand in a wave. He wore no tie, nor jacket. His shirt was unbuttoned at the collar, rolled up at the sleeves. Stomach flipping (should she have come? *Should* she?), she returned his wave, then, unclear what else to do with that hand, or indeed her other one, she sunk both into her trouser pockets, and pushed forward, on legs that had turned fluid. She was telling him something by being here, she knew she was telling him something. It had felt right to do that, back in the house, it really had.

But was it right?

Was it?

She didn't know. And there was nothing she could do about it now anyway. He was already slowing down, the engine quietening to a whir as he shifted gear, drawing inexorably closer: close enough for her to feel the tug of his eyes meeting hers, then see him glance over his shoulder, and . . .

Confusion pulled her brow.

Was he speaking to someone?

Even as the question sounded in her mind, he steered sideways, bringing the boat alongside the wharf, revealing two passengers behind him, sitting low in the runabout's sunken second row: one, a woman, in a silk summer dress and cloche hat; the other, a very small child, curled up, sleeping, in the woman's lap.

Violet realized immediately who the pair were. Even had she not seen those photographs in the atrium, she'd have placed Cressida as James's sister from her colouring; those dark, oval eyes. And James had told her about his niece: Cressida and Dicky's one-year-old daughter, Teddy. She, with her dark curls, and dark lashes that rested on her curved, cream cheek, was very obviously an Atherton, too.

All of this, Violet thought to herself in the second it took for Cressida to raise her attention to her, and for the two of them to exchange a smile. Cressida's was rather wan. Really, she looked exhausted. Beautiful, startlingly so, but faded, diminished somehow from that girl who'd stuck her tongue out in the photograph, for all she was still only twenty. A world away too from the spiteful, spoilt socialite that the more sensationalist papers had painted her as.

Violet, who'd never been fool enough to take much of what those tabloids had said seriously, had felt badly enough for Cressida at the time. She, after all, knew something of what it was to be on the receiving end of malicious gossip: bad enough when muttered, let alone printed in mass-produced headlines.

Now, though, looking into Cressida's washed-out eyes, she was struck afresh by the hideousness of the vitriol she'd suffered. The vindictiveness of it . . .

James cut the engine, and Teddy stirred, grizzling a protest.

As Cressida hushed her, Violet turned to James.

'Hello,' he said, with a smile that wasn't remotely wan. Throwing the rope over the wharf's bollard, he pulled the runabout alongside. 'This is a very nice surprise.' *Aren't you full of surprises?* 'How are you?'

'Fine. And you?'

'Better now.' He jumped onto the wharf beside her, and she felt her own smile grow, because he was back. He was back. He was *here*. 'The sun suits you. You've got a tan.'

'I thought I'd take a holiday while you were gone.'

He laughed.

So did she, her eyes on his face, reabsorbing everything about it; the strength, the energy, his cheeks that she longed to reach up and touch.

She'd done it again, she realized. Forgotten quite how much she liked it.

His eyes lingered on her. It was almost like he might be remembering too.

Then he turned back to his sister, now standing, and holding Teddy, who was awake, blinking dozily, and chewing her chubby fist.

'This is Cressida,' he said. 'And her little girl, Teddy.'

'It's lovely to meet you,' said Violet, and didn't fail to notice that he'd introduced Cressida as well as Teddy by their first names. Were they to do away with formalities, then, at last? 'I'm Violet,' she said, following his lead, Gareth's too, resolving there and then that they should.

'It's very nice to meet you,' said Cressida, and sounded, if such a thing were possible, even more drained than she looked.

Was she unwell, Violet wondered.

Is that why James had brought her?

But then why hadn't Dicky come too?

'I'm sure Teddy would say hello,' Cressida went on, 'but so far her only word is *no*. It's a useful word, at least.'

'She's very sweet.'

'Isn't she?' Cressida pressed her lips to her head. 'Although I'm afraid I won't be finding her particularly endearing at midnight, which she'll now inevitably be awake until.'

'You could have brought the nanny,' said James, reaching down to help them both ashore.

'What, and ruin Dicky's fun?' said Cressida, stepping up.

So that's what it's about, thought Violet.

Then, *What a fool Dicky must be.*

'I can help with Teddy,' she offered, wanting to say something useful. 'I'm afraid I don't have any experience . . . '

'Thank you, but I'm not allowed to ask you anyway. James has been very firm about that.'

'I don't mind . . . '

'You will,' said James, reaching into the back of the boat for the luggage. 'I don't want you treated as some hired help.'

But I am a hired help, Violet almost, but didn't, say.

She'd done more than enough of that.

And she liked that he'd looked out for her like this with his sister.

She really did like it.

'God, it's strange to be here,' said Cressida, moving Teddy onto her other hip, staring up at the island. She turned, taking in its length, her attention sticking, momentarily, on the lighthouse. Thomas was no longer there. He'd gone inside, probably. *On shift.* 'Very strange . . .'

An unmissable tremor shook her voice.

It made Violet wonder just how long it had been since her last visit.

Whether she'd returned at all, since Elizabeth's death.

She hadn't.

She – who Violet quickly came to realize wasn't one to leave any elephant in a room unacknowledged – told Violet that as the two of them waited with Teddy, at the base of the cliff stairs, whilst James stowed all the luggage they didn't need that night in the boatshed, ready for collection in the morning.

'I didn't feel able for it,' she said, pulling her necklace from Teddy's grasp. 'It all left rather a sour taste in my mouth.' She watched her brother. 'Does James talk about it?'

'Not to me.'

'Nor me.' She frowned. 'God, what a mess.'

Violet thought she meant everything that had happened that autumn. Her own arrest.

But then Cressida talked on.

'I'm getting a divorce, you know,' she said, and exhaled a sigh. 'I'm going to be a divorcee.'

'I'm sorry.'

'Yes,' said Cressida. 'So am I.'

Violet had no opportunity to be alone with James for the rest of the evening.

They all walked together across the fields to the house, James carrying Teddy and his own overnight bag, Violet taking Cressida's, and Cressida Teddy's, all the while sticking to her brother's side, as though afraid to leave any distance between them.

When they arrived at the house, they had even more company, in the form of Mr and Mrs Hamilton, both of whom were waiting inside the porch to welcome James back, and both of whom stared, mute for some several seconds, when they saw who else he had with him. It was James who ended the discomforting silence, apologising for not having had time to send warning, and then it was all activity, Mrs Hamilton fussing, as much as Violet had ever known her to fuss, over what Teddy was to be put to bed in since the house had no cot, and Teddy staring fixedly at Mr Hamilton's mask, her bottom lip wobbling, only to dissolve, the second he winked at her, into screams of horror, which was awkward, but not nearly as awkward as Cressida refusing, with as much steel as Violet had seen her display all evening, to so much as countenance either Teddy or herself sleeping in the room she and Dicky had used the last time they'd come, which, Violet deduced, wasn't in the east wing at all, but up on the second floor of the house.

'We'll be fine in one of the guest rooms,' said Cressida, her voice raised above Teddy's wails.

'Miss Ellis has the best one,' said Mrs Hamilton, glancing from Teddy, to poor Mr Hamilton, seemingly at a loss over what to do about either of them.

'Then I'll take the second-best,' said Cressida. 'Or third. I really don't care.'

'What's wrong with your old room?' asked Mrs Hamilton.

'It's next to Elizabeth's,' said Cressida, and just like that, brought her into the house, making her real, for the very first time, in Violet and James's shared company.

Stunned, Violet turned to him, watching for his reaction.

But he, cradling his hysterical niece, hardly reacted at all.

'What's that got to do with anything?' he said to Cressida, like it really was an irrelevance.

'I can't be where she was. I won't.'

'For God's sake. It was your room long before she came along.'

'I don't care. She's poisoned it for me.'

'She's not here,' said Mr Hamilton, speaking at last.

And Violet, feeling very much as though she shouldn't be either – finding this sudden, collective acknowledgement of Elizabeth's existence too bizarre to affect carelessness over, even if the rest of them seemed set on doing that very thing – made her excuses and left, returning to her room.

There she sat on the edge of her bed, wondering how it could be that the night, which had seemed so full of promise, such a short time ago, could have dwindled so rapidly to nothing.

She was still sitting like that when, a few minutes later, a bustle of opening doors and shifting furniture at the end of the corridor let her know that Cressida had got her way, and was to be her neighbour. That at least felt like good news. She was glad that she wouldn't be alone in the wing any more.

Still, it wasn't enough, not nearly enough, to improve her mood.

She wanted to see James.

She closed her eyes, feeling again the happiness of his smile when he'd come ashore, *this is a very nice surprise*, and really, really wanted to see him.

She needed to see him.

She was horribly afraid that, unless she did, they'd meet tomorrow, and he'd call her Miss Ellis, and she'd call him Mr Atherton, and it would be like she'd never summoned the courage to meet him at the wharf at all.

She had no reason to leave her room, though.

Diana brought her dinner, just like she always did, and told her, when she asked, that Cressida was also eating hers in her bedroom.

'Is Teddy asleep?' Violet asked.

'No,' said Diana. 'But we've made her a cradle, in a trunk.'

'What's she eating?'

'Same as you, chopped up. Chef had to make it stretch.' She looked at Violet's plate of chicken and salad. 'I hope you're not hungry.'

Violet wasn't.

She ate the salad, but didn't finish the chicken, and, leaving her tray on the side table by her door, dejectedly went to her bathroom to get ready for bed.

When there was another knock at her door, she, pulling her nightdress on over her head, assumed it was Diana, arrived to fetch the tray.

'Come in,' she called to her, like she always did, and reached for her comb, brushing her hair.

The door opened. It shut.

A silent stillness followed.

Bemused, she returned to her room, only to jolt to a stop, her heart entering her throat, because it wasn't Diana who was there at all.

It was James who'd come, still in the white shirt and slacks he'd worn to travel in, a cardboard box in his hands.

He was standing at her window, beside the copy of *The Painted Veil* that she'd left on the seat, looking not at its cover, but at her, in her thin cotton nightdress, looking at him.

'Is it all right that I'm here?' he said.

'Yes,' she replied, only vaguely conscious of what she said.

Her heart was beating so fast.

'Good.' His voice carried the hint of a smile. 'I hoped it might be.'

'It is.'

'I wanted to apologise about all that earlier. I couldn't let the day end without saying it.'

'You don't need to apologise,'

'I do. You came to meet me, and then . . . '

'It's fine, really.'

'It's not, Miss Ellis.'

'Please, you don't need to call me that.'

Oh.

Oh.

Had she really just said that?

She had.

She really had.

But it was all right, wasn't it?

It really did seem all right.

Because he was truly smiling now.

He was smiling at her.

He took a step forwards. 'I'm afraid I saw your book.' He dropped a rueful nod in its direction. 'I'm sorry about that too.'

'I don't mind.'

'You're sure?'

'Yes,' she said, feeling her heart quicken all the more, realizing what she was going to say next. 'I already think of you when I read it anyway.'

His eyes shone. 'We have that in common then.' He continued walking towards her, stopping just a foot away.

She needed to breathe.

She couldn't breathe.

He offered her the box. 'I brought you a gift.'

'For me?'

'For you. Open it, please.'

Taking it from him, feeling the heat of his eyes on her face, she did just that.

Slowly, carefully, she pulled out the heavy ornament inside, then laughed, really laughed, seeing what it was: a snowglobe of the gates of London Zoo.

'You went to the zoo,' she said, and loved that he had.

'I went to the zoo.'

'Did you see the zebras?'

'I saw the zebras.'

'I wish I'd been there.'

'I wish you had too.'

They fell silent.

Conscious, so conscious of his proximity, she felt a flush spread through her skin. Needing to distract herself, distract them both, she re-examined the ornament and, shaking it, watching the snow fall, turned for her bureau and placed it there.

'I really love it,' she said. 'Thank you.'

'I should go,' he said, and didn't move.

'Yes,' she said, and didn't move either.

'Right then,' he said.

'Don't,' she said. 'Please.'

'Fine,' he replied, and they both smiled.

Drawing a long breath, he moved back to her window, looking out at the night.

'I see your light from my office . . . '

'Yes,' she said. 'I see your light from here.'

'I haven't known . . . It didn't feel right to ask . . . anything, of you. But then, when I saw you earlier, waiting for me at the wharf . . . '

'I missed you,' she said, and was amazed by how easy it suddenly was to say.

Slowly, he turned his head, looking at her once more.

For a second, all was stillness.

Then he once again moved to join her, not stopping this time, but closing the distance between them almost entirely, leaving no more than a wisp of air between them.

Still, they didn't touch.

She didn't breathe.

She couldn't breathe.

'I thought about you,' he said. 'I think about you, all the time.'

'I think about you too.'

'Violet,' he said, 'Violet,' and did then touch her, running his hands around her waist, his fingertips moving up her spine.

Legs dissolving beneath her, she tipped her face to his.

This was happening.

It was happening.

'I've been so selfish,' his lips brushed hers, 'bringing you here.'

'No, not selfish.'

'Yes,' he said. 'Very selfish.'

But she was no longer listening.

Because, gathering her close, he kissed her; not impatiently, nor clumsily, as she'd been kissed, pressed against the walls of alleyways, by those boys with their mother's packed lunches. But hungrily, dizzyingly, making her forget everything, and everyone else.

She didn't think of the Hamiltons, walking home to their cottage.

Or of Diana, and when she might arrive to collect her tray.

Or of Thomas in the lighthouse, and the lamp he turned, illuminating the waves.

Or of Cressida, or Teddy, or even of Aoife.

She thought only of him: herself in his arms.

The thrill of his lips on her neck, her throat.

And that everything had changed.

She felt the euphoria of it, all through her.

Nothing, she knew, would be the same again now.

NEW DEVELOPMENT IN ATHERTON CASE

Cressida Thompson was seen leaving Scotland Yard in a private automobile last night, escorted by her brother, with whom she is now reported to be staying under conditions of bail. Tellingly, Dicky Thompson has neither visited his wife in gaol, nor did he attend her departure. One assumes the whiff of murder has rather diminished her appeal. Unquestionably, she'll be relieved to be living once more in the luxury to which she's accustomed. One quails to imagine the histrionics her custodians have been forced to endure from her behind bars.

Unusually, the police have not disclosed the amount Mrs Thompson's bail was set for, and nor have they revealed the evidence that has been brought against her. What this reporter has, however, ascertained, from his exclusive source, is that Mrs Thompson is carrying a child. Do we pity her, then, this young woman who regularly broke school bounds to drink and smoke, and has pursued a lifelong disrespect for authority? This reporter cautions against it. Better pity the innocent child she carries, especially if its mother really does prove guilty of the crime we fear.

May 1934

Cressida's back?
What can she be thinking?
What are you thinking?

Chapter Fourteen

Elizabeth

June 1932

'I hate her, I hate her, I hate her.' Grabbing the nearest item to her on her vanity – a rouge brush – Elizabeth flung it across the room, where it landed, with a dissatisfying puff, against her wall, trailing a red stain down to the cream carpet, leaving her hating that too.

She hated Laura, arms folded on the edge of her bed, looking at her like it pained her to do it, in the sage green bridesmaid gown Elizabeth had selected in a fit of pique, but which had ended up suiting Laura's fair curls far better than she'd intended. She'd *intended* to punish Laura, not only for the endless pints of disapproval she'd by now poured on her, but also – and this was so much worse – for becoming engaged herself, to Rupert, *Rupert*, back at the start of May, before Elizabeth had even had the chance to make certain enough of her own engagement to James to announce it.

She hated James for having made her wait so long to do that.

Despised him for having fought her on their marriage, so determinedly.

She hated Rupert for having given up on her, and their happily ever after that he'd been chasing, gangly legs scrambling, from the night they'd met.

In that moment, she hated Amy, perched beside Laura on the bed, eyeing Elizabeth's door with such blatant longing, not even troubling to conceal that she'd rather be anywhere but where she was. Her hand was resting on the budding curve of her sage green stomach. Elizabeth hated her for that as well, because how dare she be so despicably wholesome, and glowing, and fecund?

Most of all, though, she hated Cressida.

Cressida, who wouldn't be attending the wedding ceremony that afternoon, had banned Dicky from doing the same (what a weakling he truly was), but who hadn't bothered to inform Elizabeth that they were to be absent until just that morning. She'd called personally at Cheyne Walk to pass on her and Dicky's regrets. Elizabeth hadn't seen her – nursing another splitting head, feeling entirely unequal to any more confrontations with Cressida, she'd sent her maid, Helen, out to the hallway to make her excuses – but she'd listened to Cressida as she'd explained, quite coolly, to Helen, that she'd rather remain at home, stitching her eyelids together with hairpins, than sit silently by and watch her brother tie himself to such a cold, soulless, faded has-been as Elizabeth.

Before Cressida had gone, she'd requested leave to visit the bathroom. Helen – in a sulk herself, ever since Elizabeth had let it be known that Cheyne Walk's small staff would have to find new employment after she'd moved to Aoife's – had told her to do as she liked. Which Cressida had. Going upstairs, she'd run the sink's taps, made use of none of the amenities, but located Elizabeth's room, slashing holes through her veil, and the back of her exquisite hand-stitched ivory gown, instead.

She'd been very neat about it. Very subtle.

Elizabeth had only discovered her handiwork a minute before, when – her hair done, her make-up pristine – she'd gone to dress, and found everything ruined.

God, but she wanted to hurt Cressida.

Standing as she was, in nothing but her underwear and robe, staring at her stained carpet, clenching her teeth so hard they ached, she wanted to cripple her.

But she couldn't cripple her.

The power she held to do that, was the one power she had over James.

Not even Amy knew what it was. Laura most certainly didn't.

And Cressida mustn't.

If she ever found out, James would divorce Elizabeth.

He'd left her in no doubt of that.

I'll do it so fast, and so publicly, it will make your conniving head spin.

Amy rose, walking across the room, and crouched to pick up the rouge brush.

'Should I fetch someone to clean this?' she suggested, once again eyeballing the door.

'Leave it,' Elizabeth said. 'The whole house will be shut up tonight anyway.'

Rising, Amy scuffed the stain with her toe, then, with a shrug, tossed the brush back to Elizabeth.

'Are you sure about going to this island?' she said. 'I really do feel that a honeymoon on the riviera would be more your thing.'

'Not again, Amy, please,' said Elizabeth, touching her fingertips to her temples. If only this headache would ease. She couldn't take more pills. She'd already swallowed too many. 'I can't wait to get to Aoife's Bay.'

'It's *Aoife's*,' said Laura. '*Eee-fuh's*. Not *A-if's*.'

'Fine,' said Elizabeth. '*Aoife's* Bay. I can't wait to get there.'

'*Why*, though?' enquired Amy. 'What on earth are you going to find to *do* with yourself?'

'What one normally does on a honeymoon, my darling.'

'Well, I can see the appeal in that at least. One might even be a shade envious.'

'One sympathises,' said Elizabeth, looking not at her, but at Laura, who, maintaining an irritatingly dignified silence, got up from the bed and moved to Elizabeth's wardrobe, where she set to re-examining the holes in her gown. 'Leave it, Laura. It's beyond saving . . . '

Laura let the silk slip from her hands.

Turning back to face Elizabeth, she said, 'It seems Cressida rather hates you too.'

'It seems she does.'

'Did she find out about you and Dicky before the wedding?'

'Not that I know of.'

'So, this is just about you marrying James?'

'You don't need to sound so smug, Laura.'

'I'm not smug, *Lizzie*. I just wonder if you've thought about what she might do next?'

'She won't do anything. She'll be here, and we'll be there. Just the two of us.' Dropping her fingers from her head, Elizabeth smiled. Dazzlingly. 'It will be wonderful.'

Better anyway, at least.

It had to be.

Companionship wasn't in the deal she and James had struck.

Love most certainly wasn't.

The terms, thrashed out between them, hadn't been sullied by sentiment of any kind.

But so many men had fallen in love with her, over the years.

Too many men to count.

James couldn't be so different.

Elizabeth was sure that, given some time, some peace, she'd finally win him over, too.

The ceremony was at Chelsea registry office, and Elizabeth, with little choice, went in the same snow queen costume she'd worn to Dicky and Cressida's engagement, on the basis that it was the only other vaguely bridal thing she owned. It felt tacky, though, in the drizzly grey light of the Tuesday afternoon; over the top and

181

inappropriate.

Laura, somehow, had ended up looking better than her.

She and Rupert, and Henry and Amy, were the only witnesses that day to the ceremony. Elizabeth had elected to keep the guest list small when James had refused to have the service in a church, but now, thanks to Cressida and Dicky's absence, the gathering was verging on pathetic. There was to be no reception afterwards, either, since that was another thing James had refused to countenance. Elizabeth had considered foisting a meal upon him – dinner at the Ritz, or some such – until he'd warned her that if she attempted to do anything of the kind, he'd toast her with a speech the humiliation of which she'd never forget.

She hadn't considered calling his bluff.

He, it had dawned on her, was not a man one did that with.

'You've been a fool, Elizabeth,' he'd said to her, the last time they'd met – in his London office, since that was the only place he *would* meet her. (*This is a transaction, is it not? The filthiest I've been involved in, but a transaction nonetheless.*) 'There are only so many concessions you can extract from someone who has so little they care about losing. And you've shown your hand. It's you, not me, that minds what anyone else thinks.'

She did mind. He was right about that. She minded very much. She needed it believed that he wanted to be with her, because otherwise, how could she bear it?

'This isn't a life sentence,' she'd said to him in his office, airily, affecting a careless smile. 'I really have no desire to end my days in the back of beyond.'

'I really have no desire for you to do that either,' he'd said, coldly, from behind his desk.

'Good then. So, I'll stay just long enough for it to seem we're blissfully happy.'

No more than a year, she'd promised, before they put it out that west country life was too rural for her, and returned to their separate lives. They'd visit one another just enough, she'd said, to keep the gossips at bay, and leave no one in any doubt that their marriage was a success, and that she – who, as everyone knew had never *wanted* to be tied into a marriage of any conventional kind – was loved, adored, *missed*, not by some fop of a man like Dicky, or Rupert, but by her husband, James Atherton.

Was known, in short, to have won.

She looked sideways at James, standing beside her before the registrar in a funeral-dark suit, the muscles in his face rigid with control as he repeated his vows.

No more than a year.

She wouldn't need nearly so long as that.

She'd make him want her to stay with him, well before a year was out.

Really, he'd thank her for all this, in the long run.

At the end of the service, they left together in his motor for Paddington. Elizabeth had already sent most of her belongings ahead by courier to Aoife's, and another bag containing a change of clothes for the journey, and various other essentials, was waiting for her, care of Helen, at the station. She was hoping it would do her and James some good to be on a train together again: remind him of how much fun they'd had before, in that carriage from Oxford. Regardless, she was ready, more than ready, to go.

In the misty, lacklustre rain, she kissed the Astleys, Laura, and Rupert, goodbye, poutingly repeating her regret at not treating them all to a breakfast – 'We're just desperate to get away, you know' – and slipped into the motor's backseat, next to James. There, she smiled at the others milling on the pavement, and willed the driver to hurry the hell up as, pushing her door shut, he walked around the motor, climbed into his own seat, and started the ignition.

She exhaled as they pulled away, and looked to James, who was turned away from her, staring through his window at the damp street.

'Here's to our wedding night, I suppose,' she said, and immediately wished she hadn't, because of course it would irritate him.

It was discomforting, how often he made her question the words that came from her own mouth. He was the only person, other than her parents, who ever had.

She didn't expect him to respond to her quip.

She expected him to ignore her. It was what he normally did, when annoyed.

She endeavoured not to care.

But then he moved his attention from the window, to her, the expression on his handsome face as hard and detached as she'd known it.

'Your wedding night, Elizabeth,' he said. 'You'll be travelling to Aoife's alone. I have business in the north now for several weeks.'

She cared, very much, about that.

He wanted her to remain in London, of course. He'd already tried to convince her that she should, far too vehemently, for her to doubt that this sudden business trip could be anything but a ploy to bully her into doing just that.

He'd told her, so often, that she'd regret moving to Aoife's.

'You'll be miserable, and you'll be lonely,' he'd said. 'Why leave your home where you're happy?'

'Because I'm not happy,' she'd replied. 'Not any more.'

'So, you'd rather be miserable where no one can see you? Drag me down with you?'

She'd smiled. 'You see, now you're catching on.'

He thought her too weak to face journeying to Aoife's by herself, she supposed. Too cowardly to be equal to spending her first weeks there alone. He believed she'd give in; return to Cheyne Walk until he returned from the north, by which point he undoubtedly intended to have come up with some other way to put her off.

She really had underestimated him. This man she'd tied herself to, until death did them part, truly was, as Laura had warned, not someone to let anyone control him. Frustrating as that was, it was also a large part of his appeal.

Still, this move he'd played now, abandoning her mere minutes after they'd exchanged their vows, was not one she'd seen coming.

But he'd underestimated her too.

She took some joy in showing him that.

'That's fine,' she told him, resting her throbbing head against her seat. 'I'll get myself settled, ready to welcome you home for whenever you're ready to return.' She tilted her head, raising a brow at him. 'No rush, though, my darling. I can be terribly patient when I want to be.'

He didn't remain in the motor with her to the station. Issuing her with a curt set of instructions on how to reach Aoife's, he told his driver to stop by the gates of Hyde Park, where he got out and, letting go the maddening restraint he was usually so adept at keeping, slammed his door on Elizabeth, then walked away from her through the rain.

She'd won the point, but knew no sense of triumph.

Left alone in the backseat of the motor, in her extravagance of a gown, she felt only hollow.

Worse yet when she reached Paddington's First-Class lounge to find a table prepared, as per her stipulation, with a bottle of champagne on ice, and two flutes beside it.

'Should I pour?' the waiter enquired, uncertainly.

'No,' she snapped, 'you should fetch my bag.'

As soon as he returned with it, she went to change in the ladies' room, gave her snow-queen dress to the attendant as a tip, then returned to the lounge where, deciding she'd waited long enough, she swallowed two more pills with a glass of champagne, chased that with a sleeping draught, and – boarding her train, slumping into her solitary cabin – knew nothing else until the conductor shook her awake at Penzance.

The rest of the journey passed in a blur best forgotten. With no taxicabs to be had at the station, she had no choice but to catch the bus to St Leonard's: a quayside hamlet of fishermen homes, postal sorting office, public house, church, and general store that she might have found moderately charming, had she not been so dismayed that it was, henceforth, to be her closest point of civilisation.

A boatman ferried her, along with the postman, to Aoife's. She took an instant dislike to them both: the boatman, for his watchful silence; the postman, for his inability to be silent at all. The water was still at least, and she remained on deck for the crossing, ignoring the postman's chatter, then whistle, studying the horizon, waiting for her first sight of the island to come into view.

Which, when it did, impressed her even less, with its weathered cliffs, and lone lighthouse, than St Leonard's had.

What, *what*, had compelled James, who could have his pick of any place on earth to live, to make his home here?

It was so remote.

So . . . *silent*.

A man with a mask was waiting to meet her at the wharf.

'Mr Hamilton,' he introduced himself as.

'You look like you had rather a difficult war,' she said, and – just as with James – was filled with instant regret, because why had she said it?

Her mood and weariness getting the better of her, probably, and now she'd insulted the first servant she'd met.

She thought she should probably apologise.

But she didn't want to apologise.

'Who's that?' she asked Mr Hamilton, as a diversion, pointing at the man watching from the lighthouse.

'That's Thomas Browning,' Mr Hamilton said, picking up her case. 'You'd do well to stay away from him.'

For the rest of that day – jogging to keep up with Mr Hamilton as they crossed the fields, then meeting his icy wife in the entrance hall, and being shown by her around the admittedly spectacular house, then up to her rooms on the second floor – Elizabeth kept her own mask on: one of calm indifference to the dislike she felt, not only from Mrs Hamilton, but from everyone else too.

She smiled when, in the offices, Mrs Hamilton introduced her to an irksomely pretty young secretary called Delen Phillips, and even though Delen didn't smile back at her, told her that she was pleased to make her acquaintance.

She smiled again in her bedroom, where Mrs Hamilton made another set of introductions, this time to a satisfyingly plain girl called Nelle, who was to act as her lady's maid.

'I'm sure we'll get on wonderfully,' said Elizabeth.

'Are you?' said Nelle.

And did Mrs Hamilton smirk?

Did she?

Rising above their rudeness, Elizabeth dismissed Mrs Hamilton, said *please* when she asked Nelle to draw her a bath, and nothing at all when Nelle – deliberately, she felt sure – ran it too cold.

She held on to her manners through lunch in the dining room, then almost all the way through dinner, right up until the point when one of the footmen – Simon, or was it Alan? Elizabeth truly didn't care – coughed, and, with concerted clumsiness, spilt wine on her plate, finishing off her patience, so that before she knew what she was doing, she was picking up that plate, lifting it high, and shattering it to pieces on the table.

'You might want to clear that up,' she said, to the staring pair. 'And never spill anything on purpose again.'

With that, she left, running up the stairs to her bedroom, where, shaking at her own unleased rage, she slammed the door, sunk to the ground, and, alone in this mansion, miles out to sea, with not a friend for many more – if indeed she'd ever had any friends at all – she wept.

Chapter Fifteen

Elizabeth

Delen Phillips was the one to blame, Elizabeth decided.

She woke the next morning holding her entirely to account for the hostility she'd been faced with. It had to have been her who'd turned everyone against Elizabeth. James would never have lowered himself to seeking the sympathy of his staff. Little as he'd permitted Elizabeth to know of him, she felt certain of that. No, there'd clearly been gossip in his London offices: gossip that had been fuelled by Elizabeth's visits to see him there, and which had made its way to Delen's desk.

'Do I have that correct?' Elizabeth demanded of Delen, heading direct to her office, just as soon as she was dressed. 'You've decided that James is somehow *unhappy* in our marriage?' She gave a short, baffled laugh. 'Unhappy with *me?*'

'Well, he certainly had no urgent business to take him to Lancashire this month,' Delen riposted, with astounding impertinence. 'And Cressida told me that he refused to even have a reception.'

'Mrs Thompson to you,' snapped Elizabeth. (*Cressida.* Of course it had been her who'd written to Delen.)

'No, not Mrs Thompson to me,' said Delen, with such smug composure, Elizabeth wanted to slap her. 'I've known her since she was twelve. Now,' she glanced at the stack of papers beside her typewriter, 'if that's all, I'm very busy.'

'Are you jealous, Delen?' Elizabeth said, the words coming of their own will. 'Is that what it is? Have you been sitting here in your little hidey-hole, tapping away at your little machine, fantasising that one day you might become Mrs Atherton?'

'No,' said Delen, and started tapping.

'Are you sure? I think you might be blushing . . . '

'I'm not blushing.'

'Oh, but you are. How sweet. How utterly adorable.' She stretched her lips into a smile. 'Just wait until I tell James.'

Delen continued tapping.

The insolence of it.

The *insolence*.

Elizabeth felt her own skin start to burn.

'Has Mr Atherton mentioned to you what date he's coming home?' Delen asked.

'Yes,' Elizabeth lied.

'Oh, good,' said Delen, tapping, 'then I won't need to.'

Elizabeth stared.

Did she know?

Had James told *her*?

Elizabeth couldn't ask.

How could she ask?

'*Is* there anything else, Mrs Atherton?'

'No,' said Elizabeth, and, before she could once again lose her grip on her self-control, turned and left.

She wouldn't forget this, she resolved.

She wouldn't let Delen forget this.

As she returned down the corridor to the main house, she started a list of those she intended to punish, and Delen's name was at the very top.

*

190

In the week that followed, she heard nothing from James, but, as the days passed with excruciating slowness, plenty of others made it on to her list.

She hadn't come to Aoife's intent on making enemies. She'd *intended* for everyone to like her, so helping James to realize how blind he'd been, all this time. Indeed, for several days after her arrival, she remained at considerable pains to build bridges with all the island's residents (except Delen Phillips). She smashed no more plates, remembered her pleases and thank yous, and smiled, constantly. It was a herculean effort, and not one of them deserved it. Not Nelle, who persisted in running her bath to every temperature but the correct one, and sniffed, snottily, *all the time*. Not Simon, nor Alan, who spilt nothing else, but ruined Elizabeth's every meal simply by merit of their silent, resentful attendance. Not Chef, who meal after meal, despite Elizabeth's well-intentioned feedback, persisted in serving her tepid, flavourless food. Not Mr Hamilton, who barely acknowledged Elizabeth whenever she had the misfortune to cross his path, and turned her stomach every time she did, because how could one look at that mask without imagining the wreck of his face behind?

And certainly not his witch of a wife, with her habit for entering Elizabeth's room with barely so much as a knock, then sighing whenever Elizabeth requested anything of her – be it pressed sheets, or softer towels, or a refreshed vase of flowers – and who, much like Delen Phillips, seemed to be labouring under the inexplicable misapprehension that it was she, not Elizabeth, who held the authority to speak and do as she pleased.

Somehow, Elizabeth held on to her temper with her. She held on to it all the way up to her first Saturday evening on the island. But then she returned to her room from her bath and found Mrs Hamilton by her bed, holding the bottle of pills she kept in her bedside cabinet.

'These were on the floor,' Mrs Hamilton said, cool as you like, setting the bottle on the cabinet.

'They weren't,' said Elizabeth. 'You were going through my drawers.'

'No,' Mrs Hamilton said, quietly, her green eyes snapping indignation. 'I was not.'

'Don't answer me back.'

'Don't accuse me of something I would never dream of doing.'

And then Elizabeth was shouting, 'Don't you dare answer me back!'

'Calm down, Mrs Atherton.'

That did it.

'Calm down?' Elizabeth screamed, crossing the room towards her, unclear what she was thinking, only that she wanted to wipe Mrs Hamilton's superior expression from her face, just as she'd wanted to wipe Delen's from hers, only this time she didn't stop herself. She raised her hand then brought it down, hard, on Mrs Hamilton's cheek.

Her palm burnt.

Her breath came thick and fast.

What had she done?

What had she *done*?

Slowly, Mrs Hamilton raised her own hand, touching the red welts already rising on her skin.

'Who do you think you are?' she said to Elizabeth.

'Your mistress,' Elizabeth replied – refusing to betray her shock, or concede any further moral high ground to Mrs Hamilton – using the same cold tone she'd always employed to such effect to diminish her staff at Cheyne Walk.

But Mrs Hamilton wasn't diminished.

'I've been mistress of this house for seven years, Mrs Atherton,' she said. 'I see no reason for that to change now.'

*

Elizabeth had crossed a line, she did realize that. She'd never hit anyone before (apart from Helen, after Cressida had ruined her wedding gown), but now that she had, she accepted that there'd be no return. Mrs Hamilton wasn't going to forgive her, and nor, Elizabeth felt sure, would her husband.

Given that, given everyone else had proven so unpliable, what was the point in trying with any of them, any further?

There was no point.

None.

They were servants, she consoled herself. Just servants.

When all was said and done, what did they matter?

They didn't. Not at all.

She reminded herself of as much again the next morning when, from her bedroom window, she saw them all in what looked to be their Sunday best, leaving up the front path for the fields. They were going to church, she guessed, and hadn't invited her. She'd have liked to have gone. She'd taken lately to attending Sunday services in London, finding the words, and rituals, and trust in a world beyond, rather soothing. It angered her, immensely, that no one had thought to give her that option. That they'd left her out.

She'd never been left out of anything, her entire life through.

Mutedly, she heard their voices, their chatter drifting up to her open window.

Were they talking about her?

Undoubtedly, they were talking about her.

Narrowing her eyes, setting her jaw, she resolved to forget them, and went to the dining room for her breakfast, where she stopped at the door, seeing that the table was bare, the lidless serving dishes empty of any food at all.

Cursing Simon and Alan's laziness, she carried on down to the kitchen, expecting Chef had left everything laid out for her there.

But he hadn't. There was no sign of her breakfast, nor anything for her morning tea, nor for her lunch. There was nothing on the scrubbed worktops whatsoever, beyond the readied components of the evening roast dinner: vats of potatoes, vegetables, and dishes of marinading chickens.

Tapping her toe, Elizabeth studied that carefully prepared food. She studied it for some time.

Then, deciding that if she was to be left hungry, then so should everyone else be, she got to work, throwing it all out, with the exception of one chicken which, when everyone returned, she – first summoning Chef to the drawing room – ordered him to roast directly for her.

'I'm sure it won't surprise you to learn that I'm really quite hungry.'

Chef didn't roast that chicken.

He told Elizabeth she could roast it herself, and find a new chef whilst she was at it, since he'd work for her no longer.

'You do realize, madame, that there are people starving in this world.'

'Yes,' said Elizabeth, 'and I'm one of them.'

It was Mr Hamilton who convinced him to stay until James returned – as Mrs Hamilton told Elizabeth the next morning, back in the drawing room, where Elizabeth had been playing Solitaire.

'He's written to Mr Atherton too,' said Mrs Hamilton, her bruised face set above her silk blouse, 'asking that he return. I'm here to request a hiatus on any further histrionics until then. As I'm sure you're aware, good staff are not easy to find, and I doubt Mr Atherton will appreciate you haemorrhaging his.'

'Oh, I don't know,' said Elizabeth, moving a five of spades to a six of diamonds. 'I can't say they seem much good to me.'

'This has always been a contented house . . . '

'All I request is a civil one.'

'That's all any of us want, Mrs Atherton.'

'Fine,' said Elizabeth, pressing the back of her hand to her head, in no mood for another argument. The post had come earlier, bringing a letter from Laura, full of entirely unbelievable concern that Elizabeth was all right, given the rumour circulating that James had left her to travel to the west country alone. (Who had started that rumour? Cressida again, assuredly.) Elizabeth had received another letter too. One that, unlike Laura's, she couldn't attempt to ignore.

'I need to go away for a couple of days anyway,' she said to Mrs Hamilton. 'Do you think that if I ask your husband to take me to the mainland, he'll be able to resist the urge to throw me overboard?'

'I'm sure he'll manage,' said Mrs Hamilton.

Elizabeth left the following morning, which, in contrast to her frame of mind, was sunny. Mr Hamilton didn't throw her overboard on the crossing to St Leonard's, but nor did he speak to her, other than to tell her where to sit. He was just as taciturn when they got to St Leonard's, wordlessly leading her to a motor parked at the end of the quayside, in which he drove her (wordlessly) to Penzance.

'Well, this has been most diverting,' said Elizabeth, at the station.

'You're welcome, Mrs Atherton,' he said.

And she left him, heading inside to catch her train to Reading, and from there to Oxford.

She was gone for three nights, and returned on Friday morning, which was another fine one.

She'd told Mr Hamilton to be waiting at the station when she got in.

It was James, though, who was there.

She saw him, much to her surprise, as she left the steam-filled concourse, waiting in the early sunshine by the same motor Mr Hamilton had taxied her from St Leonard's in. And how funny, really, that he should once again be keeping her company after a visit to Oxford.

She'd fibbed to him, back in that April of 1929, when he'd told her that he'd been visiting a friend in the city.

So have I, she'd said. *What a coincidence.*

How many times had she been to those dreaming spires since? She'd lost count.

She could tally Mr Claymore's invoices, she supposed.

She didn't want to do that, though.

It would be too depressing.

She studied James, who, bearing no trace of the geniality he'd shown her in their first-class cabin, stood with his arms folded, his dark eyes trained on her. He was dressed in a shirt, slacks, and open jacket. His tense face was bathed in the golden dawn rays. Elizabeth felt a kick in her chest, seeing it, seeing him, and then, more anger, that he'd done that to her, when it was all too obvious from his immovable expression that he felt nothing of the kind, seeing her.

'I hear you've been making friends among the staff,' he said, as she joined him.

'Yes. We're all intensely simpatico.'

'I've apologised to them. Told them I was thinking too much of myself, and not enough of them, letting you loose on them, alone.'

'I'm not an animal, James.'

'An animal would have caused less damage.'

'I'm tired.' She held out her case for him to take. 'Can we please go?'

'What has this all been about?' he asked, ignoring her case. 'Were you trying to punish me, using them?'

'That's rather egotistical of you.'

'They're good people, Elizabeth. Decent people. And if they don't work at the house, they'll have to leave their families. There's nowhere else for miles.'

She said nothing.

She wasn't sure what he expected her to say.

I'm sorry?

He could whistle for it.

Like the postman.

It was an odd thought.

He was so unlike the postman that it made her smile.

Which made him frown.

'Where have you been?' he asked.

'Where have *you* been?' she countered. 'Lancashire, was it? For your urgent business that Delen's been so good to tell me wasn't urgent at all.'

'You're to leave Miss Phillips alone.'

'I'm not a member of your staff,' she said, holding out her case again. 'I don't take instructions.'

Still, he refused to relieve her of the case.

'Where were you?' he repeated.

Briefly, she flirted with telling him the truth.

Letting it go. At last.

But how could she?

And what would it mean to him, anyway?

'Come now, James.' She went to the trunk, opening it, throwing her damn case in herself. 'Let's not pretend that you care.'

They spoke as little to one another on the return journey to Aoife's as Elizabeth and Mr Hamilton had spoken on the way to Penzance. Elizabeth – who, in another set of circumstances, might have seized this opportunity of being alone with James to attempt to charm him – was too tired, and too humiliated, to try. Instead, she huddled sulkily in the rear of the runabout he sped them back to Aoife's in, seething that, whilst she'd been having a hideous time of it in Oxford, he'd been apologising about her, *her*, to his *servants*, when his only concern should have been apologising to herself, for them.

Why would she want to win him over?

She didn't want to win him over.

Not that day.

That day, she decided he belonged on her list.

So, she put him there.

Next to Mr Hamilton. She didn't forget that he was no innocent bystander in her humiliation.

No, it was him who'd summoned James home.

It was partly to show him how little she cared for his opinion, about anything, and partly to show James that she didn't crave his good one, that she did what she did when they finally reached Aoife's wharf, and disembarked back onto that hateful island of hateful haters.

Thomas was at the lighthouse again, looking down at them.

James, securing the runabout to its mooring, ignored him.

Elizabeth didn't.

She studied him.

You'd do well to stay away from him, Mr Hamilton had said.

Elizabeth hadn't thought much about his words of caution, since.

But she thought about them now. She felt rather intrigued. Comforted too, that she wasn't the only person in this place, disliked.

Thomas must have some interesting stories to tell, she decided.

Stories she might quite like to hear.

'Where are you going?' James called after her, as she headed off.

'To make a friend,' she told him.

Do you remember what you said to her, that night she went?

You told her she'd never belonged on Aoife's. That she never could.

You never admitted that, did you, when the police questioned you?

You never told them how fiercely you despised her.

Chapter Sixteen

Violet

May 1934

That night James returned to Aoife's was the first night Violet slept through to dawn without waking.

She slept in his arms.

They were interrupted just once, by Diana, who arrived to collect Violet's dinner tray within moments of that first, earth-tilting kiss, tapping on the door, stilling Violet with alarm in James's hold.

'Oh, God,' she whispered. 'Diana.'

'Ignore her,' said James. 'Pretend you're asleep.'

'I can't.'

'Yes,' he continued kissing her, 'you can.'

She wanted to.

She closed her eyes, and really did want to.

But Diana knocked again.

'She'll have seen the light,' said Violet.

'So?' said James.

'So, she knows I'm awake.'

'Miss Ellis?' came Diana's voice, in confirmation. 'Are you all right?'

'Yes,' Violet managed to respond, somewhat strangled. 'I'm fine.'

'Shall I come in?'

'Just a second. I'm changing.' She pushed James towards the

bathroom. 'Quick. You have to hide.'

'Hide with me.'

'I can't.'

'You can.' He pulled her with him.

'She might come in.'

'We'll lock the door.'

'Shhh,' she said, laughing, trying not to laugh, pushing him more firmly, even as he resisted, then shutting that bathroom door on him.

Leaning back against it, spinning with everything happening, she called to Diana to come in.

'Sorry,' she said. 'I was . . . indisposed.'

Diana eyed her. 'Are you poorly?'

'No.' She pressed the backs of her hands to her cheeks. 'Do I look it?'

'Feverish.'

'Well, I'm not.' Was her nightdress straight? She fought the urge to adjust it. 'It's the weather, probably.'

'It's cooled off now.'

'It's still warm.'

'You're all blotchy, though.'

'I'm fine, really,' said Violet, unclear as to why Diana was being so suddenly talkative, and acutely conscious of James, barely a foot from her, on the other side of the door, listening. 'Here.' She moved to fetch the tray, carrying it to Diana.

Diana took it, but didn't move herself.

'Is there something else?' Violet asked her.

'Mrs Hamilton's said we're not to tell Mr Atherton about Simon and Alan after all.'

'Oh. Right . . .'

'They seem relieved.'

'I'm sure,' said Violet, weakly.

She glanced backwards, in the direction of the bathroom.

'You won't tell on them, will you, Miss Ellis? Mrs Hamilton told me to say you mustn't.'

'I won't tell,' said Violet, and, determined now to send Diana on her way before she could say anything else they'd both regret, went to her bedroom door, opening it for her, and – thanking her, bidding her goodnight – held it open until she left.

Then she closed it, firmly, behind her.

Resting her forehead against the wood, she inhaled deeply, exhaled slowly, and inhaled again, attempting to muster some degree of calm before James emerged, only then she heard the click of the bathroom door behind her, felt his presence in a pulsing all through her skin, and a long way from calm, nonetheless turned to face him, because she simply couldn't resist.

He'd been laughing. She saw that from the enjoyment in his dark eyes.

'I'm glad you've been amused,' she said, as he joined her.

'Concerned, he said, running his hands back around her waist, electrifying nerve, after nerve, after nerve.

'Concerned?' she said, the word catching in her throat.

'That you're blotchy.'

'Am I really?'

'No.' He kissed her again. 'You're beautiful . . . '

'I'm not beautiful.'

'Yes, you are.'

'No . . . '

'Yes, Violet.'

She didn't argue any more.

Backing her against the wall, he moved his hands lower, to her hips, down to her thighs, lifting her up, and she once again stopped thinking at all.

She wrapped her legs around him, kissing him harder, growing hotter, *feverish*, overcome by an urgency she'd never known, at once unbearable, and too blissful for her to ever want to end. His lips found her neck, her collarbone, and she tilted her head back, lost in the sensation, and then he was carrying her to the bed, setting her down on the mattress.

He pulled away then, looking down at her, his stare intent in the soft lamplight, his chest rising and falling as he fought, visibly, for restraint.

'Please . . . ' she said, taking his hands, pulling him towards her.

'Have you . . . ?'

She didn't answer.

Standing, she kissed him more, so that he could ask her nothing else, because she didn't want him to know that she'd reached the age of twenty-seven and lived to such a limited degree. She didn't want to turn anything that was happening into some kind of expectation of what must come next between them. She had no interest in a transaction of I'll give you this, if you give me you. All she wanted was this thing that was happening, now.

Him, now.

He guessed the truth, though.

She sensed that from the way he was with her, rushing nothing, but unbuttoning her nightdress, coaxing it from her shoulders, tracing his fingertips over her bare skin, turning her to liquid as it dropped to the floor. Holding her close, his warm body pressed against hers, he gathered her back up and, setting her down once more on the bed, removed his own shirt. She touched his chest, above his heart, smiling at the beat beneath, then moved her hand, down his body, feeling the reflexive rippling of his muscles responding, and then he was kissing her again, covering every beating part of her with his touch: slowly, reverentially, thrillingly, like he truly did believe her the most beautiful woman he'd ever done such a thing with.

She was inexperienced, but not naive. She knew what was coming, and that babies had a habit of resulting, but she also knew that they didn't always, and that, in that moment, in her bed, with him, she didn't care anyway, and nor, it seemed, did he. Staring into her eyes, his own darker than she'd ever known them, and focused solely on her, he became still, for seconds that felt as though they stretched to minutes, then, just as she thought she might actually die from waiting, he smiled, leant down and spoke in her ear, making her smile too, then he was moving again, and there was none of the pain nor discomfort that Violet had heard others speak grimacingly of, only him, and her, on this island apart from the rest of the world, not dying, but living, blissfully entangled.

Together.

I never want to let you go.

That was what he'd said, when she'd smiled.

'I don't,' he told her, afterwards, as they lay, collapsed on the pillows, the lamps' flames flickering, the lighthouse beam skimming the ocean beyond the balcony doors. There was another aglow liner making its way towards America; only dimly, did Violet register it. She paid it no further attention once she had. She needed no thread to anything or anyone else that night. 'I haven't wanted to let you go from the second I saw you again, when you walked into Quaglino's in that red coat, your face all pink from the cold.'

'My face wasn't pink from the cold. I was mortified in that coat. All those glamorous women everywhere . . . '

'All I saw was you. No, don't look at me like that. It's true.'

She wanted to believe him.

It was hard, though, even after everything that had just happened, to see herself like that, through his eyes.

He talked on, running his fingers up and down her bare back, telling her of how he'd watched her at the door of the restaurant, convincing the maître d' to let her in, then crossing the dining room towards him.

'A woman dropped her napkin, and you picked it up for her.'

'Did I?'

'Yes. You handed it to her, and she didn't even thank you. She didn't look at you. And you didn't blink.'

'I was quite distracted.'

'You were kind, effortlessly, and she wasn't. She was incredibly rude. I couldn't stop thinking about it all night. How you, who've had so little kindness, could give it, so freely, and a woman like that hold it so short.'

'Ah, so you *did* pity me.' She said it as a tease. A ploy to cover the confusion of her emotion that he'd noticed such a thing.

Thought about it, all night.

But he didn't play along.

He shook his head.

'No,' he said, 'not pity. The more I talked to you, the more determined I became that no one should ever neglect to say thank you to you, for anything, again.' His hand stilled, resting in the small of her back. 'I think actually that the moment you picked up that napkin was the moment I first started to fall in love with you.'

Could a heart stop?

She thought her heart might have stopped.

'I haven't wanted to love anyone,' he said.

'No,' she said, her voice seeming to come from someone else entirely.

He'd said he loved her.

'I've been afraid to,' he went on. 'I was engaged before . . .'

'I know,' she said, believing he meant to Elizabeth.

To her surprise though, he shook his head.

'No,' he said. 'Someone else. A very long time ago. I won't talk about it.' His brow creased. 'I'm sure you don't want to hear about it, but she caught influenza at the end of the war and died. My mother had died before I went, my father before I came back, then she went almost as soon I did. We'd only just buried her, and then I had to go to another funeral. Old family friends who'd died

205

from influenza too. Their daughter, Laura . . . she was in pieces.'
His gaze filled with pain. 'I've seen so much death, Violet. Here,
over in France. I had Cressida when I came back, but I didn't want
anyone else. I didn't want to . . . feel. I thought it would leave me
too exposed, too vulnerable again.' His frown deepened. 'I've been
hiding, I realize that now. I decided solitude was peace, strength.
And it was. For me, it was. For years. But then I met you.' His hand
tightened on her back, holding her closer. 'When I came back here
in February, for the first time, it felt empty, too quiet.' He dropped
his head against hers. 'You've made solitude, loneliness, Violet, and
I don't want to be lonely any more. I want to be with you.'

Silently, she soaked in his words.

She felt them move through her, filling her up from the inside,
and, as they did, tears pricked her eyes.

No one had ever said anything like it to her before.

Not even close.

Reaching up, she touched his face, and he turned, kissing the
palm of her hand.

'I want to be with you too.' She took a breath, her chest
tightening on the truth she'd utter next. 'I love you too.'

She watched him smile. Saw the warmth, the happiness, filling
his eyes, and thought, *I did that.*

Me.

It still felt too fantastical to be real.

'I can't imagine living here any more, Violet, not knowing that
one of the lights in the window belongs to you.'

'You think I'm going to leave?'

'I think it was very wrong of me to bring you.'

'You said that earlier.' *I've been so selfish.* 'Why, though?'

'Because you've barely lived.'

'I've lived plenty.'

'No . . .'

'Yes.'

'No, Violet. And are you really happy here? Truly happy?'

She considered it.

Considered Mrs Hamilton's aloof manner. The scullery maids' hushed giggles. Alan and Simon's nudges.

Thomas's stares.

'No,' she said, honestly, 'not when you're gone. But now I am. Now I don't want to be anywhere else.'

'I don't want you to have to hide.'

'I don't mind.'

'You should, Violet. You should know that you deserve better. Demand better.'

'I don't want to demand. Not of you. I know what it's like to be on the receiving end of that.'

'You're not your father.'

'No, I know. I just . . . Well, I want only what you want to give me. Otherwise,' she shrugged, rustling the sheets, 'it's just obligation.'

A crease formed in his brow. 'You think that anything could feel like obligation to me, with you?'

'I hope not.'

'You should know not.'

He had scars on his shoulder, more on his stomach. They were barely visible in the dim light, but she noticed them, as they lay there, talking; touched the smooth puckering in his skin and, knowing how little he liked to dwell on his war, nonetheless asked him about them anyway, because they were a part of who he was, part of what had brought him here, and she wanted no voids in her understanding of any of that.

'Are you sure?' he said, disbelieving.

'I'm sure.'

'All right,' he said, and – first pausing, stealing himself – told her that the ones on his shoulder were from a shell wound he'd received at Arras, in the snowy spring of 1915, and the ones on his stomach from a machine gun at Ypres at the very end of 1917.

'You were hit by a machine gun?' she said, appalled.

She wasn't sure why that idea, specifically, shocked her so much. There must have been millions of others who'd suffered the same.

But he wasn't millions of others.

He was him.

It had happened to him.

'You could have died,' she said.

'But I didn't.'

'How did it happen?'

'Which one?'

'Both.'

'Violet,' he gave a shuddering sigh, 'do you really want to know this?'

'I do. And actually, I think you should talk about it.'

'Why?'

'To get it all out from inside you. Exorcise it . . . '

'Exorcise it?'

'If you can.'

He raised a brow.

She thought he might be going to refuse.

But then, with another sigh, he said, 'I don't remember much of Arras at all. It was very cold. We were attacking through a wood, hundreds of us. It was . . . bedlam.' He broke off, a distance coming over him. 'Our shells were going over our heads, the Germans' were landing all around us. There was ice all over the ground. In the trees. One of my men slipped and fell. I stopped to help him, and a second later, a shell exploded, a few yards in front of us. The next I knew I was in a field outside a clearing station, and it was snowing again. Freezing. There were rows of us there. Rows and rows.'

'Was the man you helped with you?'

'He was fine. Not hurt at all. Then he was killed a week later.'

'I'm so sorry.'

'Yes,' he said, sorry too. 'It was what it was like there, though. Day after day after day.'

'Did you come back to England to recover at least?'

'Not that time. I was sent to Etaples. But I did after these.' He laid his hand over hers, still resting on his bullet scars. 'It was the last time I saw my father.' He paused. 'I have that machine gunner to thank for that at least.'

'Do you remember more of that?'

'I remember everything. It was a pain I can't . . . describe. The force of it. I managed to drag myself into a shell hole. It was full of water, other bodies.' He fell silent, leaving her again, returning there. She laced her fingers through his, reminding him where he was, and felt his tighten around her. He talked on, describing the hours he'd waited in that hole, the incessant sound of the guns, the pounding of the heavy artillery, his thirst. 'When it got dark, the verey lights started. You know, the flares.'

She nodded.

'Arnold had seen me go down. He came looking for me, carried me in.' Easily, Violet pictured Mr Hamilton doing it. 'He saved my life that night.' He let go a long breath. 'I owe him my life.'

'Is that why you gave him this post here?'

'I'd have done that anyway.'

'Did he know my father?'

She wasn't sure why she'd never asked the question before. She'd had enough opportunities. She supposed, now she considered it, that she'd been too worried about the answer. Mr Hamilton probably had known him, after all.

Or at least, known of him.

'He did,' said James, confirming it. 'They met during training, and were in the same unit, for a long time.'

'So, he knew him well.'

'Yes. Much better than me.'

'Does he know who I am?'

He left a second before answering.

A second that said it all.

'You told him?' said Violet, shifting away, not wanting to be angry, but unable to help herself.

'No.' He pulled her back. 'No. He guessed. He knew I'd gone to your father's funeral, and pieced the rest together.'

'Has he told Mrs Hamilton?'

'I expect so, yes. I'm sorry. I know you didn't want anyone to know. I thought it would be easier for you to think they didn't.'

'It doesn't matter,' she said, except it did, but what was there to be done about it? Mrs Hamilton would have been glad to have been given another reason to dislike her, anyway. 'I hope they haven't told anyone else, though.'

'Arnold knows they're not to. He liked your father, Violet. Certainly, at first. Before . . . '

'He changed.'

'Before he was changed, yes.' He smiled, sadly. Back with her again. Properly back with her. 'You should ask him about your father, when you're ready. I'm sure he has some stories you'd like to hear.'

She arched a brow. 'Are you?'

'I am. He told me that your father carried a photograph of you with him everywhere. Looked at it constantly.'

'Really?'

'Yes.'

'I never knew that.' She found herself picturing him now too, crouched in a trench, her photograph cradled in his hands. Those hands that had once tucked her into bed; lifted her onto his shoulders. 'How is it possible that I never knew that?'

'I don't know,' said James, kissing her. 'You should have.'

She kissed him back. 'Has it helped to speak about it all?'

'No,' he said, deadpan. 'It was incredibly painful.'

Violet didn't notice when the ocean liner outside disappeared. Only vaguely was she aware of her bedroom clock striking eleven, then midnight, then one. The two of them didn't only talk, but, as the night outside deepened, and the house around them slept, they did talk a great deal: about his lost fiancée, a little, since she pressed him to (Isabel, she'd been called; he'd met her, the daughter of an English professor, in Oxford, before the war. 'She deserved a much longer life than she had,' he said, 'but she's been gone a long time now, and I was a different person when we made that promise to each other.'); they spoke of Violet's past beaus, too, since he pressed her on them ('None of them went to Oxford, or Cambridge,' she said, 'can we please leave it at that?'); even, briefly, finally, of Elizabeth.

'If you didn't want to feel,' said Violet, 'what about her?'

She asked it hesitantly.

It was infinitely more discomforting talking about her than it had been Isabel, for endless reasons, not least that there was no question mark hanging over Isabel's death.

Violet had to do it, though.

She couldn't go on not doing it any longer.

But, for the first time, James turned from her, looking away to the other side of the room. 'What about her?'

'You felt for her, I assume.'

'She gave me very little choice.'

'I don't know what that means.'

'It means that there were no good feelings, of any kind. It's the time in my life I'm most ashamed of.' He moved, facing her again, his every muscle straining with emotion. 'It wasn't a marriage, Violet. It was an arrangement. I realize now that she wanted to hide too, and saw me as a way to do that.' He was angry still. She saw it in his eyes. 'I had to let her.'

'Why?'

'Because she knew something. Something she threatened to use.'

'About you?'

'About my mother. For a long time, I couldn't think how she'd found out. It was through one of the partners at our old law firm.'

'Hence your change to Firth Knightly.'

'Hence my change.'

'And hence our dinner in Quaglino's.'

'Yes.' His eyes softened. 'Hence that too.'

She wanted to ask him what it was about his mother that Elizabeth had discovered.

But he spoke first.

'I will tell you the rest. You should know it. But not now, please.' His stare held hers. 'She has no place in this room.'

Slowly, Violet nodded. He was right, she realized. It would upset him, upset them both, to push it now, and the night had been too perfect for her to ruin like that.

So, she let it go for another time, and mentioned nothing of her run-in with Thomas, nor her difficulties with Mrs Hamilton, nor anything else that had been needling at her whilst he'd been gone, either.

Truly, cocooned in his hold – caught up in the delirious, incredulous happiness of being where she was – none of it could have felt less relevant.

He told her more of the time he'd just spent away, his impatience to return to her, and relief that he'd convinced Cressida to come with him. 'She's safe here. Dicky won't dare to follow her here.' They spoke of Teddy, and James's conviction that it would only be a matter of days before Cressida relented and summoned the nanny.

'But I thought she and Dicky were . . . ' said Violet.

'No,' said James, 'Cressida was being facetious. You'll see she's good at that.'

They talked of Harbury, where he said Cressida had retreated after the newspapers' hounding had made remaining in London impossible for her, then Violet's own weeks in that city before she'd moved to Aoife's, and Mr Barlow's indignation that James had never asked him for a reference, which James was most pleased to hear about. He'd been quite deliberate, it seemed, about not giving Mr Barlow the satisfaction of requesting one. Although his staffing department had, to Violet's surprise, secured one from Violet's old firm in Banbury.

'Did you read it?' she asked.

'No. I didn't need to. But I assure you it was all filed and above board.' He shifted on the pillow. 'Have you really been worrying about this?'

'Not worrying. Just . . . pondering.' She frowned. 'I wish Mr Barlow had known. He said you obviously weren't interested in my typing skills.'

For a second James laughed.

Then he became serious. 'He said that to your face?'

'Yes. And that everyone here would think you'd brought me for your fun.'

'What?' His entire body turned rigid. '*What?*'

'It's fine.'

'It's not *fine*. It's outrageous. Why didn't you tell me?'

'How could I have told you?'

'In much the same way as you *just told me*.'

'No . . . '

'Yes.'

'No. And anyway, here we are. Here I am.' She bit her lip. 'Here for your fun.'

She was fishing. She wanted him to contradict her.

He knew it.

Fixing her with a look, he leant over her, and, although she managed not to let go her laughter, she felt it, in her cheeks, her eyes.

'I never wanted you here for my entertainment, Violet. Although . . . '

'Although?'

'Although,' he dipped his head, kissing her, 'you are entertaining.'

'You're quite entertaining too.'

'Quite?'

'Moderately.'

'I'll let that go.'

'Will you?'

'Yes. On one condition.'

'What's that?'

He kissed her more. 'You tell me what I'm not meant to know about Simon and Alan.'

Her laughter erupted.

'Is something funny?'

'No, and I can't tell you.'

'That's fine,' he said, moving on top of her, pulling the sheets over them both, 'I don't really want to talk about them anyway.'

They were still awake when the clock struck two.

She didn't hear it chime three.

With her head on his chest, her legs entwined in his, she fell asleep to the wash of the waves below, and the rhythm of his heart.

He left at first light.

She woke briefly as he moved from the bed, kissing her head, and fell dozily back to sleep. When she woke again, it was to a much brighter sun blazing through the windows neither of them had thought to pull the drapes across.

She stared at the rays, watched a gull swoop past, then turned to look at the space he'd left in the bed beside her, and might have wondered if it had all been a dream, had it not felt so entirely, blissfully real.

She smiled, laughed, flung back her arms, then, quickly, rose, jumping from the bed: desperate, already, to be with him again.

Chapter Seventeen

Violet

As she bathed and dressed that morning, she found herself constantly stopping, smiling more, as memories of the night came pouring back. She bundled her sheets up for the laundry, leaving them by the door for Diana; it was nothing less than she'd done before, and she knew Diana wouldn't question it, just as she didn't question the necessity of keeping what had happened between her and James a secret. She didn't question that they must go on in secret, because how could they do anything else in this place where there was always someone watching?

It never occurred to her that James might disagree.

She expected that, when they saw one another again that morning, he would, if there was anyone else around, call her *Miss Ellis*, and she'd call him Mr Atherton. They'd take their breakfasts separately, as usual, and, at some point in the day, when they were alone, he'd catch her eye, she'd smile, and they'd steal a kiss. It felt so obvious to her that that was the way it would be, it was almost as though it was already written.

She supposed she forgot to reflect properly, in the chaos of her feelings, on the man she'd just spent the night with. She let the lines blur too much between him and the few others she'd walked out with, and neglected to consider what it might mean when someone like James Atherton told you that he loved you: a man who'd never clocked in and out, nor carried a briefcase for show, nor refused to attend a late matinee at the pictures because everyone else went to the half past eight showing, but had survived shells and machine guns and four years of war with his compassion intact, lost his parents, then raised his sister, all the while building one of the most successful businesses in the country, and creating an entire world on an island because he'd decided solitude was strength.

She realized her mistake, though, when, on letting herself into the atrium, she found him waiting for her by the cold fireplace. As she took him in, working on a stack of papers at the table – a table that, for once, was bare of any breakfast for her – it dawned on her not only that he didn't mean for her to eat there that morning, but also that he of course wasn't someone who was about to start skulking around his own house.

He wasn't someone who'd accept her doing it.

I don't want you to have to hide, he'd told her, in bed.

'Good morning,' he said to her now, setting his papers aside, standing as she continued towards him, dissipating her nerves, if not her unease, with his smile, the warmth in his low voice. From upstairs came the sound of Teddy, chattering. 'Hungry?'

'I am actually, which is unfortunate, given my breakfast seems to have disappeared.'

'It hasn't disappeared. It's in the dining room.'

'Hmmm, I suspected it might be.'

He gave her a quizzical look. 'You don't want to have breakfast with me?'

'Of course I want to have breakfast with you.'

'But?'

'But . . . ' She turned, hearing footsteps coming up the servants' stairs.

'Violet.'

'Yes?'

'Violet?'

'What?'

'Look at me, please.'

'There's someone coming . . . '

'So?'

'So,' her brow creased, '*James.*'

Sighing, he took her by the arm, steering her into the west wing, closing the door behind them.

'I can't have it like this,' he said, as it clicked shut.

'Yes, I've gathered that.'

'You want it to be some clandestine thing?'

'No . . . '

'Then what are you afraid of? Being seen with me? Having breakfast with me? Cressida and Teddy are there.'

'It will still look . . . ' She stopped, trying to think how to put it.

How *should* she put it?

'I'm not a man,' she began.

'No, you're not,' he agreed.

'I'm not you, either,' she went on, the words coming to her now. 'I have no one and nothing but my name, and I've already had to change that once.'

'You don't want to do it again?'

'I don't want to *have* to,' she said, hitting her stride, not pausing to unpick his question. 'Knowing everyone here suspects . . . something . . . that's been all right. No, actually,' she frowned, 'not all right. Not all right at all. But I've managed with it. I've been able to manage because I've known they were all wrong about me. To be . . . brazen now, though . . . I can't.' She stared into his perplexed face, entreating him to understand. 'I can't do it. I need to be able to look everyone here in the eye.'

'You think I want anything less for you?'

'I think it's easy to forget something matters when it's not something that matters to you.'

'It matters to me.' He took a step towards her. 'Violet,

everything about you matters to me. I'm not about to play . . . *fast and loose* . . . with your name. Why do you think I left you so early this morning? Hid in your damn bathroom last night?' He wrapped his arms around her. 'I swear to you, I will do nothing and risk nothing that will give you a moment's difficulty. But I also won't treat what you've become to me as something to be ashamed of.'

'I'm not ashamed.'

'Good. I'm relieved.'

'But shouldn't we just keep it to ourselves for now?

'To what end?' A dent formed between his eyes. 'I won't lie to Cressida. Apart from anything, she's been lied to enough. As for the staff,' his frown deepened, 'what does it matter if they see you eating upstairs?'

'They'll guess.'

'That we spent the night together? No, they won't.'

'The rest, then. That I'm . . . ' She broke off again.

What even was she?

'More than just your secretary,' she plumped for.

'You're a lot more than that. You've always been a lot more than that. And let them guess it. They're going to work it out one way or another soon enough.'

'They already hate me.'

'No one hates you.'

'I think you're wrong.'

'How could they hate you?' He kissed her, and, in spite of herself, she felt herself soften, lean into him. 'Please, come to breakfast.'

'I don't know . . . '

'Violet.' His lips were still touching hers. 'You don't need to worry. Not about this.'

Was he right?

Perhaps he was right.

She wanted him to be.

She really didn't want to go on eating alone.

She *wanted* to be with him.

She did have another worry, though. One that was harder to admit to.

Almost impossible.

But she still made herself do it.

'I can't sit where Elizabeth sat. I can't be wondering if that's what I'm doing.'

His gaze became pained. He drew breath . . .

'I mean it,' she said, before he could try to tell her it didn't matter. 'I can't.'

'Then you won't.'

She hesitated a moment longer.

'Please, just come.'

'All right,' she agreed.

'Thank God.' He kissed her again. 'It will be fine, you'll see. And, Violet . . . '

'Yes?'

'You don't have no one.'

He told Violet, as they went upstairs, that he hadn't yet spoken to Cressida that morning.

'I came straight down to wait for you.'

'What are you going to say to her when you do?'

'That you're more to me than a secretary.'

'And I thought she was meant to the facetious one.'

'She is.' They came to the top of the stairs. 'She's also no fool.' He carried on across the landing, towards Teddy's babbling. 'I've told her already how I feel about you. Honestly, I doubt I'll need to say anything much else at all.'

He was right about that.

Violet realized as much from the moment the two of them

entered the dining room, and Cressida – who was feeding Teddy, on her lap, from a bowl of porridge – turned to look at them. It was the glint in her dark eyes as she appraised them; the slant to her tired smile: she, it was clear, had guessed if not all, then enough.

Alan was in attendance. His nose had almost reverted to its normal size. Simon, Violet presumed, was lying low until his eye had done the same. She wondered, as she sat in the chair James pulled out for her – glancing around at the other empty ones, second-guessing their past inhabitants – if Mrs Hamilton had simply been doing both footmen a kindness in deciding to keep their fight from James. Or had she another reason for hiding it? James, Violet was certain, would never actually dismiss them for such a thing. Mrs Hamilton must know they didn't really need protecting.

James sat beside her, and Alan came forward, pouring their coffee. Violet kept very still as he did it (did coffee always take so long to pour?), watching Cressida as she continued to feed Teddy her porridge – not very successfully; Teddy, lips clamped shut, deflected every spoon – and James turned to Alan, asking him where Simon was.

'He's not feeling himself today, Mr Atherton.'

'I'm sorry to hear that. Is he unwell?'

'Just not himself,' Alan repeated.

'In what way, not himself?'

'Just . . .'

'Not himself?' supplied Cressida.

'Yes, exactly, Mrs Thompson.'

'Let's use Miss Atherton, shall we?'

'Very good, Miss Atherton.'

Was it possible he felt even more uncomfortable than Violet? Violet thought it might be.

'How was everything while I was away?' James asked him.

'All well and good, Mr Atherton.'

'Nothing I should know about?'

Violet shifted in her chair.

'No, Mr Atherton.'

'Really? Because I have to say, you don't seem quite yourself either.'

'I'm fine, Mr Atherton.'

'You're sure?'

'Yes, Mr Atherton.'

James studied him, narrowing his eyes.

Alan swallowed.

'All right,' said James, 'off you go for now. We can manage here.'

And off Alan went. At pace.

'He's going to think I told you something,' said Violet to James, just as soon as he had.

'He won't. He's got a bruised nose.'

'Hardly.'

'Nonetheless, I'm not blind. I assume he and Simon fought?'

'Yes.'

'Why?' asked Cressida.

'I don't know.'

'And why am I not to be told?' said James.

'I don't know that either. You'd better ask Mrs Hamilton.'

'Perhaps I will.' He looked over at Teddy, holding back another spoonful of oats with both hands. 'I don't think she likes that.'

'I don't think she does either,' said Cressida. 'But she needs to eat it. Her nanny says it's the only way for her to start the day.' She frowned. 'Teddy always eats it for her.'

'With how much sugar?'

'I have no idea. God, Teddy, please . . . '

'Give her to me. I'll try.'

'You think she'll take it from you, and not me?'

'She might.'

She did.

Perched on James's knee, absorbed by the fastening on his wristwatch, she ate like an angel.

'Just like her daddy,' said Cressida to Violet. 'She'll do whatever James tells her to.'

Cressida ate very little herself. Just some eggs that she picked at, swallowing the tiniest of mouthfuls from a single prong of her fork. To Violet's relief, she didn't appear remotely resentful over her own presence at the table, for all the jealousy she'd been accused of, and for all she was at the end of her own truncated love story. Rather, she chatted, mutedly, with the same unabashed candour as she had the night before, asking none of the normal questions Violet might have expected from a new acquaintance, but things like, whether Violet believed in heaven ('It depends how optimistic I'm feeling,' said Violet), and which point in time she'd go back to, if she were to be given the opportunity to start over from there again.

'I don't know that I would,' said Violet.

'You've had that good a life?'

'No. But I'm not sure that the things I'd change were ever things I had the power to.' It wasn't the first time Violet had considered the matter. She'd pondered it often: whether, in another life, she could have convinced her mother not to leave, or stopped her father from enlisting, then self-destructing. As a child, she'd believed herself entirely to blame. Now, her only real regret was that she couldn't go back and sit with that girl, assure her she had no control over any of it. 'What about you?'

'Nineteen thirty-two,' said Cressida, without hesitation, shocking Violet not at all. 'Everything that year was mine to change.'

'Not everything,' said James, in a tone that suggested this was not the first time Cressida had pondered the matter either. 'And it's done. You'd be much better off focusing on what's ahead.'

'I don't know that I can see anything ahead.'

'Because you keep looking back.'

Cressida pondered that too, her tooth pressed to her lip, her

223

eyes cast down to the congealing eggs on her plate. She was in another silk summer dress – lemon today, with a lace trim – but hadn't waved her hair, or used any make-up. She hadn't bothered with jewellery either. Her ring finger was bare. She looked painfully adrift, sitting there on the other side of the table; lost, and unbearably sad.

'What are you going to do this morning?' James asked her, gentler now, seeing it too.

'I don't know. Unpack, I suppose, once everything's here.'

'Arnold's organising that. Why not go out for a walk in the meantime?'

'No.' She sighed, and set down her fork. 'No, I don't think so.'

To Violet's knowledge, she didn't leave the house at all that day. Much of it, she spent in the west wing with herself and James – shadowing Teddy as she crawled up and down the corridor; building towers for her out of books; houses from cards – scared, all too obviously, to be alone. Sorry as Violet felt for her, it was impossible not to be frustrated by the constancy of her company. Whatever the truth of how much she'd already guessed, Violet couldn't be at her ease with James so long as she was there. She could hardly bring herself to call him by his name.

She didn't at first.

'I need your signature here, Mr—'

'No,' he said. 'No.'

Whilst she got better at that, each time their hands brushed over a file, or she met his gaze, she found herself transported back to her room, taken over by some moment of the night before – fighting, with every strained fibre of her being, to pretend it wasn't so.

He, who suggested to his sister several times, with increasing voracity, that she and Teddy might be more comfortable in the library, or the drawing room – 'Or anywhere else really at all, Cressida,' – clearly felt the burden of her presence too.

'Of course I feel it,' he said, pulling Violet to him when Cressida left them, briefly, to change Teddy before lunch. 'I can't think straight.'

'Nor can I,' she said.

And she needed to. They both *needed* to, not least because it was suddenly a very busy time. Whilst James had been away, the company had begun negotiations to acquire a number of sites for new, larger department-style stores that were to be positioned on the outskirts of towns across the country. Starting the process was the main reason James had decamped to London (rescuing Cressida from Habrury was, Violet now deduced, another), and he'd returned with a mammoth amount of follow-up.

'You could have warned me last night,' Violet said, as he kissed her.

'My mind was on other things. And I didn't want to upset yours.'

'Too late for that.'

There were contracts to be amended, endless letters to be dictated and typed, and that was on top of all the usual business that had arrived in that morning's post (*not* sorted by postmark: tellingly, Mrs Hamilton hadn't done that again since Violet had brought her up on it). There was no conversation about whether they should eat lunch in the dining room, because they ate it in the office, and although Cressida did disappear for a couple of hours afterwards, taking Teddy back to her room for a nap, there was too much to do for Violet to even consider that she and James might escape themselves.

Adding to the general hecticness, was Mrs Hamilton, who never normally came to the offices, but appeared frequently that day, first to let Cressida know that she'd written to Selfridges to order Teddy a cot and highchair, then, armed with a cup of warmed milk for Teddy, then, with a plate of chopped fruit for her, and again with another of shortbread. James, so busy, didn't appear to mark her presence, but Violet did, intrigued by the way Mrs Hamilton was with Teddy: kneeling down in her pencil skirt to clap hands with her, smiling, with her *eyes*, when Teddy smiled at her; even getting into a game of peekaboo.

'Was she the same with you when you were small?' Violet asked Cressida, late in the afternoon, after Mrs Hamilton had once again been and gone, this time with a bowl and spoons for Teddy to play with. They were out in the corridor. Violet was on her way to fetch a file, and Teddy was once again crawling laps.

'She never knew me when I was small,' said Cressida. 'I was eleven and troublesome before I met her.' She arched a wry brow. 'Very troublesome.'

'Was she nice, though?'

'Nice enough, I suppose. Nothing like this. I still call her Mrs Hamilton, for God's sake. She's always been very formal. Stiff, you know?'

Violet nodded. She did know.

'She's a funny one.' Cressida leant down, taking Teddy by the hips, adjusting her path. 'I think actually that she'd probably like a Teddy of her own.'

Violet had been thinking much the same.

'She doesn't seem to like me at all,' she said.

'She might. She's the kind of person who can make it seem like she doesn't when she does. I don't expect anyone here really believes she likes them.'

'Mr Hamilton must.'

'You think?'

'You don't?' said Violet, taken aback.

'I don't know. It's always felt a bit . . . imbalanced . . . between them to me.' She shrugged. 'I'm not sure Mrs Hamilton's ever been especially happy here. Look at the way she dresses. She's hardly a country mouse.'

'No,' Violet agreed.

'She has magazines delivered every month to keep up with it all,'

Cressida went on. 'And every year, before Christmas, she spends a week in London, just for the buzz.'

'I thought she was grateful to your brother for bringing her and Mr Hamilton here.'

'At first, maybe. Now, though . . . ' Another shrug. 'I think she probably resents it. Or the promise she made Arnold anyway, when she believed their marriage would be something different.'

'Before he was injured, you mean?'

'No. Not that. I doubt that she minds that. I'm sure she *loves* Arnold. I mean before he sentenced them both to a lifetime out here.'

Violet thought about it.

Thought back to that unforgettable April night Mrs Hamilton had come to her room and spoken to her of Aoife's legend.

A man brought her, she'd said, staring into the blackness. *It was a man who decided she should come.*

Perhaps Cressida was right.

Perhaps Mrs Hamilton wasn't happy.

And perhaps that was part of why Mr Hamilton doted on her so. Because he felt guilty over the enormity of what he'd taken from her.

There is nothing that man would not do for his wife.

'Elizabeth made it all even more of a misery for her,' Cressida continued. 'They absolutely hated each other.'

'Gareth told me.'

'Did he?' Cressida smiled. 'You've met him then?'

'He gave me a glass of elderflower wine.'

'Oh, dear.'

'What does he actually do here?' Violet asked. 'I can't work it out.'

'He roams, sand buckets on standby. Especially when it's dry like this. There has to be a fire warden on the island. Something to do with the law. And more importantly,' she crouched, moving Teddy again, 'James knows Gareth would never find a job anywhere else.'

'What about the Brownings?'

Cressida looked up sharply. 'What about them?'

She sounded so suddenly guarded, Violet wished she hadn't asked.

But since she had . . .

'Does your brother employ them?'

'No.' She got back to her feet. 'The council does.'

'I've never seen Francis.'

'No?'

'No.'

'Well, I suppose he must be getting older. And he's not a watchdog like his son.'

'Has Thomas always been like that?'

'For as long as I can remember.'

'I spoke to him. He told me Mrs Hamilton doesn't want me here.'

'Thomas says a lot of things he has no basis for.'

'I heard the two of them arguing, though. Here, in the house.'

Cressida frowned.

Then she shook her head.

'No,' she said. 'Thomas would never have come here.'

'But I heard him.'

'You must have been mistaken. And honestly, stay away from him.'

'That's what everyone keeps telling me.'

'You should listen. I like you, my brother certainly does, and that man isn't someone you want anything to do with.'

'But what has he done?'

'He ruined my life, Violet.' She swooped, picking Teddy up, cradling her close, as though to remind herself that she could. That her daughter really was there. 'His lies are why I ended up in prison.'

Cressida didn't expand on her pronouncement.

With an agonised look that left Violet in no doubt that the matter of her arrest wasn't something that she – so candid, about so much – could tolerate going into, she kissed Teddy, declared that she could do with a drink, and, returning to James's office, requested a brandy.

He didn't give her one.

'Cressida,' Violet heard him say, 'I'm working. I have to work.'

'You've been working all day.'

'And if you keep interrupting me like this, I'll be working most of the night . . . '

Violet really hoped he wouldn't be.

Pushing that intolerable prospect from her mind, she carried on to the filing cabinets, and thought about what Cressida had said. She could only guess at what Thomas might have done for Cressida to blame him like that. Whilst she'd long known that Cressida – three-months pregnant with Teddy at the time of Elizabeth's disappearance – had remained under suspicion of having had some hand in it, right up until the discovery of Elizabeth's body had freed her, no one had ever managed to discover what had led to Cressida's arrest in the first place. The reporters had hypothesised, endlessly, but whatever the police had known, or thought they'd known, about Cressida had been kept carefully guarded.

That brother of hers has paid them off, Violet's father had said.

Perhaps he had.

And why not, after all? Why not have saved his sister from whatever exposure he could?

Still . . .

What evidence *had* the police been given by Thomas?

Violet wasn't left to wonder over it for too much longer.

She wasn't left to wonder either about why, if not because of the nanny, Cressida had left Dicky, and returned to this place that she hadn't set foot on since she'd been taken away under police escort.

Nor was she left to wonder about Elizabeth.

Because although James did work that night, he also stopped, and when he did, he came to Violet's room. At his suggestion, they went out for a walk, and, as they walked, he finally did as he'd promised he would.

He told her everything.

Chapter Eighteen

Violet

She has no place in this room.

That's what James had said of Elizabeth, when he and Violet had spoken about her in bed.

It was the reason he asked Violet to leave the house with him that night.

'Let's be somewhere none of it will linger,' he said, running his hand wearily over his face at her door. 'I owe you an explanation, I know that, but I don't want it to be here.'

It was close to eleven. He, who'd insisted that Violet call it a day and leave the office at seven, had worked for almost thirteen hours straight. They hadn't eaten dinner together because he'd had his at his desk. Cressida had taken hers in her room with Teddy, so Violet had done the same in hers. She'd since had time to bathe, wash her hair, change; *breathe*. James, in contrast, wore the same clothes he'd been in all day, and Violet knew that he'd only just left his desk, because a minute before, she – keeping vigil at her window – had seen his light go out. He'd come straight to her, and was so patently exhausted, she almost told him it didn't matter, that they could talk about it all another time.

Let's just go to bed.

In so many, many ways, it was all she wanted them to do.

But she did want this explanation too.

And she needed to get it over with.

He, she realized – from the way he took her hand, turning to head back down the corridor – did too.

They didn't speak as they passed Cressida's door and continued into the atrium. He'd brought a lantern with him, but aside from its crackling flame, all was darkness, all was quiet. Violet shivered; it had been a much cooler, overcast day, a chill breeze picking up at sunset, and her dress was a thin one. Beneath the fabric, her heart pumped, too quickly. It was unsettling knowing he was about to tell her so much, with no inkling as to how any of it was going to leave her feeling.

'Here,' he said, quietly, at the porch, setting the lantern down, and reaching for the jacket he'd loaned her the first time he'd taken her walking, down to the bottom of the old lighthouse stairs. 'Put this on.' He smiled as he helped her do it, remembering too, and, dipping his head, kissed her. At the warmth of his lips on hers, she felt her anxiety vanish. But then he pulled away, picked the lantern back up, and it returned.

They still didn't talk as they walked through the gardens for the cliff stairs. Around them, the path's pools rippled in inky shades of blue and black and darkest purple, reflecting the sky above. The clouds moved quickly, fracturing, giving fleeting glimpses of the stars and almost-full moon behind.

'Your hand is shaking,' said James, squeezing it tighter.

'I'm nervous,' she admitted.

She waited for him to tell her she shouldn't be.

But,

'Yes,' he said. 'So am I.'

At the top of the stairs, he steered them right, along the cliff edge towards the opposite end of the island from where the lighthouse was. The wind was stronger now they were so exposed, although nothing like as fierce as it had been when Violet had first arrived on the island. Nonetheless, she was edgy enough that, as it blew, frisking the grass, carrying the smell of baked earth and salt, she pictured Aoife, roaming the night too, filling it with her haunting despair.

And, for the very first time, she mentioned her to James.

'Do you ever imagine her out here, when it's windy like this?'

'No.' He gave her a quizzical look. *Aren't you full of surprises.* 'You do?'

'Yes.'

'It's a story. Just a story.' His eyes, bright in the darkness, were bemused. 'Who told it to you?'

'Mrs Hamilton.'

'Really?' He looked even more taken aback. 'When?'

'The first night I arrived.'

'You never said.'

'No, I know.'

He stopped, turning to face her properly, about to ask her, she was certain, what else she might have neglected to mention.

In the breath before he did, she realized just how much she wanted to finally confide in him: not only about Mrs Hamilton, but every strangeness she'd encountered since she'd arrived on the island, starting with her journey over from St Leonard's and that loaded question the boatman had asked of her. *You sure you're built for island life?* She would tell him, she resolved, but not just yet.

She couldn't let them become side-tracked.

He needed to go first.

'Is that right?' he said, when she told him as much.

'It is.' From somewhere within her, she mustered a strained-feeling smile. 'I demand it.'

He didn't smile. He sighed.

A long, ragged sigh.

'Fine,' he said. 'Fine. Where do you want to start?'

'Wherever you like.'

So, he started with Cressida.

His father had blamed Cressida for their mother's death. He told Violet that as they walked on into the blustery darkness, and that, although his father had eventually come to regret his behaviour, sorely, he'd already been a dying man himself by then. 'He wasn't at Harbury when Cressida was born, and at the end was afraid to let her see him. He was very frail. Not the man he'd been.' He stared out at the ruffling, velveteen ocean. 'He never met her. Never held her.'

The revelation stunned Violet. From all James had told her of his father, she'd thought only of him as someone kind, full-hearted. James had loved him, she'd felt that in his every word, every tale; she'd felt it only the night before when he'd spoken of his gratitude to that machine gunner for sending him home to see him for one last time. She couldn't marry that love with a man who'd refused to see his own daughter and left her alone with no mother.

Not even her own father had stooped so low.

James talked more: of the grief he'd carried to France, his guilt over Cressida. 'I visited her before I left. She was tiny, only a couple of weeks old, and in this vast cot. She didn't cry, or make any noise. She just stared up at me like she couldn't think what this lonely world was that she'd been born into. It would have broken our mother's heart.' He'd written to his father, he said, every month, imploring him to return to Harbury. His father in turn had drawn up a new will, specifying that Cressida should inherit nothing in the event of his death. 'He'd always suffered with typhus, he'd caught it in Africa, and was getting older. I think he probably suspected he didn't have long, and blamed Cressida all the more for stealing what time he and our mother had had left.'

234

'Weren't you angry with him?'

'I was furious. But it wasn't straightforward.' He halted, seeming to summon the will to go on. 'He knew that Cressida wasn't really his.'

'What?' Violet, stopping too, more breathed than spoke the word. It was the very last thing she'd expected him to say. 'Who . . . ?'

'I . . . ' he began, then grimaced, reaching up, pinching the skin between his eyes. 'Shall we sit?'

'All right,' she said, unthinkingly.

So, they sat on the hard-baked earth, facing the water, the lamp nestled in the grass beside them. He took her hand, lacing his fingers with hers, and, jaw set, containing his pain, his rage, spoke of the attack his mother had suffered during a weekend party, care of an old army associate his father had invited to their house: an attack that had left her carrying Cressida. 'The man was prosecuted, sent to prison, but my mother's name was kept out of it. She was . . . utterly broken by it all. She hated that I knew, and wanted no one else to. Certainly not Cressida.'

Violet felt sick. In her mind's eye, all she could see was that photograph in the atrium of James's mother, so happy.

'My father hardly left her side afterwards,' James went on. 'He didn't intend to reject Cressida. That wasn't who he was. At the start of that October, I got my disembarkation orders, and he came to visit me at the training ground before I shipped out. We went for lunch, and whilst we were eating, Cressida arrived early, and my mother died.' His voice fractured on the word. It made Violet ache, physically hurt, to hear it. 'The only people with her at the end were people who were paid to be.'

'And Cressida,' said Violet, needing to say something. 'She was there.'

'Yes,' he agreed, with infinite sadness. 'She was.'

'James, I'm so sorry.' Dropping her head, she rested it on his shoulder, and felt him lean against her.

For a few moments after that, they were silent: Violet, staring at the black horizon, replaying everything he'd told her; he, she didn't doubt, remembering his mother.

When he spoke again, it was to tell her about the final time he'd seen his father, at the convalescent hospital he'd been sent to following his injuries at Ypres. It was the start of 1918 by the time he'd returned to England, and the hospital was in Yorkshire, yet despite that, despite his father's grave health, he'd travelled the distance to be with him. 'I can't tell you what it meant when I woke up, and saw him there, next to me.' He'd been full of remorse, full of shame, and had rewritten his will, putting Cressida back into it. 'She'll get everything this October when she turns twenty-one. He asked me to promise that she'd never know anything of the way he'd behaved, and that I'd look after her.'

'Which you obviously have.'

'Not as well as I should have. I've left her alone too much. Sent her away to boarding school so that I could live here, then let her go back to Harbury after she finished. She was only eighteen. I should have been there.' A new toughness edged his voice. 'Stopping Dicky Thompson from setting a foot near her.'

They'd been at school together, he said. He'd never liked him. 'Hardly anyone did, certainly not for long. He was a born sycophant, entirely self-serving, always waiting for the next head to tread on. He had this vindictive streak too, especially with the younger boys. We all had to watch him. The masters didn't care.' They hadn't crossed paths in the war. Dicky's father had secured him a desk job at GCHQ. 'Honestly, I forgot about him, gladly. But he remembered enough of me to go looking for Cressida as soon as she turned eighteen. He believed she'd have a dowry, of course. I knew nothing about any of it until he wired inviting me along to their engagement party . . . '

'Why didn't Cressida tell you?'

'She knew I'd try to stop it. Which I obviously did. But she was determined to push ahead regardless, and I couldn't lose her, Violet. I couldn't leave her with no one.'

'No.' Violet understood that. 'I assume you didn't give her a dowry, though?'

'No, I had our lawyers see to it that Dicky wouldn't be able to touch anything I gave her. I thought he'd lose interest when he realized how little was going to be in it for him. But,' he let go a humourless laugh, 'Cressida told him about her inheritance. I doubt it was in his plan that they'd divorce before she received it.'

'Did he love her at all?'

'He swore blind he did. But no,' he looked down, studying their entwined fingers, his strong face contemplative in the blackness, 'there's not a single part of his involvement with my sister that could be construed as love.'

He told her then about Dicky's affair with Elizabeth, turning her rigid with shock. He felt it, saw it – she saw that from his raised brow – but didn't stop talking. He kept on, clearly impatient, now that he was at last doing it, to get it all out. The breeze blew, the grass shivered, and he spoke of Elizabeth's rage that Dicky had chosen Cressida over herself, the panic he believed her to have been in that every other one of their friends was either married, or marrying. Her determination not to be left behind.

'I think she'd believed herself ageless, invincible. Time had stood still for her, and then suddenly it began to race away. She was thirty-two, and ill. Extremely ill.'

'Ill?' Violet frowned. She'd had no idea. 'In what way?'

He took a moment to answer.

She wondered what could be so hard to say.

Then,

'Syphilis,' he told her, 'she had syphilis.'

And she stared, shock coursing through her all over again.

'I,' she began, then stopped, her mind filling with every terrifying public health poster she'd ever seen – outside hospitals, in bus shelters, railway tunnels – trumpeting their dire warnings about that all but unspeakable illness.

The Great Crippler, those posters had called it.

The Scourge.

Who have YOU exposed? they'd demanded.

And Elizabeth had had it?

Elizabeth, who'd had an affair with Dicky . . .

'She couldn't have passed it on,' said James, with a grim look, guessing the line her thoughts had taken. 'It's only contagious in the initial stages, and she was long past that by the time she became involved with Dicky. She never spoke of it. I only found out because the specialist she'd been seeing in Oxford, Mr Claymore, wrote to me after she disappeared.'

'How long had she been . . . unwell?' asked Violet, rediscovering her voice.

'Years. She first saw Claymore with symptoms in her early twenties. He treated her with arsenic injections, and believed her cured. But then she became unwell again, returned to see him, and he realized they'd ended her treatment too soon, left traces of the syphilis latent.'

Silently, Violet absorbed it.

'Claymore felt terrible,' said James. 'Obviously.'

'Obviously,' echoed Violet. Then, 'I suspect Elizabeth felt worse.'

'Yes. I'm sure she did.'

'When was that?'

'The spring of nineteen twenty-nine. It's how we met. We ended up on the same train out of Oxford together.' He shook his head. 'It got stuck, we were together for hours, and she wouldn't stop talking, all about herself. I saw her again the next day on Regent's Street. She called out to me, but I got away before she could cross the road. I had no desire to speak to her again. I forgot about her.'

238

'But she remembered you?'

'She did, yes.'

Violet could empathise with that much at least.

'Claymore put her through another course of salvarsan that spring. It's less effective in later stages, but he had some hope it would work. Elizabeth refused to entertain the possibility that it wouldn't. I gather that when we met on the train, she decided that I was a lucky sign, latched on to that.' He sighed. 'Claymore said she disappeared again after the treatment, ignored his letters asking her to return for re-testing. He thinks she convinced herself the syphilis was gone, and was too afraid to be told otherwise.'

Violet could understand that, too.

'By the time of Cressida and Dicky's engagement,' James continued, 'she'd become much more unwell. She was always taking these pills. I assumed they were recreational, but, according to Claymore, she suffered from the most appalling headaches. Eventually, they got so bad that she returned to see him, discovered the syphilis wasn't gone at all.' His brow pinched. 'He told her there was little point in administering more salvarsan, but she convinced him to have a go. By then, I'd run into her at Cressida's engagement party, and she'd become . . . fixated . . . with this idea that we should be together. She kept appearing at my business lunches, running into me on the street outside my house. Claymore suspects she wasn't entirely in charge of herself. He said he'd always found her difficult, but she became much more volatile as her neurological symptoms progressed. It terrified her, apparently. She had this absolute horror of anyone finding out what was wrong with her.' He paused. 'Everyone would have, of course, if there'd been a trial. I'm sure it would have all come out, then.' He expelled a sound, much less than a laugh. 'That would have appalled her.'

'I think it would probably appal most people,' said Violet, because who *would* want such a thing publicised?

'Yes, but she was obsessed with everyone believing her life perfect.'

'It certainly looked perfect to me,' said Violet, picturing all those photographs that had been printed of her in the papers; that glittering smile.

'It wasn't,' said James. 'I don't think it ever was. Not even her parents gave her much love. Perhaps that was part of what made her so greedy for admiration . . . I don't know.' He stared out at the ocean. 'Regardless, she was chillingly narcissistic.'

'But to keep something like that to herself.' Violet couldn't comprehend it. 'She really didn't tell *anyone*?'

'No. One of her friends, Laura Ratcliffe, the woman whose parents' funeral I told you about . . . '

Violet nodded, remembering. *She was in pieces.*

'She suspected something was wrong, said Elizabeth had changed. I honestly couldn't understand how the two of them had ever become friends. Laura was, *is*, lovely. They were obviously close, though. Elizabeth left her everything. But all her friends found her difficult in the end.'

'You said last night that she knew something about your mother. I take it . . . ?'

'Yes. She'd found out everything.'

'*How?*'

'Through Amy Astley,' James replied. 'Her brother, Edwin Firth, used to be a partner at our family's old legal firm. They'd kept everything on file there. The arrest of my mother's attacker, my father's changed wills . . . everything. Not long before Cressida's wedding, Edwin invited me to a dinner party at Amy and Henry's. I didn't know Elizabeth was going to be there, he said nor did he, but after it she asked him if he knew of anything that she could use against me.'

'Edwin Firth?' Violet's labouring thoughts moved. 'Of Firth Knightley?' She frowned. 'Your *current* firm?'

'Yes.'

'*Edwin* told Elizabeth?'

'No, no, he refused to help her, but she realized he was hiding something and approached one of the other partners to go digging for her. She offered him too much money to say no to. He ended up buying himself a new house, bragging about the whole thing to one of his friends, who told Edwin, who, seeing his chance to set up his own firm, came to me, inviting me to entrust my business to him and Patrick Knightley.'

'And you do trust him?'

'I do. He handled it all pretty smartly. And he and Patrick jumped through the hoops I set when I put the business out to tender . . . '

'But surely he should have told you that Elizabeth had approached him. Warned you what she was about . . . '

'I don't think he realized how serious she was. Or imagined that she'd lower herself to shopping around anyone else.'

'He got that rather wrong.'

'He did, yes.'

'And Elizabeth threatened to tell Cressida what she'd found out?'

'Yes.' He stared into her eyes, his own hard now with fury. 'I couldn't let her. I knew it would shatter Cressida. I'd sworn to my father that I'd protect her.'

'Would Elizabeth really have done it, though?'

'Without question.' He went on, describing the cool way Elizabeth had approached him at Cressida and Dicky's wedding, threatening not only to divulge the secrets she'd gleaned to Cressida, but her own continuing affair with Dicky, too. 'Until that moment, I'd believed it in the past. I told Elizabeth to go to hell, she said she didn't want to do that. She wanted to get married.'

'Surely you fought her?'

'Yes, I fought her. I offered her money that she didn't need. I threatened to have her prosecuted for blackmail, which she knew I'd never do, because then Cressida would have found out everything anyway . . . ' He let go another non-laugh. 'She trapped me.'

Violet said nothing, fighting to take it all in.

She couldn't fathom anyone behaving so manipulatively, however unwell.

Or, why anyone would want to marry someone who didn't want to marry them.

Then, she recalled what James had said to her the night before, about Elizabeth wanting to hide.

'You really think that's why she did it?' she asked.

'It had to have been part of it. Claymore had warned her that if the salvarsan failed again, she'd deteriorate quickly. Apparently, she refused to believe it could happen, but I'm sure she must have, deep down, and was desperate to disappear before it did. Happily, so far as everyone else was concerned. And she really did despise Cressida and Dicky. I have no doubt she wanted to punish them too.'

Violet considered it, shifting her weight.

'I've been so sure you must have adored her. She was so beautiful . . . '

'No.' He said it firmly. 'She wasn't, Violet.' His eyes bored into hers, as though to make her believe it. 'She was hard, and she was cruel, and not beautiful at all.'

'Were you glad when she died?' Violet had to ask it.

She couldn't leave it unasked.

'I wasn't sorry.' His gaze on hers didn't falter. 'But I had no hand in it.'

'I've never thought you did.'

'Good.'

'Did anyone have a hand in it, though?'

'I don't know. I hope not.'

'Do you think not?'

242

'I really don't know. There were very few people here that night who didn't have some reason to hate her.'

It reminded her of what Gareth had said.

There were certainly enough of us here who wanted her gone.

Thinking of him, and his daughter, she said, 'Gareth told me she drove Delen away.'

'She made her life here extremely difficult, yes.'

'You told me she didn't like the isolation.'

'Did I? When?'

'When I first arrived. In your office, by the fire.'

He thought about it, then nodded, remembering. 'It's not untrue. She was ready for London, loves it there. She lives with friends, is always out. Honestly, I don't believe she's looked back.'

'But Elizabeth was the one to push her away?'

'She was a grim catalyst, yes. Gareth isn't the kind to hurt anyone, though, if that's what you're thinking.'

'It's not. Really. I liked him.'

He gave her a curious look. 'When did you meet him?'

'On Monday.' She could have gone on then, told him about her exchange with Thomas, but she still had too much else to say, and ask. 'I don't think he believes what happened to Elizabeth was an accident.'

'No.'

'James, what *happened* that night?'

'Too much.'

'Tell me, please.'

So, he did: of how Elizabeth had planned the entire house party behind his back, and been on savage form from the off, unpleasant to everyone from the moment they'd arrived, and incensed to learn that Cressida was expecting. 'She hadn't known about it until that night. I hadn't told her.'

'She was jealous?'

'Bitter. She wanted to ruin it for Cressida, so she did.'

243

Violet didn't ask how. She could see, very clearly now, where this was going.

'She found her in her room,' said James, 'told her everything, about her and Dicky, our mother, father . . . All of it.' He set his jaw. 'She'd already reduced Laura to tears, Amy as good as. Mrs Hamilton had gone home thanks to her, Diana and Nelle had both been crying too . . . I lost my temper, told her that I was going to start divorce proceedings, she said, over her dead body, then left.' His expression remained very still. 'I never saw her again. Everyone except Thomas and Gareth claimed they never saw her again.' He drew in a long breath, then let it go. 'Perhaps no one did.'

'But you don't know.'

'No. I went to see Cressida, obviously, but she was beside herself, refused to let me in. She'd locked Dicky out too. He said he went to the library for a drink, everyone else claimed they were in their rooms, getting dressed for dinner. None of us were together again until it was called. That was more than an hour later.'

'So, anyone could have gone out?'

'Diana *was* out, walking to the wharf to meet her father, John. You know how he takes her home on Saturdays?'

Violet nodded.

'She's always said she saw nobody, heard nothing. Gareth saw Elizabeth from his window, of course, but said she was alone. Thomas, though, he claimed he saw Cressida out on the fields, chasing Elizabeth after she'd left him at the lighthouse. Elizabeth had told him everything about what she'd said to Cressida, and he told the police that too. They decided Cressida had a decent motive.'

'Did you pay them to keep it from the papers?'

'I didn't need to. Dicky got there first.'

'He must have cared for her a little then, to want to protect her?'

'He wanted to protect himself, Violet. He never visited her

244

whilst she was being held. Didn't set a foot near her until she was cleared. I was the one who moved with her to Harbury. She was . . . crushed. Still is. But I know her, Violet. I *know* her.' His eyes fired with conviction. His whole body was taut with it. 'She's got her faults, but I've seen through hundreds of her lies. I'm certain she didn't leave her room that night.'

'Why did Thomas lie?'

'Maybe because he knew how happy it would have made Elizabeth to see Cressida suffer.'

Violet broke off a blade of grass, tying it in a knot around her fingers.

'Do you think he might have been trying to protect himself?'

'Possibly. I've gone over and over it, believe me. *Could* he have hurt Elizabeth?' He gave her a long look. 'Yes, absolutely. *Would* he have?' He shook his head. 'I can't see why.'

'Gareth said the same.' The blade of grass ripped. 'What about Thomas's father?'

'Francis? He's harmless. And he had no reason to hurt Elizabeth either.'

'How did she get herself away in that boat, though? Could she sail?'

'Not that I know of. But she was in enough of a state to try.'

'Why, though?'

'To scare us all, by disappearing?' He frowned. 'God knows. But that dinghy belonged to her.' He turned, glancing over his shoulder, back across the fields in the direction of the wharf, seeming to think of it there. 'She bought it for herself a couple of months after she arrived. Said she needed an escape route that didn't involve me or Arnold.'

'Would she really have risked such a thing at night, in a storm?'

'Well, she got to that cave somehow. And she's gone. It's over. Please,' his eyes implored hers, 'can we let it be?'

She didn't want to.

She wanted to keep dissecting it until, together, they found some sense in the nonsensical.

But she also realized that, if sense there was to be found, he, who clearly had combed over the night's events ad nauseam, would have already discovered it.

And it was obvious how hard it was for him to relive everything again now.

She couldn't cause him more pain.

'Yes,' she nodded. 'Yes, of course we can.'

They returned to the house after that.

It was as they walked that he told her about Cressida's divorce, and why it was only now that she was pursuing it. It was another bleak tale: Dicky, a doting if disloyal husband up until Cressida's arrest, had apparently become much less so afterwards, seldom appearing at Harbury, berating Cressida for her dullness whenever he did, insisting that she was the one to blame for his ongoing faithlessness, threatening to take Teddy from her if she attempted to leave him.

'I didn't know how bad it had become,' James said. 'Cressida kept it from me, afraid of losing Teddy. She tried to keep everything from the staff too, but in April our housekeeper wrote to me saying how worried she was. I asked Delen to pay Cressida a visit. The two of them have always been friends. She went, got to the bottom of it all, and now the divorce is in motion. Not before time.'

'What about Teddy, though?'

'What about her?'

'Will Dicky take custody?'

'He can't. I had Edwin hire someone to look into his affairs. His father cut him off last year. He hasn't settled a single bill since. I'm currently the only thing standing between him and debtor's prison, and he knows I'll get out of the way the second he puts a

246

foot wrong.'

'How do you know his father won't help him?'

'He's riddled with his own debts. Teddy's safe. Cressida is. She just needs to get used to it.' He looked at her sideways, appraising her in the inky night. The wind blew, tousling his hair, rippling the fabric of his shirt. 'You're safe too, you know. You don't need to worry about Aoife.'

She smiled. 'I thought you might have forgotten about that.'

'No.' He stopped. 'You sounded very uneasy.'

'I'm fine. I've just been giving into a . . . childish fear of the dark, I suppose.'

He narrowed his eyes. 'What exactly has Mrs Hamilton been saying to you?'

She almost dismissed it. She no longer felt the compulsion she had earlier to be open about it. Maybe it was the seriousness of all he'd just told her, but her concerns about boatman's warnings, and centuries-old myths, and trifles in the post, really did seem suddenly very . . . *trifling*.

Yet, he'd been so honest with her.

And, if she wasn't with him now, it would undoubtedly become harder to be.

She might, in fact, never do it, and her silent anxieties would turn into something they never spoke about: a lie, by her own omission to talk.

She couldn't have that.

Didn't *want* that.

So, with a pained grimace, she did as he'd done for her, telling him everything, becoming gladder of the cloaking darkness, the longer she spoke, because it really did all feel so very ridiculous.

He didn't treat any of it as ridiculous, though.

He listened, seriously.

'And why am I only just hearing about all of this?' he asked when she finished.

'I honestly didn't know how to tell you before.'

'You've been sleeping with your suitcase against your door. Or not sleeping, by the sound of things.' He looked, and sounded, confounded. 'I hate that you've been afraid.'

'I haven't all the time. Honestly.'

'You shouldn't have been at all. The boatman . . . Eric's his name, by the way . . . forget what he said. He's always been opposed to any of us being here. His sister was married to Francis Browning before she died. Thomas is his nephew. He's adamant the whole place is cursed.'

'James, that doesn't make me feel better.'

'You believe in curses?'

'I don't *want* to.'

'Then don't.'

'How did Thomas's mother die?'

'It was years before I got here.'

'And . . . ?'

'She fell.'

'*Fell?*' Violet stared. 'Too?'

'No, not too. There isn't any too. Aoife probably never even existed.'

'She probably did.' Violet looked around into the dense blackness, a chill snaking her skin. 'The story came from somewhere . . . '

'Yes, an overactive imagination. You can't let it bother you. Stay away from the lighthouse and Thomas won't bother you either. As for everyone else . . . ' A frown furrowed his brow. 'What do you think they've been getting in the post?'

'I *can't* think. Honestly, I've wondered if you'd had something too. Those letters that came before you went . . . '

'Which letters?'

'They were marked confidential. You put them in your drawer.'

'Them?' He frowned more. 'They were from the investigator

looking into Dicky.'

'What about that wire you sent, the day I got here?'

'That was to Edwin, after Delen wrote about Cressida. Violet,' he shook his head, 'you should have talked to me.'

'I know.' She should have.

'And you really think you heard Thomas in the house?'

'Cressida said it can't have been him.'

'I don't think it can. He never leaves the lighthouse.'

She nodded.

'Do you want me to talk to Mrs Hamilton? Find out what it's all been about?'

'No, please. It will only make things more awkward between us.'

It wasn't only that. She kept thinking about how Mrs Hamilton had been with Teddy earlier: the uncharacteristic neediness in her as she'd knelt to play peekaboo. And, of the things Cressida had said about how unhappy she'd always been. It had given Violet a new empathy for her: enough to not want to risk causing her more trouble.

Besides,

'It was weeks ago now. When I asked her again about the trifle, she told me she'd forgotten about it.'

'You believed her?'

'No. But what if I'm wrong? What if I'm the one with the overactive imagination?' It was at least a possibility. Look at the torture she'd created for herself with Aoife. 'I'll seem an idiot, and they'll all hate me more.'

'No one hates you,' he said, as he had that morning.

'Dislike, then. Distrust.'

'Violet . . .'

'Please,' she tugged his hand, 'leave it.'

He didn't respond.

She watched him, weighing it up.

'Please,' she repeated. 'At least for now.'

'You'll tell me if anything else happens?'

'Straight away.'

'All right.' He dropped his head to hers. 'All right.' Another gust of wind blew, spiralling them in the scent of grass. 'But I swear to you, Violet, you're not in any danger here.' He kissed her. 'I would never have asked you to come if I believed you were.'

Chapter Nineteen

Elizabeth

August 1932

Elizabeth bought herself the dinghy at the end of her second month on Aoife's. The idea came to her one rainy August morning when, sitting in the Oxford office of her really rather charming specialist, Mr Claymore (was there a Mrs Claymore? 'Let's try and leave my personal life out of things, shall we, Mrs Atherton?'), she noticed a new and rather intriguing addition to the collection of gilt-framed pictures on his wall. It was of a tufty-haired, wholesomely happy-looking chap, standing beside a sailboat on a pebbly beach. She stared at his sweet face, and was reminded, out of nowhere, of her long-dead brother, Anthony. She didn't usually let herself think about him; he'd been killed in the war, she'd loved him more than anyone, ever, and it hurt too much to remember that he was gone.

But, seeing this boy now, it was almost like Anthony was trying to reach out to her. Remind her of how much he'd loved her, too. That she wasn't, in fact, alone.

'Who is that?' she asked Mr Claymore, gesturing at the photograph.

'My son. But Mrs Atherton, I need you to focus—'

'Your son?' (So, there was a Mrs Claymore.) 'How old is he?'

'We're getting personal again, aren't we?'

'I'm simply curious about his age.'

'He's eleven.'

She smiled.

She'd been seven, when Anthony had been eleven.

He'd used to take her scavenging for conkers.

'Does your son like conkers?' she asked Mr Claymore.

'I think so, yes.'

'And sailing.'

'Indeed.'

'Did he win some kind of competition?' Elizabeth asked, eyeing the medal around his neck.

'He did.'

'By himself?'

'All by himself. Now, Mrs Atherton. About these memory lapses you've been experiencing . . . '

'Just quickly, where might one procure a boat like that?'

He sighed. 'I'll have my secretary pass on the shop's details.'

'Thanks ever so.'

'Now, can we please focus?'

'No,' she laughed. 'Not lately. You know that.'

'It's really not a laughing matter, Mrs Atherton. I need you to take this seriously. I know you've been rather depending on the treatment working.'

'I have rather, yes.'

'I'm so sorry. What I've told you must have come as a significant blow. I do wish your husband was here with you . . . '

'Oh, wouldn't that be nice?'

'You've always said that meeting him felt like a charm . . . '

'How personal of me.'

'That it gave you hope . . . '

'He has that kind of face.'

'You will tell him when you get home?'

'Tell him what, Mr Claymore?'

'That we're ceasing the salvarsan injections.'

'Are we?'

252

'Yes, Mrs Atherton. Like I've just said, they cause you significant distress, and simply aren't having any effect.'

'Mr Claymore, I must say you're being quite half-empty today.'

'Mrs Atherton, there is no half-full about this. The syphilis is becoming much more aggressive. These latest images we've taken indicate continued swelling of your meninges arterial walls. And these spots in your vision are a concern . . .'

Elizabeth, tuning out, returned her attention to the boy in the photograph.

Eleven years old.

Surely if a child could master bobbing around in such a boat, she could too.

Anthony would want her to have a go, she was certain.

It might even be fun.

It had been ever such a long time since she'd had a hobby. She'd once played the piano, ridden too, although never as well as her parents would have liked. They'd used to scold her for her lack of application. *No one respects mediocre, Elizabeth.*

She could apply herself to sailing.

She *would* apply herself.

'I'm excited,' she said, interrupting whatever Mr Claymore was saying. (Nothing good, if his expression was anything to go by.) 'Might you ask your secretary for those details now?'

'Details of what, Mrs Atherton?'

'Your little boat place. I'm going to become captain of my ship.'

She became captain of nothing.

Oddly, once she returned to Aoife's ('Where have you been?' James asked. 'London,' she lied), she forgot she'd so much as ordered a dinghy. It stunned her when, on the second Wednesday of September, it arrived on Aoife's.

'Where do you want Arnold to put it?' asked Mrs Hamilton, who sought Elizabeth out in the drawing room to tell her it had been delivered.

'The boatshed,' said Elizabeth, drily, covering her confusion with disdain. 'Isn't that the traditional home for such vessels?'

'You don't want to take it out?'

'Not today, no. It's overcast.'

'A good wind, though.'

'Not today, Mrs Hamilton.'

'Do you know how to sail it?' James asked her, much later, stopping by her bedroom as she was with Nelle, readying herself for yet another dinner he'd refuse to join her for.

'Of course I know how to sail it,' she snapped, batting Nelle's limp, indecisive hands away from her hair. 'God knows I need a means of escape from this hell.'

'Take it,' James said. 'By all means, take it.'

'Question for you,' said Thomas, the next morning, a Thursday, as the two of them sat on the damp ground outside his cottage, drinking tea from his dead mother's china. 'Do you know how to sail?'

'No,' she admitted. 'What about you?'

'Not me. Only Dad.'

'How disappointing.'

To make a friend.

That's what she'd told James she was going to do, the first time she'd come to the lighthouse, back on that sun-speckled morning James had collected her from Penzance: scolding her for her treatment of his lacklustre staff.

Had she made a friend?

No.

What she shared with Thomas wasn't comfortable, it wasn't *genial*; she couldn't say that she ever precisely *enjoyed* her visits with him, not as she'd used to her mornings spent with Laura on the King's Road. She missed those, missed Laura, not, of course, that she'd told her so.

I'm terribly sorry I forgot your birthday, sweet thing, was the kind of thing she filled her letters with, *I'm blaming James. He barely gives one pause to spare anyone a thought* . . .

In truth, she'd felt bad about the forgotten birthday. To salve her conscience, she'd had a case of champagne delivered to Laura, and would have rather liked to have cracked into it with her; they'd have drunk, gossiped, and the hours would have scooted by, just as hours with Laura, by and large, always had. Not like the time Elizabeth expended with Thomas. That mostly jerked along, and whenever she left him, she did so overly hot, and acutely conscious of him behind her, watching her go.

And yet, back to the lighthouse she'd kept returning, all through the summer, for, if not with Thomas, then who else had she to spend her time with? Delen Phillips was gone, now. She'd left for London on a misty August morning. Thrilled as Elizabeth had been to see her speed off into the fog in James's runabout – she'd watched it happen from up at the lighthouse with Thomas; watched Gareth too, on the wharf, sinking his head into his craggy hands, clearly weeping (where had his dignity been, really?) – it had irritated her enormously that James had couriered her. More galling yet was how, in the time since, she'd come to mourn the diversion of her daily run-ins with Delen.

They really had, by and large, been larks.

You're to leave Miss Phillips alone, James had told Elizabeth, outside Penzance station.

How that curt, snapped instruction had needled at her, scratching and itching at her peace of mind ever since. Because how dare James have pitched himself as that precocious little upstart's protector, against her?

Had there been something going on between them before Elizabeth had arrived?

James had denied it, when Elizabeth had put it to him. 'For

Christ's sake,' he'd said, 'must you tarnish everything?' But even if he'd been telling the truth, Elizabeth simply couldn't credit that Delen herself hadn't had designs on him. Her pathetic presumption had disgusted her, quite as much as her rudeness had angered her.

Not leaving her alone, Elizabeth had got into the habit of calling by on her at the office whenever she knew that James was elsewhere, perching on her desk, swinging her legs, and remarking on the lengths Delen had clearly gone to, to make herself look nice in her cheap, nasty clothes. 'Has James even noticed, though?' she'd mock whisper. 'I know he must have smelt that perfume you're wearing. We can *all* smell that.'

'I'm not wearing perfume,' Delen would claim.

'Careful, darling. James doesn't like fibs.'

'I'm not your darling. And I'm not fibbing.'

'Shall I tell you what he does like?'

'Not again, if you don't mind.'

'But I do mind,' Elizabeth would reply, and, leaning towards her, would lift her hair back from her ear: laughing at the inevitable shiver of goosebumps that broke out on her skin.

Then,

'Listen carefully,' she'd say, before sharing one of the many tricks Dicky had so relished. 'You're blushing again, darling. You know it's terribly common to be so proper, don't you? Well . . . don't you? Delen, can you hear me? Hello? Is anyone at home?'

But, increasingly, Delen had clammed up, stubbornly refusing to respond.

Infuriated by her silence, Elizabeth had looked for other opportunities to goad her into a rise, bumping into her whenever she'd left the offices for the bathroom, taunting her with anything and everything that had sprung to her mind – from the mean little cottage she lived in, to the oddness of her reclusive father, to the dullness of her unremarkable life, to the jokes she and James shared about her, behind her back – but still Delen had remained tight-lipped, hurrying away from her.

'Why the rush, Delen?' Elizabeth would ask, raising her voice for the benefit of whichever of the other servants might be nearby. 'Are you that desperate to get back to my husband? You're shooting too high, you know. Someone really should have broken that to you before now. God, speak, won't you? Don't be such a pushover, stick up for yourself . . . '

But Delen hadn't stuck up for herself.

James, though, Delen's valiant protector, he'd stepped in.

'Don't imagine me oblivious,' he'd told Elizabeth, catching her one July morning as she'd been on her way to breakfast.

'Oblivious to what?' she'd asked, massaging a new pain in her temple.

'Your bullying of Miss Phillips.'

'I'm not *bullying* her. We're not at school, James.'

'No, you're in my house.'

'My house, too . . . '

'No, Elizabeth. *My* house, in which I've always welcomed Miss Phillips, and have never wanted you.'

That had hurt.

Hand falling from her temple, she'd stared at him.

'So, you are in love with her.'

He'd looked at her like she was mad. 'What is wrong with you?'

'What's wrong with *you*? Do you not see her? Do you not see *me*?'

'I see you, Elizabeth. I see a monster . . . '

'A monster?' she'd said, with a smile she hadn't felt.

What she'd felt was even more upset.

Sad.

Monster.

She'd hated that he'd called her that. Despised that that was how he'd come to see her.

All because of bloody, damnable Delen.

'Do you get a thrill out of coming between us?' she'd demanded of her, shadowing her home that night across the fields. 'Why are you running? Stop running . . . '

But Delen hadn't stopped running.

And she hadn't responded.

So, Elizabeth had followed her home again the next night, and the one after that. She'd kept following her every night from then on in, chasing her through the long grass – questioning her on her day, what she'd talked about with James, pondering on what it might do to her father if anything bad ever happened to her ('Didn't your brother have some kind of accident? Are you all he has left, Delen?') – until, at the end of July, determined to crack her resolve, *force* her to speak to her, she'd grabbed her, wrenching her to a halt as they'd approached the far side of the island, and dug her fingers into her plump milkmaid arms until she'd felt bone.

'Stop ignoring me,' she'd said. 'I demand your respect.'

'My respect?' Delen had asked, finally snapping from her silence, her eyes all round and glassy and defiant. 'I've never in my life encountered someone less worthy of it.'

She'd claimed, afterwards, that Elizabeth had shoved her then, multiple times, towards the cliff edge.

Elizabeth had no recollection of doing any such thing.

And although she did remember telling Delen that she wanted her gone, she'd never actually meant dead, no matter what Gareth – who'd come running to his daughter's aid – might have accused her of to James.

Regardless, gone Delen had been, within a matter of days, to London.

'Satisfied?' James had asked Elizabeth.

'Yes, actually,' she'd said.

And she had been. Until she'd grown so *bored*.

Mrs Hamilton, now smugly ensconced at Delen's desk – lauding it over the west wing, like she lauded it over everywhere else – really wasn't nearly such fun. Truly, she, who walked out of any room Elizabeth walked into, and had by now several times asked James to remove Nelle from Elizabeth's service ('If you can't learn to keep your vicious tongue to yourself, Elizabeth, you can do your own bloody hair'), was no fun at all.

Nelle, snitching Nelle, wasn't fun either.

Chef, who'd barred Elizabeth from the kitchen, wasn't either.

Nor was sneering Simon, nor average Alan: both just hoping, Elizabeth could tell, for her to humiliate herself by smashing another plate.

Nor was anaemic, skinny Diana, who'd arrived to work in the house at the start of the month, and who, in her baggy, oversized uniform, wordlessly collected and delivered Elizabeth's laundry daily, except on Saturday evenings when, for some unfathomable reason, she was permitted the night off and disappeared back to the mainland with her fisherman father, *John*.

Thomas, candidly, wasn't much fun either, but he was welcoming at least.

He always *wanted* to see Elizabeth when she arrived, walking down the peninsula to meet her, that raw hunger snapping in his heavy, brooding eyes. And he was stirringly handsome, almost as much so as James, with a festering energy about him, straining from within his every, honed muscle.

He didn't know about her little illness. (She refused to pay it the respect of a name.) Whenever away in Oxford, she'd said she'd been visiting friends, and although she had, at other times, occasionally let slip about a headache if a particularly vicious one had stopped her calling by on him, mostly she'd bitten her tongue. She didn't want him to guess that she was unwell. He desired her, more with every passing day; she knew it, saw it, not only in his stare, but the beating vein in his neck whenever she rested her hand on his thigh; the laboured way he swallowed, watching her run her tongue over her lips. She'd been starved enough of such admiration not to want to risk tarnishing his with any hint that she'd succumbed to something so appalling as that germ, that *imposter,* that had taken up residence within her.

For much the same reason, she hadn't been honest with Thomas about how she'd come to marry James. No, she'd told him, the morning they'd met, that James had begged her to wed him, sworn *blind* that he'd make her the happiest woman on earth, only to turn on her as soon as they'd said, *I do.*

They'd been at the top of the lighthouse tower. Elizabeth had asked Thomas to show her around, feigning fascination in its tight, winding staircase, rusting emergency bell, the huge lens in its pool of liquid mercury, and Thomas's excruciatingly articulated explanations as to how the lens was turned, the frequency with which the cogs beneath were wound, the shifts he and his father shared (God, so much, really), determined to charm him, where she'd kept failing so singularly to charm James.

'I don't know what I did to upset him,' she'd said, voice wavering, her bottom lip curled in a pout. 'He's become so cold. I think it must have been my money he was interested in . . . '

'I doubt that,' Francis, also in the tower, had chimed in. He, a whiter-haired, stockier version of his son, had fixed Elizabeth with a distrustful look, and, silently, she'd added him to her naughty list. 'Mr Atherton's got plenty. And it don't sound a bit like him to be fickle.' He'd sniffed. 'I've never known a less fickle type.'

'I don't expect you know him at all then.'

'Strikes me I've known him a deal longer than you.'

'Strikes me, not as well.'

Francis hadn't become any friendlier, as the summer had progressed. Most of the time, he'd avoided Elizabeth as studiously as everyone back at the house had taken to avoiding her, remaining wherever she was not for the duration of her visits. On the rare occasions that they had crossed paths, he'd greeted her with nothing more than a sniffed, 'You again,' before disappearing, either into the lighthouse, or his home.

Elizabeth had asked Thomas what his objection to her was.

'He clearly has one,' she'd said, with a hurt sigh.

'He just don't like having company,' Thomas had replied. 'Thinks we're best as we've been.'

'What, lonely?'

'Alone, at any rate.'

Unlike his father, Thomas had grown, if never quite verbose, then gradually more talkative, the more time Elizbeth had invested in him.

And he *did* have stories.

Not about the island's other residents: he'd disappointed Elizabeth again on that front.

But stories that she had, nonetheless, been most keen to hear.

The first he'd told her, back at the start of July, was Aoife's.

It had been a rather inconsequential morning, too hazy to be called sunny, too bright to be termed cloudy, and the two of them had been perched beneath the cottage's empty washing line, staring at the sea from a pair of decrepit deckchairs. Elizabeth, filling the silence between them, had asked if one might have a drop of tea, and he'd shown her into his excuse of a kitchen, fetching cups and saucers, the floral pot. She, amused by the incongruity of such fine china in his large, workman's hands, had asked if he'd selected the set personally.

'No,' he'd answered, seriously, missing her tease, as he really did tend to miss most of her subtleties. 'My mother did. She liked nice things.'

'You've certainly kept them nice.'

''Course we have.' Carefully, he'd filled the pot with water.

'They were hers.'

'How did she die?'

Silently, he'd scowled at the pot.

'Thomas?'

'Like Aoife,' he'd said.

'What does that mean?'

And, raising his attention from the pot, he'd stared across at her, with eyes so wide she'd been able to see all of the whites surrounding his grey pupils, then relayed that Irish maiden's sorry tale; spooking Elizabeth, quite as much as he'd entertained her.

'Have you heard it?' she'd been unsettled enough to ask Mrs Hamilton when she'd returned to the house, catching her in the entrance hall.

'I have.'

'Do you believe it?'

'It's a myth, Mrs Atherton.'

'Thomas told me his uncle thinks the island's cursed.'

'Yes,' Mrs Hamilton had replied, coldly. 'It's certainly started to feel like it might be.'

Later, after another solitary dinner, after Elizabeth had gone to bed, she – battling the insomnia that increasingly stalked her night-time hours – had risen again, and left the house. She hadn't known where she'd wanted to walk, only that she'd needed to be outside. But, as she'd paced the island's black fields, trying to exhaust her muscles, her nerves, she'd felt Aoife's presence all around her. Each night that had followed, she'd ventured further, feeling Aoife still, exhilarating herself with her own vulnerability in the darkness, the wind and Aoife's flitting shadow, relishing her terror for how alive it proved she still was.

Sometimes, she'd jerked to a stop, spinning, believing she might catch Aoife in her sights before the veil separating their worlds descended. She'd laugh when she saw nothing, her hilarity evaporating into the salty air, for how, *how*, had she come to this:

chasing ghosts on an island, marooned in the Atlantic?

Thomas never went on any walks.

He never strayed further than the lighthouse's peninsula.

That was the second story he told Elizabeth: why it was he contained himself to such a small scrap of land. He didn't *want* to tell that particular story. Eventually Elizabeth got it out of him, though: how his mother had tumbled to her eternity, back at the start of the war, at the point the peninsula joined the bulk of the island. Thomas hated going near the spot, he said; couldn't bring himself to pass it.

'Not unless I got to.'

'Did you see her fall?' Elizabeth had asked, not teasing for once: rather feeling chilled by the idea. For what a thing to witness.

'No,' he'd said, shortly.

'You don't need to snap. It was just a question.'

'I told you I don't like talking about it.'

'Were you very sad?'

'Question for you. Wouldn't you have been if you'd lost your mum?'

'I did. Years ago.'

'How?'

'A motoring accident. I lost both my parents.'

'And you weren't sad?'

'I was *upset*, but I don't recall being especially sad.'

'Why?'

'I wasn't close to either of them. And my mother wasn't particularly nice. Horribly self-obsessed, actually.'

'Mine wasn't. She didn't think much of herself. Only me.' He'd gone on, speaking of the schooling she'd given him, teaching him his letters, and numbers, and catechisms. 'No reason for it. It wasn't like she or Dad ever let me leave.' His father, especially, had always loved the island. 'Says there's no other place like it. Calls the air here nectar. I've never known any other.' He'd wanted to go to

263

school on the mainland, he'd said. Wanted siblings too. 'Never got them.' He'd frowned. 'I wanted to join up, when the war came. Mum and Dad wouldn't have it. Said lighthouse keeping was a reserved occupation . . .'

'Wasn't it?'

'Mum could have stepped in for me. Refused, though.' He'd dug the toe of his boot into the earth. 'I've been bored all my life.'

'Is that why you always watch everything?'

'That? I got to do that.'

'Why?'

'If I don't, something else bad might happen.'

'Such as?'

'I don't want to find out,' he'd replied, ominously.

The third story he relayed to Elizabeth, he told to her the same September morning she sat with him, stewing over the damned boat she'd bought.

As moods went, she was certainly in one of her fouler ones. She'd got better at recognizing her dark spells by now, if not the warning signs that another was circling. Rather, they came upon her so stealthily, filling her with such rage and panic at the sinister trespasser within her, that by the time she'd realized it was happening, she was already in too deep to see her way out. She'd find her way, eventually, of course. One always found their way out. Yet, until that happened, and light returned, any light at all felt impossible, and everything so unbearably bleak.

And, that morning, really quite frightening. Because how could she have forgotten that she'd made such a purchase? What powers had her imposter now amassed that it should have been able to create such a blank space in her mind.

There was nothing wrong with her actual memory. No, since she'd been prompted, she'd recalled everything about the order she'd placed with Mr Claymore's sailing club. She'd remembered too, quite abruptly, everything Mr Claymore had said to her about the futility of further treatment. (And should she trust him? Or get a second opinion? She rather thought she might . . .) Still, even with that onslaught of recollection, she couldn't think what had possessed her to buy a bloody boat. She'd rather ride a horse than sail a boat, and she'd always loathed riding. All that bouncing around in the saddle. It had been a deal more fun bouncing around in the stables with her instructor, before he'd been conscripted.

Now, she'd applied herself to *that*.

Would such a thing count as contributing to the war effort?

She frowned.

Laura would undoubtedly say not.

Tapping her fingernail to her teacup, she stared down at the boatshed and wondered what her friend would make of her useless dinghy inside, doomed to unuse. Would she consider it amusing? Or troubling?

Wasteful.

'Probably,' Elizabeth said, out loud, not realizing she had, until Thomas asked her,

'Probably what?'

'What?'

'You said probably.'

'Did I?'

'Yes.'

'I didn't mean to.'

'You all right?'

'Yes, yes, quite all right.'

Not wanting to dwell any more on the boatshed, she brought her gaze up to the three cottages above. Gareth was in his garden, hoeing his herbaceous borders. The Hamiltons' green door was shut, their windows closed, both of them out working: Mrs Hamilton typing with her index fingers at Delen's desk. Plod, plod, plod, *plod*. God, how her slowness must grate on James.

Elizabeth found a small smile, thinking of that.

She moved her focus to the middle cottage: the empty one, never used. It was different to the other two, she noticed: not markedly, not enough for her to have seen it before – the trio were all built from the same grey stone, in the same boxy style – but clearly older, more weathered; its paintwork, faded; its garden, overgrown.

'Was that here before the others?' she asked Thomas, pointing at it.

'It was.'

'How long for?'

'Before I was born. Your husband built the other two when he arrived. That one there doesn't belong to him.'

'Who does it belong to?'

'The council.'

'The council?' She turned to look at him, curiosity thoroughly aroused. 'What do they do with it?'

'Nothing now. My dad and me used to live there, with my mum.'

'When did you leave?'

'When your husband built the others.'

'Why?' Elizabeth asked, astounded. She hardly needed to glance back at the tiny cabin behind them, with its tin roof and steel chimney and curtainless windows, to remind herself of how inferior it was, in every, single, way, to the inferior-enough cottage opposite. 'Were you punishing yourselves?'

He didn't answer.

It was Francis who spoke.

'I think you best head home, Mrs Atherton,' came his voice, from behind.

Startled, Elizabeth turned, eyeing him.

He, arms folded at his front door, stared back at her.

Had he been eavesdropping?

It seemed fairly clear he had been.

The realization didn't anger Elizabeth.

No, it intrigued her.

What was he worried about Thomas telling her?

Determined to find out, she said, 'I don't want to go home.'

'It's still time you went.'

She turned to Thomas. 'Do you hear the way he's speaking to me?'

She expected him to spring to her defence.

But for once, he, jolting to his feet, sided with his father.

'You best had go. I've got work to do.'

That angered her.

As she walked away, burning at the thought of not only him, but his father too, watching her leave with her tail between her legs, Thomas's treachery (and no, she didn't believe that was too strong a word) angered her a great deal.

It was to punish him that she stopped at the point his mother had fallen and peered over the cliff edge, all the way down to the ocean lapping the jagged rocks below. Then, in part to punish him more, but mostly because she was curious, she headed quite purposefully *not* for the house, but the cottages, ignoring Gareth as she passed him in his garden, letting herself through Thomas's old front gate, leaving it to clang shut behind her. Circling the cottage, she approached each one of its murky downstairs' windows, holding her face close to the glass, her hand up to her eyes, narrowing them in her effort to cut through the dust and cobwebs accumulated on the inside of the panes, and see into the rooms within. To her amazement, they were furnished still, with the shapes of tables, chairs, sideboards, lamps, all discernible through the gloom. That floral tea-set must have been one of the few things Thomas and Francis had taken with them to their new bolthole. Then again, they hardly had room up there to swing a cat.

Again that question: why had they swapped this much roomier, copiously furnished place for the windswept lean-to they eked out their days in now?

He just don't like having company, Thomas had said, of Francis.

Had they moved simply to avoid having neighbours?

Elizabeth couldn't credit it. They were living in comparative purgatory. There had to have been more to it than simple introversion.

But what?

Chapter Twenty

Elizabeth

She waited to do her digging until she could get Thomas alone again.

It was a couple more days before she managed it, thanks to Francis, who became suddenly, gallingly, much more present for her visits, following herself and Thomas wheresoever they went: out to the garden; back into the kitchen; up into the lighthouse's tower. His hawking behaviour was more than enough for Elizabeth to promote him to the very top of her naughty list, and become absolutely certain that there was something he didn't want her to know. None of them spoke of the visit she'd paid to his and Thomas's old cottage, and she rather suspected, as the days wore on, that both men might be hopeful she'd forgotten all about it, which was at least an entertaining thought.

She didn't forget, though. Not like she'd forgotten about that dinghy.

She *remembered*.

And when, on Sunday, Francis went off with Mr Hamilton to church, she – first having an explosive argument with James about a white blouse that Diana had brought back from the laundry grey – returned to the lighthouse, seizing her chance to get to the bottom of it all.

*

She found Thomas up the tower, oiling the cogs beneath the pool of mercury. She crouched beside him, and still smarting from her row with James, vented her spleen, as she had so often done with Thomas, unable to properly concentrate on the matter at hand until she had. He listened, like he always did, and, once she'd begun to feel calmer, she fell quiet, watching him work.

'Rather mystical looking, isn't it?' she observed, of the liquid metal. 'One might cast a spell with it.'

'Like a witch?'

'I suppose.'

'Question for you.' He applied more oil. 'What spell would you do?'

A vanishing spell, she thought. *I'd erase this thing that's taking me over.*

'I'm not sure,' she said. 'What kind of spell would you like?'

'One to make you happier.'

'Thomas. Would you?'

'Yes.' A flush crept up his weathered neck. 'And to get you away from that husband of yours.'

'That's *very* sweet of you.'

'I don't say it to be sweet. I say it because it's the truth.'

'Oh,' she pouted. 'But what about you? Wouldn't you do anything for yourself?'

'Getting you away from Mr Atherton would be for myself.'

'*Thomas.*' Truly, she was almost touched. He'd never said anything like it before. Never so much as attempted to put words to the feelings she'd observed building in him.

Still, they'd fallen off track.

This wasn't what they were meant to be talking about.

'What about your mother?' she asked, recentring them.

Did he stiffen?

'What about her?' he asked.

'You wouldn't bring her back?'

'I can't.'

'But if you could?'

'I can't, and that's that.' He recommenced his oiling. 'We shouldn't be talking about her.'

'Why?'

'Because I don't want to.'

'Or because your father told you that you mustn't?'

'Because I don't want to,' he repeated.

She narrowed her eyes.

He really was being most displeasingly closed.

Out of nowhere, she heard Laura's laughter.

Then, her voice:

I think, dearest, that you simply detest being told, no.

When had Laura said it?

Elizabeth couldn't recall. No matter. The timing was irrelevant. What *was* relevant was that Laura had been correct. Elizabeth did hate being told no.

Despised being resisted.

Leaning closer to Thomas, her gaze on his blackened hands, testing the cogs, she made it so that her face was less than an inch from his; her body so close that she could feel the heat emanating from beneath his coarse shirt.

He still hadn't touched her. In much the same way as he'd remained silent on his feelings, so too had he restrained himself physically, keeping his hands to himself with such determination that Elizabeth had begun to think he might be afraid to let himself go. *Ravage her.*

She'd never really felt the urge to push him to do it before, nor any temptation to ravage him herself. Whilst she'd *wanted* to be tempted – for the thrill of it; the insult to James – and had teased herself, endlessly, with what it might be like to be intimate with such a rugged, brooding *working man*, the possibilities had only ever managed to intrigue her in a detached, mildly curious, kind of way.

271

Put bluntly, easy as Thomas indisputably was on the eye, he was, when it came down to it, simply too . . . troubled, too . . . *unhinged-*seeming . . . to arouse her desire, for all she'd enjoyed how sorely he'd come to desire her.

Although . . .

Was enjoy the right word?

Perhaps not.

It felt a little too light-hearted. Too *happy*.

Savoured, then? Would that do better?

Or, *relished*?

Neither of them felt quite right either.

Needed, a voice inside her suggested.

A voice of her imposter's creation?

Or her own voice?

One she should listen to?

But she didn't want to listen to it.

Didn't want to be needy.

Was she needy?

She couldn't think. Couldn't be sure. It was so unutterably hideous, this guessing game, every moment of every day, of whether one's mind was or was not behaving as one's right one. And now another part of her thinking machinery was whirring into gear.

A right part, or a wrong part?

She didn't pause to evaluate. The mechanisms clicked, and she decided, resolutely, on what she must to do to win Thomas's trust.

And – strange thought – did she, after all, want to do it for herself, too? *Need* to do it, craving a touch, any touch, because it had been so very long since she'd been touched, or held, by anyone?

It felt too pathetic to contemplate.

Not contemplating it, she placed her hand on Thomas's shoulder, dropping her chin to his other. It was bonier than she'd anticipated. It didn't feel at all like she'd imagined James's would.

And how still Thomas had turned.

She observed his oily hands, clenched now, over the cogs. Slowly, she moved her own from his shoulder, tracing the contours of his arm, all the way down to his fist: dry, and tense, and cold.

'Elizabeth . . . '

'Are you nervous, Thomas?' She felt her own heart beat a steady, plodding rhythm. Much like Mrs Hamilton at her typewriter. *Plod, plod, plod.*

But why was she thinking of Mrs Hamilton?

She turned her head, pressing her lips to Thomas's clammy, stubbled cheek.

'Elizabeth,' he repeated, voice cracking.

'You don't need to be nervous.'

'You can't want someone like . . . '

'Shhh, Thomas. I won't hear it.'

'My dad said I mustn't ever . . . '

'Be happy?'

'No. Lose control with you.'

'What's wrong with losing a little control?' she whispered, into his ear. 'Nothing, Thomas. Nothing.'

'I've never . . . '

'I know. But I have.' She moved, between him and the mercury, so that she was facing him. 'Let me show you.'

Still, he tried to resist. For several seconds more, as she unbuttoned his shirt, he stared down at her fingers and held himself rigid, unresponsive. Then, she reached for the belt of his trousers, and he groaned.

After that, she really didn't have to show him very much at all.

Could she tell it was his first time?

Yes, she could.

Pinned beneath him on the hard, lighthouse floor – her head pressed painfully against a steel beam – she tried to fool herself that he was James. But Thomas was too clumsy, extremely quick, and her imagination, much like him, wasn't up to the job.

When he was finished, he lay on top of her, heavy and panting, then raised himself up, staring into her eyes like she'd just handed him the world.

'Like that, did you?' she said.

Silently, he nodded, and shifted his weight, laying his head on her chest.

With her own head still wedged against the beam, she held him, and saw how much oil he'd got on her dress. It was a nice one, of palest blue, and now she'd have to throw it out, like her blouse. The realization annoyed her.

His failure to enquire whether she'd liked anything about what they'd just done, annoyed her.

Why *had* she done it?

'Do you miss your old house?' she asked, remembering.

'No,' he said, dozily, his defences most definitively down.

Not wanting to risk them coming back up, she proceeded with care, reminiscing about her own past houses: the country pile she'd grown up in; the London townhouse she'd sold to buy Cheyne Walk; Cheyne Walk itself.

'I left all my furniture there too.'

'Did you?' he said, and sounded almost asleep. 'We didn't leave everything.'

'No, you brought the tea set.'

'Other things too.'

'Not much.'

'Not much room, is there?'

'No.'

She let another silence fall, and drift along; his breath grew deeper, more regular.

'Who built your new cottage?' she asked, and felt him start on her chest. 'You and your father?'

'We did a bit.' He swallowed a yawn. 'Your husband's builders helped.'

'Why didn't you build a bigger one?'

'No space.'

'I suppose it must be a deal more convenient for you, living so close to work.'

'Yes.'

'And you must have had to pass that bit where your mother fell all the time before.'

He nodded. 'Didn't have no choice.'

'But that's not why you moved?'

He didn't immediately answer.

He lifted his head, more awake now, his stare no longer grateful, but guarded. 'What is this? Why do you want to know?'

'I'm curious, that's all. I feel like it might have had something to do with your mother.'

'Who told you that?' he asked, so quickly, she knew she'd struck gold.

Now her heart raced.

It galloped, in triumph.

'No one's told me anything. It did, though, didn't it?'

'No . . .'

'Thomas, you can tell me. Talk to me . . .'

But he, climbing off her, pulling back on his trousers, was, quite evidently, not about to do any such thing.

Cursing him, cursing his father – cursing the steel beam digging into her skull – Elizabeth jammed her heel painfully against the lighthouse wall, and cursed that too.

Honestly, what a waste of a good dress.

She consigned that dress to the kitchen bin before James could see it, anyone else return from church, and Chef once again eject her from his domain. Running through the house in her negligee, she went to her room, where she washed Thomas from her skin. It had occurred to her on the lighthouse floor that they were taking no precautions. She hadn't worried for Thomas; she couldn't have done him any harm, just like she'd never been able to do Dicky harm. Mr Claymore had been adamant on that matter. But, as she bathed, she pondered whether her and Thomas's rushed scramble might produce James an heir. Mr Claymore had told her she must never, not ever, risk such a thing.

He was a worrier, though.

And how furious it would make James.

The prospect gave her reason enough to permit Thomas several repeat performances through the week that followed: performances that Thomas was never anything less than eager to give, speedily, before Francis could catch them in the act. Then, in the closing days of September, she got her monthly, which enraged her – so much so that Nelle was once again temporarily removed from her service, replaced by Diana, whose mute incompetence only enraged her more – but, as soon as it was done with, she let Thomas back at it.

She had her other reasons for carrying on with him too.

First, that need – entirely shameful to admit to, and which she could hardly bear to acknowledge – to be held, *wanted*; and her hope, however reliably disappointed, that she might start to enjoy it.

Then, much more acceptably, there was the matter of her interest in Mrs Browning.

It had come to her as she'd walked home from her and Thomas's first fumble what he and his father were hiding, and that Francis must have had some hand in his wife's fall. Perhaps it had been accidental – for all Francis's myriad faults, he didn't seem the murderous kind – but nonetheless enough to get him into a deal of trouble. Thomas, Elizabeth decided, had seen it happen – it explained perfectly why he'd been so cagey when Elizabeth had asked him if he had – and Francis, terrified of him betraying some hint of it to one of their new neighbours, had removed him to the peninsula to stop him doing that very thing.

How convenient for him, really, that his traumatised son was such a neurotic, petrified of passing that point his mother had fallen. Francis (calculating, selfish Francis) must have realized he'd only become more so with each passing year that he wasn't forced to do it.

He'd trapped him.

Trapped his own son.

Imprisoned him, to gag him, so he wouldn't be imprisoned himself.

The more Elizabeth thought about it, as those September days gave way to October, the more certain she became that she was correct.

But she still needed Thomas to admit it all.

If he didn't, it would be like losing, which she abhorred, quite as much as being told, *no*. She refused to lose to Francis, who, with his long looks and sniffed insults, had more than held on to his prime position on her naughty list. She *couldn't* lose to him, not when she was so tantalisingly close to securing the means to get rid of him, like she'd got rid of Delen.

All she needed was Thomas's trust.

His *confession*.

He kept refusing to give it to her, though.

Willingly as he continued crushing her to the lighthouse floor, pumping away – *adoringly*, as he looked down at her afterwards, pressing his sweaty face to hers in a kiss – he clammed up, without fail, every time she entreated him to please just do it, for goodness sake, tell her what had *really* happened to his mother.

'I have told you,' he insisted. 'My dad would never have done anything to hurt her. He couldn't hurt anyone.'

'Then why did he bring you up here?'

'Because we're better alone.'

'No one's better alone.'

'Maybe not.' He gave her another damp kiss. 'I don't feel better without you any more.'

'That's nice.'

'You won't ever stop coming, will you?'

'No, no. Not while I'm here.'

'You can't leave.'

'I might have no choice,' she said, thinking again, much against her will, of her imposter.

And then of Laura, who'd written to say that she and Rupert had set their wedding date for the following May.

Will you come?

How unenthusiastic the enquiry had looked, in black ink.

Then, of Amy, who'd written too, mostly about her pregnancy, due to end in November, a month after James's thirty-seventh birthday, which Elizabeth had recently discovered was on its way, thanks to Mr Hamilton, who she'd overheard asking James if there was anything he particularly wanted for a gift. (What a lickspittle, really.)

Goodness, what fun it would be to surprise James with her own pregnancy as a present.

A party too?

Would that be fun?

Or madness?

And was Thomas still talking? Saying something about not being able to bear it if she did leave him?

She wasn't sure. She stopped listening again, her mind (right or wrong?) returning to the party she'd just decided to throw.

Hadn't she?

She had!

A party. She'd invite the Astleys, Laura and Rupert, stage a show of marital bliss and put a stop to Laura's naysaying once and for all. Elizabeth would write to Dicky too, get him to bring Cressida along. That way James would have to cooperate. *Act his part*. Cressida wasn't going to want to come, of course, but Dicky would have to find a way to convince her. Elizabeth could tell him that if he didn't, she'd tell Cressida of how often the two of them had spent the night together throughout their engagement.

'What fun,' she said.

'What?' said Thomas, confusedly.

'You'll see,' she told him, elated enough to deposit a kiss of her own on his lips. 'You'll see.'

My little bird,
You're late with your report. And your last one was far too short.
What is going on, over there?
What on earth is going on?

Chapter Twenty-One

Violet

May–June 1934

It was on the Monday following James's return to the island with Teddy and Cressida, that Teddy's new cot and highchair arrived from Selfridges, brought over by the boatman, Thomas's uncle Eric, with the morning post. Alan and Simon (eye now healed) fetched the furniture, which they brought back to the house with the help of the postman. The postman got no cake when he arrived in the kitchen (he didn't like to grumble, but it had been some time since he had), and nor, for once, was he greeted by Mrs Hamilton. Mrs Hamilton was in Cressida's room, supervising the installation of Teddy's cot. So, in her absence, Chef handed out the staff's mail, and, a few hours later, another woman nearly fell from Aoife's cliffs.

It was Nelle who slipped. She – who Violet now learnt had only recently returned to work after a prolonged illness – had, at lunchtime, apparently complained to Mrs Hamilton of feeling unwell, and asked to be excused for a walk to clear her head. She'd gone all the way over to the other side of the coast and stumbled where the mainland met the lighthouse's peninsula, and the subsiding cliffs had been fenced off. Gareth Phillips, out for a walk himself – patrolling the dry fields; checking his sand buckets – had seen her fall and run to help her before she could slip any further.

'She's very shaken,' said Mrs Hamilton, who came to the west wing to report on the incident to her husband – himself there requesting James's permission to proceed with repairs to the roof of the empty cottage by the wharf, arguing that if they kept waiting on the council to get to it, the roof would fail entirely. Cressida and Teddy were also present, on the floor of Violet's office: Cressida fashioning animals from scrap paper; Teddy – just risen from her first nap in her new cot – ignoring her mother's endeavours, and staring warily in the direction of Mr Hamilton and his mask. 'She's twisted her ankle,' Mrs Hamilton went on, 'and has several grazes. I don't need to tell you that it could have been a great deal worse.' She sounded shaken herself. 'I can't think why it's taking so long for the netting to arrive.'

'It's a very particular kind,' said Mr Hamilton.

'Have you chased it?'

'Yes. Twice.'

'Then while we're waiting, you'd better put some stronger fencing up.'

'The fencing is strong enough. Nelle must have got past it.'

'She shouldn't have been able to.'

'What was she doing so close to the edge, anyway?' asked James.

'Looking for the seals?' hazarded Mr Hamilton.

'She hasn't said,' said Mrs Hamilton, distractedly. 'She really doesn't seem well.'

'Does she want to go home?' asked James.

'No, she says not. I've sent her to bed with a draught.'

'Best place for her,' said Mr Hamilton.

And he, who'd do anything for his wife, except leave Aoife's, didn't reinforce that fencing either.

'It's not necessary,' he told James. 'Everyone just needs to use a bit of common sense.'

Two days later, Nelle returned to work, hobbling a little, but, according to Diana's shrugged observation, more or less back to herself.

'She's quite quiet anyway,' said Diana, rather richly.

After that, Violet thought little more of the matter. She'd never had much to do with Nelle in the past, other than when she'd come across her dusting her bedroom, and although her accident had obviously been a terrible scare for her, it had also ended well enough. No one else, to her knowledge, dwelt on it, so why should she?

Besides, she had much, much else to distract her.

You'll tell me if anything else happens? James had asked of her when they'd returned from their midnight walk.

Straight away, she'd promised, and had meant it.

But, aside from Nelle's accident, there was nothing untoward, in the month following his return, that *did* happen. Not to Violet's eyes. To *Violet's* eyes, those weeks of lengthening days and shortening nights, carrying them all towards the summer solstice, were a time of heady, unblighted bliss. The sun didn't always shine – some days it was grey, threatening drizzle, if never actually delivering it – but mostly, it was bright, and when, eventually, Violet could bring herself to look back on that short, happy interlude, *the calm before the storm*, it was always in technicolour: the golden blue of the sky; the glinting cerulean of the ocean; the luminous white of the house.

She'd known, from the moment she and James had kissed, that everything was going to change, but she hadn't for a second imagined that life could change as much as it did. She hadn't been prepared for the luxuriant joy of each morning, waking up in sheets still twisted and warm from his body, or the happiness of finding him again, waiting for her in the atrium, ready to go with her to breakfast. Or the charged delirium of the hours she spent with him in the office: hours, which, even with Cressida and Teddy so often near – even with all the work that kept pouring in from

London – nonetheless flew by in a haze of caught smiles, dizzying kisses, and the anticipation of what was coming when they were once more alone.

She'd come to realize, eventually, that she allowed herself to become too distracted; failed to take note of too much. Such as the coincidence of not only Nelle's accident, but also Alan and Simon's fight before it, having occurred within hours of a postal delivery. And the preoccupation in Mrs Hamilton's manner when she'd reported on Nelle's fall to James and Mr Hamilton. *She doesn't seem at all well.*

She became increasingly disconnected from the staff, too, seldom going down to the kitchen any more, other than to drop the office mail for collection – which she always did hurriedly, eager to return to James. In her haste, she ceased paying attention to who was, and wasn't, hovering there ahead of the postman's call, and who did, and did not, seem themselves.

By the same token, with less room in her thoughts, she afforded Diana less space, and, to her shame, noticed no warning signs of how deeply anxious Diana, already so withdrawn, was becoming. Once she'd ceased eating dinner in her room – which she did, quickly, because why would she want to be there, when she could remain with James? – she saw much less of Diana too, with the result that, little as she'd ever gleaned from her by way of insight into the rest of the household, she ceased gleaning anything at all. And although she did continue to notice the occasional anomaly in the way she found her belongings in her room (a blouse placed above a jumper in her drawer, when she'd left it below; a book positioned spine in on her shelf), they were very occasional, and by June, stopped entirely.

And what of James? Did he do as he'd proposed, and speak to Mrs Hamilton of all the things Violet had told him about on their walk?

No, he didn't.

Violet had, after all, asked him to let it alone, and he – working such gruelling hours; dealing with Cressida, and her divorce; giving his every free thought to Violet – never considered doing otherwise.

He did, however, ask Mrs Hamilton about Simon and Alan's fight. And, when Mrs Hamilton told him that she'd discovered it had all been over some girl, nothing worth bothering him with, he gladly let it go.

Ignored too much, too.

But he really was so very busy.

Both of them were incredibly busy.

And, for the first time in as long as either of them could remember, happy: intensely, elatedly, happy.

Was it really so wrong that neither of them wanted to go looking for reasons not to be?

Really, when all was said and done – given their pasts, given everything they'd each been through, and the loneliness they'd endured – who could blame them for not doing that?

Chapter Twenty-Two

Violet

They had just under five weeks, before the solstice. Such a short time, and yet so much within it that etched itself into Violet's memory. Not all of it involved James. Violet didn't become so entirely consumed by him that she forgot *everyone* else.

His sister, certainly, wasn't someone anyone could forget.

Violet grew to like her: more, the better she came to know her. Yes, she'd clearly spent her life being over-indulged by her guilt-ridden brother – every day, she appeared in a different, obviously expensive, outfit; continually, she demanded either James's, or Violet's attention, interrupting them as they worked with questions as to how much longer they'd be doing it, or what they were doing; and, when she asked Mrs Hamilton to order Teddy new toys because she'd left so many of her favourites at Harbury, she did it carelessly, with no reference whatsoever to the cost – but she never came across as spoilt. Rather, she was intensely vulnerable, constantly looking to James, as though to bolster herself with his presence. She was clever too, chatty and companionable, and did *try* to help around the office, offering to stuff envelopes, and proofread Violet's typing. She didn't remain entirely oblivious to the amount they had on.

What most endeared her to Violet, though, was her obvious love: for James, who she orbited so closely, and most of all, for Teddy, who she all but enslaved herself to.

She never did send for the nanny.

James had been quite wrong about the inevitability of her doing that.

'I can't,' she admitted, over another frustrated attempt at feeding Teddy porridge. 'She might try and steal Teddy away for Dicky.'

'How do you suppose she'd get off the island?' James asked.

'Elizabeth managed it.'

She rarely let Teddy out of her sight, and only ever then if James, or Violet, or Mrs Hamilton, agreed to watch over her. She wouldn't leave her with anyone else; certainly not Diana or Nelle.

'Nelle doesn't seem to be on the same planet as the rest of us any more,' she said to Mrs Hamilton, not long after Nelle had returned to work. 'What exactly was wrong with her when she left last year?'

'A nervous complaint.'

'I suppose that's hardly a surprise.'

'Why?' asked Violet.

'She was Elizabeth's lady's maid.' Then, again to Mrs Hamilton, 'Is she having some sort of relapse? Should she see a doctor?'

'She says not.'

'Well, I'm not leaving her with my daughter anyway. She'd probably forget she was meant to be watching her.'

'You know I'm more than happy to watch her for you,' said Mrs Hamilton, the new softness to her voice already becoming more familiar, 'any time.'

'Yes, Mrs Hamilton, I do know, and thank you. But I won't take advantage.'

She didn't take advantage.

Cressida, not Mrs Hamilton, was the one who supervised Teddy when she slept. Cressida was the one who shadowed her wheresoever she crawled. And whenever Cressida herself went out for a walk, it was always with Teddy strapped to her in a sling, and then only for short strolls through the gardens and up to the cliffs above. It was obvious how terrified she remained of losing her daughter, no matter James's reassurances that she was safe, but equally obvious, it seemed to Violet, was that there was another fear nagging at her.

'Are you worried about going near Thomas?' she asked her.

'Wouldn't you be?' said Cressida.

Feeling awful for her wandering about, aimlessly alone, too scared to stray from the house's view, Violet took to offering to go with her. Cressida always accepted. And, as the two of them walked, so did they talk. Gradually, Cressida expanded on all James had told Violet, relaying ruefully how in love she'd believed herself with Dicky ('What an arrogant simpleton I was'), then speaking quietly, clearly painfully, of her anger at how much had been hidden from her, then revealed, of her parentage.

'Can you imagine being someone who'd trade a secret like that?'

'No,' said Violet, who still couldn't.

But, encouraged by Cressida's confidences, she did, in turn, open up about her own less than straightforward past: haltingly, hesitantly, but nonetheless wanting Cressida to know that she wasn't alone; give her misery some company.

'My misery's grateful,' said Cressida. 'How's yours?'

'Quite grateful too,' said Violet, honestly.

Because although it really hadn't come easily to her, being so candid with someone she'd so recently met – or being candid at all, with anyone who wasn't James – it was a relief to do it. The shame she'd held so close felt lighter, shared.

Day-by-day, walk-by-walk, the two of them spoke of all sorts of other things: from their pasts, to their presents, to the island ('Can you truly bear it?' Cressida asked. 'For now, I can,' said Violet), to Cressida's guilt that James had done what he had to protect her, and her fury at him, still, that he hadn't just told her the truth from the off.

'If he had, he'd never have had to get married.' She bent,

picking a dandelion, holding it up for Teddy. 'Elizabeth would have crawled back into her Cheyne Walk hole.' She twirled the dandelion. 'She'd never have come here, I wouldn't have been arrested, and I wouldn't feel now like she's still inhabiting half the rooms in the house.'

'She's gone,' Violet was compelled to remind her, just as James, and Mr Hamilton had, the night she'd arrived. 'She's not in the house. She's not anywhere.'

'She's everywhere, Violet,' said Cressida, blowing Teddy's dandelion, sending seeds fluttering, and ice through Violet's veins. 'She's absolutely everywhere.'

It was the only one of their walks that Violet endeavoured to forget.

Even as they returned to the house, she was trying to force Cressida's disquieting words from her mind. They were fancy, she told herself. Pure fancy. Ghosts weren't real. They *weren't*. Whatever her own irrational fixation with Aoife, she knew, deep (deep) down, that it *was* irrational. Spirits didn't haunt the sane.

She refused to let them haunt her.

Still, she was relieved when she got to the office and found a distraction waiting for her in her pile of mail, care of Mr Barlow, who'd written expressing his *deep regret* at whatever insult he might have unwittingly paid her before she'd left his employment. *I'm sorry if you took offence at what I said.*

'It's one of those apologies that isn't really an apology at all,' she said to James, showing him the letter.

They were alone. Cressida and Teddy had been intercepted at the porch by Mrs Hamilton, who'd whisked them down to the kitchen for elevenses.

James pulled her onto his lap.

'Shall we make him send another?' he asked.

'How did you get him to send this one?'

'I simply suggested that he consider doing it. Told him you were really no fun at all.'

'You did, did you?'

'Yes. But if you want to prove me wrong . . . '

She did prove him wrong, right there on his desk; breathless, with the thrill of it.

That, she wanted to remember.

It was a few days later that she had the conversation she'd been half-dreading, half-hoping for, with Mr Hamilton.

I'm sure he has some stories you'd like to hear, James had said, when he'd rocked her with the confirmation that Mr Hamilton had not only known her father, but guessed too that she was his daughter.

James had meant nice stories, Violet knew. The kind in which her father had carried her photograph, laughed over the mis-sized socks she'd knitted him, and perhaps even kicked a football during the 1914 Christmas truce.

Fond reminisces.

Certainly not the revelation she persuaded Mr Hamilton into granting her.

She was in the atrium when he came across her. It was late May, a sunny Wednesday morning, thick with heat and the scent of cut grass from the freshly mown lawns outside. For the past half hour, Mrs Hamilton had, with Cressida's permission, been playing in the gardens' pools of water with Teddy. Violet, on the way back from her bathroom (no baby on its way; she was relieved, she was), had run into them as they'd come inside, all damp and breathless. Mrs Hamilton, handing Teddy back to Cressida, had apologised to her for how wet she'd become, and, hearing the affection in her voice – seeing the enjoyment illuminating her cool, green eyes – Violet had found herself smiling at her, and, to her shock, Mrs Hamilton had smiled back: quickly, rather awkwardly, but with more sincerity than Violet had ever had from her before.

Oddly buoyed by that smile, Violet had commented on how happy Teddy looked.

'I don't think she minds being wet at all, Mrs Hamilton.'

'She doesn't seem to, does she?' Mrs Hamilton had replied, dropping a kiss on Teddy's cheek, then laughing as Teddy had grabbed her perfect hair – her delight convincing Violet, once and for all, that beneath those pressed silk blouses of hers, a heart did most certainly beat.

A more generous heart than Violet had, for too long, given her credit for. A heart that had compelled her to hound Mr Hamilton's plastics hospital until the nurses had allowed her in to see him. One that had helped her convince him to marry her, then turned on her, bringing her to live in this place that he, not she, had been happy.

A heart that had led her to Violet's room, that long ago April morning, there to warn Violet, whatever her own grievances against her, to keep away from the lighthouse.

Violet had still been mulling how differently she'd come to view Mrs Hamilton since then, when the postman's approaching whistle had carried through the open porch. No longer laughing, Mrs Hamilton had left for the kitchen, and Cressida had taken Teddy to change.

As Cressida had gone, she'd suggested to Violet that they head out for another walk afterwards. 'It's too beautiful to be inside typing.' Agreeing, Violet had lingered, waiting for her, and, to kill time, rotated the room, once again perusing its array of photographs. Finding herself back at the one of the soldiers in France, she'd studied their faces, wondering, as she had countless times before, which, if any of them, had been the one to report her father's supposed crime.

'Have you found me yet?' Mr Hamilton asked, from across the room, appearing through the servants' door.

'I have,' she said, pointing at a very young, handsome man. It hadn't taken her long to make the connection. His eyes were just the same. And he was twice the size of everyone else. 'Where were you all?'

'Ypres,' he said, joining her. He pronounced it, *Wipers*. 'It was at the start. See how most of us are smiling? That didn't last long.'

'Who took it?'

'James. Hardly anyone here survived. He keeps it up to remember. He visited every one of their families, you know, after the armistice.'

'No, I didn't know,' said Violet, but could easily believe it.

It was the kind of thing he'd do.

Her thoughts returned to her father, this time to the reams of letters he'd written to the police and the newspapers raging over the lives James had lost under his command, labelling him a murderer, *a man with the death of thousands on his conscience, and more than capable of killing another*. Too many of his letters, far too many, had been quoted, printed. James would have read them, she had no doubt about that now. He'd have read them, and then he'd have come and tortured himself with this photograph.

'I'm very ashamed,' she said to Mr Hamilton, only realizing as she spoke that she'd resolved to. 'I want you to know how terribly I feel about everything my father did. I think about those letters he wrote, every day. Every morning, I wake up and think about that man he killed.' She turned, looking Mr Hamilton in the eye. 'I wish so much that I could have stopped him.'

'I know that, Miss Ellis. I'm sure the man your father used to be would have stopped him too.' The skin around his eyes crinkled, kindly. 'Let's blame the generals, shall we?'

She nodded, gave a small smile of thanks, and returned her attention to the photograph.

'Why isn't my father in it?'

'He'd have been somewhere else. These were all officers, apart from me.'

'Were any of them my father's CO?'

'That one,' he pointed at another young face, 'until he was killed.'

'Was he the one to report him?'

'No. He died long before. It was another private did that. He didn't make it to the end either.'

'Oh.'

'Yes.'

'I've never wished that on him.'

'No.' He sighed. 'It's what it was like there, though.'

'That's what James said.' She stared down at the picture, not really seeing it any more, but imagining her father, out of frame, polishing his boots; his revolver. 'He told me he didn't know whether my father really shot himself.'

'No one knew that, except your dad.'

'How did he get away with it, though?' She'd been pondering the matter, ever since that grey, rainy dawn when she and James had first spoken of it, and had become ever surer, in the time since, that there had to have been more to it than a benevolent judge. 'So many others were shot. He should have been shot.'

'He should, yes.'

'Then?'

He sighed again.

'Mr Hamilton, please. Just tell me what happened. I'm his daughter. I deserve to know.'

He considered it.

For several seconds.

'Please, Mr Hamilton.'

'I don't know . . . '

'*Please.*'

His brow puckered. 'You sure you want to know?'

'I am.'

'Really?' he said, sceptically.

'Really,' she replied, firmly.

'You can never tell James I told you.'

'I won't . . . '

'All right.' He nodded. 'I do think you deserve to be told the truth. I think James deserves to have you know it . . . '

It was her turn to frown. 'What do you mean?'

He let go yet another, even longer, sigh. 'James paid the judge to pardon your dad. Gave him a lot of money to let him free.'

Violet stared, stunned.

What? she might have said.

Only, she couldn't summon the word, any word.

Couldn't think.

James had bribed the judge?

'Your dad found out he'd done it,' Mr Hamilton continued, 'took it to mean that James had a sore conscience because he was the one who reported him, which he wasn't, but your dad blamed him for everything after that. Said your mum ran off because she was ashamed of him. Claimed that no one would give him work because of his record. He didn't know about this place, not until all the nastiness in the papers, but he wrote to the offices in London, all the time, asking James for more money.'

'Did he give it to him?' Violet asked, appalled.

Please don't let him have given it to him.

'Not a penny, and your dad hated him even more for it. Then James saw you at your dad's funeral, and hated himself for leaving you short, all that time.'

Mutely, she stared up at him, struggling to take it in.

She thought back to the way James had looked at her in Pentonville – that calm he'd given her, with the warmth in his eyes – and felt tears prick her own. She couldn't bear that he should have carried guilt, any guilt, over her. It made her ache, deep in her heart, that she'd done that to him. And yet she loved him all the more, too, for having cared, even then.

'Why didn't he tell me?' she asked.

'He wanted you to think that the judge believed your dad was innocent. He wanted to give you that.'

She started, hearing the east wing door open, and turned, seeing Cressida and Teddy come through it.

'You really mustn't tell him I told you,' said Mr Hamilton.

'I won't,' said Violet, still reeling.

And, knowing the pain it would cause James if she did, she kept her word.

She didn't tell him.

But, before she left with Cressida, she went to see him in the office, where he was sitting by his cold fire, working on more contracts. He looked up, seeing her, and she watched his serious expression lift in a smile.

Going to him, taking his face in her hands, looking into his dark eyes, she kissed him.

And, dropping his papers, he kissed her back.

It was another memory she held on to.

Cherished, along with everything else.

Yet, above those memories, above all else that she saw, and heard, and felt during those golden, cerulean, too short, not-quite-five weeks, there were certain times in particular that she held especially close: times that she knew, even as she was in them, would endure as some of the happiest of her life; times that she and James spent alone together, not in her bedroom, nor in the office, nor out on the fields in the pitch dark, but hidden from everyone, hidden from view, down in their rocky cavern at the base of the old lighthouse stairs.

Chapter Twenty-Three

Violet

They started going there again on the Saturday afternoon following his return, when the sun was out in full blazing force, and the water, lapping the rocks, every bit as spectacular as he'd said it could often be, all the way back on that distant wintry dawn when they'd first visited the cavern together. Unlike then, when the ocean had rolled huge and grey, it shone brilliantly, so still, so clear, that Violet, at its edge, could see the sun's rays glinting from the scales of fish darting across the seabed; the ripples of its beams, painted on stones.

Cressida, supervising Teddy's nap, hadn't asked to follow them on their walk. No one had followed them. Nor did they the next day, nor the next, nor the next, when, regardless of work, they kept returning to the cavern.

'We need to,' said James, who, on that first baking Saturday, discovered the thing that meant he simply *wouldn't* stop insisting that they down tools, if only for a half hour, to go back. 'The only way past this is through it.'

'Or we could leave it?' Violet suggested.

'No,' he said. 'We're not doing that.'

'It all started when, on that first Saturday, Violet, in observing how inviting the water looked, unwittingly prompted him to suggest they go for a swim.

'I don't have a costume,' she said.

'I don't think that matters.'

'I also can't swim.'

'Well, that matters a bit.'

She laughed.

He didn't.

'Come on,' he said, unbuttoning his shirt. 'I'll teach you.'

'No, I don't think so.'

'I do.' He shrugged his shirt off. Removed his trousers.

'Stop getting undressed,' she said, their intimacy still, at that point, new enough that she laughed, struggling to believe she was saying such a thing at all. 'I'm not going in.'

'It's not safe, you living somewhere like this and not knowing how to swim.'

'I've been fine until now.'

'That's not an argument.'

'I'm too old to learn how to swim.'

'That's not an argument either.' He, stripped down to his undershorts, turned, and dived. She, biting her lip, watched him disappear, then break the surface. Pushing his hair from his face, he swivelled, grinned, *refreshed*, and swam back to her, holding his hands up. 'Come on.'

'Is it cold?' she asked, warily, at once full of temptation, and fear.

'Not really. No, don't you dare put your toe in. You just need to do it. Wham. I won't let you sink.'

'I don't know . . .'

'Yes, you do.'

And she supposed she did, because somehow she was unbuttoning her blouse, shrugging it off, then her skirt too. Stripped down to her own undergarments, she leant forwards, placing her dry hands into his wet ones, which were definitely chilly . . .

'Ready?' he said.

'No. Count to three.'

'One,' he said, then pulled her in, and she felt her breath leave her, because the water wasn't chilly, it was freezing, absolutely *arctic*, and there was nowhere for her to put her feet.

'Oh, I hate you,' she gasped. 'How deep is it?'

'Not that deep. I'm standing. Violet,' he sought her eye, held it, 'I'm not going to let you go. Not until you tell me to.'

'I'm not going to tell you to.'

'Has no one ever taken you swimming?'

'No, I didn't grow up with a lake in my back garden.'

'It's at the front actually. Anyway, kick your legs. No, don't kick me.'

'That was for pulling me in.'

'You need to relax.'

'I can't *relax*.'

'Violet, I know you can.'

'*James*, I know I can't.'

But he wasn't having it. He held her, close, teasing her, and kissing her, and coaxing her, until she stopped shivering, and, forgetting the sheer expanse of water around them, the *creatures*, felt her muscles slowly unclench. Still holding his hands, she even managed to float.

For a second.

Several swimming lessons later, she floated like that for a little longer; several more after that, she let him let go of her, and managed to float all by herself: lying on her back, staring up at the beating blue sky.

There were times – quite a few of them – when they forgot that she was meant to be learning to swim, and, on the warm, dry rocks, became preoccupied with other endeavours. But then they'd remember, and back into the water they'd go, where, at the start of the first week in June, Violet took her first tentative strokes. Two days later, she finally gave in and submerged her head.

'How did that go?' Cressida asked, when she returned to the house.

'It could have been better,' said Violet, who still felt as though she had a nose full of salt.

'She breathed in,' said James.

'Disaster,' said Cressida.

And,

'I've got a present for you,' she told Violet, the next morning, when, seeking her out at her desk, she presented her with yet another delivery from Selfridges: a two-piece costume, imported from Paris, in bright, blinding red. 'Better than swimming in your unmentionables, I think.'

'Cressida, thank you. This is the nicest thing I've ever been given.'

'Really?' She pulled a face. 'James, did you hear that?'

'I did.'

'You might want to up your game.'

A little over a week later, and in that two-piece, Violet swam the length of the rock's shelf, quite alone, then she swam all the way back again.

'Look at you,' said James, grinning at her from the rock's edge.

'Look at me,' she said, grinning right back at him.

It was a Sunday: her favourite day of the week. The day when, much as she'd improved in the art of brushing off the cool distance that so many of the staff still treated her with – detached as she really had become from all of them – she didn't have to worry about brushing off anything, because they were all far away, over on the mainland.

The house above the cavern was, save for Cressida and Teddy, blissfully empty.

James, insistent that they needed to celebrate her triumph, returned up into it to fetch champagne.

Whilst he was gone, Violet hauled herself from the sea, squeezed out her hair, and lay down, drying herself on the toasty rocky surface.

Are you really happy here? James had asked of her, the first night they'd spent together.

Can you truly bear it? Cressida had enquired of her too, out walking.

For now I can, Violet had told her.

I can, she thought to herself now. And although she knew in her heart that she wouldn't be able to forever – that she, like Mrs Hamilton, would struggle to tolerate a life forever cut off from the world, especially in a house where it was only on Sundays that she could completely relax – in that moment, lying in her two-piece, with the sun bathing her damp skin, casting patterns on her closed eyelids, she was so incredibly, *really happy*, that it felt like enough.

She sat up when James re-joined her, watching him over her shoulder as he came out of the cliffs' shadows. Taking the glasses he handed her, she made a comment about how she hadn't drunk champagne since they'd last eaten together in London, he said that that was rather remiss of him, and cracked the bottle, letting the cork fly high into the clear sky. She watched him fill their glasses, trying to read the movement of his thoughts behind his suddenly tenser-seeming face.

'To you,' he said, raising his glass to hers.

'To me,' she said, clinking distractedly, still studying him.

He didn't look away from her. Taking a drink, he smiled, then laughed, running his hand through his damp hair, realizing, obviously, that she'd guessed there was something on his mind.

'Everything all right?' she asked.

'It's all right.'

'You're sure?'

'Yes.'

'I don't believe you,' she said, but moved anyway, leaning against his bare, warm shoulder, and felt his arm come around her.

For a little while after that, they remained silent. He ran his hand up and down her arm, she sipped her champagne, the cool bubbles fizzing on her tongue, sliding down her throat, and waited for him to get to whatever it was she felt, in her not quite steady heart, coming.

As, at length, he did.

'Do you remember telling me that you didn't want to have to change your name again?'

'I do,' she said. It had been the morning after the first night they'd spent together. She hadn't read anything into his question at the time; she'd been too worried about everyone in the house guessing that she'd become more to him than his secretary. She was sure that they must have all long since cottoned on, and she wished it didn't bother her, but it did. Just not as much, not nearly as much, as the idea of spending any less time with him.

'I don't want you to *have* to do that either,' he continued.

'No,' she said, and, at his emphasis on *have*, felt her heart quicken all the more.

She was starting to read something into what he was saying now.

'I know you said you were relieved the other week about there being no child. I was too. In a way . . . '

'A way?'

'Yes, a way.'

'James?' She moved, needing to see his face.

And he gave another short laugh, struggling, as much as she'd ever seen him struggle, to find the words.

'I don't want you to ever have to do anything, Violet.'

'I know that.'

'I need you to feel that you belong wherever I am. I want to wake up next to you every day and not have to sneak away . . . '

'I want you to do that too.' Was she smiling?

She felt like she was smiling.

She knew she was trembling. Her champagne wavered,

shimmering in her glass.

He took it from her, and, setting it on the rock, his own beside it, pulled her to him, resting his head against hers, so close that his deep, glinting eyes were all she could see.

'I don't want to have to be relieved that we're not going to have a child,' he said. 'I don't want to . . . *worry* . . . that neither of us have ever talked about the fact that we keep doing nothing to prevent one. I've never in my life wanted children, and now I can't think why that was. What could have been wrong with me . . . '

'James . . . '

'I never believed I'd marry anyone again, Violet. I didn't think it possible that there was anyone who could make me want to. But I want to marry you.'

'You do?'

'I do.'

She laughed, then breathed, and laughed again. 'Am I dreaming?'

'I hope not.'

'James.'

Why did she keep saying his name?

Her heart was threatening to burst through her ribs.

He'd asked her to marry him.

Marry him.

'Do you want to marry me?'

'Do I want to?' This wasn't a dream. It wasn't. 'What do you think?'

'I know what I hope. But I also know it's all very quick. And a big question.'

'Not that big a question. Not to me.'

'That's a yes?' he said, just as he had back in snowy London, when he'd asked her to move to Aoife's as his secretary. He'd look anxious then; wary, almost.

Now, he looked delighted.

His gaze was electric with it.

'It's a yes,' she said, kissing him, delighted, *ecstatic*, too. 'Yes, please.'

And his *smile*.

Out of nowhere, she thought of the photograph upstairs of him as a child. It had made her ache, the first time she'd seen it; his happiness had seemed so lost.

She didn't ache now.

Now, she threw her arms around him, and kissed him more, as, laughing, heart pounding too, he kissed her, pulling her down on top of him as they fell backwards against the rocks.

They stayed down on those rocks that day for hours. By the time they returned to their champagne, it had grown warm, so they never drank it, but they talked, they talked and talked, deciding, over the course of that glorious, glimmering afternoon, that they'd marry as quickly as could be arranged, and honeymoon in Tuscany afterwards.

'You must have a ring,' he said. 'I can't let my sister have given you the nicest thing you own.'

'I forgot the snow globe.'

'I think I can probably do better than that snow globe.'

'What shall we tell Cressida?'

'That we're getting married.'

'And everyone else?'

'The same.'

'Today?'

'Yes. Why not?'

By nightfall, they all knew.

Cressida, Violet went with James to tell. When, eventually, they returned to the house, they found her up on the first-floor landing, playing with Teddy by the library door.

'Thank God you haven't drowned,' she said, on all fours,

running a train around the tracks she'd had Mrs Hamilton order.

'We have news,' said James.

'Yes,' she gave her daughter a knowing look, 'we had a hunch you might, didn't we, Teddy?' Then, smiling, she stood, kissing first James, then Violet. 'Congratulations, really. I have every confidence yours will be a much longer marriage than mine. And I'll come to this wedding, James. I promise.'

The staff, though, James told alone.

'Would you?' said Violet, when, as evening fell, the clatter of them all returning from St Leonard's carried out to the atrium's veranda, where, in the lingering heat, they were sitting with Cressida and Teddy, sharing a fresh bottle of champagne.

'Fine,' he said. 'But you can't keep on like this with them.'

'I know.'

'You are allowed to tell him that you don't want to keep on with them at all,' said Cressida, once he'd gone. 'I hope you know that, too.'

'This is his home . . . '

'It doesn't have to be. Certainly not all the time.' She leant forwards, moving her glass from the reach of Teddy, who was tottering around the low table before them. 'Has he asked you if you want to go on living here?'

'It hasn't come up.'

'Perhaps you should bring it up.'

'Perhaps.'

Cressida narrowed her eyes. 'Don't be too grateful, will you? You don't need to be grateful at all.'

'He's changed my life.'

'And you've changed his.' She moved her glass again. 'What are you worried about with the servants, anyway?'

'They never talk to me.'

'They hardly talk to me.'

'They also stare.'

'Yes,' she sighed, 'I suppose I have noticed that.'

Did they stare at James when he announced that Violet was to be their new mistress?

'Some of them,' he said, when he returned. 'Not Arnold.'

'He was pleased?' asked Violet.

How eager she was to hear that he had been.

'He was.'

'And Mrs Hamilton?'

'She certainly wasn't displeased. She asked me to pass on her congratulations.'

'Really?'

'Really.'

'What about Diana? And Nelle . . . ?'

'They needed to be told, and now they have been.'

'Oh,' she grimaced, 'that doesn't sound very encouraging.'

'They were fine.' He reclaimed his seat, and his drink. 'You don't need to think about it any more.'

That night, she didn't.

That night – after they'd emptied the champagne beneath the pinkening sky, eaten an early dinner with Cressida and Teddy, and after Cressida had taken Teddy to bed – Violet went, for the first time, with him to his bedroom.

He held her hand as they walked up the stairs to the first floor, then again up the next flight to the second. They came to a wide, high-ceilinged landing, the far wall of which was, like the atrium's, all glass, with no land visible: only the panorama of the sky, pricked by the night's first stars, and the vast ocean below. The earth-less view made it feel to Violet like the house might almost be floating. It wasn't a comfortable sensation; rather, it reminded her of the vertigo she'd been struck by when she'd first come to Aoife's: that fear that this palatial building wasn't entirely safe; not entirely to be trusted in.

To her right, were two doors; to her left, just one: James's, she quickly discerned, as, still holding her hand, he moved towards it.

She didn't follow.

Rooted to the spot, unable to draw her eyes from the pair of closed doors he'd turned from, her hand fell from his.

What's wrong with your old room? Mrs Hamilton had asked Cressida, the night she'd arrived.

It's next to Elizabeth's, Cressida had replied.

'Violet?' said James now.

Turning back to him, she saw, from his frown, that he'd realized the line her thoughts had travelled.

'Why did you have her up here?' she asked. 'Why not have put her downstairs?'

'I wasn't here when that decision was made.'

'Which one was hers?'

'Why do you want to know?'

'I don't know. But I do.'

'All right.' He moved back towards her, and gestured at the door nearest the window. 'It's just a room. There's no one in it. Certainly not her.'

'I know,' she said, and she did.

Still, looking at that door, she felt her sense of instability deepen.

Should she say something?

Cressida would, she knew.

Don't be too grateful.

'Can we go to my room instead?' she asked. 'I don't like it up here.'

'Violet.' He looked pained.

'I mean it. I really don't . . . '

'At least come in first. See if you feel better inside.'

It wasn't an unreasonable request.

So, she went with him.

And she did feel better inside his room. She'd wondered about it for so long, it was a distraction, seeing it at last. There were

306

no lamps burning, but the night outside wasn't yet entirely dark; through the open balcony doors, a muted light came, bathing the four-poster bed, wooden floors, and furniture in a silver glow. The space, at once large, and uncluttered, and *his*, was peaceful.

His arms, coming around her, were reassuring.

'Can we stay?' he asked.

'All right.'

'You're the only other person here, Violet. The only person I've ever wanted here.' He stared down at her. Behind him, through the balcony doors, the lighthouse's beam skimmed the water. There was no breeze. Not even a whisper of one. Aoife, for the present, was at rest. 'You do believe that?'

'I do.'

'You must.' The skin around his eyes creased in a smile. 'You have to.'

Scooping her up, he carried her to the bed, and, as they sunk down onto it together, she closed her eyes, arching her back at the sensation of his kiss. Losing herself in his touch, she let the last remnants of her disquiet go.

She let her thoughts of Elizabeth go.

In the stillness of the night, the millpond ocean barely made a sound. The silence was broken only by a lone bird, singing, oblivious of the late hour. It was 17 June, after all. The summer solstice, *the longest day*, would come with the following weekend.

And change everything, all over again.

They're engaged?
He's asked her to marry him?
I don't believe you.
I won't believe it.
I think I'd better come and see for myself.

Chapter Twenty-Four

Elizabeth

October 1932

The party had, after all, been madness. It was far too late, though, for Elizabeth to do anything about it. The dining room was being prepared, all the guests were in residence, and what, *what*, had she imagined she was doing, inviting them to stay?

It wasn't as though any of them had wanted to come. Amy had tried to cry off, feigning anxiety over her looming confinement, which was still an entire month away, for God's sake. She'd written to Elizabeth twice with her nonsense concerns about travelling so far, compelling Elizabeth to go to the effort of writing back, talking her around. *Remember, darling, you did promise not to become a bore.* That in itself had been humiliating enough, but not nearly as shaming as the letter that had arrived from Laura the week before, making it clear that she, not Elizabeth, had been the one to guilt Amy into attendance.

I've just come from the Astleys', she'd written. *Please don't fret, they're both coming. We all want to know you're all right, Lizzie. And I might as well mention this, but you really needn't have sent all that champagne in the summer. My birthday's in January, remember? It was Amy's thirty-third that you missed. I've passed your gift on to her. We can use it to wet the baby's head . . .*

Mortifyingly, Elizabeth had wept, reading those words, at once appalled by her own mistake (of course she knew Laura's birthday was in January), and overcome by a debilitating wave of fear, and yes, jealousy too. For how could she not be jealous at the thought of Amy and Laura together, drinking *her* champagne, with not a worry to speak of in their imposter-free worlds?

That same post had brought another letter from Dicky, damnable Dicky, who, even at that eleventh hour, had still been trying to squirm out of his and Cressida's own invitation.

I can't say I trust you not to misbehave anyway and ruin my marital bliss, he'd said.

You're just scared of facing James again, Elizabeth had riposted, by return, once she'd composed herself.

In this instance, it's you who most terrifies me, he'd replied, in the next mail run.

How unbecoming, she'd written, the Monday just gone. *You'd better grow a backbone, quickly, otherwise the next letter I write will be to Cressida. And remember, you can't tell her you're coming until you're on your way. This is to be a surprise for James, and if you let Cressida ruin that, I'll ruin you both.*

Do that, and I'll ruin you too, he'd threatened in his final letter, which he'd obviously spent some time stewing over, because she'd only received it the morning before. *We shall see you on Saturday, though, with a surprise of our own.*

Ridiculously, she'd discounted that promised surprise as nothing more than another baseless attempt by Dicky to rile her. She hadn't been *pleased* that he'd finally agreed to do her bidding. It had irked her, tremendously, that he hadn't just done as he was told from the off. Worse, she'd started to panic, even as she'd tossed Dicky's letter into the fire, as to why she'd become so determined to throw this party in the first place. And, why she'd wanted Dicky, and Cressida, and everyone else, as guests.

For the fun of it?

What an absurd notion.

How could she ever have thought any of it might be fun?

Dimly, she recalled believing she might prove to Laura how happy she was, but that only felt more absurd yet. James was never going to have let her get away with such a thing, not even with his sister in residence. Elizabeth couldn't control how he behaved. She couldn't control anyone on the island. Not even, on her bad days, herself.

So, was it her imposter, then, who was to blame for this lunacy she'd set in motion? Had it once again got the better of her judgement? It felt too much of a leap – first a dinghy, now a house-party; she didn't want to believe it could have grown so influential.

She wouldn't believe it.

The idea was far too frightening to contemplate.

The dark and wild October night that she ran out into now, fleeing the house behind her with a coat thrown over her evening gown, galoshes pulled onto her feet, was frightening.

Everything she'd done and said, from the moment her and James's six guests had arrived that morning, was frightening.

And the party, which she wished she'd never conceived of, was already, at not even seven, an unmitigated disaster.

The day had, perversely enough, started well. She'd woken to her alarm, set for five, and, with no sign still of her monthly, had felt a ballooning of satisfaction. Igniting her bedside lamp, she'd dressed, then left her room. James had already been awake too, she'd seen that from the seam of light at his door, but, tempted as she'd been to go into him, get his birthday off to a bang with the news of her pregnancy – or even, at last, a touch, a kiss: one that he might, at such an early hour, be defenceless enough to respond to (she hadn't entirely given up on it) – she'd pressed on. Hastily, conscious of the time, she'd left the house, and crossed the fields for the Hamiltons' cottage. She hadn't spotted Aoife in the gathering wintry light, but the wind had already been picking up, so she'd heard her, all around, cheering her on.

She'd enjoyed that.

Enjoyed, too, the Hamiltons' bleary-eyed shock when, hammering on their green door, she'd brought them both to it in their nightrobes.

'You'd better get a move on,' she'd told Mr Hamilton, in his painted mask, which he had, thank God, taken the time to put on. (Or did he sleep in it? She'd often wondered.) 'You need to hightail it to St Leonard's. We've guests arriving into Penzance in just under an hour.'

'What?' not he, but his wife, had demanded. Her silky black hair had still been in its curlers, and her face, naked of any make-up, had looked startlingly young. She might almost have appeared sweet, had it not been for her incensed green stare.

'Guests, Mrs H,' Elizabeth had said. 'So you'd better chop-chop too. They all need rooms preparing. Cressida and Dicky can go next to me, of course . . .'

'They're coming?'

'They *are*, Mrs H.'

'Stop calling me that.'

'Stop telling me what to do, and get on with your work.'

'Don't speak to my wife like that.'

'I'll speak to both of you how I please,' Elizabeth had replied, leaving. 'And, *Mrs Hamilton*, if you'd be so good as to let Chef know that there'll be eight of us to cater for now, I'd be grateful.'

She'd enjoyed that too: the idea of Chef's inevitable panic at how he was going to feed them all. As she'd walked from the Hamiltons, she'd pictured him in his larder, counting his *ouefs*, measuring his *sucre*, weighing out his . . . No, she knew no further French. Proficiency in anything other than one's language was, in her view, simple showing off. Regardless, *ouefs* and *sucre* had been more than sufficient to gratify her.

In the bleak dawn, the lighthouse's burning lamp had still been visible, but she hadn't gone to call on Thomas, for several reasons, the most pressing of which being that she'd wanted to get home, sink some pills for the splinters of pain in her head, and, finally, invite James to his party.

She'd found him in his office: working, always working, even on a weekend; even on his birthday. She'd knocked on his door, giving him her felicitations – smilingly laying it on him that they were so shortly to have company – which was when it had begun to unravel.

He hadn't reacted like she'd planned. Hadn't lost control, nor shouted, nor railed. Just simply stared at her, with such cold, deep hatred in his dark gaze that it had taken her every ounce of resolve not to back away.

For several seconds, he hadn't spoken, and when, at length, he had, he'd done it quietly, with complete calm.

'I presume Dicky hasn't told Cressida she's coming. That's why I don't know?'

'Yes.' Elizabeth had raised her chin. 'It will have been a lovely surprise for her too.'

'You'd better not be planning any more surprises,' he'd said.

Which would have been a perfect time for her to have stunned him with her other news.

Except, it had been then that she'd felt it: that tell-tale tugging in the pit of her stomach.

Without another word, she'd left, running to her bathroom, where she'd discovered that Thomas had failed her, *again*, and in her frustration, her winding disappointment, had smashed not a plate, but her own pulsing head, with the flats of her cold hands.

The next thing she'd known, she'd been lying on her floor, without any idea of how she'd got there. A seizure? Mr Claymore had warned her that they'd almost certainly start to come, but she couldn't permit it to have happened already.

And yet somehow, she'd bruised her shoulder. Bitten her lip.

Those injuries had frightened her too.

They'd upset her, very much.

Like the cramps of her emptying womb had upset her.

They'd still been upsetting her when she'd reached the wharf, just as everyone had been disembarking Mr Hamilton's boat into the wind and drizzle. James had already been there. He hadn't waited for Elizabeth at the house, nor had he turned to acknowledge her as she'd advanced along the wharf's wet, slimy wood. His attention had been all Cressida's, who he'd smiled at, kissed, and had the temerity to apologise to, in front of everyone, for dragging her such a long way. *I'm sure you could have done without this nonsense.* Still ignoring Elizabeth, he'd turned to Laura, kissing her too, then shaken Rupert's hand, every inch the gracious host, which perhaps Elizabeth should have been grateful for, except she'd known he was doing it to madden her. It *had* maddened her. He'd even been genial to the Astleys, telling Amy how well she looked, when, to any sane person's eyes, she'd grown appallingly fat, *all over*. And how Elizabeth had loathed it, watching as Henry had helped her along the wharf to the shore, so solicitously. Rupert had made an awful fuss as well, fretting about Laura not slipping, sparing barely so much as a glance in Elizabeth's direction.

And Cressida.

Cressida.

'Are you quite all right?' she'd asked Elizabeth, at the base of the cliff stairs, frowning, as though in concern. 'I know it's only been a few months, but honestly, you've changed. I might have thought it years.'

'Might you?'

'Yes.'

'How funny. And here was me thinking that you still look young enough that Dicky should be placed under arrest. Plump too.' She'd caught Amy's eye. 'It seems to be the theme.'

And from there, the unravelling had continued, apace.

Amy, hardly one to shy away from deploying her own sharp

tongue, had, with a look at Laura, bitten it, saying nothing in response to Elizabeth's jibe. Her silence – which had all too obviously been born of a consensus between the pair of them to indulge Elizabeth, be *kind* – had only served to make Elizabeth feel all the more isolated, and determined to get a rise from Amy. As, eventually, she had. It had taken effort – she'd thrown another dig her way as they'd crossed the fields ('How one waddles when *enceinte*'), then more back in the house, over morning tea ('Maybe spare the biscuits, Amy darling') – all of which Amy had ignored, but then they'd sat down to luncheon. Chef had produced various salads and quiches (clearly he'd found enough *oeufs*), and Elizabeth, observing Amy request a slice of Lorraine, had advised her to stick with leaves.

'No wonder you were so reluctant to come, darling. Honestly, I turn my back for a few short months . . . '

'Oh, do just shut up,' Amy had snapped.

And had there been a quiver in her voice?

Henry, reaching for her hand, had certainly thought so.

James – dining with Elizabeth for the first time in their marriage – had too.

'Perhaps you should go upstairs and rest,' he'd advised her, much as he might have a troublesome child.

'I don't want to.'

'Then leave me alone,' Amy had said.

That time, there'd been no doubting the tremor.

Old Elizabeth might have felt quite sorely over it.

Ignore me, she'd have probably said. *It was a silly jest, darling.*

But old Elizabeth had been absent a while now.

And new Elizabeth was hurting.

'Tell me,' she'd persisted, 'are you giving Henry special dispensation to stray until you get yourself back on form? Or does he even need it?' She'd shot Dicky, to her right, a smile. He (who could have also done with sticking to leaves) hadn't smiled back,

315

because he'd had his mouth crammed with quiche. 'What do you think, my sweet?'

'Enough,' James had said.

'Leave Dicky out of this,' Cressida had chimed in.

'I don't want to do that either,' Elizabeth had replied.

And Dicky had chewed, frantically.

'You're miserable, aren't you, Elizabeth?' Amy had said, and Elizabeth had realized just how upset she was, from her use of her full name. 'You can't *bear* that any of the rest of us might not be.'

'Amy,' Laura had cautioned, 'let it go.'

'Fine,' Amy had said, and, pushing her plate away, heaving herself to her feet, had left.

As had Henry, but not before he'd first served Elizabeth with some choice words that she'd elected not to listen to.

'Are you happy now?' James had asked her.

'Do I look happy?'

'Lizzie, what's come over you?' That had been from Laura.

And, before she'd known what was happening, Elizabeth had turned on her, telling *her* to shut up, stop looking so smug. 'Don't you realize Rupert's only settled for you because he couldn't have me.'

'Right,' James had said, and, pushing his own plate away, he too had left.

Cressida had gone with him.

Had he asked her to do that?

Elizabeth hadn't been aware of it.

Ignoring them both, she'd felt her chest heave in shock at what she'd said.

Rupert had gawped, shocked too.

Then,

'I haven't settled,' he'd piped up. 'It's always been Laura.'

'For God's sake.'

'It's true.'

'She's a strawberry, Rupert.'

'A *what*?' Laura had said.

At which point Dicky had left the room too.

'A strawberry,' Elizabeth had repeated, appalled to feel yet more tears spilling down her cheeks. 'Inoffensive, likeable, but nothing extraordinary.'

'Lizzie,' Laura had breathed, her own blue eyes swimming. 'Where have you gone?'

'I don't know,' Elizabeth had heard herself say.

And then, hating herself, hating her own honesty, had left as well.

That had all happened at just after one.

There'd been many, many more tears in the six hours since.

At three, Diana had been the one to cry when Elizabeth, feeling much calmer for having taken another dose of tablets, and having had a short rest (*was* she becoming a troublesome child?), had risen and gone down to the kitchen. She'd broken Chef's embargo, intent on salvaging the day. She'd wanted to talk to him, civilly, about what he was planning for the meal, and ensure that Mrs Hamilton and the rest of them had everything in hand. But Mrs Hamilton – apparently catching up on some typing (plod, plod, plod) – hadn't been there, and Elizabeth had found the rest of them clustered around the table, drinking tea, eating cake (more *oeufs*), with no discernible sign of any effort being gone to for the evening ahead. Elizabeth had torn a strip off them all, naturally, rebuking every one of them in turn, and telling Diana, who'd visibly quailed beneath her stare (such a mouse, really), that she could forget about going home to her parents that night, all hands were needed on deck.

'But I always go,' she'd whimpered.

'Not tonight you don't.'

'But my dad'll be here at eight.'

'What a shame for him.'

'Get out,' Chef had commanded.

And Elizabeth had gone, gladly.

She'd expected Mrs Hamilton to pay her a rebuking visit, and Mrs Hamilton hadn't disappointed. At four, she'd arrived in her room, all pinched and angry.

'I've tidied your mess,' she'd said. 'Again.'

'You needn't have.'

'Diana looks forward to her trips home all week. You can't just rip that from her . . . '

'Well, I have.'

'No, you haven't. I've told her that she's to meet her father as usual.'

'You told her what?'

'I don't like repeating myself, Mrs Atherton.'

'How *dare* you?'

'How dare *you*?'

'I can't tolerate this.' Elizabeth had shouted it. 'I can't tolerate you.'

'The feeling is mutual, I assure you.'

'I hate you. I hate all of you. I hate this place . . . '

'Then leave.'

'I wish I'd never come.'

'Really?' Mrs Hamilton had sneered. 'You must have known what you were getting yourself into.'

'I had no idea . . . '

'Oh, please. You made this bed . . . '

'And now I have to lie in it?'

'Now, unfortunately, we all have to lie in it.'

'I'll give you something to lie in,' Elizabeth had said, realizing as she'd spoken that her threat had made no sense, which had enraged her more. She'd raised her hand, wanting to slap Mrs Hamilton again, but Mrs Hamilton had raised hers too, stopping her.

So, Elizabeth had spat in her face instead.

And Mrs Hamilton had gone home.

At six, whilst Elizabeth had been dressing, Nelle had ended

up in tears as well. Elizabeth couldn't even say how it had happened. She really hadn't said or done anything particularly out of turn to her. But Nelle, ever a wet rag, had become so terribly morose of late. Sympathising with that at least, Elizabeth had handed her a kerchief and found herself patting her shoulder, at which Nelle had first flinched, then looked confused, and, finally, cried more.

Leaving her to it, resolved to at least make amends with Laura and Amy before dinner, Elizabeth had set off for the east wing.

Cressida and Dicky's door had been shut tight. She'd heard them talking from the landing, but, focused absolutely on the apologies she'd felt choking her, hadn't troubled to listen.

James, she'd passed on the stairs.

Wordlessly, he'd moved, permitting not a brush of contact between them.

And, wordlessly, she'd carried on.

She'd heard Amy and Laura talking too, when she'd stepped into the east wing. They'd been with Henry and Rupert in the bedroom closest to the wing's entrance. Rupert had been standing at the room's door, already dressed in his evening tails, facing inwards, propping the door open so that everyone's voices inside, their cigarette smoke and perfume, had spilt out into the darkness. None of them had heard Elizabeth arrive. They'd been too noisy, speaking over one another.

Arguing about her.

Neither Amy nor Henry nor Rupert had been very nice. Elizabeth refused to let herself dwell on the things *they'd* said. Laura had been marginally kinder, fretting over how thin she'd grown, how drawn she'd turned (was it true?), and what her marriage to James – clearly the sham they'd all long suspected (had they?) – could have been about.

'Whatever it was, he's obviously had enough,' Henry had said. 'Not sure I'd want to mess with him . . .'

'I like him,' Amy had said.

'Yes, darling, you always have had a thing for the stern, handsome type.'

'No, I'm serious. I do like him. My brother likes him. He deserves better than this.'

'He does,' Laura had agreed. 'But disgraceful as Lizzie's been, so does she . . . '

'How can you say that?'

'Because she's obviously unwell. I'm not sure she can be sleeping. You must have noticed those shadows.'

'I can't say I much care.'

'Yes, you do, Amy darling.'

'No, Laura, I don't.'

Amy had been angry. Elizabeth had realized that. She'd understood it. *Preferred* it to Laura's worry, over which she, in the cold corridor, had felt at once indignant, and even more afraid.

Then,

'She is very keyed up,' Rupert had volunteered, musingly. 'Twitchy . . . '

'I rather think James has refused to bed her,' said Henry.

'Can't say I blame him,' Rupert had replied, for Laura's benefit, without doubt, and yet Elizabeth had still felt her burning cheeks work. 'Perhaps that's why she's been so detestable to you, Amy. She wants a baby too.'

'For God's sake, Rupert, women have other ambitions besides procreation you know.'

'Elizabeth has never wanted children,' Laura had added.

A truth. Elizabeth *hadn't* ever been interested in motherhood. Her own mother had hardly acted as much of an advertisement for the role. No, her desire to make a child had been purely about James. Or, perhaps, not purely that. Perhaps, she'd felt another need too: to hold an imposter that was living, not killing, within her.

Was that terribly selfish?

'Still,' Laura had gone on, 'heaven knows how she's going to react when she finds out Cressida's expecting.'

And Elizabeth had felt as though she'd been struck.

Spinning on her heel, she'd left, slamming the wing door behind her (let them all know she'd heard their poisonous chatter), then headed back upstairs, taking them two at a time in her fury that Cressida, *Cressida*, should have been granted a living imposter, care of Dicky. *Dicky*.

A surprise, he'd promised Elizabeth.

It wasn't right.

Wasn't fair.

Resolved to redress the balance and finally do as she'd wanted to for a very long time, erase Cressida's happiness from her, she'd steamed into Cressida's room.

Cressida had been on the bed, Dicky with her, his podgy hand resting on her stomach.

'What do you want?' Cressida had asked of her, rudely, quite calmly, no inkling of the pieces Elizabeth had been about to shatter her world into.

Dicky, though, jumping to his feet . . .

He'd misbehaved enough to be worried.

Elizabeth had relished that.

'I gather congratulations are in order,' she'd said, throwing Cressida a smile. 'Although, darling,' her blood had coursed, 'I hope the baby doesn't kill you, like you killed your mother.'

That had got her.

Cressida had turned ghastly pale at that.

'Leave,' Dicky had commanded.

But Elizabeth, going nowhere, had only just begun.

'Have you ever wondered, Cressida, if you killed your father, too. All that grief you caused him. Although,' she'd tsked, 'Papa Atherton wasn't really your father at all, was he?'

'What do you mean?' Cressida had asked, or rather, whispered.

She'd been sitting upright by then, clenching the blankets beneath her, as though for balance.

'I mean,' Elizabeth had said, taking a step towards her, 'that you're not really an Atherton.'

'You're lying,' Dicky had said, with a vehemence that had done nothing to disguise the jolt of shock, and confusion, Elizabeth had caught in his eyes. Again, it had pleased her. Clearly, he really hadn't had an inkling about Cressida's true father. 'She's lying,' he'd insisted to Cressida. 'She's a liar . . .'

'Takes one to know one,' Elizabeth had countered. 'But in this instance, I'm not. Ask James if you don't believe me. He's been determined to keep it all secret. You may as well know my helping him with that is how we came to be married. You see, Cressida's real papa ended his days behind bars. Couldn't take no for an answer, forced himself on her and James's poor mama . . .'

'No,' Cressida had said, even quieter than before. Barely audible. She'd stared at Elizabeth, so still, and Elizabeth had known it wasn't really herself that she'd been seeing. No, she'd been picturing her mama. The crime that had given her life. Slowly, she'd shaken her head. 'It's not true . . .'

'Of course it's not,' Dicky had blustered.

'But it is,' Elizabeth had insisted, and knew that Cressida had believed her, because her eyes had, gratifyingly, filled with tears. 'How she must have loathed carrying you, Cressida. A little viper in her nest.'

'Stop . . .'

'Do you think she worried about whether she'd ever be able to love you?' Elizabeth had continued, twisting the knife. 'I expect she must have.'

'That's enough,' Dicky had said, moving now, around the bed, towards Elizabeth.

'You killed her, Cressida,' Elizabeth had persisted, moving too, away from Dicky. 'You never even gave her the chance to try and love you.'

'Stop,' Cressida had repeated, pathetically.

'James's father didn't love you either,' Elizabeth had gone on. 'He never so much as laid eyes on you. Not once. He only left you all that money because he felt bad for you, the babe of a rapist . . . '

'Get out,' Dicky had said, altering course.

Again, Elizabeth had dodged him.

'You mustn't worry about Cressida's inheritance,' she'd told him.

'I'm not . . . '

'Good, because it's quite safe. Well, unless Cressida divorces you, of course.'

He'd stopped.

Stared.

And she'd smiled.

Before her eyes, he'd turned as pale as his child bride.

'Leave,' he'd said, voice cracking. 'Now.'

'I want to stay,' Elizabeth had replied, smiling more, her final blow ready.

For a second, she'd held it hovering above them both, enjoying herself, however briefly, for the only time that night.

She'd looked from Dicky's sickened face, to Cressida's frozen one.

Then, as a single tear had escaped Cressida, riding her cheekbone, and dropping onto her fisted hand on the sheets, Elizabeth had let the blow fall.

'You'd better hope, Dicky darling, that Cressida never finds out how many nights we spent together through your engagement. Oh,' she'd slapped her hand to her mouth, 'did I just say that *out loud*?'

'Get *out*!' not Dicky, but Cressida had screamed, at a shocking volume.

Quite loud enough to have alerted James, who'd appeared just as Cressida had been clambering to her feet, shakily, like a drunk deer, pushing Dicky away, even as he'd moved to her, reaching out, pitifully, to hold her.

'Don't be too hard on him,' Elizabeth had told Cressida, feeling James's grip close around her own wrist (a touch, at last!), 'he really couldn't help himself. And he always talked about you in bed. He never forgot you . . . '

'What have you done?' James had said, swinging her around to look at him. And God, he'd been livid. She'd seen him so before, of course, but not like this. Never like this. The muscles in his face had strained with his rage; his dark eyes, trained on her, had been murderous. 'What have you *done*?'

'Simply shared some overdue truths,' she'd said, eyebrow arched, not wanting to betray how, in the face of his fury, her enjoyment had, abruptly, evaporated, replaced by a crashing realization of the power she'd just bankrupted herself of.

He'd realized, though.

Oh, he'd realized.

Stopping only to cast his by then sobbing sister a very different kind of look – of pain; *love* – he'd dragged Elizabeth out on to the landing.

'I want you out of here tomorrow,' he'd said, pushing her from him. 'I'll start divorce proceedings on Monday.'

'James,' she'd begun, with no idea what to say next.

He'd interrupted her anyway.

'It's over, Elizabeth. You should start packing.'

'I'm not packing.'

'You damn well are.'

'I'm damn well not.'

And she hadn't packed.

She'd run.

Now here she was, in her overcoat and galoshes, stomping through the dark, whipping rain.

She didn't know what she was going to do. Not yet. She was still thinking on that. But she did at least know where to go.

There was only one place left that she *could* go.

The lighthouse.

Chapter Twenty-Five

Elizabeth

She felt no relief, approaching the lighthouse that night. On the contrary, the closer she drew to its tall, overbearing silhouette, and white, swooshing beam, the colder, and more manic, her already thrashing heart became. Its beat was erratic: no plodding, but a frantic protest. It had dawned on Elizabeth as she'd left the fields what it was that she now needed to make happen, and although the wind had howled, buffeting her with Aoife's support, *yes, go, go,* it was clear her heart still needed some convincing.

She hadn't belted her overcoat. It flapped open, her gown beneath it wet through. Her face was slick with rain, her neck too, and her diamond choker slid, bouncing uncomfortably. (She must really have lost weight.) Reaching up, she detached the necklace, then, pocketing it, ploughed on.

It had been almost a week since her last visit to the lighthouse, the Sunday before. There'd been a scene that afternoon, care of Francis, who, cottoning on at last to his son's new recreational pursuits, hadn't, for once, gone to church, but had instead been waiting to intercept Elizabeth on her way to Thomas, stopping her at the exact point his wife had fallen to her death. He'd wanted to ban her from the lighthouse just as Chef had tried to ban her from the kitchen. (Really, all these men presuming she'd permit their will to take precedence over her own.) She'd told Francis to go to hell, he'd told her to leave his boy alone, find someone else to alleviate her boredom with, at which she'd laughed, because what had her clinches with Thomas been, if not the sweaty, desperate definition of boredom?

'I'm begging you,' Francis had persisted, his long white hair flying in the gusty October afternoon, 'stop this, before he ends up hurting any more than he has to. He was happy before.'

'He wasn't *happy*.'

'Settled, then. You're going to break his heart. He thinks you love him.'

'Francis, stop.'

'Stop what?'

'Pretending that you care. I know it's only yourself you're worried about.'

'*What?*'

'You're terrified that he's going to tell me.'

'Tell you what?'

'That it was you who killed your poor wife.'

She'd gone on, enlightening him with everything she'd then been so sure to be true: that he himself had been behind Mrs Browning's fall, and had moved Thomas up to the lighthouse to ensure Thomas never betrayed his crime to their new neighbours. At some point in her diatribe, it had come to her that she might, after all, have got it wrong; it had been Francis's incredulous frown that had stirred her into doubt; the disdain in his creased face.

Oh, dear, she'd thought.

'How dare you?' he'd said to her, just as Mrs Hamilton had, *so many times*. 'I loved my wife. I wasn't anywhere near her when she fell. It was Thomas saw her go.'

'*He* pushed her?'

'No one pushed her.' He'd yelled it, so defensive it had made her suspect she might just have stumbled on the truth.

327

Could she have, though?

Could Thomas have killed his mother?

Her right or wrong mind had struggled to decide.

But, as Francis had talked more, she'd listened without further interruption, too intrigued, in that moment, to want to hear anyone else's voice but his, even if that had meant swallowing her own. He'd told her that before his wife had fallen, she'd argued with Thomas; he'd been trying to convince her to help him enlist. 'We couldn't let him try. What if some recruiter had agreed to have him? He wouldn't have survived five minutes.' When Thomas had grown angry, his mother had left their cottage for the lighthouse to fetch Francis, and Thomas had followed her. It had been raining, and she had, according to Francis, slipped. 'Didn't die straight away neither,' Francis had said. 'The two of us got her back up, into her bed. She lived for a week before she went.' His eyes had grown glassy. 'Thomas blamed himself, but she didn't. Called him her sweet boy.'

'Sweet?'

'He was, as a little one. No one sweeter.' He'd stared. 'Changed, though, didn't he, when he got to working age. Started with his nightmares . . . '

She'd frowned. Thomas had never mentioned having nightmares to her.

'Bad ones,' Francis had gone on. 'Got to seeing things, too.' (Again: news.) 'All his mum wanted was to know I'd look after him once she went. Make sure he didn't give off to anyone that he might have hurt her. Protect him.'

'So, you incarcerated him up here?'

'I moved him, yes. And now,' his craggy face had twisted, 'I'm telling you to keep away.'

She had kept away. Not because Francis had asked her to. Absolutely not. But because what he'd told her had unsettled her. Horrified her, really. For how could it be that she'd permitted the many, *many* liberties she'd by then granted Thomas, to a madman? And not just any madman, but a *working* madman.

A *lighthouse keeper*.

One who still required a parent to soothe him from his nightmares, and who she'd no longer believed she had any need for. Because *he* couldn't help her punish his father. No, it seemed he'd never had it in his gift to do that. And she'd already indulged him more than enough on the lighthouse floor. At that stage, her monthly still hadn't come; she'd considered her pregnancy a *fait accompli*. So, pushing Thomas from her overtaxed thoughts, she'd concentrated them on James's party.

That damnable party.

Squelching in her galoshes towards the lighthouse, clenching her choker inside her pocketed fist, she pictured the scenes unfolding back at the house behind her: Dicky, forlorn, ejected from Cressida's room; James, writing to his lawyers; Amy rolling her eyes at so much messy emotion; Laura shaking her head in sorrow.

Lizzie, where have you gone?

'It doesn't matter where I've been,' Elizabeth told not her, but Aoife, now sending mist swirling around the lighthouse walls. 'It's where I'm going that counts.'

And with that, she pressed her shoulder to the lighthouse door; it hurt, bruised from her incident in the bathroom earlier (had it only been that morning? How long ago it seemed), but she rammed against the wooden door anyway, until it gave. Then, she climbed the pitch-dark spiral stairs.

It was Francis's assistance that she really needed that night. Thomas wouldn't be any use; even if he could bring himself to leave the peninsula for her, he'd never manage the rest of it. Apart from anything, he, who she didn't doubt was in love with her, wouldn't be able to bear it.

Francis, though, who'd made no secret of wanting her gone, would. Nothing would give him more joy than to help her leave the island.

But she wanted to talk to Thomas first.

She did, after all, need one more thing from him.

He was delirious to see her.

'Elizabeth,' he exclaimed, rising from where she found him sitting on the lighthouse floor, his head pressed back against the wall, his vacant eyes on the lamp. They glowed with feeling as he took her in: delight, relief; such *gratitude*.

She'd have to have been a monster not to feel *something* at the sight. And she wasn't a monster. She *wasn't*. Hadn't she given Nelle that kerchief earlier? Patted her shoulder?

'I've missed you,' she gave to Thomas now. 'I've missed you so much.'

She didn't say it to butter him up for the act she was about to ask of him. Her words were, genuinely, for his benefit. She didn't want to leave knowing she'd broken his heart.

What an appalling thing to have to carry on one's conscience.

He opened his arms, and she went to him, granting him a kiss. And perhaps that was a little for herself too. For she held on to him as he held her, stealing comfort, however slim, from the pressure of his chest, the warmth of his embrace.

She was so very cold.

'I need your help, Thomas.'

'What with?'

'Just a small thing.'

'I'll do anything.'

'Thank you, Thomas.' Was she crying again? 'Thank you.'

*

She'd resolved, as she'd left the rain-sodden fields behind, that she wouldn't let James divorce her. She couldn't. She found it hard enough to bear the mortification of his rejection privately, let alone having it made public. She couldn't permit the leak of any detail pertaining to their marriage: not her imposter, not James's misery, and certainly not that she'd had to blackmail him into wedding her in the first place. (Had she truly done that? How desperate it felt in the cold black of night.) She'd expected him to fall in love with her, of course, and whilst she wasn't sure when, exactly, her belief in that eventuality had disappeared, it was long lost to her now.

Over, as James had said.

He'd caused her more than enough pain with his stubbornness. She refused to let him ruin the rest of her life. She planned to live a long time yet (what did Mr Claymore know? She *would* get a second opinion) but couldn't conceive of doing that humiliated.

She wouldn't.

The issue was, of course, that everyone back at the house already knew far too much. She didn't trust any of them not to use it against her, start spreading malicious gossip. Or perhaps she was being unfair to Laura. Laura really did seem to still love her.

And why not, after all?

Yes, Elizabeth had fallen off form of late, but for years they'd had such fun together. Such happy, easy fun.

Now when had *that* fallen by the wayside?

On the night of Dicky and Cressida's engagement?

Or before that hideous event?

Elizabeth had an uneasy suspicion it might even have been before . . .

No matter.

The point was that, since 1919, the pair of them had been one another's everything. That kind of friendship didn't just disappear. No, Laura, Elizabeth could depend on.

But Rupert, Henry and Amy had all turned. Dicky assuredly had too. Cressida was Cressida (*Cressida*), and James, Elizabeth had played her hand with. She had nothing left in reserve with which to control him, or silence any of them, so what choice did she have but to create something?

Something that would mean none of them would ever breathe a word of ill-feeling about her to anyone, because they'd be too scared of incriminating themselves. The same something that would, with a fair wind, leave Cressida in a great deal of trouble.

Elizabeth's plan was a simple one. She was going to disappear. Not for ever. Just for a few days. Enough time for everyone to become terribly worried about where she'd gone, and for those that needed to, to remember how much they loved her. The police would be called in, they'd all of them bear false witness, perjuring themselves, James included (*I've no idea what could have compelled her to run off like that. I'd never want to do anything to harm her. I love her, dearly . . .*) from which it would be impossible for them to backtrack without risking prosecution. Cressida – who'd stolen Dicky, ruined Elizabeth's wedding day, and unquestionably warped her brother's mind against her – would have a particularly unpleasant time of it because Thomas was going to arm the police with both motive and evidence to arrest her on suspicion of doing Elizabeth harm.

'You're to tell them that you ran after me when I left here because you were worried about me,' Elizabeth instructed him. 'Say that you saw us together, and that Cressida shouted at me, then I walked away, and she followed. Say you presumed we were heading back to the house and never imagined anything terrible could come of that . . . '

Once Cressida was safely in the clink, Elizabeth would emerge with some kind of story about a fall or a concussion, or . . . she wasn't sure. She hadn't properly thought that bit through yet. Candidly, there were several components of her simple plan that she hadn't yet fleshed out (such as where she was going to hide whilst she disappeared, and what she was going to do for clothes and food and money), but that would all come to her, she had every confidence. The important thing was that when she did emerge, she only *wouldn't* implicate Cressida in her injuries if James agreed to drop his nonsense about a divorce.

'Then I'll be back here with you,' she assured Thomas. 'It will be like nothing ever happened.'

It was a lie. She didn't intend to ever live on this cursed island again. She'd claim to anyone who asked that she was too traumatised after her accident (whatever it was going to be), and find somewhere else to establish herself. Somewhere with shops and restaurants and *life*. Not London, though. Or at least, not until she was better. It was too much of a goldfish bowl. She wasn't sure where she should go. Oxford? No. Not there. Mr Claymore really was an insufferable pessimist. She needed to find that second opinion.

So many things to do.

Setting them aside, she focused on the matter of the moment, which was getting off the island without detection before James could set his divorce wheels in motion.

She told Thomas, as she stood in his arms, that Cressida was behind James's threats to divorce her.

'I only told *her* everything about her parents because she told James about you and me.'

'How did she know?'

'She guessed.'

'How?'

'I don't know. What does it matter?'

'Don't suppose it does.' Around them, rain thrashed the lighthouse's windows. *Hurry up*, counselled Aoife. *This is taking too long*. 'Question for you, though,' said Thomas, over her. 'Why not let him divorce you? We could marry then, you and me. Be happy.'

333

'No, no,' she said. (*No, no,* Aoife screamed.) 'I couldn't live here with you. Not with James so close by.'

'I could leave. Go with you now.'

'Thomas, I can't take you with me. What about your father? What would he do?' She didn't give him time to consider. 'And how would you even manage to leave this place?' Again, she left no pause. 'The only way for us to be together is for James and me to stay married. You surely understand that?'

He struggled to.

It was too irksome, how intransigent he suddenly became.

But she gave him more kisses.

Slowly, *taking too long*, she convinced him.

He still didn't want her to go from Aoife's, though.

'I'm scared,' he said, squeezing her.

'You don't need to be.'

'I can't know you're somewhere else, not here.' His arms grew tighter. 'I can't.'

'It's only going to be for a few days.'

'That's what you say now . . . '

'Thomas,' she said, struggling to keep her impatience from her tone. Struggling for breath too, in his hold. 'Please . . . '

Downstairs, the door creaked open.

Heavy footsteps on the stairs followed.

Francis.

It was the first time Elizabeth had been grateful to know he was on his way.

Thomas released her, she gathered herself, and Francis appeared, lumbering through the doorway, filling what remained of the small space.

He'd got wet outside. His clothes smelt of damp wool, and stale tobacco. Raindrops beaded his hawkish nose.

'What's going on?' he asked.

'I'm leaving,' said Elizabeth, still a bit choked. 'With your help.'

334

'Are you now?'

'Yes,' she said, and told him the rest: how, shortly, she was going to make her way down to the boatshed, there to wait for him to join her, *unseen*, and sail her away to the mainland in her dinghy.

'And how am I meant to do that in this weather?' he asked. 'Without any light.'

'I'm sure you can devise a way if it means getting rid of me.'

'You're set on coming back, though.'

'I am,' she agreed, for Thomas's benefit rather than his own, because without Thomas's cooperation with Cressida, none of it would work.

It was Thomas's shadowed face that she studied for a reaction to her words.

His nod of compliance that she drew satisfaction from.

She didn't look at Francis, so had no idea what he made of her assurances that she'd go on living on the island.

For the time being at least, she really couldn't have cared less.

She noticed Gareth Phillips at his lit window as she left the peninsula, and knew that he was watching her, but also that he conveniently lost interest, pulling his curtains shut. Erring on the side of caution anyway, she detoured inland, past the rain-swept dairy, and returned to the coast on the far side of the cottages.

There, she stopped, hearing, over Aoife's lament, a chugging engine. Frowning, shivering, she peered out into the darkness, her eyes settling on a lantern-lit boat, approaching through the swell. It took her a moment to realize who it could be, but then she had it: it was Diana's fisherman father, of course. Frown deepening, she wiped rain from her face. Damnable Diana and her damnable Saturday nights off.

Also, this damnable weather, and the damnable waves.

They looked a great deal bigger to her, now that she was about to set forth on them.

In a dinghy. With no light.

Was it madness to do that?

Her right mind seemed to think it might be.

Had Francis said something about it?

Been worried?

She didn't think so. She certainly couldn't recall anything.

Where was Francis, though?

She was shivering uncontrollably. Her teeth were chattering. She tried to clench them to stop them, but bit her tongue instead, tasting blood. She needed to move, warm herself up, but where to?

Not the stairs.

Diana couldn't be far away.

Here was Francis at least, loping towards her.

He'd come the long way around as well.

Did anyone see you? she wanted to ask.

But the words didn't come.

She couldn't seem to move her lips.

Or her eyes.

She was staring.

Staring, staring, staring, at Francis, approaching her fast now.

It was her last conscious thought.

And then, there was nothing.

When she came around, the world around her looked narrower. Blurred and tiny. Her eyes, which hurt, wouldn't fully open. Her cheekbones hurt. Her hip hurt.

Her head *hurt*.

She was wet. Still very cold.

Still outside. Rain battered her face, stinging her broken skin.

Where was she?

She moved her fingers (that hurt) and felt sand. Dimly, she became conscious of the crashing of waves. Wincing, tilting her head, she looked around her, and found that she was lying in a small cove. In the distance, Diana's father's boat was sailing away from the island, back towards civilisation.

Gone already?

How long had she been unconscious?

And what had happened?

Where was Francis?

As if in answer, a wrinkled face peered over her own.

'You pushed me,' she said, and it hurt, it *hurt*.

'You fell.'

'No, you pushed me. I saw you . . . '

'You went into convulsions . . . '

'Don't be ridiculous.' It came out *rithicilush*. 'Why would I have convul . . . convul . . . ' No, that wasn't happening. She gave the word up for lost. It was an awful word, anyway. 'You pushed me.'

'I didn't push you.'

'You did.' Now she had him. Now she could make him regret the shameful way he'd treated her. 'Just like Thomas pushed . . . ' She broke off.

What was she trying to say?

Who had Thomas pushed?

'Thomas never pushed his mother.' (That was it.) 'I never pushed you.' He sounded panicked. *Me thinks he doth protest too much*. 'You need to stop this nonsense.'

'It's not nonsense.' *Nonshense*. 'Wait until I get to the police.' She made to move. Her hammering head swam.

'You're not going to the police.'

'Yes, I am.' She got to her feet. The whole world was swaying. 'I am . . . '

'You want to go away, remember?'

Did she?

337

Yes, perhaps she did.

Francis talked on, telling her how she'd never belonged on the island, never could, and never would, and another recollection came to her, hazily: that it was Cressida who she most wanted in trouble that night.

She was the one who really belonged at the top of her list.

But now Francis, in close second place, would benefit from Cressida's downfall, too.

If only she could find a way to punish them both. And Mrs Hamilton, and Nelle, and average Alan, and . . .

Who else?

There were too many people who'd done her wrong. She couldn't seem to hold them in her thoughts. They leaked through her skull, and she raised her swollen hands, clutching her head, trying to stop them, but they kept going, oozing through her fingers.

And now she was staring again.

At Francis.

Who really did look panicked.

And then, nothing.

When she woke again, it was to more rain landing like grit on her face, and a swaying sensation beneath her. She appeared to be in a great deal of pain, and lying in some kind of dinghy, with a full sail above her: hauntingly white beneath the heavy night sky.

Where had the dinghy come from?

Had she bought it?

Yes, yes, she had.

Mr Claymore had told her she should get one. Learn to sail. *A new hobby might be just the thing.* What preposterous advice, really.

And she never had learnt.

So, what was she doing out on this dinghy alone, with what felt

338

like a badly battered face, and ribs that turned to shattered glass every time she breathed?

She tried to push herself up, and, at the agony of the movement, sobbed.

In a rush, the events of the night came back to her, and with them the realization that Francis had done as she'd asked, got her off the island, just not with him.

He'd pushed her off alone.

In a storm, in a dinghy that she had no idea how to sail.

Now he was back at the top of her list again.

He was right at the very top.

She just wasn't sure any more that there was anything she was going to be able to do about it.

ELIZABETH ATHERTON'S COAT FOUND

In a grim development, the remnants of a tailored overcoat - since identified by James Atherton as a close match to the one his wife was last seen in - were discovered yesterday, washed up a mile west of St Leonard's.

The police have now confirmed that they are officially treating Mrs Atherton as missing, presumed dead.

My patience has run thin.
It's just about run out . . .

Chapter Twenty-Six

Violet

June 1934

The solstice that year fell on the penultimate Friday of June when, at dusk, Aoife's Bay was to empty, the staff crossing over to St Leonard's to celebrate the longest day. It had been from James that Violet had first learnt of the annual festivities held in that harbour hamlet: the bonfires, music, and dancing that people travelled from miles around to be a part of. He'd mentioned it as something that she might like to cross over to the mainland for, too.

'You've been on the island for almost three months now. You must be ready for a change of scene.'

She was.

There was some uncertainty, though, right up until the day of the solstice itself, as to whether the celebrations should be permitted to go ahead in their full traditional glory. The bonfires were the main concern. The weather, dry for so long, had left the countryside like kindling.

'Any wind, and it will be off,' said Mr Hamilton, who heard as much from the builder's merchant he visited on the Thursday, collecting materials to fix the Brownings' old roof. 'Can't risk the sparks.'

But there was no wind that Friday.

The June morning dawned still and clear, and static with heat. In an effort to keep the house cool, all the doors and windows were left open. A gull, drunk on flying ants, flew into the dining room at breakfast, just as Alan was bringing in fresh toast, and caused havoc in its panic, battering itself against the wall, then the table, making Teddy scream, all before knocking itself out against Alan's head.

'You all right?' asked James.

'Yes, Mr Atherton,' Alan said.

The postman came not long after, and when he did, his whistle travelled through the open windows too, not flying, rather drifting, flat and limp in the close, sticky air.

He brought another private and confidential letter with him. Not for James this time, but for Cressida. Mrs Hamilton found Cressida with it out on the atrium veranda, where she'd taken Teddy to play in the shade after breakfast. Once Cressida read it, she came direct to Violet and James in the office.

James was at his desk, and Violet was at hers. She was tired. She'd struggled with sleep again that week. The heat hadn't helped. Nor had it that, ever since Sunday, she'd continued to spend her nights in James's room. The staff were all scandalised, engagement or no, she didn't doubt it, but it wasn't their disapproval that had kept her up. No, it was her disquiet: that same unease she'd felt the first time she'd gone with James to the second floor, and which, even in his room, had continued to haunt her, waking her, regularly, as he slept.

The night before, not long before dawn had broken, she'd found herself rising and silently padding from his room, out to the landing beyond. She'd stood at Elizabeth's door, thinking about opening it, and then, pulse racing, *had* opened it. The room inside had naturally been empty; no red-headed ghost sitting on the bed. It had been stuffy too, airless and overly warm, and Violet had felt sweat bead beneath her robe. Moving further in, the furniture hulking around her, shadowy and unused in the moonlight, she'd approached the bureau, her strained reflection staring back at her from its mirrors. Reaching out, she'd taken the doors by their handles and, heart racketing, opened them. She'd expected to see clothes and shoes inside, but had found nothing but an empty cavity. Not even a trace of perfume.

'Her friend Laura took everything,' James had said, making her jump by being so suddenly behind her.

She'd turned, facing him, and he'd frowned: perplexed, and yes, impatient too.

'What are you doing, Violet?'

'I wanted to see.'

'Why?'

'I don't know.'

And she hadn't known.

But as she'd gone with him, back to his bed, where neither of them had slept again, or really talked, she'd kept thinking of what Cressida had said to her, when they'd been out walking.

She's everywhere, Violet. She's absolutely everywhere.

She'd wondered if she'd ever manage to forget those words.

She'd started to fear she might never be able to forget Elizabeth.

Not in this house, anyway.

Not her. Not Aoife.

'Someone's helping him,' Cressida said now, slamming into the office, and her letter on James's desk. She had Teddy on her hip. There was a trail of sweat snaking down the back of her pale-green dress. 'Someone has to be helping him.'

'Helping who?' asked James.

'Dicky.'

The letter had been sent by the solicitors he'd apparently gathered the means to instruct. James read it, and as he did, Cressida turned to Violet, filling her in on the letter's contents: specifically, that not only had Dicky retracted his agreement to testify to his own infidelity so that she might divorce him, he'd also threatened that, unless she and Teddy returned home to Harbury directly, he himself would divorce Cressida on

344

grounds of abandonment and sue for full custodial rights to their daughter.

'What a lovely man,' said Violet. 'Really.'

'I can't imagine who he thinks he married,' said Cressida, her dark eyes flashing. She'd become, in her fury, a different person entirely to the Cressida Violet had grown accustomed to. Teddy observed it as well. That much was obvious from the unblinking awe with which she looked up at her mother.

James, in contrast, seemed entirely unfazed by this version of his sister before him. He, focused on the letter in his hands, had clearly met her before.

Violet had encountered her too, of course: those photographs in the atrium. She wondered what Dicky would make of it that he'd triggered Cressida into rediscovering that version of herself now. He'd be rather worried, she suspected.

It was a good thought.

'How can he believe I'll go running back?' Cressida demanded. 'Play the chastised wife. I won't. I can't . . .'

'Of course you can't,' said James, setting the letter down. 'He'll be bluffing. We'll sort it out.'

'What if he's not bluffing?'

'Then we'll sort that out too.'

'You're not worried?'

'Not especially, no. It's Dicky, for God's sake. We can handle him.'

He left directly for Penzance, there to contact Edwin Firth, instructing him to notify Dicky's creditors that they'd be receiving none of their promised payments, and asking him, too, to get to the bottom of whether Dicky really did have another source of funds and, if so, who that was.

Violet didn't go to the mainland with him. It wouldn't have felt right to leave Cressida alone, and sure enough, the instant she offered to stay on the island with her, Cressida accepted. They

345

agreed that the three of them – herself, Cressida and Teddy – would head over later with the others, in Mr Hamilton's boat, and meet James for the festival.

'I don't want Teddy to miss it,' Cressida said, resting her cheek against her daughter's black curls. 'She'll love the music. I'm not going to let Dicky ruin her fun.'

Violet went with James to see him off from the wharf, where his runabout was already out of the boatshed, on the water, fuelled and ready for the evening. It had been a while since she'd crossed to the other side of the island. *Thomas's side*, as she'd come to think of it. She had, much like Cressida, been steering clear of it, ever since she'd discovered the lies Thomas had told the police. It was jarring to see him up at the lighthouse again, watching her and James together.

'Ignore him,' said James, 'please.'

So, she did, looking towards the spot Nelle had taken her tumble instead. Mr Hamilton had been wrong, she realized: the fencing didn't look particularly robust any more, rather lopsided in part, as though it had been pushed apart.

By Nelle?

What had she been up to?

She could have died . . .

Averting her thoughts from that morbid scenario, Violet carried on with James, their feet crackling on the dead, parched grass. They held hands as they walked, and did talk, just not about her expedition into Elizabeth's room. But she was sure, as they switched subjects – from Cressida, to Dicky, to work, to the solstice – that he must be thinking about it still, just as she was, and it was discomforting, it was, to have something come between them that they couldn't seem to discuss.

It was when they reached the wharf that she noticed the discolouration blurring the horizon: not clouds, not yet, but a darkness, looming. Seeing it, she felt more uneasy yet, unsettled by a growing sense of foreboding. It was like the perspiring day was taking on a strange momentum of its own, running out of order, out of control: first, her absurd urge to go prying for Elizabeth's things; then, that gull at breakfast, and Cressida's letter; now, James going off, so abruptly, with a possible storm brewing.

What else might be coming their way?

'What will you do whilst I'm gone?' asked James, looking not in the direction of the bruising sky, but down at her. 'Don't try and work, it's too hot.'

'No, all right. I suppose I'll see what Cressida wants to do.'

'Go for a swim?'

'Maybe.'

'Not to that room again, though,' he said, addressing it at last. 'There's nothing there.' He stared into her eyes, not impatient now, but troubled. 'I can't stand you upsetting yourself with it.'

'I'll stop, really.'

'Yes?'

'Yes.'

'Good.' His dark gaze, still fixed on hers, softened. 'I'll see you in a few hours.'

'You will.' She summoned a smile. 'Good luck.'

'It will be fine.'

'I hope so.'

'It's Dicky,' he said, just as he had in the office. 'He can be managed.'

'You couldn't stop him marrying Cressida,' she felt compelled to point out.

'No, it was Cressida I couldn't stop marrying him. This is different.'

'What about whoever's helping him?'

'We don't know that anyone is. And if they are, I suspect they're only doing it because they want to be bought off.'

She nodded, wanting to believe it, and leaning down, he kissed her.

She held his hands, pulling him closer, hit by a sudden instinct not to let him go.

But how could she ask him to stay?

She couldn't, of course.

So, she released his hands from hers, and, with another kiss, he left.

And she stayed at the wharf, watching him go, until his runabout had disappeared from view.

All was industry up at the Brownings' old cottage, where Mr Hamilton and his men had started the repairs on the roof. They'd been on their way inside when Violet and James had passed by before, heading up into the loft, but now Mr Hamilton was at ground level again, outside the front door, talking with Gareth.

Violet stopped to say hello, and, as she did, pointed up at the second figure who'd appeared outside the lighthouse with Thomas. 'I assume that's Francis?'

'It is,' said Gareth.

'He does exist, then?'

'He does that.'

'I haven't seen him before.'

'He hasn't been out much lately,' said Mr Hamilton, who, now she gave him her full attention, was clenching something in his fist. Something that glinted through his fingers. 'He's grown frail these past weeks. I'm not sure how much longer he'll be able to go on up there.'

'How old is he?'

'Just turned eighty.'

'Eighty?' Her brow creased. 'Shouldn't he have retired years ago?'

'He's kept on for Thomas. God knows what he'll do when Francis goes.'

She looked up at the pair again. It had been a while ago that James had told her how this cottage had used to be their home; she'd asked him then why they'd moved out and hadn't queried his explanation that Francis hadn't wanted his son living among strangers. She had met Thomas, after all. But she did question now what they both must be making of this work being done to their old house.

'Do they definitely not mind?' she asked.

'It's not theirs to mind,' Mr Hamilton replied, his grasp tight around whatever it was he was holding. 'It belongs to the council, and I cleared it with them yesterday.'

'What's that?' she asked, squinting at his hand.

'It's nothing. Just something I found inside.'

It was the quick way he said it, like he'd been waiting for her to ask.

The frown Gareth cast her.

'It's obviously not nothing,' she said, moving closer to get a better look. 'Is it jewellery?' It was. Glinting, chunky jewellery. Mr Hamilton couldn't hide it, no matter how hard he seemed to be trying to. 'A necklace?'

'Really, Miss Ellis, it's not for you to worry about.'

'She will anyway.' This from Gareth. 'Best tell her and have it done.'

'Tell me what?' said Violet, feeling her clammy skin prickle in conviction that the day was about to take another far from welcome turn.

Sighing, Mr Hamilton opened his bearlike paw, revealing not a necklace, it was too short; more, a choker.

A diamond choker, with a very distinctive clasp.

A clasp shaped as an 'E'.

Violet stared at it, her mind filling with the scores of newspaper

349

pictures she'd seen of Elizabeth: smiling, laughing, with these diamonds wrapped around her neck.

'Where was it?' she asked.

'Beneath the floorboards, at the top of the stairs,' said Mr Hamilton. 'I was lifting them for a better look; rot's set in with all the rain that's been getting through. It caught the light.' He shifted in his mud-encrusted boots, as awkward as Violet had known him.

She supposed it must feel fairly awkward, breaking it to a man's new fiancée that you've discovered the necklace of his dead wife in a place it categorically should not have been.

'What was it doing there?' she asked, and her words seemed to come a long way from her.

Had Elizabeth been wearing the choker the night she'd disappeared?

Judging from Mr Hamilton's strained manner, he certainly believed she had been.

'She might have given it to Thomas before she left,' said Gareth. 'A keepsake.'

'Then why doesn't he have it?' said Violet.

He didn't have an answer for that.

'What are you going to do with it?' she asked Mr Hamilton. 'You'll have to show James.'

'I know.'

'Will you tell the Brownings you've found it?'

'No. Not yet.' He glanced in their direction. 'Let's see what James says first.'

'It probably don't mean anything,' said Gareth, and, planting his hands in his pockets, surveyed the dusty, anaemic grass. 'I'm more worried about this tinder box we're all standing on.'

Cressida was out in the front garden with Teddy and Mrs

Hamilton when Violet returned to the house: Teddy, tottering around in one of the shallow pools; Mrs Hamilton behind her, holding her hands.

Violet told them about the choker. She'd been thinking of nothing else on her walk home, and saw no reason to keep it secret. Everyone would know soon enough, she was sure.

They were both taken aback.

'Are you sure it's hers?' said Mrs Hamilton. Teddy tugged her hands, but for once she ignored her.

'Quite sure.'

'That cottage was searched, though,' said Cressida. 'I remember.'

'Obviously not very well,' said Violet. '*Was* she wearing it that night?'

'Definitely,' said Cressida. 'I vividly remember thinking how scrawny her neck looked beneath it. And that I wanted to strangle her with it.'

'Where is it now?' asked Mrs Hamilton as Teddy stomped her foot, making a splash.

'Mr Hamilton still has it,' said Violet.

She nodded.

Then, without ceremony, handed Teddy back to Cressida and left, up through the garden for the fields.

'A shilling to whoever can guess where she's going,' said Cressida.

'Do you think she knows something?'

'What could she possibly know?'

Violet, of course, had no idea.

Neither she, nor Cressida, saw Mrs Hamilton for the rest of the day.

When, at seven that evening, they, along with the rest of the staff, assembled on the wharf to cross to St Leonard's, Mrs

Hamilton didn't join them, but remained at home.

'I'm afraid she's not up to it,' said Mr Hamilton, as everyone else took their seats on his boat. 'It's this weather.'

It was a reasonable excuse. Over the course of the afternoon, it had become increasingly muggy. The clouds Violet had seen foreshadowed on the horizon had massed, blanketing the beating sun, trapping the intense heat of the day beneath them so that the close air pulsed with its constricted energy. The sea had remained eerily calm – a deep turquoise mirror, made all the darker for its reflection of the brooding sky above – but there was a hint of a breeze murmuring that hadn't been present even a half hour before.

'Aoife's stirring,' Violet had said to Cressida, as they'd crossed the fields.

And Cressida had nudged her, smiling.

The breeze wasn't cooling, not at all. Not even the gulls sang. Violet for herself felt at once sluggish, and oddly restless. Really, if it hadn't been for the promise of James waiting across the water, she'd have gladly run a cool bath, and spent the night in it.

But she didn't believe that's what had motivated Mrs Hamilton to stick to her house. No, she'd been too shaken earlier for her absence now to be credited as a plausible coincidence.

'Chewing it all over, probably,' said Cressida in Violet's ear.

And, probably, she was.

Gareth wasn't among the passengers for St Leonard's either. He, of course, wasn't one for socialising, but even if he had been, he couldn't abandon his post.

'It's not the night for it,' said Mr Hamilton, frowning at another ripple of wind. 'There could be lightning. I'm not sure I should be going anywhere either.'

'You can't let them all down,' said Cressida, with a look towards the staff, seated now on the boat, all of them decked out in their best. Diana fanned her face with her hand. Nelle chewed her nail, looking out over the swollen water. Simon and Alan sat apart, in silence. Only the chatting ground staff, Chef, his kitchenhand, and the scullery maids, seemed to be happy about their night off.

Thomas was nowhere to be seen up at the lighthouse: a relief to Cressida at least, as they'd crossed the fields.

Francis wasn't there any more either.

Nor was he coming to St Leonard's.

He, who, to date, had apparently never missed the solstice celebrations, had called by on Mr Hamilton earlier to let him know that this year, he would.

'*Did* you tell him about the choker?' asked Cressida.

'Not my business to,' Mr Hamilton said.

'Why did he say he wasn't coming?' asked Violet.

'Doesn't feel up to it either. Now, are we ready?'

'I'm not sure Teddy is,' said Violet, looking down at her, sound asleep in her sling.

Mr Hamilton looked at her too, his eyes creasing in a smile. Teddy had, if not precisely warmed to him lately, at least ceased being quite so wary, no longer staring at his mask so much; even throwing him a shy grin, from time to time.

'She'll be rested for the party at any rate,' he said.

Violet, climbing onto the boat, wished she felt the same.

She turned, helping Cressida on with Teddy, and the two of them sat on a free stretch of bench.

Another rustle of wind blew.

'Aoife's sending us off,' said Cressida, with another nudge.

'Yes,' said Violet, and, in the eerie, sticky calm, it really did feel like she might be.

Mr Hamilton pulled free the mooring ropes, started the engine, and, in their depleted numbers, off they went, leaving the island almost, *almost*, empty. Just the Brownings, Gareth, and Mrs Hamilton left behind.

353

As they chugged away, Violet turned in her seat, checking again to see if Thomas was out. But he wasn't. He was watching from inside the lighthouse, though, she didn't doubt it. It was the tingling in her skin. That invisible pressure she felt weighing on her.

They were all being observed, she felt sure.

I'm coming.
I'm on my way . . .

Chapter Twenty-Seven

Elizabeth

October 1932

What was it that propelled Elizabeth out of the dinghy that night?

Her fury? The white rage she felt towards heartless, murdering Francis for placing her in it?

Or fear, at ending her days alone, on such a cold, dark night?

Or hope, in the flip of the wind that buffeted her back in the direction of Thomas's swooping beam rather than away from it.

Or the wave that came, capsizing her as she moved, agonisingly shedding her coat and galoshes, preparing to swim?

Perhaps, without that wave, she mightn't have gathered the nerve to dive.

She mightn't have been able to.

She was in so very much pain.

And the water was so penetratingly, chillingly cold.

Quieter, beneath the surface, though.

Silent, almost.

Calm.

Numbing.

As she sank down into it, her hair floating above her, she clutched her diamond choker in her fist. It had been a gift from her brother, Anthony. He'd given it to her the morning he'd left for France in 1915. He'd told her he wanted her to have it to remember him by, if the worst happened.

'It won't,' she'd insisted. 'It can't.'

But it had, at Loos, less than a month later.

'Why him?' their mother had demanded of Elizabeth when the telegram had arrived. 'Why did it have to have been him I had taken from me?'

Elizabeth had never told anyone about that. Not even Laura.

She'd never talked to anyone about Anthony.

Like Laura said, it really did no good to dwell on one's grief.

But oh, Elizabeth had grieved for Anthony.

The world had become an emptier, far more brittle place, after he'd gone.

She'd had his choker at least. She'd always thought of it as carrying a part of him.

She moved her hand now, tightening her bleeding, swollen fingers around it, and it burned.

The sensation stirred her from her strange, submerging lethargy, and two realizations came to her.

The first was that it had been Aoife who'd changed the wind, and sent that wave to knock her into the water. She'd wanted to help her.

Her second realization was that she was about to die, and she really didn't want to.

She needed to help herself.

She was thirty-two-years old. Thirty-two years she'd walked the earth, and had, in that time, learnt many, many things: like, how to ride a bicycle proficiently, a horse passably, not sail a boat at all, but dance the Charleston, a foxtrot, drink endless bottles of champagne without slurring a word, and, in Highgate ponds, swim.

She could swim so well that, with Aoife's help, she managed to do it that night in the pitch-dark Atlantic, covered in cuts and grazes, with a bruised shoulder and battered ribs.

She learnt something else too, as the waves carried her on, pushing her towards Aoife's shore: how wily Aoife was. Because she didn't steer her into the lighthouse's beam with her wails of encouragement: not into Francis's view, nor anyone's else's sights, nor, indeed, against the rocks.

No, she deposited her into the safety of one of her coves, the island's rocky arms coming around Elizabeth as she crawled onto the sands, as though to cradle her.

Hush, hush, you're safe now.

Dripping and breathless and still clutching her choker, Elizabeth closed her eyes.

What time was it?

She had no way of knowing.

But she could, quite easily, have slept.

She could have slept and slept and slept.

But she mustn't sleep.

Her eyes jerked open.

She wasn't safe.

Not yet.

How could Aoife have made her feel that she might be?

Was she turning on her after all? Lulling her into slumber out here, exposed to the elements, with the tide creeping in, because, after all her centuries of loneliness, she wanted to steal her as a forever companion?

Or was that madness?

Was all of it just madness?

Utter madness, whispered Elizabeth's mind. (Her right one, she suspected.) *Get up you fool.*

So, Elizabeth got up.

She didn't remember much after that.

A long walk.

Lots of rain.

A stop to be sick.

Another stop to avoid what appeared to be a lantern-holding search party, calling her name (why did she avoid them? Might it not have been easier to let them find her? Already, it felt too late), then a further one to rest, press her hands to her head, and wish that she had her tablets with her.

Somehow, she must have found her way to the Brownings' old cottage, because the next thing she was aware of, she was blinking her eyes open on the floor of its kitchen, surrounded by the abandoned furniture she'd last observed from out in the garden, looking in. It was still night, still raining. The storm rattled the windowpanes, and a drip was striking the floorboards above her. She felt the sound, like a nail in her skull.

She was shivering.

She *hurt*.

And she wasn't alone.

Wincing, she turned her head, taking in the two men crouched beside her.

Oh, God, she thought.

It's time, old thing.
It's time.

Chapter Twenty-Eight

Violet

June 1934

It had grown darker by the time they neared the mainland, the thickening clouds obscuring the sun. From the sea, the glow of shoreside bonfires, blazing on pontoons, was clearly visible. Violet smelt them, the woody scent drifting on the hot, restive air, bringing music, laughter. Cressida stood, holding up Teddy to see – she'd woken very much ready for the party – and the scullery maids squealed, jubilant about the fires. Mr Hamilton had suggested on the way over that, given the turn in the weather, they might most sensibly be left cold.

'But they can't be,' the girls had chorused. 'It won't be the same.'

Clearly the village organisers had agreed.

The breeze was, after all, still too light to be properly called a wind.

It was there, though.

It felt like it might be growing.

And from far away, beyond the horizon, came the low murmur of thunder: a growl, and occasional flash.

They steered through the burning pontoons to reach the quay, and Violet felt the force of their flames on her sweltering body. She spotted James's runabout instantly, moored at the harbour wall, but couldn't see him on the packed quayside. Anxiously, she searched the thick crowds for him, overwhelmed, suddenly, by the shock of being around so many strangers, after so long in such isolation. It was foolish of her, she knew it was – she'd lived in London, after all – and yet, as Mr Hamilton bumped the boat alongside the quay wall, and someone in the crowd let off a firecracker, she felt her clammy chest constrict.

Oblivious, the scullery maids urged Mr Hamilton to hurry and lower the gangplank, which he did, letting first them, then the others, disembark. Violet paid no attention to them all going, but continued combing the furore for James, her eyes darting from flushed, anonymous face to flushed, anonymous face, failing, repeatedly, to find his.

Had he even arrived?

It struck her that he might not have. That something might have happened to him.

She'd been so anxious earlier, letting him leave.

Feeling a fresh stirring of alarm, she looked around again, this time for his motor, but could see no sign of it either. She didn't even know where he normally left it parked.

And now Cressida was leaving the boat with Teddy, holding Mr Hamilton's hand to cross the gangplank. Mr Hamilton looked not at her, nor Teddy, but back across the dead calm ocean, the skin between his eyes strained by a frown. He'd told the staff he wanted them all on the boat again by ten for the return journey to Aoife's – then, when the scullery maids had protested, by no later than eleven – but it seemed to Violet that he'd rather be making the crossing now, and his disquiet put her all the more on edge.

Cressida seemed suddenly quite serious too, her dark gaze roving the throngs for her brother as well: impatient, undoubtedly, to discover what had come of his attempt to talk with Edwin Firth.

Making to join her, Violet approached the gangplank, thanking Mr Hamilton as he distractedly held out his hand to help her over.

'What are you going to do now?' she asked him.

'Oh, I'll wait here,' he said, climbing back aboard.

Violet didn't try to change his mind. She realized that he, like Gareth, was hardly one to relish a night among strangers.

Far from relishing it herself, she nonetheless turned to Cressida, suggesting that they press on and try and find James, with which Cressida agreed.

It was as they headed into the sweaty furore that Violet thought she heard her name being called. She stopped, pulling Cressida to a halt with her.

'Did you hear that?'

'Hear what?'

'James. Saying my name.'

'No . . . '

'I'm sure I did.' Violet turned on the spot, raising herself up on tiptoes, craning her neck to see above the melee. A passing woman bashed into her, knocking her sideways without apology, and she ignored her, looking around again.

'It must have been someone else,' said Cressida.

'I suppose it must,' said Violet.

Only then she heard her name again: closer now; unquestionable. And, in the same second as she looked to Cressida to see if she'd heard it too, and watched her face move in a smile of recognition, she felt his arms come around her, and his kiss, on her neck.

She laughed, partly in shock, but mostly happiness, spinning to face him.

'Well, that's better,' he said, his eyes bright, his shadowed face lit up with his own smile beneath the dismal sky. And how different his was to those of all the overheated strangers she'd been scanning the features of before. 'You looked worried . . . '

'I didn't think you were here.'

'Where else would I be?'

'I don't know,' she said, which she didn't, but it hardly mattered anyway, because he was here.

He was with her.

This fraught, charged, longest day would feel better from now on, she was sure.

For the couple of hours that followed, edging them towards a grey, sweltering sunset, and beyond into a barely cooler night, it really did feel better.

James filled Cressida in on everything he'd managed to achieve in Penzance, which was no inconsiderable amount. He'd spoken at length to Edwin on the telephone, several times over the course of the afternoon, ascertaining that Edwin not only knew of the solicitors whom Dicky had engaged to act for him, but had already begun enquiries into who was footing their bill. He'd also discovered that none of Dicky's debts had yet been settled, and whilst it was to be presumed that Dicky believed he had someone up his sleeve to help him do that, Edwin was as confident as James that they'd have a price.

'Which we'll pay,' said James to Cressida, 'as soon as we find out who it is.'

'And what if they don't have a price?' asked Cressida.

'Then Edwin will build a case for you to petition for custody of Teddy. You have a great deal more on your side than Dicky does.'

'I was arrested for suspected murder, James.'

'And cleared.'

'Nearly expelled too . . . '

'But never actually.'

'Thanks to you.'

'It doesn't matter who it was thanks to. It never happened.'

'Dicky will say the same about whatever we accuse him of.'

'He can say what he likes. Edwin's gathering witnesses, testimony. He's confident his sister will stand for you . . . '

'Amy? Really?'

'Really. No one is going to take Teddy from you, Cressida. I promise. We won't let it happen.'

Slowly, she nodded.

Then, kissing Teddy, she smiled.

It was the most reassured Violet had seen her look all day.

She felt reassured.

More so, as James ran his arm around her again, pulling her closer, and asked her what she'd like to do. 'Have a drink, food . . . Hook a duck?'

'Duck,' parroted Teddy.

So, with James's help, Teddy hooked a duck.

They all hooked a duck, winning peppermints, and humbugs, and chocolate mice. Then, they bought Teddy lemonade, a parcel of vinegary chips, glasses of beer for themselves, another for Mr Hamilton, which Cressida ran to him on the boat, after which she returned to the packed quay, and the heady night carried on. As the light slowly faded, the wind did pick up further: enough to trigger the odd uncomfortable look in the direction of the bonfires, but not so much that any resolution was reached to extinguish them. For the present, the murmuring storm remained a distant menace, rather than a near reality, raging far away at sea. Over the thunder's bass, the band played their jigs, drowning it out; hogs were roasted, Teddy laughed at a man juggling sticks of flames, screamed in terror at a performance of Punch and Judy, and, with her tummy full of chips, once again fell asleep, cocooned in her mama's sling.

The sun had set by then. The night was almost completely black, with only the barest trace of light left on the electric horizon.

It was in that enveloping darkness that the happy mood of the night shifted.

The wind was the first thing to alter, surging, quite suddenly, sending hats flying from heads, whipping the water beyond the harbour walls into waves, and triggering the hasty departure of several boatloads of men out to the pontoons, armed with pails to quench the fires. As they went, jeers of protest rang from the quayside, escalating in volume as the fires began to fizzle out, making the blackening night blacker yet. It was all done in outward jest, but there was an edge to the shouts: an undercurrent that made Violet, sitting beside James and Cressida on the harbour wall, think back to her earlier discomfort.

She scanned the yelling crowds and spotted the scullery maids balanced on bollards, the postman below them, all with their hands cupped to their mouths, forming horns for their own mocking calls. It came to her that she hadn't seen much of the rest of the staff all the night long: only Chef at the beer stall, and the groundsmen at the hog roast. Not a glimpse of Simon, nor Alan, nor Diana, nor Nelle.

Where had they been?

Had they all gone to their homes rather than join in the party?

Perhaps they had. None of them had seemed too thrilled to be heading to it when they'd left Aoife's, after all.

Why shouldn't they have been, though?

Because of the choker?

Had they been as unsettled by its discovery as Mrs Hamilton had?

Violet frowned at the thought. She hadn't yet mentioned the choker to James. Nor had Cressida. They had reached no prior agreement to keep it to themselves, and yet they both had. Violet wasn't sure why.

A reluctance to ruin the night?

Certainly, she hadn't wanted to mar it.

Given her and James's earlier discord over her trip into Elizabeth's room, she hadn't wanted to bring her up.

But she should have, she realized now.

She should have told him as soon as she'd seen him.

He needed to know.

And she needed to not have deliberately kept it from him.

366

So, turning back to him, she interrupted him talking to Cressida about taking Teddy back before the wind got worse, and did tell him.

'I'm sorry,' she said. 'I've no idea why I didn't mention it before.'

'I'm sorry too,' said Cressida, with a rueful grimace at Violet. 'I think it was all the excitement with the ducks.'

James didn't respond.

Just stared at Violet, apparently lost for words.

'I can't think how it could have got there,' Violet said, supplying some for him. 'I suppose an animal could have taken it in.'

Still, nothing.

Just a deepening frown.

'Or a gull,' she hazarded.

'Poor Alan, with that gull at breakfast,' said Cressida.

'It can't have been a gull,' said James, rediscovering his voice. 'Or an animal.'

'How do you know?'

'Because that choker was on Elizabeth's neck when they found her.'

And that revelation rather altered the mood of the night, too.

Elizabeth's body, exposed to the elements for a month, had been in a grisly state by the time it had been found, James said, as they all returned to Mr Hamilton's boat, there to make sure of the specifics of exactly how he'd discovered Elizabeth's diamonds. Her body had been taken to London for the post-mortem, where the inspector running the case, a man called Jenkins, had called James in to sign the identification documents. He'd notified Elizabeth's lawyers too, who in turn had told Laura: the sole beneficiary of Elizabeth's estate.

'Laura was already at the mortuary when I arrived. She'd been in to see Elizabeth, and was pretty distraught. Elizabeth's bones were undamaged, but the rest of her . . . ' he frowned, 'you can imagine. That choker was how Laura knew it was her. And her hair. She'd still had bits of her gown on her too, and her wedding band. It had got wedged beneath her knuckle . . . '

Against her will, Violet pictured it.

Cressida, lips turned, clearly couldn't help herself either.

'Did you see her?' she asked.

'No. Jenkins said I could sign the papers on the basis of Laura's identification, and I saw no reason to do otherwise. Laura was upset, I didn't want to leave her alone. I certainly had no desire to see Elizabeth. Jenson offered to have the wedding band and choker released to me, but I had no interest in them. I just wanted it to be over, and to get back to you, Cressida, so that I could tell you it was.'

'Did you ever see the choker?' asked Violet.

'*Yes*. Jenkins had it, right there on the table. Elizabeth's ring too.'

'I'm surprised the newspapers didn't print anything about it,' Cressida said. 'They didn't spare their ink on much else.'

'Laura was adamant they weren't to be told specifics. It's why,' he raised a brow, 'I never mentioned it to you. Laura didn't want any of the sordid details made public. She said Elizabeth would have despised that.'

'And Arnold doesn't know?'

'No, he knows. I told him.'

'He must have told Mrs Hamilton,' said Violet. Then, to Cressida, 'That's why she was so stunned, earlier.'

'Was she?' said James.

'You could have knocked her over with a feather,' said Cressida.

'Christ,' he said, 'what a bloody day.'

It had indeed been that.

Such a strange and perverse one, in fact, that it didn't even seem particularly remarkable when they reached Mr Hamilton's boat to find another surprise waiting, this time in the form of Delen Phillips. She was perched with Mr Hamilton in his cabin, sharing a cone of chips. The smell of the grease and vinegar filled the contained space. Delen's smile, as she turned towards them all in the doorway, lit it up. Violet needed no explanation to realize who she was: she'd seen Gareth's portraits, and Delen, with her bobbed waves, round eyes and full grin, was the living incarnation of them.

When she spoke, she did so in a whisper, her eyes on snoozing Teddy.

'I've been looking everywhere for you,' she said, her voice a throaty, west country burr.

She'd been close by in St Just, visiting her mother for the day, she told them, once they'd all greeted one another, and Violet had been introduced. She'd hitched a lift over to St Leonard's to catch the boat with everyone else back to Aoife's.

'You might have told me I had until eleven,' she said to James. 'What was all that nonsense about getting here by ten?'

He frowned. 'What do you mean?'

'You said ten.'

'When?'

'In your wire.'

'I didn't send you a wire.'

She laughed.

He didn't.

And she stopped, clearly realizing his confusion was no tease.

'I got a wire,' she said, serious now. 'Yesterday afternoon. It said you needed me here and to come directly. That I wasn't to risk missing the boat back.'

He turned to Violet in question.

'It wasn't me,' Violet said. 'How would I have sent a wire?'

'How would I have sent one?' he said. 'I didn't . . .'

'Well, don't look at me,' said Cressida, even though nobody was. 'I couldn't have done it either.'

369

'Sounds like someone's playing silly buggers,' said Mr Hamilton, which by that stage was rather stating the obvious.

Still, it was unnerving to hear it said out loud.

Because who was doing it?

None of them had any idea.

'Whoever it is,' said James, staring in the direction of his tinder box home, 'they want you over there, Delen.'

'I don't know that I much want to go any more.'

Violet didn't know that she much blamed her.

James didn't either.

'I'll go on ahead,' he said. 'You wait here.' He glanced at his watch. 'It's already ten anyway. Come with the others. All right, Arnold?'

'Of course.'

Cressida elected to remain behind as well, with Teddy.

'And what about you?' James asked Violet, turning to her with a smile that she knew was intended to make light of everyone's unease: reassure her, and perhaps himself too. 'Will you stay?'

Yes, she could easily have said. *If you don't mind.*

He wouldn't mind.

He, who'd already done so much for her, would, she knew without question, do this thing as well: let her stick with the crowd, and leave him to cross the dark ocean and sort out all this strangeness – whatever it was – alone. Just like he'd shouldered so many other things, alone.

He's changed my life, Violet had said to Cressida, the night they'd become engaged.

He had changed her life. He'd done that entirely, and irrevocably.

He'd been doing it since before she'd known him.

And you've changed his, Cressida had said to her.

Violet had dismissed those words at the time. She hadn't thought they could be true. For how could she, with so little, have changed the life of someone with everything?

370

Now, though . . .

Now, for the first time, she accepted, really *believed* that Cressida had been right.

Because as she looked at James, she saw, beyond his smile, deep in his eyes, a request that he probably wasn't even aware of making, but which was nonetheless there, asking her to *not* leave him alone. Not that night.

She realized that he, who for years and years hadn't been able to need anyone, did now need her.

'I'm not staying,' she said.

'No?' he said, holding out his hand for hers.

'No,' she said, taking it. 'Of course not. I'm coming with you.'

Chapter Twenty-Nine

Violet

They had just a single light at the front of the runabout to illuminate their path across the churning ocean, back to Aoife's. The night had turned so deep around them, that they might have been travelling through a void, the rest of the world vanished entirely. The conditions weren't as rough as they had been the April morning Violet had arrived, but they were still *rough*. She felt no nausea, though. She didn't become green as a cabbage. Rather, as James opened the throttle, steering them at an angle across the waves, and the runabout leapt their crests, smacking down onto the water with almighty cracks, adrenalin coursed through her veins.

'The belly won't break, will it?' she asked of James, yelling to be heard.

'No. You're safe, I promise.'

'All right,' she said.

But, she didn't feel safe.

It was so dark.

So very dark.

They saw the lighthouse's beam, long before they could make out the shadow of Aoife's. For once, it wasn't moving. It shone, straight and unwavering.

'What the hell is going on?' said James.

'I don't know,' said Violet, edgier yet.

The storm had drawn closer, as they'd crossed the ocean.

There was still no rain. The night remained bone dry.

But soon, a flash of lightning came overhead, illuminating the shape of the island, and she knew that they were almost there.

They'd been spotted coming.

Two figures were waiting for them at the end of the wharf: one was Gareth, the other a man whom Violet had never met before but, just as with Delen earlier, knew anyway who he was.

He looked the same as his son, with his strong, angular face, and sunken eyes.

Dressed the same as his son, in a flannel shirt, and corduroys belted tight at the waist.

And, when he spoke, he sounded the same as Thomas, too.

The same as someone else, as well, Violet realized with a cold jolt.

She really had had it wrong.

All this time, she'd had it wrong.

It hadn't been Thomas she'd heard Mrs Hamilton arguing with on the servants' stairs, that morning she'd arrived.

It had his been his father, Francis.

We'll talk about this later, he'd said to Mrs Hamilton then.

'She's here,' he said to James, now. 'She's come.'

Chapter Thirty

Elizabeth

October 1932

She supposed it was inevitable that she was found that night. Given the search parties combing the island (for her, for *her*; through her blanketing pain, the first spikes of satisfaction poked), it would have been too much to expect that the Brownings' old kitchen should remain unexplored. Was there anyone who Elizabeth might have been happy to see inside it? She considered it as she stared up through her swollen salt-stung eyes at the aghast, moonish faces of first Alan, then Simon, her thoughts darting from possibility to possibility, settling, depressingly, on nobody. She didn't factor Thomas into her calculations; for the present, he, stuck to his lighthouse, with his assassin of a father, was an irrelevance. And the rest of them were too angry, even Laura. Alan and Simon at least had no especial call to be. Elizabeth had given them no recent reason to hate her.

Had she?

No, she didn't believe she had.

It was a decisive tick in their favour.

A piece of good fortune, then, that they'd come.

Had Aoife sent them?

She must have.

Thank you, Elizabeth silently told her, then swiftly retracted the gratitude, recalling that that princess had wanted her dead too.

374

But wait . . .

Hadn't she resolved not to believe in her?

Decided that she was madness?

Madness, she thought.

'Madness,' she said out loud, and it hurt, appallingly, to speak.

It was an agony to breathe.

'Madness?' said Simon.

What was he talking about?

Elizabeth had no idea.

'Are you all right?' Alan asked her.

'No,' she said, angry now, because why should Alan force her to answer such a question when it must be patently obvious that she was a very long way from being all right?

Could it be possible that he was stupid as well as average?

Elizabeth hoped not.

She needed him to not be stupid.

She needed his, and his sidekick's, help.

'We'll fetch help,' Alan said, making her wonder if she'd mistakenly spoken the last bit out loud.

'You mustn't,' she said, and that much she was confident she had put voice to, from the splintering in her head.

Forcing herself to talk again, she said, 'You can't tell anyone I'm here.'

'Everyone's looking for you.'

Again, that satisfaction.

Then: alarm.

'They need to not find me.' She tried to push herself up. 'I need you to tell them you found this place empty, and help me get away.'

'Why?' said Simon.

'Because I asked you to.' She managed to sit, which was excruciating, and that upset her, but not nearly as much as Simon's guarded tone, because he really did sound so insultingly reluctant to cooperate.

Where was his compassion? Really.

'I want them to believe I've had an accident,' she went on, voice cracking with the effort. 'That I've hurt myself.'

'But you have hurt yourself,' said Simon.

'Not like this.'

'I don't understand . . . '

'Would you find it easier if I paid you?'

A brief silence followed.

Then,

'How much?' said Alan.

'A lot,' Elizabeth told him.

And he, at least, wasn't remotely reluctant after that.

He was desperate for money, even more so than Elizabeth might have expected of a provincial footman, which was to say: extremely desperate. Elizabeth decided to take his acute neediness as confirmation that the fates really had been conspiring to help her, in spiriting him her way.

Or – intriguing thought – perhaps his appearance *was* down to Aoife's handiwork, after all.

Perhaps Aoife did exist, was full of remorse for her treachery, anxious to redeem herself, and quite right too.

Elizabeth rather liked that possibility.

Already, she'd grown to miss Aoife.

Regardless, Alan was ripe for a bribe, thanks to an unemployable father (the war, *again*), and a younger sister who'd achieved where Elizabeth had failed and got herself pregnant, *sans* husband.

Not that Alan entrusted Elizabeth with that information.

No, it was to Simon who Alan spoke of it all, plucking his little violin, reminding his pal of his myriad plights, persuading him into cooperation.

Simon wasn't immediately convinced.

'What if we get caught?' he kept saying.

'We won't,' Alan assured him.

'Not if you're careful,' said Elizabeth, painfully, her patience fraying.

'And if we do this,' said Alan, 'I'll be able get Nancy into that home. They'll look after her, and the baby. She'll be ruined otherwise. It'll kill my dad. You can't want that . . . '

''Course I don't,' said Simon.

And maybe he didn't.

Still, it was only when Elizabeth agreed to double the sum she'd promised to pay him, that he grudgingly fell in.

'And when will I get the money?' he asked her.

'Once you get me off this island,' she told him, through set teeth.

'All right,' he said. 'All right.'

And, at last, off he and Alan went, to plot her escape.

She played no hand in masterminding affairs. Frankly, she was in no fit state to mastermind anything, and became worse yet after they left her; delirious, in actual matter, jerking in and out of consciousness in her cold, wet clothes, on the Brownings' hard, damp floor. By the time the footmen reappeared at her side in the black Sunday dawn – bringing food that she couldn't eat, and water that she struggled to drink, but no blanket to speak of – she may or may not have cursed them with an expletive she normally considered beneath her. Simon may or may not have responded in kind. Truly, it was all a blur. Hazily, she registered them manhandling her upstairs to better hide her, *just in case*, where they crammed her behind a wardrobe and threw a dust sheet over her, which at least offered some meagre warmth.

She didn't move from beneath that sheet all day. Simon paid her one further call – informing her that the staff's Sunday trip to St Leonard's had been cancelled so that they could continue to search the island – but other than that, she spent the hours alone: sweating, shivering; dreaming strange dreams about her mother, and fretting, in her more lucid moments, that someone might come looking for her.

But no one did come looking. Nobody cared enough to go to the effort of checking Alan and Simon's assurances that they'd found the Browning's cottage empty – and what a shame it was that the storm passed, leaving clear, calm skies, because every one of them deserved to be soaked to their lazy, wretched cores.

It was much later that Elizabeth discovered – from Diana's fisherman father, of all people – that, unlike Simon, Alan hadn't remained on Aoife's for those Sunday search endeavours. Nor had James, who'd motored off across the ocean to alert the Penzance police as to Elizabeth's vanishing. (Was he beside himself? Racked with guilt? How Elizabeth yearned to know.) Alan (not-in-fact-stupid-Alan) had gone with him, having volunteered to be the one to fetch Diana back to Aoife's so that she might be present if the police needed to question her. He and Diana were cousins, it transpired. Diana's father, John, was Alan's doting uncle, and rather concerned himself about how his nephew was to keep up with his overwhelming financial obligations. Not to mention the volatility of his own ocean hauls. And the nagging worry of the engine that needed replacing in his boat. And the stiff rudder. Truly, John bore the weight of the world on his broad shoulders, and Elizabeth was to hear about it all, thanks to Alan, who took the liberty of promising his uncle more of Elizabeth's money in exchange for his assistance in whisking her off Aoife's.

Jumping on board, literally, with Alan's scheme, John ferried both him and Diana back to Aoife's to await James's return from Penzance. Then – with canny nephew and oblivious daughter safely deposited – he chugged away for an afternoon spent navigating the surrounding waters, returning stealthily to Aoife's at dusk, when he dropped anchor at the furthest most cove from the lighthouse, and waited for his nephew to call him to action.

They may well not have been able to pull off what happened

next, had luck not once again been on Elizabeth's side. But fortune favoured the deserving, and James – who'd by then returned to the island with two members of the police – called a meeting in the house on behalf of those inspectors, at six, which all residents of the island, save the duty lighthouse keeper, were required to attend. Alan once again volunteered for service, setting out into the autumnal darkness to find the last straggling search parties, whilst Mr Hamilton went to fetch his vixen wife, and Gareth, from the cottages, then Francis from the lighthouse. Alan, meanwhile, hightailed it down to the by-then black cove to alert his uncle John.

At six, John moved, avoiding the beam of the lighthouse, finding his way to Elizabeth.

'Who are you?' Elizabeth asked, when he arrived.

'Hush,' said John.

'Am I hallucinating?' Mr Claymore had cautioned her to be alert for such events.

'What a pretty thing,' whispered John, in what was to prove the peak of Elizabeth's regard for him.

Then she realized that he was looking not at her face, but at her choker, still clutched in her hand.

Vaguely, she registered dropping that choker as John carried her from the cottage. Through murky eyes she watched it slither through a crack in the floorboards, and, in the second before she once again blacked out, felt a punch of victory that John wouldn't now be able to steal it from her, as he was quite plainly intending to do.

It was only when she came to again, slung agonisingly over John's shoulders, him slip-sliding down the cliffside to the shore, that she was struck by the enormity of what she'd lost.

She started to sob then, part in pain, so much pain, but mostly, grief.

'Hush, won't you,' said John, still jogging. 'I got to get you away.'

Then they were down in the cove, clambering into a boat, and on a wing and a prayer and the tails of Aoife's cape, away they did go, far from Elizabeth's last link to Anthony, the reach of Thomas's beam, on and out into the pitch night.

Elizabeth lost consciousness again on the crossing.

By the time she woke, John was dumping her in his storage shed, and she smelt fish all around her, so had that to weep about, too.

She wept a great deal from that point on, discovering so very much, beyond her lost choker, to regret. Like, how – aside from the most fleeting of visits from John, and his surly wife, Melder – she was left almost entirely alone. And, that she hadn't tasked Alan or Simon with fetching her medicine before she'd left Aoife's. Or any money. Or a change of undergarments. As it was, the pain in her head often became so unbearable that she vomited, and, when not contending with that, she was forced to suffer the degradation of letting Melder bathe her, and dress her in her ugly fisherman wife's cast-offs.

'Stop complaining,' said Melder.

'Where's that lovely necklace of yours gone, then?' asked John.

'I threw it in the sea,' Elizabeth replied, damned if she was about to gift him a treasure map.

The windowless shed was always unlit. Melder wouldn't permit a candle; she was too afraid of detection. Often, when Elizabeth woke, it was so dark that she thought she'd been buried, and she'd sob, gagging for air, until she passed out once more. On other occasions, she'd come to relishing the darkness, because light so often hurt. And on she went, tripping in and out of consciousness, from one blackness to another. She knew she kept having seizures, from the heaps she found herself in on the shed's floor, but had no sense of them, nor of time passing.

Until, quite suddenly, her fever left her. She opened her eyes to the sight of John beside her, holding a bowl of congealing porridge, and discovered that her ribs must have mended because they no longer ached.

Discovered that she was ravenous, too.

And, from John, that it was somehow the third Thursday of November. Not only that, but that her disappearance was national news, Cressida had been arrested, and released on bail. A man called Private Nathan Edevane had launched a campaign of hatred against James; meanwhile, all of Elizabeth's fair-weather friends were back in London, and, that Sunday, Aoife's staff were to be allowed back to St Leonard's again.

'Why didn't you tell me any of this?' Elizabeth asked, panicked.

'I did,' said John.

'You can't have.'

'I *did*.'

'But you've let too much happen. Too much time has passed.' As the truth of it coursed through Elizabeth, her panic grew. 'How could you have let so much time pass?'

'Melder said we should put a stop to it all, but you told her we mustn't.'

'No . . . '

'*Yes*,' John insisted. 'You wanted our Diana to tell the police that she saw Cressida out chasing you, just like Thomas Browning did.'

That rang a distant bell. Now John mentioned it, Elizabeth vaguely recalled worrying that Thomas's word alone wouldn't carry enough weight in implicating Cressida, so, when John had mentioned that he and Melder were going to visit their daughter, she'd tasked him with instructing Diana to incriminate Cressida, too.

Actually, it had been a very clever idea.

Could Diana have been so helpful, though?

Had she spoken to the police?

'No,' said John, when Elizabeth asked, and, wordlessly,

Elizabeth promoted Diana up the ranks of her list. 'And that poor Cressida's been arrested anyway.'

'So?'

'So?' John said. 'She hasn't done anything.'

'Cressida's done plenty, I assure you.'

'She's having a *baby*.'

'I'm aware of that.'

'You have to help her.'

'Don't be ridiculous. We'd end up in even more trouble than her.'

'Why?'

'Because no one's going to believe that we could have been oblivious to this circus unfolding for close to a month.' God, a month. *A month*. The words screamed in her head. She'd only planned to be gone a few days. If she was to turf up now, everyone would realize she'd been hiding. *James* would. He'd see right through it, use it against her. 'We'll go to prison.'

'What?'

'John, how can this not have occurred to you?'

'I thought you'd make everything all right.'

'And how do you propose I do that?'

'Use your money.'

'For what?'

'What people like you use it for.'

'Even if that made sense, I don't have any money. Not here.'

'But you need to pay us. You promised you'd pay.'

'I will, eventually.' She wouldn't. Neither he nor his surly wife deserved it, banishing her to this shed, clothing her in little better than rags. How could Alan have sent her to it? He didn't deserve payment either. He'd shot up her naughty list, right alongside his mousey cousin.

She had no intention of paying Simon, either. Apart from anything, how was she supposed to get to her money? It wasn't as though she could stroll into a bank and withdraw it. She couldn't stroll anywhere. Her face, which had turned heads long before this mess, had now been pasted across every newspaper in the land.

What was she going to *do*?

It was Melder who declared that she must leave, insisting they couldn't keep her hidden forever, especially not with Diana back again that weekend. She regretted ever being dragged into the whole sorry mess. Elizabeth should be moved up the coast, she resolved, that same night, towards Penzance, into the cottage she'd been born in, and which her family had left vacant when they'd moved to St, Leonard's, years before. It was unfurnished, but remote enough to work as a stopgap until Elizabeth could think of a better place to put herself.

'What am I meant to sleep on?' Elizabeth asked, horrified.

'John'll take your mattress.'

'What am I meant to eat?'

'Food. I'll pack you some.'

Before Elizabeth knew what was happening, Melder was doing just that, and digging out a shawl and too-big boots to go with Elizabeth's shapeless woollen smock. After that, she dragged a pan of water into the boatshed, unceremoniously shoved Elizabeth's head over it, and drenched her hair in the dye she used to keep her own greys away, turning it from red to a deep, witchlike black.

Then, once the early November darkness had fallen, she handed Elizabeth a purse of coins for emergencies, and ushered her, with undignified haste, out of the shed and into John's boat, where John was already waiting.

Ready to ferry Elizabeth up the coast.

Chapter Thirty-One

Elizabeth

Melder's family's hut – a leaky, derelict hole that managed to be even worse than Elizabeth had imagined – was a half-mile trek inland from the coast. John said nothing as he led Elizabeth to it, focused on hefting her mattress across the pitch-dark fields. It was only when they reached the hut that he broke his silence, dumping the mattress on the dung-covered floor, telling Elizabeth he'd be back on Monday.

'Don't go anywhere until then,' he ordered, as an *adieu*.

Elizabeth left at first light. She'd been up since before dawn, woken by her own shivering, more excruciating pain in her head, and the taste of blood. She'd had another seizure, she realized from the torn scab on her lip. As she examined herself in the outhouse's murky mirror, she resolved that she couldn't go on a day longer as she was. She needed medicine. Needed a doctor. All was forgiven, Mr Claymore. She'd gladly crawl to his office if she had to, or indeed that of any other specialist (a second opinion, yes, *yes*), but first, she needed money, warmth, clothes. *Help*.

She was no longer so afraid of being seen. Much as her reflection appalled her, it also reassured her that she wasn't nearly so recognizable as she'd assumed: not dressed in rags, with her nest of hair that Melder had *ruined*, and her face so sickly pale after her internment. She'd have to be careful not to draw attention to herself, but she could risk an excursion.

Heading once again for the slate-grey coast, she turned, following it to Penzance. It drizzled, the rain seeping into her woollen shawl, chilling her skin, making the stale fabric stink. Teeth chattering, she grew edgier the closer she drew to the town's smoking chimneys, conviction wavering as to whether it had been her right or wrong mind that had led her to come. *Would* someone see through her disguise? She'd been noticed, her entire life through; it felt preposterous that she wouldn't be noticed now.

Ridiculous, in fact, to have chanced this expedition.

Yet, her feet took her on, and, as she first navigated the town's limits, eyes peeled as she took its measure, then made for Penzance's main thoroughfare – breathless, after such protracted inactivity, on its steep cobbled streets – no one did give her a second glance: not the worker men she passed, or the housewives with their baskets and brats, or the children on their way to school. When she reached the post office, the morning's headlines were flapping from a board at the door, announcing the discovery of a battered dinghy – *her* dinghy: the one that Mr Claymore had so recklessly urged her to treat herself to – washed up less than a hundred yards from where her coat had been found, with one of her galoshes still, somehow, contained within it.

ACCIDENTAL DEATH? asked the *Illustrated News*.

SUICIDE? demanded the *Cornish People*.

SEARCH FOR BODY NOW FOCUSED ON IMMEDIATE VICINITY, proclaimed *The Times*.

But the body's here, she thought, *I'm here,* and might have become hysterical at the preposterousness of it, had she not been so incensed at the idea of Cressida's bubbling hope of reprieve, not to mention the humiliation of anyone believing that she, Elizabeth, could have become desolate enough to have taken her own life.

And were the other shoppers heading into the post office giving her a wide berth?

Avoiding her?

They were.

They *were*.

Her shame deepened, which made her angrier yet, and more resolved than ever to do as she must.

No one approached her as she made for the telegraph counter and penned her message, leaving it carefully anonymous, to anyone's eyes but the recipient's. Coins in hand (thank you, Melder) she handed it over for transmission, to a woman who ignored her, caught up in an inane conversation with her colleague. What were they discussing? Elizabeth didn't listen. She couldn't have cared less. Honestly, how dare these people all treat her with such indifference. How little attention people paid you, when you appeared poor.

Wire despatched, Elizabeth returned to her hut, ate some of the chalky bread Melder had given her, wrapped herself up in her blanket, clutched her throbbing head, and waited.

She waited all through that day, and all through the following night. Again, she didn't sleep, but tripped awake every time she was about to lose consciousness, panicking about whether her wire might, after all, have been a miscalculation. She was terrified too of having another seizure. In the deepest darkness, she stared at the hut's low ceiling, and, hearing the wind pick up, howling around its walls, thought how much more menacing it sounded here, where she knew it was just wind, and not Aoife.

She didn't go anywhere this time at dawn. Desperate as she was to leave her hovel, and discover whether the cavalry she'd requested really would materialise, she remained where she was, because it was still too soon.

Drive, she'd instructed in her wire, *bring the motor*.

Meet me at the cemetery gates at six STOP

Not taking anything for granted, she'd selected the cemetery as an assignation point when she'd conducted her recce of the town, on the merit of its abandonment. (Plus, it had a pleasing poeticism to it.) She'd chosen the later hour for darkness, as well as to allow time for the long journey by road from London.

At five, she left the hut again, pressing out into the drizzle and mist, darting looks into the enveloping blackness, wishing, very much, that Aoife was with her. She hummed to hear a noise, any noise, that wasn't the crashing sea, or the chilling wind, but her voice shook, her teeth chattered, and she was too exhausted to set either steady. Her feet hurt too, blistered from Melder's cheap, ridiculously sized boots.

She didn't see anyone this time as she entered the town. The streets were silent, emptied by the weather, everyone inside their homes, cocooned behind their glowing windows. The icy November night smelt of coal, the sea; so many roasting dinners. And was it possible that Elizabeth envied these strangers, nestled inside their toasty sanctuaries? No. *No.* She had no need to envy anyone. The cavalry was on its way, it *was*, she could sense it. Feel it. She'd made no miscalculation, she was certain. There'd be no ambush by the police.

You have been my everything since 1919, she'd written in her wire. *I need you for so much more than a cigarette in a bathroom now STOP*

She knew her friend.

Knew she wouldn't let her down.

Don't you dare come crying to me when it all ends in tears, she'd warned Elizabeth back in the January sleet, outside the Kit-Kat Club.

What choice had Elizabeth had?

And there she was, waiting for Elizabeth at the cemetery gates beside her motor, illuminated by its beaming headlights, her face pensive, peering through the fog, so smart and snug in her unremarkable clothes: such a welcome, wonderful, strawberry.

'Lizzie?' she said, frowning as Elizabeth approached her, raw disbelief in her brimming blue eyes. 'Is that really you?'

'It's me, Laura. It's me.'

'My God.'

She had her arms folded. She didn't open them.

Elizabeth didn't care.

Because Laura had come. She'd come. And if she was angry, still, at Elizabeth, she was also happy to see her alive. She couldn't hide that. Couldn't conceal the tears now spilling down her plump cheeks. And it was nice, so unutterably, wonderfully *nice*, to be with someone, anyone who wanted her to not be dead.

Too nice, in fact, for Elizabeth to do anything but open her own arms, stumble towards her friend, wrap her rigid body in a tight embrace, and sob.

Chapter Thirty-Two

Elizabeth

Laura didn't soften. Not right away. Extricating herself from Elizabeth's hold, she instructed her to get in the motor, and, climbing into her own seat, slamming her door, *hard*, drove.

She drove for more than an hour, inland into dark, dense forest, eventually coming to the lodge her parents had once used to host hunts, before they'd caught the flu. Elizabeth had visited it before. Laura herself had thrown the odd weekend party within its picturesque, ivy-clad walls. Mainly, though, she'd left it shut up, unstaffed and unused.

Take me there, Elizabeth had written in her wire. *Will explain everything then.*

Laura made her do that, long before they reached the lodge.

'No lies, Lizzie. No more pretence. I've had my fill of it.' Her stare, trained on the motor's flipping wiper blades, was unblinking. 'I want to know everything.'

So, Elizabeth gave it to her. Relieved, when it came to it, to finally let it all *go,* she held nothing back: not the farce of her marriage, nor her misery on Aoife's, nor her imposter (she even choked out its name), nor seizures, nor Mr Claymore's nonsense about stopping treatment.

Laura had to pull over.

'You've been shouldering all this?' she said, her face no longer set, but wrung with emotion: horror, unmistakeable horror (and how unbearable it truly was to look her abhorrence in the eye), but grief too. 'Hiding that you've got . . . '

'Please, Laura, don't let's repeat it.'

'But do you know who gave it to you?'

'Of course I *know*.' What did Laura take her for? 'He was a friend of my father's.' He'd been older than Elizabeth, of course. Kind and indulgent – much more so than her father had ever been – he'd made her feel safe. Until he hadn't.

What had his name been?

She couldn't seem to recall.

Another thing she'd forgotten.

She remembered, though, that Mr Claymore had treated him too.

'He got better,' she said, eyes smarting. 'It's really rather unfair . . . '

'I'm so sorry, Lizzie.'

'Yes, so am I.'

'How long has Mr Claymore said you might have?'

'Well, I do want to see about that second opinion . . . '

'How long, Lizzie?'

'I'm not sure he's ever given me a precise timescale.' Had he? 'Maybe there was something about a year or two . . . '

'Oh, Lizzie. *Lizzie*.'

In the end, it was the one thing that Elizabeth could say in her imposter's favour: it coaxed Laura back to being on her side.

Not before Laura gave her a good serving for what she'd put them all through, though.

'We've all been beside ourselves,' she said, once they were driving again. 'Absolutely *beside* ourselves. I haven't known whether you've been dead, or somewhere scared and alone, in pain.'

'I have been scared and alone and in pain.'

'You could have said something. You should have *said*

something. The moment you returned to your senses.'

'I told you, I was too afraid.'

'You don't think Cressida's been afraid?'

'I don't want to talk about her.'

'Lizzie, her life's ruined. She could have lost the baby . . . '

'She hasn't lost anything. She's not even in prison any more.'

'She's on *bail*. You have to come clean. Tell the police she's innocent . . . '

'I *can't*, Laura. They'll arrest me.'

'Not necessarily.'

'Yes, necessarily. I really mightn't have much longer left.' Elizabeth did, she refused to accept it might be otherwise, but it worked for the present to pursue this morbid line. 'Do you really want me to end my days in shackles?'

'Of course I don't. But maybe if you went to James. Explained things to him . . . '

'He won't listen.'

'He might.'

'He *won't*.'

Laura kept arguing with her. She simply wouldn't believe that James would be so cruel as to stand by and see Elizabeth incarcerated. No, she – who'd nursed in the war, actually been loved by her parents, and had driven half the length of the country to rescue Elizabeth on the strength of an anonymous wire – had too much goodness in her for that.

But, in the end, she also had sense enough to accept that events had run well beyond the realms of control, and that gambling on James's better nature was not a risk Elizabeth could afford to take.

'I don't like it,' she said, as, in the still continuing rain, they pulled up outside the lodge. 'I don't like it one bit. But I suppose what's done is done.' She emitted a deep sigh. 'We'll just have to make the best of it.'

'So you'll help me?' Elizabeth asked, looking not at Laura, but at the lodge's alight windows and smoking chimneys: a haven for her, at last.

Distracted by the prospect of her bed inside, its soft pillows, and thick eiderdown, she didn't immediately grasp what it meant that so many lamps were burning, and the fires stoked, inside this unstaffed lodge – which was of course that somebody else was there.

It was only when Laura said, 'We'll help you,' that she realized.

'Who's we?' she asked.

And, as if in reply, the front door opened, an umbrella unfurling through it, swiftly followed by Rupert's gangling form.

'Laura,' said Elizabeth, coldly. She hadn't forgotten how unforgivably Rupert had spoken about James refusing to bed her. *Can't say I blame him.* Not at all. And now he was about to discover her secret. He'd *know*. It would repulse him. She couldn't stand it. Not from him. He'd always adored her so. 'I told you to come alone.'

'Be grateful, Lizzie. It's a good thing Rupert is here.' Laura silenced the engine. 'You're going to need both of us for what you need to pull off.'

Elizabeth was at least saved the humiliation of having to witness Laura tell Rupert everything. Immediately they were inside, Laura despatched her upstairs to bathe, in a *bath*, and by the time she returned downstairs, warm and clean and wrapped in one of Laura's robes, it was done.

Was Rupert repulsed?

He certainly didn't attempt to kiss Elizabeth, as she joined him and Laura by the drawing room fire.

He, sticking to his seat, didn't come near her.

He wouldn't even meet her eye.

Swallowing on the sting of his distance, Elizabeth sat in the armchair opposite him and Laura. What she expected to happen

392

next was that Laura would tell her she'd continue hiding her –
in comfort, with a visit arranged from a discreet doctor with a
prescription pad – whilst the investigation into her supposed death
continue to run its course.

Laura wouldn't countenance that, though.

'Cressida might yet be charged with murder,' she said.

'But my dinghy's been found,' said Elizabeth.

'So?'

'So, I saw the papers. They're saying I might have killed myself.
Which I simply can't have, by the way. We'll need to steer them
towards an accident . . . '

'We can't *steer* anyone,' Rupert said, lighting a cigarette,
studying its end. 'The police aren't going to just let this drop. Not
after all the attention it's had.' He tapped his cigarette, musingly,
then nodded, apparently decided. 'The only way that any of this
will disappear, is through us convincing the right people that it can.'

Elizabeth narrowed her eyes. 'What do you mean?'

'I mean, going to the police and telling *them* you're still alive.'

'Yes, I was worried you might mean something like that. Laura,'
she turned to her friend, 'he wants to get me arrested . . . '

'No, Lizzie . . . '

'No one's getting arrested,' said Rupert. 'We've had more than
enough of that. Leave this with me. I'll head back to London first
thing Monday, have a word in a few right ears. We'll get this
sorted.'

Rupert was as good as his promise. Laura had been right, after
all. Elizabeth had needed him. Or his connections, at any rate – of
which his family had legion, not least, in the home office, where his
father, Lord Litchfield, held some significant sway.

Within three short days, the police commissioner himself, Lord
Arden – anxious to supply the clamouring public with a solution to

the entire sorry mystery, over which he'd apparently been hauled across the coals, multiple times – paid a visit to Laura's lodge, so that he could see Elizabeth alive with his own bespectacled eyes.

Elizabeth met with him, along with Laura and Rupert, in the drawing room, where Arden told her, lip curling, that he'd known for some time about her *sickness*; apparently, Mr Claymore had volunteered her medical history to Scotland Yard when she'd first disappeared – rather highhandedly, if you asked Elizabeth ('No one is,' said Arden) – on the understanding that it would be kept confidential. He'd told James about it all, too.

'Was he sad?' Elizabeth asked, her skin, already aflame at Arden's disgust, burning all the more, because now James knew too. He *knew*.

'Sad is not the adjective I'd associate with Mr Atherton,' said Arden, who wasn't particularly sad either. Furious, actually. (*This is not the kind of underhand dealing I've built my career on,*' he'd informed Elizabeth on arrival at the lodge, '*but you have some very persuasive friends, and you're a thorn in my side I'll be glad to dispose of.*') 'His poor sister, however,' Arden continued, 'has been pitifully reduced by the entire affair, over which I feel exceedingly ashamed, and would hope you do too.'

'Of course she does,' said Laura. 'She's very sorry.'

'She's not sorry at all,' said Arden, saving Elizabeth the bother, 'and I don't for a second believe this *disease* of hers is to blame.' From behind his spectacles, he cast Elizabeth a withering look. 'I've encountered your kind too many times before, no checks or balances, thinking only in terms of yourself. But since you are, for the present, alive, and serving a sorry enough sentence, let's put this to bed as quickly as possible.'

He'd already discussed how to do that with his chief inspector on the case, Jenkins, to whom he'd promised a hefty bonus for his cooperation. (*Use your money*, John had told Elizabeth; how wise he'd been.)

'Do you have any distinguishing jewellery?' Arden asked Elizabeth.

'My wedding band,' she suggested, holding up her hand.

'What about your choker?' Laura asked.

'I lost it.'

'Where?' asked Arden.

'In the sea,' she told him, just as she had John.

Which was correct, wasn't it?

'How deep in the sea?' Arden asked.

'Very deep,' she said, thinking of the water she'd been knocked into when she'd swum back to the shore.

But *had* that been when she'd lost the choker?

It didn't feel quite right.

Regardless, as Arden, Rupert and Laura continued talking, hatching a plan for Rupert to procure a copy of the choker, with its hallmark clasp, Elizabeth let them to it. What matter, really, where she'd lost those diamonds? The end result was the same. They were gone. Anthony's last gift to her was gone, and it broke her heart . . .

'Here, Lizzie,' said Laura, softly, passing her a kerchief, letting her know that she was crying.

'We'll have to bring a couple more men in,' Arden said (not softly). 'Jenkins knows the ones. They'll have to be paid too.'

'Yes, yes,' said Rupert.

'And I meant it about that endowment to the London Samaritans . . . '

'Absolutely. Name the amount.'

'Perhaps Barnardo's, too.'

'Any charity you choose.'

'Well, that's something good that can come of this.'

The plan, Elizabeth learnt, was that James and the lower police ranks were to be informed that a body had been found, drowned in a cave, decomposed, but unmistakeably identifiable as Elizabeth's own, with no bones broken, or any discernible evidence of malicious intent.

'We'll put out that the tides got the better of her,' said Arden, talking about Elizabeth like she wasn't there, 'a terrible accident.'

'But I don't want everyone thinking of me as decomposed,' said Elizabeth, wiping her eyes. 'I can't have the papers writing that.'

'We'll go into as few specifics as possible,' Arden said. 'Less lies printed, less scope for us to get tripped up.'

'People are still going to wonder why Lizzie *left* Aoife's,' said Laura.

'Then we'll let them wonder,' said Arden.

'What body will you use?' asked Rupert.

'We'll find one. God knows we get enough unclaimed. But I'd like to avoid showing Mr Atherton anyone. He's hardly a man to be fooled with a wig on a corpse. Miss Ratcliffe,' Arden turned to her. 'This is where we'll need you to help . . . '

Laura wasn't thrilled about the role he then asked her to take in putting James off from seeing the body.

'I don't want to lie,' she said. 'Not like that. Not to his face . . . '

'Think of it as helping Cressida,' Rupert suggested.

'And me,' said Elizabeth.

'We really do need for you to do this,' Arden told her.

And, eventually, she came around, still far from happily, with which Elizabeth empathised.

She wasn't especially happy about any of it either: not Cressida's reprieve, or the idea of Francis's relief when he discovered he'd really got away with all he'd done. But what choice did she have but to go along with it?

Cressida at least had had a hell of a month.

Pitifully reduced, Arden had said of her.

And Francis would at least *believe* himself a murderer once Elizabeth's body was found. Probably, he'd consider himself lucky that the police hadn't found any trace of the cuts and bruises Elizabeth had been covered with when he'd cruelly despatched her into the night, and then feel guilty at his own fortune. He was a religious man. He'd believe hell to be waiting, Elizabeth was sure.

And Alan and Simon might believe themselves culpable in her death too, simply by merit of not having done more to help her. Especially Alan, who'd so heartlessly sent her to hide with John and Melder.

John and Melder would feel terrible as well, and so they should, banishing her to that derelict hovel.

Mrs Hamilton might even regret her vitriol towards Elizabeth.

Delen might.

Actually, now Elizabeth properly considered it, there really were all number of people who'd suffer, knowing her to have perished.

She enjoyed that idea.

The next day, Rupert travelled to London again, back by the weekend with a shiny new diamond choker (*use your money*; how helpful it was), and, the Monday following, left once more, to escort Laura to the mortuary.

'It's done?' Elizabeth asked her, when she and Rupert returned.

'It's done,' Laura said, unbuttoning her coat.

'How was James?' Elizabeth asked, because how could she not?

'Kind,' Laura said, with a deep sigh. 'I feel terrible. Dirty . . . '

'You're not dirty, and you're not terrible,' said Rupert. 'You're wonderful.'

And Elizabeth might have rolled her eyes, had she not feared the pain of the motion.

She did fear the pain, though.

She continued to fear more seizures.

But, although a visit from a discreet doctor with a prescription pad was duly arranged, he – a Mr Pullman, personally recommended by Rupert's family's private physician – provided Elizabeth with no second opinion that she wanted to hear. Rather, having perused Mr

Claymore's records, passed on to him by Arden, he sang exactly the same pessimistic tune as Mr Claymore had.

'Can I not at least try more injections?' Elizabeth asked him.

'There's no point, Mrs Atherton. Given the episodes you've been having, things have become much too advanced. All that salvarsan will do is make you feel worse. And look at my hand again, follow it . . . You can't see it now, correct?'

'I can.'

'Then how many fingers am I holding up? No, don't turn your head . . .'

'Three.'

'My hand is a fist, Mrs Atherton.'

She didn't believe him. *Couldn't* believe him.

She moved to look, and he gave her a sympathetic frown that made her want to scream.

'We can't reverse things now, I'm afraid.' Sorrowfully, he shook his head. 'But I can help you with your pain. And I'll see you fortnightly, to monitor how things are progressing. I'd like you to keep a diary of your pain, grading it from one to ten, then your episodes, their timing, how you feel afterwards, before, any further loss of feeling you might have, sight difficulties . . .'

And, on he went.

Elizabeth liked his pills at least.

But not even they helped with the grimness of her December funeral, which she talked Laura and Rupert into letting her attend, and at which bleak, drizzly affair she remained hidden in the back of Laura's motor, peeking out of the window through the mist at the gut-wrenchingly pitiful number of people grouped at her graveside.

Henry and Amy, flush with the joy of their new arrival (another Henry, after all), hadn't bothered to attend. Neither Dicky nor Cressida had come either. And although the Hamiltons were both there – Mrs Hamilton putting on a laughable pretence of subdued respect, no hint of the hatred she'd shown Elizabeth in life – neither Francis nor Thomas were in attendance (Elizabeth pictured Thomas, sobbing at the top of the lighthouse), whilst James, dressed in what looked to be the same suit he'd worn to their wedding, appeared bored, assuredly just waiting for the entire, inconvenient affair to be done with.

There weren't even as many reporters present as Elizabeth had expected: just a small handful, clustered beneath the shelter of black umbrellas, the rest of them probably distracted by the latest murder to have hit the press.

Clerk at Illustrated News bludgeoned to death by Private Nathan Edevane.

Elizabeth had rather approved of Private Edevane, up until that point. She'd liked how vehemently he'd fought her corner. But to have stolen her thunder like this?

It was too incredibly vexing.

At the start of 1933, Laura officially inherited all of Elizabeth's wealth and, at Elizabeth's request, withdrew several thousand pounds for Elizabeth to keep at the lodge, for no other reason than that Elizabeth never wanted to be without money again. And, although Laura refused to stomach facing James again after the funeral ('I can't do it, Lizzie, I simply can't . . . '), she sent two of her maids to Aoife's to pack up Elizabeth's clothes and belongings.

'Was James there?' Elizabeth asked Laura, when she came to deliver it all.

'Apparently not,' Laura said.

'What about the rest of them?'

'One assumes so.'

'I hate them, Laura. I hate them all so much. I hate that they're all just carrying on there. They made my life unforgivably hard . . . '

'Hush now, Lizzie. It's gone. Done with.'

It wasn't, though. Not to Elizabeth's mind.

But, for the ensuing sixteen months, she, prematurely living her death, remained hidden in Laura's lodge, sometimes with Laura there, occasionally Rupert as well (he never kept anything less than a concerted distance), but all too often, alone. She had to hide whenever the char Laura sourced came to clean and stock the kitchen, and, reluctantly, learnt how to cook her own meals, almost always resorting to *oeufs*, on the basis that they were very difficult to ruin.

The only person, other than Laura and Rupert, who she was permitted to see, was Mr Pullman. Much as she craved company, though, she didn't enjoy his, not like she'd used to enjoy Mr Claymore's. Mr Pullman, ancient and condescending, wasn't nearly so easy on her good left eye.

Still, she kept her diary for him, only lying a little when it came to the frequency of her 'episodes', as Mr Pullman euphemistically called her seizures, but not at all in terms of her pain, because she couldn't risk him lowering her opioid dose.

'Please don't worry about that, Mrs Atherton,' he said. 'That's not a course I'm considering pursuing.'

In the April of 1933 – four years after Mr Claymore had broken it to Elizabeth that his supposed cure had failed her, and she'd despondently boarded that train for London, so meeting James (and what a wonderful time they'd had together; hadn't they?) – she suffered her first seizure whilst Mr Pullman and Laura were both in attendance. That was when Mr Pullman declared that the time had come to recruit a nurse to live with Elizabeth permanently at the lodge. 'It's too dangerous for you to continue as you've been, Mrs Atherton. Your capacity to care for yourself is beginning to diminish very quickly.'

Elizabeth cried. She couldn't help herself.

Laura cried too.

She was very upset.

Nonetheless, she managed to rally sufficient cheer to marry Rupert in May, on a beautifully sunny Saturday ('I wish so much that you could have been there, Lizzie.' How Elizabeth wished it, too), and was pregnant with his child by September.

By that point, the sight in Elizabeth's right eye had gone completely, and she had a new and constant companion in the form of a middle-aged nurse called Ruth Flinders. She cleaned, so that Laura's char didn't have to, and had her own motor for collecting provisions. Better yet, she also had a wonderful knack for massaging Elizabeth's head – not to mention listening, with infinite sympathy, to the hideous hand that life had played her.

It was to Ruth that Elizabeth confided how unfair she felt it that Laura should be living so happily, whilst she was hardly living at all.

'And to think she's got all your money too,' said Ruth.

'Not that she needs it,' said Elizabeth.

'Do you really want her to have it in the long run? She stole Rupert, after all.'

'And my friend Amy. It was always me that was closer to her before.'

Ruth tutted. 'They've become quite the chums, I expect, up there in London. They'll be getting even closer too, now Laura's expecting.'

'Apparently Amy is again as well.'

'There you go.'

'It makes me sad, Ruth.'

'Of course it does, my sweet.'

'I don't like being sad all the time.'

'I don't like seeing you sad. Maybe you should think about who you do want your money to go to.'

'Do you mean, you, Ruth?'

Another tut. 'What an idea.'

'It might as well be you, as anyone, I suppose. But I'd rather keep it for myself.'

''Course you would.'

'I'm rather afraid of dying.'

'Aren't we all.'

'I suppose I should put some thought into what I want to happen when I do, though . . . '

'When you're ready, my sweet.

'I'm sure Laura will respect my wishes. She's that kind.'

'You mull it over, then.'

'I will, Ruth.'

'Would you like me to rub your head again?'

'Yes, please.'

And, as Ruth rubbed, Elizabeth did mull: *not* over who she wanted to leave her wealth to, as Ruth assuredly intended (what an idea, indeed; Elizabeth was ill, gravely – she could admit that now – but not naive); rather, closing her eyes, she thought, once again, of those who'd hurt her.

James, Francis, Cressida, Mrs Hamilton, Alan, Diana, Delen . . .

In all that increasingly slipped from her malfunctioning mind, their names she never forgot.

She had them on her list, and she checked it, morning, noon, and night.

As Laura's pregnancy advanced, she visited Elizabeth less, but wrote to her often from London. Elizabeth struggled to read her letters, thanks to her defunct right eye, and head that throbbed whenever she strained to do anything, so relied on Ruth to read them aloud to her. Mostly, they were dull – full of repetitive tales of Amy's little boy; the kicks in Laura's own belly; Rupert's shoots; restaurants the pair of them had visited ('Aren't they living the life of Riley,' said Ruth) – but nonetheless, provided a diversion.

But then, in February of 1934, Laura mentioned that Amy

402

Astley's brother, Edwin Firth, had, along with another lawyer, Patrick Knightly, set up a new firm.

I gather he finally got to the bottom of who it was that told you James's poor mother's secrets, Lizzie. I wish I could have persuaded his name out of you myself. Truly, Elizabeth could no longer recall it. *It would have been something I could have given James, to make up for all the lies I've fed him. And his mother was such a wonderful woman. I rather idolised her.*

'Ugh,' said Elizabeth to Ruth.

Anyway, it seems James is to be Edwin and Patrick's first client. And that woman you hated, Mrs Hamilton, won't be James's secretary for much longer either. He's hired a new one. A girl called Violet Ellis. She's to move to Aoife's in April . . .

'Read that last bit again,' Elizabeth asked Ruth, sitting straighter.

Ruth did. 'Lovely name, isn't it? *Violet.* I wonder how James has convinced her to move to that island.'

Elizabeth, wondering much the same, had her write by return to Laura and ask.

Also, how old this Violet was. And, when, precisely, in April she was to take up residence on Aoife's.

Plus, anything else Laura knew about her.

Is she pretty?

Try not to fret over that, Laura replied, which obviously meant that Violet *was* pretty. *I doubt James offering Miss Ellis the position has anything to do with her appearance. I gather from Amy that there's a degree of history between the pair of them. No one's really meant to know, but she's the daughter of that man who hated James so much. The one who hanged in June, Private Nathan Edevane . . .*

Elizabeth remembered him.

He hadn't slipped from her mind, either.

Cross, still, about the reporters who hadn't been at her funeral, she'd devoured the newspapers that had eventually covered his, at Pentonville. There'd been a blurred picture of the back of his daughter's head. She'd been sitting all alone. Young, assuredly.

Young, and pretty.

Imposter free, too.

Elizabeth couldn't bear it.

Couldn't bear that James had invited Violet to Aoife's, actually *wanted* her there, on that island where he'd made her so brutally unwelcome.

She couldn't tolerate that he, or anyone on that island, might be happy, when she was so deeply and damnably wretched.

'I need them all to be wretched too,' she told Ruth.

Ruth didn't attempt to hush her, as Laura might have.

No,

'That's understandable,' she said.

Which it was.

Understandable, and entirely reasonable.

'I think I'll have to make them wretched,' Elizabeth said.

'How?' Ruth asked.

'I don't know,' said Elizabeth, which she didn't.

Not immediately.

But, she thought on it.

She *mulled*.

Slowly, it came to her.

By the end of March, she knew what she wanted to do.

Chapter Thirty-Three

Elizabeth

Her plan wasn't an entirely clear one.

Just as when she'd fled from Aoife's, she hadn't thought every part of it through.

Truly, *plan* was probably too considered a word.

Idea might do better.

Or, *vision*.

Yes, she had a *vision*: one in which she inveigled her way back into the minds of those on her list, and upset them, *needled* at them, just as they had her.

The first letter she wrote, she penned herself, and it was agony, it took her almost an entire day to do it, with her arms and hands that had become so weak, but determinedly she pressed on.

'I'm afraid you need to, my sweet,' said Ruth, patting her shoulder. 'Laura will never believe it, if I've written it.'

That letter, marked to be opened in the event of Elizabeth's death, was addressed to Laura, pledging all that remained of Elizabeth's wealth to Ruth.

Use your money, John had counselled.

Elizabeth could think of no better purpose to put it to now than securing Ruth's assistance in pulling off her swan song.

Ruth claimed that she'd have gladly given Elizabeth her help, even without such a carrot dangling before her. 'On my oath, I've never hoped for anything from you. I'm here because you need me. It's my privilege to care for you . . . '

Elizabeth didn't believe her.

But nor did she blame her.

Good for her, frankly, looking out for herself. Only fools believed they could rely on others – who knew that better than Elizabeth? – and she approved of Ruth not being a fool.

Plus, she really did have such a knack with her hands.

Hands that she put to work from that day forward, penning Elizabeth's missives for her, experimenting with various handwriting styles, then driving in her motor to mailboxes far and wide to send them: no post mark the same.

The only letters Elizabeth put her name to, were those she sent to Thomas.

Everyone else's – and she sent scores – she signed simply, *Anonymous*.

Thomas, she wrote to out of necessity. Whilst she'd missed his adoration, she'd never remotely missed him, but she needed someone on the island to act for her, and there was no other for her to turn to.

Making no mention of her unfortunate state of health, she told him that his father had tried to kill her, and that she, fearing another attempt – if not by him, then by James, or any of the others who so irrationally despised her – had been in hiding ever since.

'Will he believe it?' Ruth asked.

'He'll believe anything I tell him,' said Elizabeth.

'And he can definitely read?'

'Yes, yes, his mother taught him. They've all of them been schooled.'

Help me, she entreated Thomas. *I need you to tell me if everyone is still there on Aoife's, and what they've all been up to. I know how*

you watch, my darling. Address your letters to Miss Ruth Flinders
and send them to the below address. I promise they'll find me.

Thomas replied within the week.

'Like an obedient puppy,' said Elizabeth.

In messy, oversized letters, he expended several paragraphs on his joy that Elizabeth was still alive, and the grief he'd suffered when he'd believed her dead.

I felt like I might as well be too. Thank God I'm not. Now I can breathe again. Live again. Just knowing you're still here, it's everything.

'Sweet, isn't he?' said Elizabeth to Ruth. 'Read the bit about how angry he is at Francis again, will you?

I can't bring myself to speak to Dad any more. I can't look at him. I hate him for having done that to you. I'll hate him forever.

Yes, Elizabeth really did like that part.

I'll hate him forever.

It was no less than Francis deserved.

After that, Thomas bored her with too much that was inconsequential (the weather; Mr Hamilton's ongoing church runs; a near miss for a ship, *I wish you could have seen how quick I helped with the beam . . .*), causing Elizabeth to yawn, then press worriedly at her face, feeling how the muscles in it really had begun to fail, only to sit straighter as Ruth relayed Thomas's revelation that Nelle had left Aoife's not long after she herself had, suffering with nerves ('She was always exceedingly wet,' Elizabeth said), but had returned to the island the month before, needing her wage, her labourer father having suffered some kind of injury.

'Poor man,' said Ruth.

'Yes, yes,' said Elizabeth, gesturing, with her enfeebled arm, at the bureau, as her right mind whirred, telling her what she must do with her next letter.

That, she sent to Nelle, timing it so that it would reach her at that start of the week Laura had said Violet Ellis was due on the island. Elizabeth placed several pound notes in the envelope ('Don't worry, Ruth, there'll be plenty left for you'), and wrote to Nelle that she, who wished to remain nameless, needed her assistance in a most sensitive matter.

'Which is?' asked Ruth.

'Keeping an eye on things for me in the house,' said Elizabeth. 'And making sure everyone there is as horrible to Violet as they were to me.'

'Oh, you are clever.'

'Thank you, Ruth. Now, let's carry on . . .'

Questions are being asked about whether Mrs Atherton's death was really an accident, she dictated, cackling inwardly. *The commissioner is under scrutiny, and has been asked to find someone to blame. I'm told that he doesn't care who that is, just so long as someone can be seen to pay. He might even come after you, Nelle. You and Mrs Atherton didn't entirely see eye to eye, did you?*

Now don't be afraid. With me on your side you'll be fine. But I need you to stay alert, act as my little bird, keeping me informed of what is going on, especially with regard to Miss Ellis when she arrives. If you do well, you'll receive further payments, which I happen to know you can't afford to pass up.

Miss Ellis is no simple secretary. She, in the employment of the commissioner, has been sent to spy on you all. I know, it's extremely shocking.

'Bit farfetched?' suggested Ruth.

'Nelle is a very simple girl,' said Elizabeth. 'And exceedingly malleable.'

She'll attempt to gain everyone's trust, she went on, *I'm relying on you not to permit that to happen. You can't breathe a word of this letter – the consequences for you will be dire if you do – so you must find other ways to turn your colleagues against Miss Ellis. Her father was none other than Private Nathan Edevane; perhaps you can find some plausible way to tell them all you've discovered that.*

A friend in service in London, perhaps. Say Miss Ellis has a terrible reputation for loose morals, and is after Mr Atherton's money. Pretend you caught her sitting on Mr Atherton's lap. Do whatever you must, Nelle, and take every opportunity to watch Miss Ellis: examine her things, search her room, then report everything back to me. Leave your letters in an unmarked envelope at the foot of the lighthouse peninsula, beneath a rock you'll find at its edge, painted with a white cross. They'll find their way to me.

And they did.

Care of Thomas, who Elizabeth instructed to paint and position that rock, then collect, and despatch, Nelle's mail.

Postie thinks I've got a new girlfriend, he wrote.

Don't break my heart, Elizabeth replied.

I couldn't, he said, *I wouldn't.*

Meanwhile, Elizabeth, hitting her stride, had dictated a flurry of other letters, all timed to arrive on Aoife's with Violet: one to Francis (*old thing*), threatening to expose his guilt; another to Mrs Hamilton, just to torture her (*do you feel anything at all? Are you capable of it?*); then, another to Alan (*Your sister was the reason you accepted that bribe to remain silent, wasn't it?*), just to torture him too; and, finally, to Diana, breaking it to her what her parents had got up to. *You're at sixes and sevens now, aren't you?*

Elizabeth did that to punish Diana, for not having been more cooperative in helping to incriminate Cressida with the police. Because who knew whether Cressida would have been permitted off the hook, had Diana just been prepared to say that she, as well as Thomas, had seen Cressida out chasing Elizabeth on the fields?

And now Cressida was walking free, with a little girl called Teddy who Laura said looked just like her, and who Cressida adored. It was nauseating, unacceptable . . .

Enjoying concocting her letters, at least – enjoying the accounts Nelle sent her of the strained mood that had entered the house with Violet (*It's changed, I don't like it*), and the lies about Violet she'd obligingly spread (*I've got a cousin in service in London, actually*) – Elizabeth wrote more: to mousey Diana, and wicked Francis, and cruel Mrs Hamilton, and cold, clumsy Alan. (Oh, how she laughed, when Nelle informed her of the fist fight that Alan and Simon had had after her genius note, insinuating Simon had betrayed Alan. *Simon says!*)

She never considered sending James anything. He, she feared, would smell a rat. Possibly even go to the police.

For much the same reason, she didn't write to Mr Hamilton either, tempted as she became.

Mrs Hamilton, however . . . She, Elizabeth felt confident, would be too proud to come clean to anyone, either about how truly awful her behaviour towards Elizabeth had been, or, that she'd now become a victim herself.

The rest of them had far too much to hide.

How do you suppose mama and papa would fare in prison, little mouse? Elizabeth enquired of Diana.

Then, in another letter, *Dare you ask them?*

Then, in another, *Try not to fret. I'll hold on to their secret. For a little longer.*

Simon was the final penfriend she made for herself. On him, she went comparatively lightly, but couldn't leave him entirely alone – not when he'd been so reluctant to help her out of her bind, that night of James's birthday – so she sent him the odd note, fabricating rumoured reports that had been made about him to the police.

Watch your back, my friend.

And so she went on.

For a while, the idea of the strain she was putting them all under – the thought of their spiralling confusion as to who she might be, when she might write next, and what she might do to expose their sins – was enough to satisfy her.

Nelle's assurances on how universally Violet was disliked, satisfied her. Especially given she felt sure that what was discomforting to Violet, must also be discomforting James.

'He'll tire of the inconvenience of it soon,' she told Ruth. 'You'll see. We'll be hearing before long that he's got rid of her, like he got rid of Delen.'

Except, they didn't hear that.

Instead, as April gave way to May, Nelle wrote of long walks that James took Violet on, all alone. The cosy teas they shared.

I reckon the commissioner might have told Miss Ellis to make him fall in love with her. I reckon it might be working.

Elizabeth broke a vase, when that letter arrived.

Had another *episode*, too.

'Rest now,' said Ruth. 'No, don't try to talk. You know you can't for a while afterwards.'

'Get out your pad,' Elizabeth instructed her, when she was back to herself.

You must listen out for what's going on in Miss Ellis's room at night, Elizabeth told Nelle. *I want to know if she has company.*

I can't hear nothing, Nelle replied.

It's anything, Elizabeth told her, *not nothing.*

I can't hear anything, Nelle said. *And now Mr Atherton has gone away for work.*

Good, replied Elizabeth. *Keep listening, though, little bird.*

It was Thomas who informed Elizabeth that, when James returned from his business trip, he did so with his sister and niece in tow.

Cressida's back? she demanded of him. *What can she be thinking? What are you thinking?*

That she looks very sad, Thomas replied. *Very sorry.*

Don't you dare be fooled, Elizabeth said.

Then, to Laura,

Have you heard anything of Cressida lately, by chance?

I gather she's divorcing Dicky, Laura replied, *not before time. He's got himself into a terrible mess, financially. His father's had enough. According to Amy, James is settling his accounts on the condition that he lets Cressida and Teddy go without a fuss.*

'That should make you happy,' said Ruth, looking up from Laura's note, and down at Elizabeth in her bed, which she hadn't had the energy to rise from that day.

'It doesn't, though, Ruth. Cressida's got James. She's got her daughter . . .'

'Not much you can do about that.'

'Isn't there?' said Elizabeth, and pushed the matter to the side of her right mind, ready to consider, *mull*, another time.

Meanwhile, she waited for Nelle's next report.

But Nelle was late with it, so Elizabeth told her off (*What is going on, over there? What on earth is going on?*), after which, Nelle did write, insolently trying to extricate herself from her responsibilities.

I think you've been tricking me into helping you. I talked to my dad, and he said it's all wrong, that you're probably just a madman with too much money and nothing better to do with it. I like Miss Ellis. She's always so nice. And I think she might love Mr Atherton too . . .

How dare you call me mad? Elizabeth had written back. *And what do you mean you think that Miss Ellis might love Mr Atherton? What basis have you for such an absurd hypothesis?*

Again, she waited for Nelle's reply.

But it was Thomas who wrote first.

Nelle had a tumble, leaving her last letter for you. Right near where Mum went. Nearly got killed . . .

'That must have given her a scare,' said Ruth.

'I hope it's shocked her into some sense,' said Elizabeth, who'd forgotten all about Mrs Browning and her supposed tumble.

What *had* happened there?

'You don't think we better leave it all for a while now?' asked Ruth.

412

'I can't, Ruth. I just can't.'

At the start of June, Rupert wrote that Laura had given birth to a little girl – Lillian, they'd called her (might they not have chosen Elizabeth?) – and Elizabeth, whose right mind had once again done her proud, devising what she was to do about Cressida, wrote to Dicky, anonymously again, offering to help with his finances so that he might be saved the pain of losing custody of his daughter. *Write by return, care of the below post office box, intimating how much you need.*

'I didn't think you liked Dicky,' Ruth said.

'I like Cressida a lot less,' said Elizabeth.

'And how are you to get this money to him?'

'I've got plenty here.'

'Enough though?'

'More than enough. You mustn't worry.'

'I'm not . . .'

'You are. I see you are. But don't. When I go, you'll be wealthier than your wildest dreams.'

'This isn't about the money.'

'So you keep saying.'

'Maybe if you told me how much you have in the safe?'

'The key's in my bedside drawer. Fetch it if you like, have a count.'

So, Ruth had a count.

'Yes,' she said, once she was finished, 'that's quite a lot.'

Thomas wrote, several times through the first fortnight of June, telling Elizabeth the ins and outs of the plans for the solstice festivities in St Leonard's, how hot it was getting, how quiet on the island, and how old his father was seeming, sleepless in the

413

heat, anxious and uneasy. *I know he's done wrong, but I don't like seeing him like this.*

What about Nelle? Elizabeth asked him, ignoring the irritation of his concern over Francis. (*I'll hate him forever*, he'd said. What rot.) *Is Nelle back up and about?*

Seems to be, he replied, on the Monday before the solstice. *Here's a letter for you.*

I won't write again, Nelle threatened. *But I know Miss Ellis loves Mr Atherton now, because she's getting married to him. So there, she doesn't mean him any harm. Leave us all alone.*

'Read it again,' Elizabeth demanded of Ruth.

'I think you heard, my sweet.'

'It can't be right,' said Elizabeth, clutching her stomach, feeling very much like she was going to be sick.

She was sick.

Copiously.

That was partially down to her imposter – Mr Pullman had long since asked Ruth to record such incidents in her journal – but not entirely.

It was James and Violet's fault as well.

Wiping her mouth, with the back of her weak, useless hand, Elizabeth told Ruth to get out her pad so that she might write to Nelle and make absolutely sure she had her facts straight. *He's asked her to marry him? I don't believe you. I won't believe it.* Then, as her right mind once again rose to the occasion, *I think I'd better come and see for myself.*

'I'm not sure that's a good idea,' said Ruth, pen hovering.

'I am,' said Elizabeth, pushing her failing fingers to her throbbing head; gagging on another surge of bile. 'I can't spend another day locked in this lodge, enduring this . . . *pain*. The opioids don't work any more. Nothing works. I'm dying, *dying*, and I need to do this.' The tears spilt from her. 'I'm so alone.'

'You have me.'

'Only because I'm paying you. I want to be with people who want me with them. I want Aoife.'

'Aoife's not real, my sweet.'

'But she is. And I miss her terribly. I miss my brother. I've remembered now where I lost that choker. It wasn't in the sea, at all . . . '

'What?'

'It was there, on the island.'

'Oh, God . . . '

'I dropped it in Thomas's old cottage. John was going to steal it from me, you see. I have to fetch it. I want it with me when I die. But I can't *die* knowing that that will be it for all of them, over *there*.' Shaking, she looked, with her left eye in the direction she imagined Aoife's to be. 'I have to go back.' She retched again. 'I need you to help me. Will you? Please.'

Ruth frowned, shaking her head. 'It will cause so much trouble. Everyone will know these letters have been you. They'll guess I've helped . . . '

'I'll say I paid Laura's old char. It will be her word against mine. *Please*, Ruth. You can even have the choker once I'm gone. You'll have it all.'

Slowly, Ruth's frown softened.

'You'll blame the char?' she said.

'I'll blame the char.'

And, hesitating only a moment longer, Ruth nodded.

Of course she nodded.

She had her eye on her prize, and it was glinting.

Ruth pressed Elizabeth on what she intended to do when she reached Aoife's Bay.

Elizabeth couldn't tell her.

'I'm not a planner, you know that, Ruth.'

What Elizabeth did know, though, was that she needed for Ruth to drive her to St Leonard's, and pay a boatman there to courier her to the island. They resolved that Ruth herself couldn't escort her: it would be too incriminating. ('You can never let on that I've known any of it,' Ruth said, again, and again, and again.). They also decided that Elizabeth should make her journey on the solstice, when she might more easily go unnoticed in the festival crowds. Not that her sagging face, thinning hair, and patched eye, were particularly recognizable any more.

'I'm afraid not, my sweet,' said Ruth. 'We'll still colour your hair, and wrap you up in a shawl, though, just to be sure.'

Ruth went ahead to St Leonard's, the Wednesday before the solstice, to arrange Elizabeth's crossing on the pretence of acting for a relative of the Brownings who wished to visit ailing Francis as a surprise.

'You'll leave at eight from the wharf,' Ruth told Elizabeth, when she returned. 'A man called Abel will be waiting for you in a blue boat named *Bess*.'

Recruiting Abel wasn't the only groundwork Ruth laid.

Unable to resist torturing her pen pals with one final epistle, Elizabeth had Ruth write to them all, letting them know that she was inbound.

And, on an eleventh-hour whim, she asked her to wire Delen, too.

'Is that not going a bit far?' asked Ruth.

'I don't want her to miss the fun,' said Elizabeth. 'Thomas says Mr Hamilton will be bringing everyone back from the festival at ten. Tell her she needs to catch that boat. Sign it from James.'

'But what are you going to *do* when they all get there?' Ruth repeated.

'It will come to me,' Elizabeth assured her.

It would, she was sure.

Everything always did, in the end.

All that mattered for the present was that she was returning to the island.

She'd reclaim her choker, and afterwards, there'd be no more moving on.

My patience has run thin, she'd written to Nelle. *It's just about run out.*

I'm coming, she'd said to Thomas. *I'm on my way.*

It's time, old thing, she'd told Francis.

It's time.

Chapter Thirty-Four

Violet and Elizabeth

June 1934

'She's here,' Francis said to James on the wharf. 'She's come.'

'Who's come?' said James to him, as more lightning flashed.

Almost immediately, thunder growled.

Violet didn't flinch at the sound, or glance up at the dry, heavy sky. She looked at Francis, his face wrung, and Gareth, grim beside him. In the pause before Gareth answered, she felt her heart kick, not in suspicion of what name Gareth might utter – she had none – just simple dread, because whoever it was, it was obviously no one good.

More wind blew, ruffling the hot, charged air: an ill-wind, full of malevolence.

Aoife's stirring, Violet had said to Cressida earlier.

She was awake now.

'Who?' asked James again, impatience making him short.

'Elizabeth,' choked Francis.

Elizabeth.

The word, Francis's voice, seemed to come from another sphere, another plane.

Violet's own had, quite abruptly, tipped, and stopped.

Elizabeth.

It felt too absurd to be real.

It was absurd.

Yet, it was, also, apparently real.

'She wanted her choker,' Francis continued.

'I found her searching for it,' said Gareth. 'Thought I was looking at a ghost.'

'Mrs Hamilton's thrown it over,' said Francis.

James didn't speak.

His face was very still, but his eyes, bright in the darkness, moved: from Francis, to Gareth, up to the cottages; *thinking*.

Instinctively, Violet stepped towards him, in the same moment as he reached out for her. She felt his warm grasp come around hers – *This will be all right*, he seemed to say – and she tightened her own. *I know*.

Only she didn't know.

She didn't know anything.

There was another flash.

More thunder.

Elizabeth.

'Where did Mrs Hamilton throw the choker?' James asked Francis, finally breaking his silence.

It wasn't the first question that had sprung to Violet's mind.

He was reeling, of course.

'Ocean,' said Francis, strangled, quite obviously reeling too.

'Why?'

'She was angry.'

'Where are they both now?' asked Violet, and it was a relief, at least, to talk. To be *doing* something.

'Mrs Hamilton's gone home,' said Gareth, and she saw how he looked at her: the regret, and sympathy, in his kind stare.

It didn't make her feel better.

She didn't want sympathy.

She didn't want any of this to be happening.

'Elizabeth's up there,' said Francis, nodding at the lighthouse, with its motionless beam. 'Been talking about Aoife, like she's real.

Seems to think she can see her.'

It really did sound preposterous, put like that.

'I been getting these letters,' he went on.

'Letters?' said James.

Oh, my God, thought Violet.

'Mrs Hamilton has too. Turns out near everyone's been getting them. Thomas knew.' Francis drew a shuddering breath. 'He knew it all. Never said. I never guessed it could be her, writing . . . Never dreamt she could be alive.'

'Where has she been?' asked Violet, numbly.

'Not far away,' said Gareth, taking over from Francis, who, head bowed, seemed to have momentarily lost the power of speech. 'Not far at all. Seems Miss Ratcliffe, as was, has been looking after her.'

'Laura?' said James, and Violet felt him stiffen. '*She* knew?'

'She knew.'

Under his breath, he cursed.

Then,

'Right,' he said, grimly, 'right,' and, in that one word, seemed to come back to himself. 'You'd better tell us what exactly has been going on.'

Elizabeth watched the four of them on the wharf from up outside the lighthouse. She was collapsed in one of the decrepit deckchairs she'd spent so much time in during her tenure on the island, exhausted from her journey, and the events of the last two hours. Thomas stood to her left. Aoife flitted excitedly to her right. Reassured by her presence, at least, Elizabeth studied the shadows below her, fixated on the stillness of them; the occasional relief the lightning threw their silhouettes into; then, their sudden movement, towards the cliff stairs.

She'd seen Violet already, earlier in St Leonard's. She'd spotted her when she'd been on her way to find Abel, and his boat called

Bess. The second she'd glimpsed her, climbing out of Mr Hamilton's ferry behind Cressida (*Cressida*), and ebony-haired Teddy, she'd known who she was, and it had incensed her, because really, how unimaginative of James to have chosen someone so *conventional*: so utterly, obviously, unexceptionally *sweet*.

Another strawberry, in fact.

How could he? When he might have had Elizabeth, in her prime?

Furiously, she'd summoned the energy to knock into Violet on the quayside, jerking her sideways, but depleted as she herself had been by that small exertion, Violet hadn't paid her touch a moment's heed. She'd been preoccupied, looking for someone in the crowds.

Looking for James.

Elizabeth had heard him call out to her, with such warmth in his deep voice that it had been a dagger in her heart. Another had come when she'd glimpsed him making a beeline for Violet, his handsome face (that *face*) *smiling*, focused entirely on reaching her, when he'd only ever wanted to head in the opposite direction to Elizabeth.

She'd watched the easy way he'd run his hands around Violet's waist, the joy in Violet's own smile, then turned away, unable to look a second longer: not at them, and certainly not at Cressida, with her delightful, delighted cherub in her arms. Because, although she'd set Dicky well on his way to reclaiming that cherub with the several hundred pounds she'd now sent him, she'd forgotten, with everything else going on, to remind Ruth, when Ruth had dropped her in St Leonard's, to send Dicky the next tranche he'd requested.

Would Ruth do it, anyway?

Elizabeth could but hope so.

For herself, she wouldn't be returning to the lodge, or Ruth, after this night. She'd resolved on that now. Even as Abel had ferried her over to Aoife's – no hint of recognition in his weathered face, nor murmured suggestion that he might have seen Elizabeth somewhere

421

before (had she changed *that* much? To her horror, it seemed she must have) – she'd been deciding. By the time she'd felt the hot, welcoming whirl of Aoife's hold coming around her, she'd known that she wouldn't leave her again.

And, sad thought, but had Ruth realized that she wouldn't want to?

And was that why she'd agreed to help Elizabeth come back? Because she'd seen her own freedom, beckoning?

It felt all too plausible.

Elizabeth doubted Ruth would even wait around to see whether Laura would be prepared to grant her Elizabeth's endowment. No, probably she'd already emptied the safe of its more than ten thousand pounds, and run.

In her shoes, Elizabeth would be running. She'd known, deep down, that her promised lies about bribed chars were never really going to wash. No one with an ounce of sense was going to believe that she and Ruth hadn't been in cahoots all along.

God speed to her. She'd been a good nurse.

Elizabeth bore her no ill-will.

And for now, she needed to focus on the night at hand.

Truly, it hadn't gone well, so far.

First, there'd been the blow of her choker.

Desperate to have it with her, to *hold* it, hold her brother, she'd headed straight to the Brownings' old cottage from the wharf. The garden had been full of building supplies, and the floorboards inside, all awry. She'd tried to move them so that she could search beneath them, but she'd been tired, even then: shaky and breathless from her walk up the cliffside, her weak, unresponsive arms no match for the heavy, cumbersome task. Tears of frustration had built in her throat, bile too . . .

'Who are you?' Gareth Phillips had asked her, shocking her by being suddenly there.

She'd turned to look at him, with her good left eye.

He, like Abel, hadn't recognized her.

It had upset her even more.

'What have you done with my choker?' she'd asked.

And Gareth had known her then.

He'd stared, stupid with shock.

'My choker,' she'd said. 'Please . . . '

Still, nothing.

'*Gareth.*'

'Mrs Hamilton has it.'

'Where?'

'No,' he'd said, shaking his head, backing away. 'No. You're gone. You should be gone . . . '

'I'm here, you fool. And I want my choker. Where is Mrs Hamilton?'

Eventually, she'd extracted from him that he'd seen her heading up to the lighthouse.

So, to this lighthouse she'd come.

He'd insisted on accompanying her. 'I'm not letting you loose alone.'

It hadn't been a quick walk.

She hadn't had *quick* in her.

And Gareth hadn't so much as offered her his arm for support, not even when they'd reached the start of the lighthouse's peninsula, where the path had been narrowed by some rather ramshackle fencing. (The spot Nelle had tumbled, Elizabeth had guessed, from the rock she'd spotted at its edge, painted with a now-faded white cross: dull, in the long day's diminishing light.) For most of the way, Gareth hadn't spoken either, until he'd suddenly started, firing at Elizabeth the questions he'd obviously been silently scripting: about where she'd been, who with, what was wrong with her . . .

She hadn't answered him.

Owing him nothing, she'd ignored him, her thoughts consumed by her choker.

Her choker that Mrs Hamilton had taken.

Mrs Hamilton, who, along with Francis and Thomas, had seen herself and Gareth approaching, and walked down the peninsula to meet them.

And how had *they* each reacted, when it had dawned on them that Elizabeth was not only alive, but back?

Elizabeth didn't know.

Thomas had robbed her of that moment.

Robbed her, too, of the satisfaction of educating the pair of them on how cleverly she'd outsmarted them, because he'd already confessed every truth and half-truth she'd ever fed him: from her marriage to James, to how she'd escaped the island, twenty months before, to the shelter Laura and Rupert had given her, to the spying she'd persuaded Nelle into, the other letters she'd written . . . *everything*.

Mrs Hamilton had persuaded him into his treason. It seemed that Elizabeth's choker had been discovered, earlier that same day (really, it was almost as though Anthony had sensed her coming), and, when it had, Mrs Hamilton had started to fear, at last, who her own letters might have been coming from. Suspecting Francis had also been a recipient ('Aren't you clever,' Elizabeth had said), she'd come to call on him and Thomas, just as soon as her husband had spirited the rest of the island away to St Leonard's, demanding to know what they knew.

'How dare you?' she'd spat at Elizabeth, coming to halt in front of her on the peninsula's grass, the Brownings behind her. (*How dare she?* Aoife had whispered in Elizabeth's ear, and Mrs Hamilton's dark hair – loose, like she'd been tugging at it – had blown in her festering breeze.) 'How dare you be alive? How dare you have come here?'

Elizabeth hadn't immediately responded. Her right mind had left her, just when she'd needed it most, whilst her wrong one had emptied of everything but the horror in Thomas's stare as he'd

424

appraised her eye patch and scraggly, black hair.

He hadn't opened his arms to her.

She'd imagined him trying to embrace her.

Wanting to.

It had been a long, long time since anyone had.

'This is what your father did to me,' she'd said, speaking not to Mrs Hamilton, but him: the lie, coming to her as she'd uttered it, weakly, her words slurred by exhaustion.

'I never did,' Francis had claimed, his own voice cracking with emotion. He'd aged, terribly, but Elizabeth had taken no joy from it. He, haggard and bent, had looked too beaten for triumph. She'd found no joy in anything that had been happening. Only panic, and mortification. 'You've been turning my own son against me.'

'You tried to kill me. You pushed me off the cliffs.'

'You went into convulsions. I tried to help—'

'By sending me off alone in a dinghy?'

'No.' He'd shouted it. 'No. I helped you, because you told me to, and I was sick of the sight of you, but you took yourself out in that boat alone . . . '

'I didn't.'

'You did.'

'No, you pushed me. Aoife rescued me . . . '

'You're in a fantasy world.'

'You're lying.'

'I'm not.'

He is, Aoife had sung. *He is*.

Only . . . was he?

Elizabeth had forgotten so much else.

Had she forgotten what had really happened with him that night, too?

She didn't think so.

She really didn't think so.

But she didn't *know*.

It was terrifying, awful . . .

'What's the matter with you?' Mrs Hamilton had asked. 'You look extremely unwell.'

'I am rather,' Elizabeth had replied, and might have been more grateful that James had clearly never done her the disservice of betraying her ill health to them all – like Mr Claymore had betrayed it to him – had he not betrayed her so completely in every other way.

'Those pills you kept,' Mrs Hamilton had said. 'Were they . . . ?'

'Yes, Mrs Hamilton, yes.' She'd felt tears coming again. It had been hideous standing, so exposed, before them all. 'Have another gold star.'

'I want nothing from you.'

'Nor me from you. Especially not your pity.'

'You certainly don't have it.'

'Not from any of us,' Gareth had chimed in.

Elizabeth had all but forgotten he was there.

She hadn't wanted to be any more, either.

She'd wanted to be back in her lodge, with Ruth rubbing her head.

Why had she left?

Why had she come?

She'd clutched her head, trying, frantically, to remember.

'I want my choker,' she'd heard herself sobbing. 'Please, won't you just give it to me?'

'This?' Mrs Hamilton had said, opening her hand, holding it out to her.

For the first time that night, Elizabeth's heart had lifted.

Vainly, she'd reached out for it. Reached for her brother . . .

Which was when Mrs Hamilton had turned from her, hurling him, and her choker, over the cliffside, into the Atlantic.

'Fetch it,' she'd said.

And, sinking on her folding knees, Elizabeth had sobbed in earnest, whilst Mrs Hamilton had gone home.

'I wish I had killed you,' Francis had told Elizabeth, before he too had gone, with Gareth, to wait for the others at the wharf. 'You're a disease . . .'

'I'm not a disease,' she'd said, 'I'm not.'

But he hadn't listened.

Nor had Gareth.

Or Thomas.

Only Aoife.

'Thank you,' Elizabeth said to her now, in the darkness, as James, Violet, Gareth and Francis disappeared up the cliffside. 'Thank you, Aoife.'

'She's not real,' Thomas told her, not for the first time that night. (*Don't listen to him*, Aoife whispered.) 'I am, though. And I'm sorry that you've got so poorly.'

'Don't lie. I saw the way you looked at me earlier.'

'I was upset, that was all. Upset, because I loved you.'

Loved.

No *love*. Not for her.

Not any more.

'Did you love me, Thomas?' She turned, facing him, looking into his mad, mercury-tinted gaze. 'Really?'

'Question for you? Did it feel like I loved you?'

'I don't know. Not many people have loved me.' She could be honest about that now. For, if not now, then when? 'Not many at all.'

'Well, I did. You used to make me happy. Before you done all this . . . wrong.'

'It's *did*. And I haven't.'

'You have. I have too.'

'You mean your mother?'

Finally: an admission . . .

'No, I mean helping you.'

'Oh.' *Oh.*

'You told me so many lies, Elizabeth. The way I've been to my dad. All of them. Miss Ellis. You said she had it in for you. That she tried to stop Mr Atherton ever marrying you . . . '

'Did I?'

Had she?

'*Yes*. And I'm ashamed. So ashamed. It's twisting me up,' he lay the flat of his hand to his heart, 'here.'

'They hurt me, Thomas.'

'I think it's you, been doing the hurting. Dad's always telling me the past's the past. That we got to let it go . . . '

'And how has that gone for you?'

'Not well. But I think you got to try and let yours go.'

'I can't.'

'Why?'

'I'm too afraid.'

'What of?'

'Everything. I have been for years.' She turned back to look at the deserted wharf. 'I can't remember any more what it was like not to be.'

He sighed, like he understood that much.

And, perhaps he did.

She sighed too.

'I really did want everyone to come back from St Leonard's together,' she said.

'Why?'

'I just imagined that being the way it happened. I wanted to surprise them. It's too bad.' Tears pricked her eyes. 'It really is too bad.'

Lightning flashed.

Thunder cracked.

'They'll be on their way by now at any rate,' said Thomas. 'I need to set that lamp turning again.' He looked upwards. 'Storm's almost here.'

428

*

Beneath the black sparking sky, Violet approached the green front door of Mrs Hamilton's cottage. Gareth – appalled to learn that Delen was even now on her way over from St Leonard's, at Elizabeth's invitation – had returned to the wharf to break it to her, and everyone else, what was unfolding. James, meanwhile, was accompanying Francis to the lighthouse, there to deal with Elizabeth himself.

'Deal, how?' Violet had asked him.

'I'll work it out,' he'd replied.

'I want to go with you . . . '

'No, absolutely not.'

'James, please . . . '

'No, I can't have you near her. You don't want to be.'

'He's right,' Francis had said.

'Let him keep a clear mind,' Gareth had counselled. 'He'll only be worrying about you, if you're there.'

'I will,' James had said. 'Please, don't make this harder.'

Violet hadn't been able to argue with that.

So here she was, full of misgiving, heading up Mrs Hamilton's front path, alone, her mind spinning with everything that Francis and Gareth had just relayed to herself and James. James was, naturally, incandescent – at Elizabeth, and Laura, and Alan and Simon, and every other member of his staff who hadn't seen fit to come to him with what was going on – whilst Violet felt as though she'd stumbled into some hideous, nightmarish maze, out of which she was struggling to believe there might be any escape. And although she now knew, at last, what Francis's argument with Mrs Hamilton had been about, the day she'd arrived, it was small comfort, because it had, of course, been to do with Elizabeth's letters.

Francis had been angry, he'd said, as they'd climbed the cliffs. He'd received his first letter with the morning post, and been certain Violet must have had some hand in it, since Elizabeth had mentioned her.

'How had she known to?' Violet had asked.

'That friend of hers in London,' Francis had said, and James had slammed his hand against the rail. 'I was in a rage,' Francis had gone on, 'set on having it out with you, Miss Ellis. I let myself into the house, and Mrs Hamilton caught me on the stairs, asked me what I thought I was doing. I didn't mention the letter, just that I had to speak to you . . . '

'Had she read her own letter, yet?'

'No. She still hadn't been home. She tore a strip off me, saying how I wasn't meant to come to the house uninvited, especially not to accost helpless young women. I told her I wasn't finished with the matter, that we'd talk about it another time, she told me we most certainly wouldn't, and sent me packing, then followed me, just to make sure I went. Didn't dare try again after that. Couldn't face it . . . ' He'd paused, gathering his breath, looking down at Violet behind him. 'She was protecting you, Miss Ellis.'

It hadn't surprised Violet, not as it might have done back then. Not now she'd grown to know Mrs Hamilton better.

Not given the visit Mrs Hamilton had paid her, just two days later, warning her to keep away from the Brownings.

But she still had questions for her. Many, many questions.

And she didn't want to remain by herself, waiting for James to *deal* with Elizabeth.

So, she raised her hand, to knock on Mrs Hamilton's door.

And, again, when no one answered.

At length, footsteps sounded beyond it. Slowly, it edged open, Mrs Hamilton looking to see who was there, then, realizing it was Violet, she opened the door wider. She'd been crying, Violet saw instantly. Her pale cheeks were swollen. Her eyes, glassy. The neck of her silk blouse was damp.

'I'm sorry,' she said, and her face crumbled. 'I never

430

imagined . . . Never . . . I am so sorry . . . '

'It's all right,' said Violet, which it wasn't, not at all, but she needed to say something. 'It's all right.'

Mrs Hamilton shook her head, and, helplessly, Violet stepped forwards, placing her hand to her arm, half-expecting, even then, for her to push her away.

But Mrs Hamilton – controlled, calm Mrs Hamilton – didn't push her anywhere.

She reached up, gripping Violet's hand with her own cold one, and invited her inside.

They went to her drawing room, where Mrs Hamilton already had a brandy on the go, and poured Violet one. The room was as immaculate as Violet might have expected, with a gramophone in its corner, and a table neatly stacked with fashion journals; the windows were open, curtains drawn, letting the stifling breeze in.

Up at the lighthouse, the beam was once again moving.

Far out at sea, another light had appeared on the horizon: Mr Hamilton's boat, approaching.

'He's going to be angry,' Mrs Hamilton said, following Violet's stare.

'You never said anything to him?'

'I didn't say anything to anyone.'

'Why?'

'Because I haven't known what to say.' She turned her bloodshot eyes back to Violet. 'It's been a nightmare. A living nightmare . . . '

'You could have talked to me,' Violet said. 'Will you now, please?'

And, falteringly, as the two of them moved to sit on the room's settee, Mrs Hamilton did, starting with how she'd felt, discovering her first letter from Elizabeth, the day Violet had arrived. 'I'd come back here after I'd seen Francis across the fields. Arnold was down at the wharf with Mr Atherton, you remember he went to Penzance . . . '

'Yes, I remember.'

'I thought to get Arnold his lunch, and found the letter waiting. It mentioned you, asked me how I felt about your arrival. I had to check if you knew anything about it. I realized as soon as I spoke to you that you didn't.'

'Is that why you punished me with your tale of Aoife?'

'No,' she closed her eyes, 'I did that out of anger, that you'd come.'

'Because I took your job?'

'Not only that. I couldn't understand you . . . *choosing* this place, over London. *Life.*' She gave Violet a pained look. 'I never had a choice. From the moment James offered Arnold this post, his mind was made up. We hardly had any money. He never left our house. But you . . . ' Her forehead creased. 'You had a choice. Yet, you came. For Mr Atherton, I've come to realize. And I understand that now, I do. I see how you love him. I know that love, myself. But then, I resented you. I wanted to shake you . . . '

'Well, you did that.'

'And I'm sorry.' Her expression, as naked as Violet had known it, was sincere. 'Arnold had told me about your father. I should have been kinder.' Her eyes glistened. 'I know about that too, after all. What it is to live with a man changed by that war.'

'I'm sorry for that too,' said Violet, her throat tightening at such unexpected intimacy. 'Although, I don't think you should compare your husband to my father.'

'No,' Mrs Hamilton agreed. 'No . . . '

'You really did scare me, you know. I've thought about Aoife, too much.'

'It's just a myth,' Mrs Hamilton said, as she had back then. 'Put it from your mind.'

'I've tried.'

432

'Try harder,' she said, like it was so simple.

'You've never been uneasy?'

'Not about her. Only this place.' She raised her glass, draining it. 'Don't get the two confused, Miss Ellis.'

Slowly, Violet nodded.

Mrs Hamilton stood, going to the sideboard for the bottle.

'Didn't you ever suspect Francis might have had a letter too?' Violet asked, as she topped them both back up. 'It must have occurred to you . . . '

'Yes, but I didn't take it seriously. Not at first. I supposed someone was . . . *toying* with us.' She sat. 'After Elizabeth went, we all of us got scores of letters from strangers, accusing us, questioning us . . . I assumed that it was just more of the same. Nothing more than a . . . '

'Trifle?'

'Exactly. A flash in a pan. Only, the letters kept coming. Always anonymous. And whoever was writing them obviously knew a great deal. Then, Diana, Nelle, Alan . . . They weren't themselves. I asked them, naturally, if anything was worrying them, but they claimed not, so I started checking the postmarks of their mail, all the mail, trying to find a pattern.' She looked at Violet. 'You caught me out in that.'

'Did you find a pattern?'

'No, the postmarks never repeated. The handwriting didn't seem to, either.' She frowned at her glass. 'Alan admitted to me, after he and Simon fought, that someone had written to him, *annoying* him, but he said it had been about Simon talking to a girl about him. He gave no hint of what the two of them had done . . . ' She broke off. 'I didn't want to bother Mr Atherton with it. Not with his sister just back, upset enough. I saw no point. Then Nelle had that fall, and I was worried about that. I've worried about everything.' She broke off, staring into her glass.

The night outside flashed, it growled.

And, below, the waves grew louder.

'What have you thought it might all be about?' Violet asked.

'Thought?' Mrs Hamilton let go a sound, halfway between a sob and a laugh. 'I haven't known what to think.'

'You really never suspected it might be her?'

'Not until you told me about Arnold finding her choker. She was dead, buried. I never questioned that. I was at her funeral. I saw the earth thrown on her grave . . . ' She emitted another strangled noise. 'I took the choker to show to Francis earlier, after you all left for the fair. I hoped of everyone, I could convince him to be honest with me. But it was Thomas. *Thomas*.' She shook her head, as though still trying to make sense. '*He* was the one who knew everything.'

'Yes,' said Violet, thinking now of her first encounter with Thomas, at the start of May.

She doesn't want you here, he'd said.

All this time she'd believed him to have meant Mrs Hamilton.

But it had been Elizabeth.

Always, it had been her.

Outside, there was another bolt of lightning, the thunder so violent this time, it made the walls and windowpanes shake. And, in the same moment, the wind blew, with sudden strength, sending the curtains flying.

Pulse racing, Violet moved, going to the windows, looking from Mr Hamilton's boat, up towards the lighthouse. She didn't expect to see anyone – she'd been imagining James inside the Brownings' home, bolstered, *shielded*, by Francis's presence – and yet, as more lightning illuminated the island, she saw two figures on the cliff pass, where the rocks were subsiding, and Nelle had fallen. One of them was James. She knew it. *Felt it*. Her heart did too, quickening all the more.

The other figure, close to the cliff's edge, far too close, was slighter, shorter, and could only be Elizabeth: real, at last – no ghost, haunting Violet's steps, nor invisible reflection in a mirror

434

– but living, breathing.

She's everywhere, Cressida had said.

But she wasn't.

She was here, *here*, and it sent Violet's pumping blood cold.

'I need to go,' she said, realizing how true it was. 'I should never have left him alone.'

'He won't want you there.'

'I don't care.'

'Fine.' Mrs Hamilton stood too. 'I'll come with you.'

'You don't have to . . . '

'Miss Ellis . . . '

'Violet, please, for God's sake.'

'All right,' Mrs Hamilton conceded with a nod. '*Violet*. She's in a sorry state, and I expect just waiting to take it out on you. Let me help if I can, please.'

Elizabeth had left the lighthouse before she'd seen Francis and James coming.

Thomas had abandoned her, for his damned lamp, so she – with Aoife skipping beside her – had returned to the point from which Mrs Hamilton had so cruelly thrown her choker. Moving beyond a gap in the fence, she'd peered over the cliff's edge, down into the crashing waves, picturing Anthony's diamonds on the seabed below – trying to devise whether it was her wrong or right mind suggesting that, with just a few short steps, she might return to them, return to him, all of it, *over* – when Aoife had cautioned her to wait.

Look who's coming.

And, out of the corner of her left eye, Elizabeth glimpsed the pair of them on the cliff pass: Francis, stooped, his hands stuffed in his pockets; James, strong and proud and intent.

She'd all but given up on him coming.

Nothing else had gone her way, after all.

It was a shame, though, that he hadn't brought Violet.

And that the others were all still on Mr Hamilton's rocking boat.

She doubted, now, that she'd see them.

Did it even matter?

She wasn't sure. She'd had no plan, she really hadn't.

And yet, she was assailed by such an awful sense of unravelling; everything happening out of sequence, beyond the realms of her control . . .

Francis continued past her, heading for the lighthouse without acknowledgement, like she was a ghost already.

But James, he came to a halt before her, at the fence: so close that she could smell his scent, see the fury firing in his dark eyes.

And . . . something else, too?

Horror, at what had become of her?

Fear, at what she might yet do?

There are only so many concessions you can extract from someone who has so little they care about losing, he'd said to her once.

How strange that she remembered such a thing, now.

It seemed her right mind had returned.

The thought comforted her.

Aoife, blowing, bathing her skin in heat, the promise of an eternity to come, comforted her.

But the realization that it was she, not James, who was now the one with nothing to lose . . . that grieved her.

For the tides had turned, the winds had changed, and he cared, he *cared*, just not about her, only getting rid of her, before she could do him damage, do Violet damage . . .

'Have it your way,' she said, her voice raised above Aoife's, except it didn't sound how she'd meant: not strong, nor courageous, but, weak, shaky . . .

Very frightened, too.

Perhaps even more so than him.

Worse, she appeared to be crying again.

And, before her blurring left eye, James's expression shifted, into one she couldn't, not even in her right mind, recall him ever showing her before. Was it . . . concern?

Sorrow?

'What are you talking about, Elizabeth?' he said, and that was all wrong too, for he spoke softly.

Where had his fury gone?

His terror?

'I'm going.' Why couldn't she stop crying? 'I'm going . . . '

'Where?'

'To Aoife.'

'She's not real.'

'And Anthony.'

'Who's Anthony?'

'My brother.'

He had been real.

Hadn't he?

Please, she thought, *let him have been real.*

Let there have been some love in my life that was real.

She took a step backwards.

'Elizabeth, stop, it's not safe.' He stepped forwards, towards her, past the fence. 'You need help. Care . . . '

'I can't pay anyone else to give me that. Not any more . . . '

'Then . . . fine, *Christ*,' his face twisted, angry again, 'I'll do it. I'll pay . . . '

'That's not what I meant.' She took another step, and he followed with two. 'I have money, except Ruth stole so much . . . '

'I don't know what you're talking about.'

'I want to go, James.' He'd reached her now, was holding her by the arms. *A touch, a touch.* 'Please.' The sky above ignited, turning from black to white, exploding in noise. Wind whirled, Aoife in an absolute frenzy.

Do it. Now.

'I can't,' said Elizabeth, 'not alone.' She couldn't. She was too scared. 'I can't . . . '

'You're making no sense,' James said.

You don't need to be scared, Aoife crooned.

'I can't help it,' Elizabeth told her.

'Help what?' asked James.

'Anything,' she said. 'Not any more.' She couldn't. It was too terrible. Too lonely. 'I want it to be over.'

'What are you saying?'

'Push me.'

'*What?*'

'Now. Please.'

'No.'

'Yes.'

'*No.*' He said it so vehemently.

And yet, he was tempted.

She saw it.

Felt it, in the grip of his hands.

Now he was afraid again.

Terrified of what he wanted to do.

'I'll be gone,' she said. 'Just think of it . . . '

You've almost got him, sang Aoife. *He won't forget you now. You'll haunt him for the rest of his life.*

'Just one push, James.'

'No . . . '

'Yes, yes . . . '

His hands tightened.

And was that a glow, over his shoulder?

Had that last bolt of lightning struck home?

His home.

Bullseye, crowed Aoife, and her breath smelt of smoke.

'Push me,' said Elizabeth to James, again. 'Now.'

He drew breath.

She felt his muscles tense, about to move . . .

Then, a woman's voice.

Violet's voice.

For she was suddenly there, coming towards them in the blackness, her dress whipping around her.

'Enough,' she said, with a vehemence that shook the sweltering, smoky air.

Watch out for her, warned Aoife.

But where had she sprung from?

Elizabeth had been too preoccupied with James, and the glow, to notice her coming.

She saw her now, though, but the woman before her bore little resemblance to the one she'd watched earlier in St Leonard's. She no longer appeared sweet, or unremarkable; rather, determined, fierce . . . *Enraged*.

Not a strawberry, after all.

It didn't please Elizabeth.

She realized she'd liked the strawberry better.

Preferred, now that Violet had come, the image she'd had of her, cowering helplessly somewhere.

But Violet wasn't cowering. She was coming through the fence too, detaching James's hands from Elizabeth's arms. 'Enough,' she repeated. 'You can't let her do this to you.'

'Violet,' he said, and it was like a punch to Elizabeth's heart, hearing the way he spoke her name, 'you shouldn't be here.'

'Of course I'm here.'

'Move away from that edge, all of you,' said Mrs Hamilton, for she'd come too.

Violet had brought her.

Were the two of them . . . friends?

No.

No.

Elizabeth couldn't have that.

She couldn't . . .

Couldn't bear that James was no longer holding her, but Violet instead, urging her back, behind the fence.

'The fields,' Violet said.

'I know.' He glanced in their direction, then, belatedly, back to Elizabeth. 'I need to go. You need to leave . . .'

'I do,' Elizabeth agreed, and what she did next, she did in the matter of a moment, not giving herself the opportunity to think better of it.

It was like jumping into Highgate ponds on a cold winter's day.

Throwing herself into a Charleston.

Knocking down an oyster.

She propelled herself backwards, and as she did, three things happened.

The first, was that she heard Thomas – always-watching Thomas – yelling her name, and then she saw him, sprinting down the peninsula towards them.

The second, was that James released Violet and reached out for her, *her*.

The third (and Elizabeth truly didn't plan this; she hadn't *had* a plan) was that, struck by overwhelming dread of the journey she'd now set herself on – the pain that might be waiting; the unknown – she reached out, to save herself.

And perhaps, if her hands had found James, he might have been strong enough to pull her back.

But it wasn't James who she caught a hold of.

It was Violet.

Violet, whose head snapped around as Elizabeth's fingers closed around her wrist.

Violet who stumbled.

And Violet who fell, as the solid rock of Aoife's island mystically disintegrated from beneath her.

Elizabeth fell too.

They fell together.

Down, down, down, in the hot smoky air.

It's time, Aoife sang.

It's time.

Chapter Thirty-Five

Violet and Elizabeth

James's face was the last thing Violet saw, as she went.

The terror in it.

His voice, the last she consciously heard.

No.

Then, the lighthouse bell began to clang, its hollow toll filling the whooshing night, and Violet tumbled, she span, until she found herself looking into the wildness of Elizabeth's unpatched eye, staring up at her. Beneath Elizabeth's falling body, less than a second away, were rocks, and swollen, black waves; the crash of foam, and rip of currents.

That second stretched.

Elizabeth reached out, flailing to grab another hold of Violet, and Violet raised her own arms to her face: a last, desperate effort to protect herself.

She drew breath, filling her lungs . . .

Then, the second was over.

The water was cold.

Elizabeth felt its brutal smack as she broke the surface, then, a softening: an icy liquid cushion, closing around her.

She'd lived this moment before.

She thought about that, as she sank, slowly, down, watching Violet break the surface above her.

Thought about how, on the first night she'd died, twenty months before, she'd swam; fought to live.

Wanted to live.

Life now, though: it was impossible.

She'd grown so tired.

And the worst was behind her. She'd made the leap.

All she had to do, was give in.

It was nice, having Violet with her. For once, she wasn't suffering alone.

But Violet was kicking, even as the suck of the current, and her clothes, dragged her down.

Stop, Elizabeth wished she could tell her. *Let it happen.*

It's so much easier, once you do.

She turned from Violet's struggle, exhausted by it, and looked downwards.

Dimly, she heard more disruptions above.

Other bodies, diving?

James, risking his own life to save Violet's?

The idea didn't upset Elizabeth.

Nothing upset her.

She'd realized she could see again, with both eyes.

She could see so clearly.

She saw her diamonds, in touching distance. Aoife too, holding them up to her in the cup of her hands.

How beautiful she was.

And here was Anthony.

He'd come.

Of course he'd come.

He *had* been real.

Hello, Lizzie, he said, and held out his hand.

She took it.

443

She felt no pain. Not anywhere.

There'll be no more now, Aoife told her.

You're safe, Anthony said. *Time to rest*.

Yes, Elizabeth thought. *Yes*.

It's not safe, you living somewhere like this and not knowing how to swim.

That's what James had said, when he'd taught Violet.

But it wasn't safe even now she did know. Because no matter how she kicked, she couldn't reach the surface. Eyes burning with desperation in the pitch salty blackness, she thrashed, and she reached, but the churning water kept tugging her down.

No, she thought, *no*.

I can't. I can't . . .

Her chest expanded, bursting, burning, trying to force her lips open, for a breath that wouldn't be there, only ocean, which would fill her throat, her lungs. Biting her lips shut, she kept kicking, weaker now, too weakly. The surface was moving further away. It was there, though, still there . . .

And then, someone else was too.

An arm, like a vice around her waist.

Legs, kicking with hers, pulling her up.

Then, there was another, grabbing her hands, pulling as well, the surface growing closer, closer . . .

Keep kicking, a voice inside her insisted: not Aoife's, nor Elizabeth's, nor Violet's father's, but her own. *Help them. Kick . . .*

So, with the last of her strength, she did, and, as air stuck her face, she released her lips, opening her mouth, gulping on the oxygen that flooded her, whilst the dull, muffled noise of *under* fell away, replaced by the lighthouse's bell, the crashing water on the rocks, and rain, heavy rain, hammering down.

And, with the thud of a wave, all was muffled again.

She was spinning: a rag, in a mangle.

Then, within seconds, that arm, around her waist, pulling.

Not those hands any more.

Violet didn't know where they'd gone.

The arm, though, that belonged to James.

She knew it, even before the pair of them once again broke the surface, and he, dragging them clear of the break, turned her so that she was facing him, his frantic stare boring into her own, asking her if she was hurt, in any way.

'No, no.'

'Can you swim, then?' he shouted.

'Yes.'

'You have to get away from these rocks. Just another thirty yards out, and wait. Thomas went back for Elizabeth. I need to help him.'

'James . . . '

But he, diving, had already gone.

She had one moment's hesitation, of wanting to go after him, but then she accepted how foolish that would be.

So, shaking, sobbing – in shock, disbelief, and fear, so much fear, that he wouldn't come back – she did as he asked, and swam out from the rocks, over the black roll of the waves, until she had to stop, because she was shaking too much, the rain was so strong, and the waves kept pushing against her. Choking on the spray, she turned, searching for James with her stinging, tear-blinded eyes, finding nothing but the dark, jagged spectre of the island looming above her.

Was Mrs Hamilton still up there, on the cliffs?

It was impossible to see.

The lighthouse's bell had fallen silent, though; its beam was once again slowing to a stop.

Francis must have left.

To jump too?

Violet had no energy left to guess.

She wanted James.

Where was he?

Where?

She couldn't go on without him.

She couldn't . . .

And yet, as another wave struck her, buffeting her, *pushing* her, she became suddenly furious, at everything.

Her fury made her stronger.

She struck the waves back with her arms, again, and again, swimming once more, on and on, waiting, with every stroke, every gasped breath, for him to come, but he still didn't, he didn't, and it had been too long, so she kept swimming, ever deeper, to nowhere, alone . . .

Until she wasn't.

Because Mrs Hamilton hadn't been on the cliffs.

She'd run to the wharf, to get Arnold, and his boat.

His boat which, still full of passengers, found Violet – not thirty yards out from the rocks, as James had instructed, but more than the one hundred she'd swam.

Delen was the one who spotted her.

'There,' came her voice, through the darkness. 'Look, they're there.'

They're? Violet thought. *They're?*

She turned, searching the swollen, rain-obscured waters, her burning chest expanding in hope, desperate hope . . .

Her hope grew as she caught sight of the movement: arms, slicing through the waves, still some distance away, but getting nearer.

Was it him?

Was it?

He stopped swimming, searching too.

'Violet?'

'I'm here,' she called, sobbing more, for it was him, it was.

Alive, still, moving again, as she moved to him, Arnold's lamp finding them, bathing them both in its gold glow.

'I couldn't see you,' said James, holding her tight.

'I couldn't see you. But you're here . . . '

'I'm here.'

Thank God.

Violet didn't ask him about Thomas.

He was alone, after all, so she knew, she knew, and it hurt, it did, because she hadn't liked him, God knew she hadn't liked him, but he'd helped to save her life.

She didn't ask about Elizabeth either.

As James pulled her closer, she knew about her too.

Felt it, in the looseness in the air.

The sudden lightness.

There'd be no more letters.

No more whispers.

No more pain.

She wasn't anywhere, any more.

She was gone.

Francis had come out into the water too, that night.

Leaving the bell, leaving the lamp, he'd run for the lighthouse's old rowboat, as fast as his eighty-year-old legs would permit, intent on getting to his son.

It was Gareth, not Delen, who spotted him, grappling with his oars on the waves.

'He wanted to make good,' Francis wept. 'Wanted to make it right. "Got to, Dad," he said.' He stared out at the water. 'I can't find him. I need to find him . . . '

No one could convince him to come in out of the rain, and wait for morning.

447

So Gareth – knowing too well the pain of searching, helplessly, for a son – stayed with him.

At his request, Delen went to wait for him, in his cottage.

The Hamiltons went back to theirs.

And, through the downpour, the rest of them returned to the house.

It was still standing. The fire, quenched to nothing but blackened grass, hadn't reached its walls. It was only when Violet saw it, untouched, that she realized part of her at least had been hoping it had burned.

'Yes,' said James, much later, after Cressida – stunned, like everyone was stunned – had taken Teddy to bed, and the staff had wordlessly gone to theirs. James had told them he'd speak to them in the morning about what should come next. 'I hoped it, too.'

They were in Violet's room, not his.

He hadn't asked which one she wanted to go to.

He'd known.

Now, as they stood at her window, staring out at the lighthouse's stilled beam, he told her how sorry he was, for all of it.

'What do you want, Violet? Where do you want to be?' His hair was still wet. Neither of them had yet changed their sodden clothes. 'I should have asked you, long before now . . . '

'I shouldn't have waited for you to.'

'So . . . ?'

'I don't know,' she said, honestly. 'But not here.'

'Then, we'll go.'

'You're sure?'

'I'm sure. It's never given me what I've needed. You're the one who's done that.'

She turned, looking into his eyes, and smiled, however sadly.

'What about everyone else?' she asked.

'We'll work that out. Together.'

She nodded. 'Together.'

Moving closer to him, resting her head against his damp, salty chest, she returned her attention to the window.

In her mind's eye, she saw Elizabeth again, so wretchedly ill and wasted, falling beneath her.

She thought of Thomas, taking her hands, *making good*.

She'd never forget either of them now; she was certain.

James, silent beside her, wouldn't either, she knew.

But it was over.

The two of them were leaving.

And the sky outside was already beginning to lighten on the new day.

A shorter day, thank God.

A grey one, too. It was still raining, as torrentially as it had been on the April morning of Violet's arrival.

But the lightning had passed.

The wind had fallen.

Aoife, wherever she'd gone, was at rest.

Epilogue

Violet

Three months later

It was on a golden September Friday that, together, they returned to the island for a final time. The morning was mellow with warmth, not yet ready to let go of summer. The sky was entirely clear.

Still.

Gareth was there to meet them at the wharf. He operated the lighthouse now, along with Alan and Simon, who took it in turns to travel over for their shifts from St Leonard's, in Eric's tug. In the end, the two of them had been the only ones who James had dismissed from his staff. Violet had agreed that he should. Cressida had too.

Strongly.

'They could have got me out of that cell with a word,' she'd said. 'Let them try prison. See how they like it.'

But James hadn't reported them to the police.

In the end, after all the recriminations, and excuses, and regret, had been done with – no one sorrier than Lord Arden, the commissioner – he hadn't pursued charges against anyone.

Not even Laura.

'Enough,' he'd said, just as Violet had to him, when she'd pulled his hands from Elizabeth on the cliffside. 'It's enough.'

The island was all but empty now: the cows, Lettice included, moved to Harbury; the house, closed up.

Francis was the only other, besides Gareth, who'd remained permanently in residence on the bay. He no longer worked, though. He – who'd aged another decade in the course of that single rain-soaked night he'd spent searching for Thomas – was no longer able for it. But he slept in the hut he'd shared with Thomas. He drank his tea from the set his wife had loved.

Gareth often joined him.

'What do you talk about?' Violet asked him, as, with James, they progressed up the wharf.

'Our boys,' Gareth said. 'And my Delen. You tell her that, please.'

'All right,' said Violet. 'As soon as I'm back.'

'Still walking out with that whippersnapper, is she?'

'I'm not sure *whippersnapper* is quite how he regards himself,' said James.

Violet, smiling, wasn't either.

But,

'Yes,' she said. 'Yes, she is.'

She'd grown to know Delen much better, these past few months.

She'd come to the wedding, along with Cressida and Teddy, the Hamiltons, and Edwin Firth, when Violet and James had married, the week after the solstice, in Penzance. Violet and James were still planning to honeymoon, in Tuscany – next summer, perhaps – but, in the meantime, had moved to London, whilst the Hamiltons had gone to Kent, there to oversee the construction of the new home James and Violet had planned, *together*. It was just a few miles from Harbury, where the Hamiltons were staying, until their new cottage was built.

Cressida and Teddy were back at Harbury too.

Not Dicky. He'd disappeared, like Elizabeth's old nurse, Ruth, had disappeared, just with rather less money in his pocket.

'He had the nerve to approach Laura for help,' Edwin had told James, having had it from his sister. 'She sent him packing, of course. Apparently, his papa's keen to press him back into army life. Let them deal with him . . . '

Not far from Harbury, was a train station, with a direct connection to London.

Already, Mrs Hamilton was making good use of the service.

And James and Violet were living in James's Fitzrovia house: another mansion Violet couldn't quite make herself used to. ('You'll get there,' Cressida had assured her, laughing.) Violet and James had offered all of the staff at Aoife's, bar Alan and Simon, posts there. Chef and his kitchenhand had accepted; Nelle, surprisingly – if a little discomfortingly – had too. All the others, Laura had given employment in her lodge, which she swore she'd never again be able to bring herself to set foot in.

That was something else Violet had learnt from Edwin. He'd passed that morsel on personally, during one of his frequent visits to the London offices. He often stopped by at her desk. She'd grown to like him, much more than she'd anticipated.

'Hard not to, isn't it?' said Delen, whose desk faced Violet's, and who Edwin kept inviting out for dinner. ('And I seem to keep saying yes,' Delen exclaimed.)

Violet travelled into the offices every morning with James. She hadn't been tempted to stop working, just because they were married.

'What would I *do*?' she'd said, when James had asked her if she wanted to.

Recently, she'd become more involved in the planning of the company's new department stores. She loved it, couldn't imagine ever being inclined to step back; certainly not until circumstances compelled her into a temporary pause.

She had a few more months before that, though.

'A very few,' James said, with a grin.

He was busier in London than he had been in Aoife's. There were more people to make claims on his time, so, these days, it was Delen who Violet mostly shared her tea breaks with.

Delen who she went out for lunch with, every Friday.

Cressida came into town for those lunches as well, giving in to Mrs Hamilton's entreaties to leave Teddy with her for the day. And increasingly – thanks to Delen's involvement with Edwin, her *whippersnapper* – Amy Astley had started to come along, too.

Against the odds, Violet had found herself enjoying her company: every bit as much as she did her brother's.

She was *fun*.

Laura, however, never appeared.

'She can't forgive herself,' Amy said. 'Not until James does.'

'Then she'll never forgive herself,' said James, who wouldn't be moved, not on that.

He'd given in on Aoife's, though.

Given it up.

Violet, who'd never forgotten the peace he'd told her he craved, the night they'd met in Quaglino's, had convinced him that any peace he found would forever be tinged, so long as the island remained in his life.

'Let it become something different,' she'd said. 'A real haven, not just a hope of one.'

He hadn't needed much persuading.

He'd endowed the deeds to a charity for shellshocked soldiers. Plans had been drawn – for common rooms; wards; nurses' quarters; doctors' quarters; a swimming pool; croquet lawns – and Laura, however unforgiven, had, along with Rupert, insisted on funding the build.

I'd like to think that the Elizabeth I once knew would be happy about it, she'd written, to Violet, in one of the countless apologies she'd now sent. *I honestly can't be sure. Regardless, this gift that Rupert and I give is to salve our consciences, not hers . . .*

On Monday, the island's transformation would begin. Within a year, it would be home to scores men like Violet's father.

It was why she and James had returned that morning.

In the end, they'd resolved that they needed to say a final farewell to this place in which they had, amidst everything, found happiness.

They didn't linger in the house, when they reached it.

Instead, they returned to their cavern, their *hideaway,* at the foot of the old lighthouse stairs.

'I wonder who'll discover it next,' Violet mused, as she sat beside James on the warm rock, looking out across the shining ocean. All was calm, quiet; *spectacular.* 'A doctor, maybe . . . '

'With a nurse?'

'If she likes,' Violet said, with a smile. 'Will they have gentlemen nurses, do you think?'

He smiled too. 'Perhaps.'

She shifted, touching her hand to her fluttering stomach, and he moved, threading his fingers through hers.

'You don't regret giving it away, do you, now that we're back?' She had to ask him: it had been worrying her, ever since they'd arrived.

'Not at all.' He spoke without any hesitation. 'You?'

'No,' she said, and didn't pause either.

'Honestly, I just want to be gone now.'

'Yes,' she said. 'I think I do too.'

He leant down, kissing her. 'Shall we, then?'

'Let's.'

'All right.' He pushed himself to standing, holding his hand down to her.

And, as she took it, standing too, she felt a brush on her skin: the barely there movement of a breeze.

James, turning for the cavern, didn't appear to notice.

But, as they walked for the house, she felt the breeze again.

She *heard* it, flitting, *murmuring*, around the cavern's walls: urging them on, urging them away.

Yes, go, it seemed to say, *leave*.

It's time.

Violet glanced back over her shoulder, at the empty, sun-baked space behind her.

The ocean lapped the rocks.

A trio of gulls arched through the sky.

It's time.

Author's Note

The idea for this novel originally came to me when I happened across the strange case of the Circleville Letters. Unlike *Secrets of the Watch House*, this mystery dates back to the 1970s, when an anonymous individual preyed upon a small Ohio town, sending letters to its inhabitants, threatening to expose their most carefully guarded secrets. I was instantly caught by this eerie concept of a faceless somebody holding a population hostage with the power of their posted words, and thought how well it might work in a big house, cut off from the world. And so, Aoife's Bay was born. The island is fictional, as is the village of St. Leonard's – and, indeed, the legend of Aoife's – but very much inspired by the research trips I took to Cornwall. The time I spent walking the stunning coastline around the tin mines at Botallack, and after hours at Land's End – when the tourist buses are all gone, leaving just the sound of gulls, and crashing waves, behind – were very much with me when I was writing the descriptions of Aoife's. I've loved every moment of creating that rugged, haunted world, and very much hope you've enjoyed reading it too.

Acknowledgements

Secrets of the Watch House is, unbelievably, my seventh novel, and that I'm here at all, with another novel in the pipeline, is in no small part thanks to the incredible team I'm lucky enough to work with. Thanks to my editor, Manpreet Grewal, for her brilliant insight, support, and championing, and to everyone at HQ – Priyal Agrawal, Lily Capewell, Kirsty Capes, Sarah Lundy, Donna Hillyer, Amal Ibrahim; you're amazing. Thank you, Becky Ritchie, for all you do (it's a lot!); thank you, Euan Thorneycroft, for your fantastic support this past year; and thank you to the rights team at AM Heath for helping to get my books out across the world.

A huge thank you, too, to all the writers, bloggers and Bookstagrammers who are so generous, reading and reviewing my books, and of course to every reader who has picked one up. I count it a huge privilege to make it on to your reading pile – hearing from you genuinely makes my day, so please do get in touch.

Thank you to my friends, for your sanity-saving support and encouragement. And, as always, thank you to my husband, Matt, and to our children, Molly, Jonah and Raffy: you're highly distracting, but you also keep me going, all the time, and I don't know where I'd be without you.

Keep reading for a spellbinding extract from Jenny Ashcroft's sweeping historical romance, *The Echoes of Love*

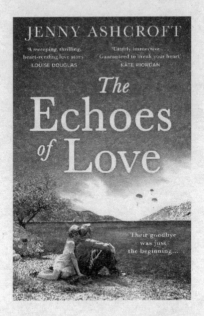

Under the Cretan sun, in the summer of 1936, two young people fall in love...

Eleni has been coming to Crete her entire life, swapping her English home for cherished sun-baked summers with her grandfather in his idyllic shoreside villa. When she arrives in 1936, she believes the long, hot weeks ahead will be no different to so many that have gone before.

But someone else is visiting the island that year too: a young German man called Otto. And so begins a summer of innocence lost, and love discovered; one that is finite, but not the end.

When, in 1941, the island falls to a Nazi invasion, Eleni and Otto meet there once more. But this time Eleni has returned to fight for her home, and Otto to occupy it. They are enemies, and their love is not only treacherous, but also dangerous. But will it destroy them, or prove strong enough to overcome the ravages of war?

Available to order now

Chapter One

Crete, June 1936

It felt like the beginning of so many summers that had gone before. Eleni, sitting beside her grandfather in his beloved Cadillac, roaring along the dusty coast road from Chania – sticky with sweat beneath her travelling clothes: the skirt suit that had been so appropriate in Portsmouth, but in Greece was too thick, too dull; grey with lingering English chill – gave not a moment's pause to the possibility that the one ahead might be different. Why should she? She'd been summering in Crete since she was a baby. This was to be her nineteenth stay. She trusted in what the island held waiting for her, entirely.

The road grew quieter, the further her *papou*, Yorgos, drove them out of Chania's bustling centre. There were no other motorcars on the winding hillside pass, just the odd farmer and laden donkey, goats that grazed in the dry, golden heat. Yorgos overtook them all, at a speed Eleni's British father would have called reckless, had he been there, but which she hardly noticed. She rested her head back, feeling the balmy wind in her tired eyes, the ebbing sun a warm cloth on her face, and, heedless of the Cadillac's wheels skimming the cliff edge, luxuriated in the relief of her three-day odyssey across Europe finally being over.

She'd travelled by herself that year. Her father, Timothy – a naval captain, and off to sea himself for the summer – hadn't been happy about it. He'd wanted her to take her usual chaperone: a retired teacher by the name of Miss Finch. But Miss Finch had, only the week before, broken her leg – playing croquet, of all things – leaving Timothy no time to recruit a replacement, and little choice but to give in to Eleni's assurances that she could manage the trip alone. Which she had. Happily. Sorry as she'd felt for Miss Finch (and really, *poor* Miss Finch), it had been such a relief, not having to spend endless hours nodding along to her tales of various nieces and nephews, so many pet rabbits, and pure liberation, deciding for herself when to have a drink, or read, or simply stare from the carriage window in silence.

And now she was here.

Here.

She tilted her head, looking down and out at the sea below; a glittering cloth tinged rose by the dusk, sliced in two by the furrows of the ferry that had brought her from Athens. Idly, she watched it steam away to the horizon, wondering who was now on it, what kind of lives they led, and all the while Yorgos talked, his gruff voice raised above the engine, grilling her on her solitary passage through France, Mussolini's Italy, speaking in rapid Greek, no concession to the months that had passed since she'd last used the language, his tolerance for it not being her mother tongue extremely low.

'Did the trains run on time?'

'They were fine,' she said; *ola kala.*

'Not crowded?'

'No.'

'You had no trouble in Italy? The blackshirts . . . '

'I hardly saw any,' she said. 'Only at the border.' Having her documents scrutinised by the abrasive soldiers was never comfortable, but she'd survived the ordeal many times before. The fascists had, after all, been running Italy since she was a child. She'd known to keep her expression blank as the men had studied her, then her papers, then her again. She'd distracted herself by looking at the posters on the railway sidings. 'Mussolini never gets older in his pictures,' she mused. 'Apparently he shaves his head so no one will guess he's going grey.'

'I don't want to waste oxygen talking about him,' said Yorgos.

'You started it . . . '

'And now I'm finishing it.' He shifted gear. 'You had enough to eat?'

'Plenty.'

'Really?'

'Yes.' She smiled. 'Really.'

He grunted, disbelieving.

Still smiling, she didn't attempt to convince him.

He'd never be convinced she ate enough anywhere but on Crete. Her diet was an obsession for him. He'd feed her now until September, not happy unless she left having gained at least a stone to see her through the British winter. She'd manage it, with remarkable ease, but couldn't be nearly so pleased about it.

'Why?' Yorgos would demand. 'What, you want to be one of these *magazine models*?'

She wouldn't entirely mind.

He'd arm her with fruits and vegetables to return to England with as well, refusing to accept that any food could be got there that wasn't brown. She'd take the heavy box, even though it was a pain to carry, the fruit would inevitably bruise, and she *really* didn't need it, because she hated denying him anything. And because she knew how his certainty that the British diet had killed her mother plagued him – as though more tomatoes and olives and spinach could have saved her from the Spanish flu.

Perhaps they might have.

'Here we are,' he said, unnecessarily, rounding the bend Eleni had been waiting for, veering on to the steep track of rocks and wildflowers that led down to the villa.

She braced her feet against the motor's floor, stopping herself from lurching forward as they sped on, feeling a wave of joy as the bougainvillea-shrouded house came into view.

It hadn't changed.

It never changed.

She stared, drinking in its perfect *sameness*.

She had no place she'd grown up in, back in England. She'd moved with her father countless times around their Portsmouth suburb of Gosport, their naval quarters upgraded with each new promotion he'd secured through the ranks (an indoor latrine, running hot water, that kind of thing). When she'd turned eleven, Timothy had spent long periods in Africa, and boarding school dormitories had joined her rotation of bedrooms. At fifteen, he'd taken a desk job back in Portsmouth and summoned her home to complete her school certificate there. She'd only just finished. She wasn't sure what should come next, only that her father expected her to be waiting in their newest house – a modern detached with both garden and garage – when he returned from his summer patrol of the Libyan Sea. (*I feel a . . . hole . . . of sorts, without you,* had been his farewell at the docks, delivered without him once touching her, or meeting her eye. *Take care now. I miss you. Dear. In my way.*)

This villa had been her constant. Perched in the elbow of land between Chania and Souda, overlooking the sea, it was, like so much of Crete, built in the style of the Venetians who'd occupied the island before the Turks had invaded, back in the 1600s. It wasn't grand, and needed repair in parts, but to Eleni, flattened by the functional monotony of Gosport, its imperfections only added to its beauty. The terracotta walls, fissured by age, battered by centuries of heat and wind, were as pale as peach flesh; the shutters, no bluer than a hazed sky. At night, they'd creak in the breeze coming up from the shore,

464

and she'd lie listening to them, soothed by the thought that her mama must have once done the same.

'And she watches,' said Yorgos, as he always did, pulling to a halt at the front door. He turned off the ignition, flooding them in a silence broken only by the song of the cicadas, the lapping waves below. 'Happy, because you are here.'

Eleni smiled.

Slowly, she climbed from the motor, drawing deep on the villa's layered scents: citrus from the lemon trees; the bougainvillaea's pollen; the thyme that grew, everywhere. She closed her eyes, losing herself in them all, these smells she'd missed too, too much.

She didn't think about Yorgos watching her, his satisfied nod at her contentment.

She didn't think about much at all.

She simply breathed.

It was her favourite breath of the year.

The breath that truly started summer for her.

The breath when her monochrome world shifted fully into colour, and her loneliness gave way to belonging.

The breath when – however impossible she'd find it to ever admit to her father – she came home.

It was dark by the time she set off to swim that night, picking her way down the stairs a long-gone Venetian had cut into the hillside. She could hear Yorgos clattering around on the terrace above, readying the grill for their dinner. The light of his oil lamp oozed into the blackness, joining the glow of the moon, helping to illuminate her rocky path downward. She wore her bathing costume beneath her robe, held a towel under her arm. The costume's new elastic was stiff, clinging in a way that made her very conscious of how little of her it covered. She'd bought it for the summer at Landport Drapery on Portsmouth's

Commercial Road, using the money she'd saved working as a weekend receptionist at Queen's Hotel.

'Don't fritter it away, now,' her boss, Mr Hodgson, had instructed, handing over her final payslip.

Did he give similar instructions to the male staff, she'd wondered.

Regardless, the costume was navy blue, cut with a sweetheart neck, down to a daring high thigh, and she loved it. It was the most glamorous thing she'd ever owned. She had no idea what her *papou* was going to say when he saw it, or the shorts she'd impulsively bought at Landport's as well.

Don't wear them anyone can see, probably.

She'd taken her time unpacking it all upstairs, unfolding her older, less controversial, sundresses, hanging them in the ancient wardrobe, then pausing – out of habit, old longing – at the bureau, staring into the photograph that stood there: the only one that existed of herself and her mama. It had been taken at a studio in Portsmouth when she'd been just a few months old, and her mama not much older than she was now; just twenty. Her mama was wearing a winter coat, and held Eleni bundled up in a blanket, clasping her hand. Eleni had her fist wrapped around her forefinger; tight, trusting. She'd known her mama, then. Once, she'd known her.

They looked alike; even Eleni could see that. Aside from the fair hair she'd inherited from her father, her mama had given her everything: olive skin, oval face; *curves.* Yorgos said they shared mannerisms, as well. *She used to sink her face in her hands when she laughed, and fiddle at her earlobe when she was trying to ignore me telling her off.* Did Eleni's father notice their similarities? He never spoke of it if he did. And he kept no photographs up. He wasn't one for ornaments or memories. Eleni wished he was, but not even a wedding portrait graced his well-ordered desk.

She shivered. The June air had cooled since sunset, and her

bare skin prickled in anticipation of the sea's liquid touch. She could hear the waves licking lazily over the cove's pebbles below. The Greeks had a word, just for that fizzing sound they made. *Flisvos*. It was a beautiful sound. It deserved a word of its own, Eleni thought.

It grew darker as the steps gave way to the small private bay, and she disappeared from the reach of her *papou*'s lamp. The sea, beyond the shallow shore break, was calm; a mirror to the stars, the beam of the white moon. She continued towards it, not hesitating as she shrugged off her robe, letting it fall to the ground. It was the only way to make herself get in, at this time of year, this time of night. No pause for thought.

Except then she did stop, startled by the crack of a branch behind her. She turned, glancing up at the shadowy hillside. An animal, she thought. A goat, or stray dog. She waited to see if it would show itself . . .

But no, nothing.

'Fine, be like that,' she said, in Greek, so it understood.

And, without further ado, she ran at the sea, diving, her breath leaving her as the biting water quenched her face, her sluggish, weary limbs. She swam deeper, on and on, diving again, reaching for the sandy bottom, lungs bursting until she could bear it no more and had to resurface, gasping for air. Sinking backwards, she floated, pulse pounding in her ears, eyes fixed on the stars – so much brighter, away from Portsmouth's city lights, so much closer – thinking of the freedom of the months ahead. The wonderful reality that she was lying in the Aegean Sea, staring at Venus, and not revising for her exams, or doing the washing up, back in Gosport.

She wasn't sure how long she might have gone on drifting like that.

Not so very long, probably. Soon enough, the sea's chill would have propelled her from her reverie.

But the call came first.

'Otto,' it rang out, high and clear from the shore, '*Otto Linder.*'

Intrigued by the unfamiliar voice, the unfamiliar name, Eleni kicked herself upright, peering through the night for the person who'd spoken, finding her easily on the dark water's edge, marked out by her white evening gown; a ghostly kind of silhouette. The gown was full-length, elegant, making its wearer appear more adult than she'd sounded. She'd *sounded* like a girl. Eleni studied her, wondering who she was, and what she could be doing on the rocks beneath Nikos Kalantis's villa. A villa which, now Eleni looked, had several lamps of its own burning. Her brow creased. She'd only ever known Nikos's home to stand empty in the past. He'd always been absent on business when she'd visited. ('This is no loss,' Yorgos had once said.)

Was he here this year?

Or had he leased his villa to tourists?

Certainly, this girl wasn't Greek. German, maybe. They were hearing it spoken more these days in England; those newsreels that played at the pictures of Hitler shouting, the ecstatic crowds cheering . . .

'Otto.' That name again. Something else followed. '*Wo bist du?*' Definitely German. And whiney. '*Essen ist fertig.*'

Then, another voice: male, deep, and so very close to Eleni, she all but lost her heart through her mouth.

'*Ich komme.*'

I'm coming?

Eleni hardly considered it.

She was much more concerned with absorbing the revelation that she hadn't been nearly so alone in the water as she'd believed.

That, and the jolt of the stranger, *Otto's*, eyes meeting hers when she spun reflexively towards him, no more than twenty strokes away.

Hand to her exploding chest, she stared.

For a moment, so did he.

As shocked as she was?

He didn't appear particularly shocked.

The night was too deep for Eleni to see him clearly – she drew an impression rather than a picture: the symmetry of his face, accentuated by the shadows; those eyes, holding hers – but it was enough for her to feel sure that he'd been a deal more aware of her presence than she had his.

Indignantly, she arched a brow.

Did he smile?

She was pretty sure his lips moved in a rueful smile.

She had no time to decide. The girl in white called for him again – '*Otto, wo* bist *du*?' – and, with a flicked glance in her direction, he bade Eleni, '*Guten Nacht*,' (she understood that) then was gone, slicing through the water for the shore.

Too stunned to move, Eleni watched him go.

He swam fast. His strokes, clean and assured, hardly made a noise. Vaguely, she made sense of why she hadn't noticed him before.

How long had he been aware of her own presence though?

Turning the unanswerable question over, she kept her attention on him as he reached the rocks, pulling himself from the sea. His back was broad, muscular, his movement easy and athletic. The woman threw a towel for him, and he caught it. He obviously joked, too, because the woman laughed, her peals slicing through the night. At the sound, their familiarity, Eleni felt the strangest tug; that hollowness of being on the outside. In the ensuing silence, she, replaying Otto's smile – certain now that's what it had been – found herself wishing she knew what he'd just said.

Much more than that though, she really was becoming freezing.

With a breath of resolution, she forced her cold body back into motion. She swam as swiftly as Otto had, not looking at him again, so not knowing whether he did, or did not, glance back at her. By the time she'd realized how much she wanted to check, it was already too late; she'd reached the shore and was wading through the shallows, Nikos's own rocky inlet hidden from view.

She stared in its direction, curiosity over Otto, and the girl, growing.

Then, teeth chattering, thinking she could quiz her *papou* on them, she reached for her towel and robe, and, wrapping herself in both, set off at a jog for the villa.

She heard no more noises on the way up; no cracks, nor rustles. It was only when she came across a kitten, curled right at the top of the stairs, that she recalled the snapping branch that had stopped her in her tracks before.

'Was it you?' she asked the tiny animal, scooping it up. It mewed plaintively, its back leg sticky with blood. 'Now who did this?'

Another mew.

Cradling it close, she carried it on with her, back into the light of her *papou*'s lamp.

'Don't bring that animal in here,' he called from up on the now-smoky terrace.

'It's hurt.'

'That's life.'

'*Papou*, you're a doctor . . . '

'For humans.'

'Just take a look at it.'

'And all the other cats on the island?'

'Please. Whilst I get changed. I won't be long.'

470

She wasn't.

And, as she and her *papou* ate beneath the stars – the kitten, clean of blood, purring at their feet ('What shall we call him?' she asked. 'Nothing,' Yorgos said. 'That's not a very good name,' she observed) – she mentioned the Germans she'd seen at Nikos Kalantis's villa. She learnt that Yorgos knew disappointingly little of them, only that they must be part of the family that had flown in that morning from Berlin to stay for the summer. *The Linders.*

'Friends of Mr Kalantis?' she asked.

'Let's hope better of them than that,' he said, and frowned, scolding her against throwing fishbones for the kitten to eat.

She ignored him on the fishbones, but let the matter of the Linders, and Nikos Kalantis, go, knowing he was only being short-tempered because she'd raised the subject of his neighbour in the first place. They'd been at odds her entire life: a dispute over land that went back generations. The island was littered with such family feuds. The story went that Eleni's grandmama had, for herself, been good friends with Nikos, before she, like Eleni's mama, had died too young, leaving Eleni's mama just a baby (a troubling family trait), but not even she'd been able to heal the rift between the pair. If anything, Eleni suspected her friendship with Nikos had made it worse. There'd been some incident involving her mama too, back during the Great War, when Nikos had lost his temper at her – Eleni didn't know why ('You think a man like him needs a reason,' Yorgos had said, when she'd pressed him on it), only that it was another thing Yorgos could never forgive, and hated remembering.

Hating that for him, Eleni had long ceased asking him to.

Dropping more fish for the kitten, she moved the conversation on, coaxing him back into a better mood by mentioning the whispered rumours of King Edward's affair with the American divorcée, Wallis Simpson, giving him – no royalist, but every inch a moralist – all the opening he needed to vent about values and duty and the importance of modesty. (*He's really going to hate my shorts,* she thought.) As he talked on – jumping from Edward, to the newly reinstated Greek monarchy, his fury at their support for yet another would-be European dictator, General Ioannis Metaxas in Athens, and from there to the welcome news that Dimitri, the owner of the harbourside café Eleni had waitressed at the summer before, had called by, offering her employment again – she did her best to keep up, fighting a smile at his gesticulations, forgetting all about her watery encounter.

But later, as she fell onto her mattress, an oil lamp flickering on the bedside table, the kitten snug on a cushion by the door, her mind moved once more to the memory of Otto's face in the darkness. The warmth in his voice. *Guten Nacht.* She stared sightlessly at her chipped ceiling, listening to the shutters creak, and thought not of her mother, but of him in his villa down the way, and about what relation the girl in white could be to him.

A sister?

Girlfriend?

Or a fiancée?

Somehow, sister felt better.

She expelled a short laugh at herself, for caring.

Then she rolled on to her side, extinguished her lamp, and wondered how long it would be before she saw him again.